SHAKE, RATTLE AND RAIN

POPULAR MUSIC MAKING
IN MANCHESTER
(1950 - 1995)

CP Lee is a lecturer in Cultural Studies in the School of Media, Music & Performance at the University of Salford. Before that he was a founder member of Mancunian Rock iconoclasts Alberto Y Lost Trios Paranoias. He has written two books on Bob Dylan, published by Helter Skelter, and numerous articles on a variety of other topics for magazines and other media. He is a frequent contributor to BBC Radio and still plays music on a regular basis.

Bob Dylan all alone on a shelf

The EDLIS series Bob Dylan all alone on a shelf exists to make available research work that could easily be overlooked by publishers but is of use to research scholars, collectors, enthusiasts and concert goers interested in the works of Bob Dylan and related areas.

The series presents work that may have existed in another form, as webpages, as an out of print book, as a circulating *samizdat* publication, or in someone's imagination. No idea is too obscure, no detail too minute, no thought too strange, to fit in this series. Its range shall be as great as the range of topics covered in Mr Dylan's own works.

If you have a suggestion for the series e-mail our esteemed editor of the series, the well known Ed Ricardo, Havana's foremost Bob Dylan connoisseur, concert goer and a long term member of EDLIS, the hard to pin down anarchical group responsible for so little but behind so much. He places his head above the parapet hoping for your support, but expecting rain.

edu@edlis.org

SHAKE, RATTLE AND RAIN

Popular Music Making in Manchester, 1950-1995

C P Lee

Hardinge Simpole

Hardinge Simpole Publishing
Potters Market
West Hill
Ottery St. Mary
Devon
EX11 1TY

http://www.hardingesimpole.co.uk
hardingesimpole@aol.com

First published by Hardinge Simpole Publishing in 2002

ISBN 1 84382 048 X Hardback
ISBN 1 84382 049 8 Paperback

Dedication

This book is dedicated to all the people from Manchester who have been, or will be, involved in making music.

Contents

Chapter 6
The Anti-Christ comes to Manchester *123*

Chapter 7
Post-Punk operatives *159*

Acknowledgements

This thesis is not my own work. It's the work of hundreds upon hundreds of musicians (and musicians' friends!) who have lived and worked in this City over the last fifty years. Many were called, but few could boogie ...

... to all of them, many, many thanks. In particular, I'd like to thank the many people I've talked to and interviewed during the time it took me to complete this work. They include, in no particular order, Bruce Mitchell, Victor Brox, Tosh Ryan, Peter Hook, Eddie Mooney, Peter Hughes, Bob Dickinson, Anthony H Wilson, Captain Mog, John Scott, John The Postman, Richard Boon, Bill Murphy, Howard Trafford, Clint Boon, Dave Haslam, Benny Van Den Berg, Fred Fielder, Barry Whittam, Andy Harris, Pete Maclaine, Scott Carey, Alan Lawson, Alan Fraser, Steve Redhead, Craig Jamieson, and every other person I have been in touch with, personally, professionally, or otherwise. Grateful thanks too to Hardinge Simpole for making the transition from thesis to book form a painless and cheerful process, to my late father James Gabriel Lee whose description of Chief Constable McKay motivated me to dig deeper, and as always to Pam Lee for her stalwart support.

Preface

The idea for Shake, Rattle & Rain was conceived in 1990, researched over a five-year period and then written up during 1996. As a thesis for PhD submission, Shake, Rattle & Rain is produced in an academic style, and much of the information gathered for inclusion has proved useful to other researchers in a variety of fields. One of its chapters has been expanded into a full-length book (Like The Night – Bob Dylan and The Road To The Free Trade Hall, Helter Skelter Publishing, London, 1998). However, I've been told often, and I do believe it, there's something in here for everyone, for people who are simply interested in Popular Music and for those who 'like a good story', because that's what this book is all about – the story of Manchester music over a finite time from 1955 to 1995

Popular Music has changed a lot since 1995, Britpop came and went, even the seemingly irresistible rise of House Music appears now to have reached its zenith, with clubs closing down or seeking new directions. As to be expected, the scene in Manchester has reflected those changes and the apparent unstoppable force of turning out of 'new product' has slowed down considerably. But the City still appears capable of encouraging and nurturing fresh talent that can appeal far beyond the confines of its boundaries, Damon Gough's Badly Drawn Boy being just one example. Manchester's profile in other areas has undergone a significant metamorphosis as it has rebuilt itself from the rubble of the IRA bomb that devastated the City centre in 1996. It has placed itself firmly on the tourist map due to a variety of cultural features, not the least of which is its rich musical history. When foreign visitors arrive they can expect to enjoy not only clubs, art galleries and the new Imperial War Museum, but also themed walking tours through the City's musical past, and coach trips that follow "The Smiths' Manchester and Salford", complete with musical accompaniment!

With this publication from Hardinge Simpole the story written so far is now in the hands of any and all readers. With the rapidly evolving changes and expanding parameters of the Manchester music scene, it is intended that future editions of this book will bring forth updates. The narrative of this edition takes its leave at a pivotal moment in the history of Manchester music, when, once again, all things seemed possible. As for the future? Well, we'll just have to wait for the next volume.

CP Lee
Manchester, 2002
http://www.cplee.co.uk

Chapter 1

Introduction

Oral Accounts, Chronology, and Culture

"Why the Hell has Manchester got so many fantastic bands? I mean, the thing that amused me about Manchester was that they were saying there was this vanguard of bands from Manchester - The way that Manchester was going to save the world with bands like the Happy Mondays and The Charlatans, Inspiral Carpets, and I used to sit there and think, what is this crap? You look at Joy Division, New Order, The Smiths. You look at James who were included in it, there were so many... But as to why Manchester has so many bands, I've no idea. You could almost be vague enough to say that it must be something to do with the water, because there's no other bloody reason!"
Peter Hook

This book is about reclamation. My aim is to allow the voices of the musicians to speak for themselves in telling their stories and to avoid falling into the common academic trap of mediating history. By reclaiming the people's voices, this is an attempt to uncover the hidden history of a local music scene, specifically to find out what happened to Popular Music and the Music Scene in Manchester from 1950 to the present day.

I have been an active participant since I played my first gig in 1964 (at the Ladybarn Folkclub), and even now I am still performing roughly once a month. My connections with the contemporary Pop/Rock scene are less active, more academic nowadays, but I still monitor developments through close associates who are presently involved in the music business; students at Salford University who are on the Popular Music Course there, and colleagues from the Institute of Popular Culture at the Metropolitan University, who are engaged in research into 'Youth Culture'.

In musical terms, Manchester isn't unique, but it is certainly special. All major cities in the United Kingdom have music scenes that have existed for decades, some thriving, others less so. Manchester's music scene was content to proceed along on its own way until, in 1988, something happened to it that had never happened before: it caught the attention of the world's media.

Manchester did have a thriving club/dance culture; it did have a lot of groups, but it had had all these things before in the 1960s and the world didn't come flocking to its doors then. Something happened in 1988; nobody is quite sure what. The aftermath of the Second Summer of Love, perhaps? Or, maybe it was a slow period for news? Whatever, something in this post-industrial city in the North West of England managed to lock into the zeitgeist of the time and reporters and film crews from international news agencies flocked to the Happening. Soviet and Japanese TV companies vied with each other for space on Oldham Street to film Affleck's Palace, home to the alternative clothes trade. The New York Times, The Sun, The Daily Mail, The Observer, Radio Four and the BBC World Service, all sent intrepid reporters to soak up the atmosphere in Manchester's vibrant nightclubs. Bewildered patrons of Joe Blogg's clothing designs gave interviews to journalists about the width of their flares. According to Sarah Champion, in her book, 'And God Created Manchester', applications for Manchester University and Polytechnic rose by 30 per cent.

"Why Manchester? 'Cos cool kids from across the globe move here year after year to start bands. 'Cos it's the Capital of the North, sucking up talent from Merseyside, Lancashire and Cheshire. 'Cos of venues like The Boardwalk, unafraid to showcase new 'local' acts; 'cos local newspapers document future heroes; 'cos Manc entrepreneurs risk cash putting out unknown bands......"
Champion. 1991. p11.

Like all media fads, this one sailed away into history too. The fall of the Berlin Wall, the Gulf War, the war in the former Yugoslavia, all came and took precedence over articles concerning the cultural importance of the Happy Mondays, Stone Roses, and The Mock Turtles. History had overtaken the myth of 'Madchester', and when it did get back into the news, the name had metamorphosed into 'Gunchester' and it was the drug wars that stole the headlines. That is until the next media circus - Britpop.

Britpop was the name given by the music press in the early

1990s, to what might more properly be defined as 'Post Modern Indie', a revival of the guitar band sound, born in the early 1960s, taken to the max in the late 1970s, and now, here in the 1990s, charging out of its underground, cult status, and regularly taking the charts by storm. Why Britpop is important to the story of Manchester music, unfolded here, is the inclusion within the Britpop ranks of the massively successful Oasis and their subsequent influence on the local music scene.

Hailing from the Burnage housing estate in South Manchester, Oasis are a copywriter's dream. Staunchly Working Class, second generation Irish, the Gallagher brothers, who form the mainstay of the band, have risen to the dizzying heights of superstardom despite, or because of, their 'laddish' behaviour. They drink, take drugs, might have been burglars, aren't afraid to boast about 'birds', wealth, etc and, almost coincidentally, have a very commercial songwriter in the form of brother Noel. They are, as of writing (mid 1996), poised on the verge of becoming one of the biggest international groups since U2, and are, without doubt, the most commercially successful band in England at the moment.

Peripheral to the band's success is the amount of media interest in the City that has been (once again) generated by the media. Record company scouts are combing the clubs of Manchester, looking for up and coming Mancunian bands, journalists are rewriting their old articles that ask the question, 'Why does Manchester produce so many groups?'

With Manchester back on the music map it seems timely that this piece of work is being written, because my argument is that, over the years, a musical infrastructure has been built up, one that is capable of nurturing and sustaining an indigenous sub-culture of musicians, engineers, designers, promoters, etc all of these elements combining to create the right atmosphere for new talent to emerge and thrive.

Having established, in terms of the media at least, that something happened within the Manchester area, I do attempt in the Conclusion to connect this phenomenon with the local issues presented in the text. However, it is stressed that I am not asking the question, why? I am asking, what happened? I am going, as far as is possible, to the source, and attempting to build an account of the history of music making in Manchester, by my own personal experiences and oral accounts given to me by the people who were directly involved in the various movements that have spanned the last (nearly) fifty years.

Methodology

Oral History

This is the chosen methodology because official history typically comprises facts gleaned by the historian from contemporary accounts, and consequently the 'historical information' is tainted and then, subsequently, there is further contamination via the historian's presentation of the work.

As a work of reclamation, and to avoid the above problems, I have allowed the participants to speak for themselves. However, as memory is a perceived thing, selective and prone to alteration, it is necessary to be aware of the pitfalls in 'taking for granted' all that is recounted. Therefore, I have used documentary evidence where possible to substantiate the contributions of the participants. Such additional evidence is either derived from contemporary texts or more recently published material.

The oral historian must be aware of avoiding leading questions or interpolating themselves too much into the interview. Fortunately, the majority of musicians are 'outgoing' personality types and need very little coaxing in order to 'perform' as it were, in front of a microphone. Therefore, I judged myself to be fortunate in the abundance of material that I was able to glean from the interviews and the interviewees.

The contributors were chosen to represent a cross section of participants in the music scene during the four and a half decades covered here. They range from people like Bruce Mitchell who started playing in the early 1950s and who is a practising musician today, through to Scott Carey who is a more recent addition to the Manchester music scene. Some of the participants have left the music business altogether, for example Pete Hughes, Howard Devoto and Richard Boon. Others continue to contribute on an international scale, for example Peter Hook and Anthony H Wilson as a musician and as an entrepreneur, respectively.

With one or two exceptions, all quotations are taken from tape transcripts. With regard to the taping sessions, all interviews took place at sites chosen by the interviewees. These varied from offices to living rooms, to the back rooms of pubs and in one case a suburban South Manchester back garden. The interviews were recorded on tape and the cassettes transcribed. All the participants were aware that the material would be used in the form of an 'attributable quote'. I discarded several interviews with people when they asked if the material could be 'off the record'.

On occasions throughout, I have intervened and placed myself within the text. While this may appear an unusual practice in the field of cultural studies, it is not so unusual in Anthropology (Willson & Kulick, 1995). Anthropologists, however (and Cultural Historians!) are expected to retain an objective distance from their subjects, to avoid personal intervention and mediation from intruding upon the gathering of 'untainted' knowledge. The academic problem facing this particular piece of research is the unavoidable fact that I was an active participant in many of the events under scrutiny and it is an advantage that I can therefore offer empirical evidence relating to certain specific occasions. Having said that, this is in no way an autobiography and I have restricted my interventions to the bare minimum.

Psychogeographics

I refer to the Situationist concept of Psychogeographics. This is used occasionally in an attempt to explain the seemingly spontaneous movements of young people and their scenes across the landscape of the City over the years. This is to say that the spontaneity is guided possibly through the psychic resonances of certain geographical spaces.

References

In too many cases, participants in Popular Music have been deprived of their voices. However, this balance is being redressed and there is a growing number of excellent studies, including some using oral history and direct field work, eg White, Finnegan and Cohen in the UK and Shank and Keil in America. Other research addresses the regulation of the night-time economy and the lived practices of contemporary music-playing, eg O'Connor et al (1996) at Manchester Metropolitan University's Institute of Popular Culture.

In this work, I have referred to existing literature where

appropriate and references to all writers and/or texts cited are provided at the end of each relevant chapter and there is a complete bibliography after the appendixes. There is no underlining in the references, but each publication is encapsulated in single apostrophes.

Definitions

Throughout the writing of this book certain concepts emerge, and these relate to questions of 'tensions', 'authenticity'. 'Popular Music' and 'scenes', defined below.

Tensions

When certain events (local, national or international) are stated by the interviewees as impacting directly on the music scene they experienced, I have chosen to chronicle them as 'tensions'. By this term I mean that oppositional dynamics are constructed, such as differing trends in fashion on pages 30-35 ('trad' versus 'modern'); Police action to regulate and close clubs in Chapters 4, 8 and 9 (law and order versus empowerment of youth culture and musicians); the structure and organisation of the music industry in Chapters 5, 6, 7 and 10 (centralisation versus decentralisation).

Authenticity

Authenticity is a reflection of 'tension' and the concept of authenticity is important, for example, to find out why young people choose one form of music over another, why some forms of music are treated with scorn and derision, what makes young people seek out forms of music alternate from the mainstream. The participants' own views on authenticity are delivered here.

Popular Music

I have used the words 'Popular Music' in the sub-title in the knowledge that a strict definition is problematic. Broadly Popular refers to Pop, meaning those genres associated with Youth music that have derived from Urban Rock, Jazz, Folk, Country and Western which has developed over the last forty years.

Scenes

'Scenes' are not specifically geographic. The word relates more to a metaphysical concept that dwells within a psychological realm of meaning pertaining to a 'coming together' of like minded people with shared interests and practices. Thus, within 'the Manchester Scene', there are a myriad of scenes that would appear to the outsider to be mutually exclusive. For example, The Fall and M People share a similar geographic position, but their music scenes differ widely, Freddie and The Dreamers and Oasis are both from 'the Manchester Scene' but decades apart.

The meat is sweeter the closer to the bone

Having stated the main argument and explained the theoretical approach, I shall now tackle the content.

Music is invariably linked with 'youth'. One of the original aims of this book was to examine that link. It then became obvious that many of the people covered by my research, who had started out playing music in their teens, or earlier, were now well into their 40s and 50s, and still playing music. The same is true of those involved in the infrastructures of Popular Music. In a sense, it became obvious that they had grown up with music, and saw no reason to change their life style just because they had reached a certain age of so called maturity. Consequently, although 'movements' can be said to be generated by young people, there is a sustaining undercurrent of involvement that does not recognise age. This observation will be reflected in this work and so, where reference is made to the Manchester music scene as 'youth culture', it should be understood that what is meant is (people of any age who are pertaining to) a music culture generated by youth.

The structure is chronological and covers themes and genres, or movements, rather than 'all' groups. That is to say, I have had to consider the overall view, rather than the story of certain individual groups. For instance, the history of The Smiths, or Simply Red, are admittedly intriguing and fascinating stories in their own right, but have been covered quite adequately in hagiographies elsewhere. Where necessary to the text, mentions are made of a variety of performers, but I have not felt it necessary to go into explicit detail. Similarly, the careers of certain other musicians have been highlighted, but only when I felt that their inclusion would contribute to the overall arguments.

Inevitably, this will lead to accusations of unfairness. Where for instance, a critic might argue, is an overview of The Fall, who have certainly been at the forefront of Manchester music for the last two decades? Why only deal peripherally with 10cc, who, once again, represented a solid Mancunian presence in the music charts during one of Manchester's fallowest periods, the early 1970s?

The simple answer is that there have been too many bands from Manchester to do them all justice. It would require several volumes to adequately cover the myriad number of musicians who have sprung up from the city over the years. I was forced by time and circumstance to be selective, and will, no doubt, puzzle or offend some people by my omissions. So must it be, but it is nevertheless worthwhile to plod through the fields rich with a crop of anecdotes and memories that I feel must be gathered in before it is too late. So much of our past is being destroyed, or lost, that it is a tragedy that we are not reaping this rich harvest. In the first appendix the reader will find a database of over one thousand groups who emerged from the Manchester area over the last 45 years, and that list is by no means definitive or exhaustive. Add to that list the number of people who worked peripherally in the business directly involved with groups: roadies, managers, agents, promoters, studio engineers, distributors, sleeve designers, photographers and such like, the total number of people affected by direct contact with Popular Music must run into tens of thousands.

Women and Rock (An Apology)

'When I first began my research I was particularly determined not to ignore women who, in several earlier studies of youth and Popular Culture, had been treated as socially insignificant, peripheral, stereotyped, or even invisible.... I was astonished, however, to find an overwhelming absence of women in the rock music scene on Merseyside....'
Cohen, 1991, pp 201/2

It is an unavoidable fact that the situation Sara Cohen found in Liverpool, generally speaking, mirrors the situation in the Manchester music scene. There have, of course, been notable exceptions. Elkie Brooks started out her professional career in the city under her original name of Bookbinder. Former Velvet Underground chanteur, Nico, spent her last years based in Manchester, and women like Una Baines in the Blue Orchids and Brix in The Fall, have been significant contributors to the music scene.

The research material here reflects the male hegemony noted by Cohen, whilst also reflecting the involvement of women active in the Music Scene in Manchester (see Chapters 9 and 10).

An outline of this book

Why Do People Join Groups?
We begin with a very basic question, why do people join groups? The resultant chapter falls into two parts, reflecting two separate strands of influence.

Part One

Music tuition at school. A certain proportion of my interviewees received formal musical training at secondary school level. The skills and knowledge gained from this enabled them to seek out like minded school colleagues, together with whom they would participate in informal Jazz jam sessions after school hours. Occasionally this was encouraged by more liberally minded teachers. Eventually, all these interviewees went on to become professional musicians, starting with Jazz bands in the 1950s, progressing to Beat and R'n'B groups in the 1960s, and subsequently following a variety of musical paths throughout the next few decades.

Part Two

The second line of musical induction was one that was to exert an even greater influence from the 1960s onwards, and that was the availability of Popular Music through the media. The introduction of television and radio programming designed specifically for teenage consumption became established on a much more regular basis. Such things as Radio Luxembourg, technological advances leading to transistorised radios and cheaper musical equipment, and the increased spending power of the post-war teenager, combined with pop TV programmes such as '6 - 5 Special', 'Oh Boy', 'Ready Steady Go', and 'Top Of The Pops', all introduced young people to different forms and meaning within contemporary cultural practices, and exerted a direct influence on viewers and listeners. Emulation of performers began to become specific within the desire to become a musician. I will demonstrate how the broadcast media exerted a seductive image of the exotic 'other' that has influenced successive generations of would be musicians.

This chapter also makes clear the importance of 'style' in terms of fashion choice for both the performer and the follower, the two, in fact, becoming inseparable within the context of recognition. Interestingly, the choice of musical preference was dictated by the fashions of the dominant forerunners. For instance, 'hip', young Mancunians in the 1950s followed the example of American West Coast, Cool Jazz players, with their Ivy League clothes, Chinos and loafers, as opposed to the more British dishabille of Trad Jazz Ravers, who sported sandals, jumpers and duffle coats.

We shall also see how style is a useful reflector of the inner tensions inherent within Youth Culture. There is the ever present tension of 'the generation gap', and quite often within Manchester music, organised resistance to trends within music orchestrated by those in authority. Here, though, we shall be concerned with the chosen, marked differences between sub-groups, a theme which re-occurs throughout the text, leading us eventually to an examination of the tensions inherent within the cultural structure of Oasis.

Folk Music In Manchester

The importance of style is also central to the next chapter, 'Folk Music In Manchester', which is historically fixated on the city's Folk scene in the early 1960s. Being generally perceived as the world of the student or intellectual, Folk was a movement which ostensibly eschewed aesthetic commercialisation, 'dressing down' was *de rigeur*. Even here though, cultural influences and sub-cultural nuances were operational. This Folk scene was not only the world of the traditionalist, inspired by manifestos on Popular Music issued by the Communist Party Of Great Britain ('The American Threat To British Culture', CPGB, 1952), and filtered through the 'Singers Clubs' established by Salfordian writer of 'Dirty Old Town', Ewan MacColl, it was rapidly becoming the world of the 'Beat', a kind of proto-hippy who was happily at home within the Folk community, or the Rock community.

It was these two camps that almost literally came to blows when Bob Dylan appeared at the Manchester Free Trade Hall in 1966. This was Dylan's infamous electric tour where he had a backing band for the second half of his concert. It was this performance on the 17th May that led to the release of a bootleg album, misleadingly entitled 'Live At The Albert Hall'. I have constructed a clearly defined argument with documentary evidence to prove that this recording was actually made at the Free Trade Hall. Positioning the events of that evening within a socio-historical context provides a clear picture of the cultural diversification of a so-called subcultural group, and will also settle once and for all, the arguments within musicological circles over the origin of the recording.

The Axe Falls

The next chapter, 'The Axe Falls', deals directly with the tensions between youth and authority. There was an explosion in Beat Music culture across Britain in the early 1960s. Young people had become a viable economic community, some of the needs of which were supplied by the converted cellars and warehouses that became the venues for live music. There were over two hundred Manchester clubs and dance halls that were active (though not all simultaneously), from 1963 to 1966. By 1967 this figure was down to little over a dozen, and by early 1971, there were three clubs left in the city that regularly catered for a Rock audience. The obvious question is, what happened?

With the assistance of colleagues from the Institute of Popular Culture I was able to obtain a copy of the Chief Constable's Annual Report for 1965, and as a result we now have a much clearer picture of what happened to the Beat boom in Manchester.

The Chief Constable had identified a problem as early as 1964, but it wasn't until the following year that the Police launched what can only be described in present day terms as a 'media blitz'. Interviews were laid on for radio and television. Press reporters, including journalists from the Times and the Guardian, were taken on secret tours of the 'underworld of teenage vice dens'. Slowly and quite deliberately, a moral panic was generated. This led to one of the most unique Acts of Parliament that had been passed, or would be passed, for a long time. The Manchester Corporation Act of 1965 went through Parliament unopposed and came into force on January 1st 1966. It was designed to ensure the closure of the Beat clubs by providing the police with an arsenal of legislation relating to the running, ownership and management of the venues. What this chapter does is provide a unique case study and analysis of a community riven by tensions between the Law (guardians of the community) and the lawless (youths operating beyond the bounds of accepted behaviour).

Research into the regulation of the night time economy is a relatively new phase of cultural studies and hopefully this chapter will provide a starting point for other cultural historians to follow.

Music Force

The legacy of club closures for working musicians in Manchester, combined with the increase in popularity of discotheques, is covered in this chapter. In 1972 musicians set up a co-operative, designed to breathe life back into the moribund music scene by starting up an agency and gig promotion service that would be run by the musicians themselves.

Music Force was officially established with a charter, treasurer and secretary, and for the next four years it provided many established and new musicians with a chance to work. It even published its own music magazine, 'Hot Flash', before those involved in the infrastructure went their own separate ways in the mid 1970s. That infrastructure is the most significant aspect of Music Force and its cultural legacy. From it stemmed the ability to start up two of the country's leading independent record labels, Rabid and Factory, and their support services which included graphic design, flyposting, record production and PA hire, were utilised to great advantage by the Punk and New Wave explosion that engulfed the music business from 1977 onwards. Many of the people then involved are still active now in all branches of the music business.

The conclusions to be drawn by the ethno-musicologist, or cultural historian, would relate to the significance of the formation of the co-operative and the eventual legacy as outlined above. Much of what was laid down by Music Force came into fruition in the 1980s with the advent of 'Madchester', and all the cultural baggage that attended it. This chapter clearly demonstrates how that groundwork was established.

The Anti-Christ Comes To Manchester

The following chapter, 'The Anti-Christ Comes To Manchester', demonstrates how the moral ethos and impetus of Punk rock was embraced by a new generation of musicians, and in particular how one event, the appearance of the Sex Pistols at the Lesser Free Trade Hall in 1976, acted as a catalyst for the disaffected and disenfranchised young people of the city. The performance can also be viewed on an international scale owing to the inspiration it offered to many who were there to witness it. These people were inspired to go out and form their own groups, several of which went on to international stardom.

One of the bands to emerge from that night, Buzzcocks, became the first Punk group in the country to release a record on their own label, New Hormones, a release which would spawn an avalanche of recordings by other groups around the globe that continues to this very day. This chapter is the first systematic use of oral history and documentary accounts to trace the development of the 'Indie' genre.

Post Punk Operatives

'Post Punk Operatives', the next chapter, is an analysis of the next four years following the original inception of Punk in Manchester and focuses on the relationship between musicians, recording, and record labels, in particular Factory, undoubtedly the most influential Manchester Indie label.

Peter Hook of New Order, among others, provides useful insights into the working relationship between management and musicians, operating under a new integrity implicitly negotiated by Punk values. The processes of creativity are also approached, as are recording and production, and negotiating with major and Indie labels for a successful deal.

From the other side of the creative divide, Anthony H Wilson provides a detailed account of what draws somebody into the record label side of the business, as well as a useful insight into network television's patchy relationship with modern music. Again this highlights an irreconcilable tension inherent in the music world, that of the artist versus the conglomerate, capitalist enterprise.

For a decade Factory was the yardstick by which Indie labels were measured. This chapter pays close scrutiny to this significant cultural phenomenon, examines the artistic designs and philosophy behind its success, and eventual downfall.

Fun In The Heart Of The City

This chapter involves the use of Situationist psychogeographics and oral history, to remap the city along emotional lines. Utilising the techniques propagated by Guy Debord and Raoul Vaneigem in the 1950s, a word picture is built up that provides an insight into what the Situationists called 'the Drift'. In this case, 'the Drift' is the movement of groups of young people from place to place, and venue to venue in the city centre over the decades. It looks specifically at the origins of the 'all nighters', precursors of the present day 'Raves' and offers an account of several places that have been at the epicentre of cultural change, namely, The Twisted Wheel and Roger Eagle's, The Magic Village.

This is followed by accounts of the city's music culture taken from the fanzine, 'City Fun'. This periodical started life as a mimeographed music fanzine dedicated to the burgeoning Manchester musical scene of in the late 1970s. It eventually went on to gain national distribution through Rough Trade. Proper layout, design and offset litho printing didn't render the magazine impotent, however, and throughout its turbulent life it retained an integrity and adherence to New Wave principles that often clashed with the rapidly altering lifestyles of the musicians featured in its pages.

In the final sections of this chapter, 'the drift' finds itself in the Haçienda during the final phases of 'Madchester', and examines the legal battles that went on to save various Manchester venues from new government legislation that came into operation as a result of the moral panic engendered by the increased use of Ecstasy and other 'Rave' drugs. The chapter closes with a juxtaposition of Manchester City Council's relationship with its musical culture, and that of Austin, Texas, as outlined in Barry Shank's seminal work, 'Dissonant Identities'.

Madchester & Scallydelia

This chapter dissects the rise of DJ culture and places it within a framework of accompanying cultural happenings that were affecting the Manchester music scene as a whole: the revival of the guitar band sound, an upsurge in live music venues, independent recording and fashion. The rise of 'Baggy' and its eventual transference into 'Scally', via such groups as the Stone Roses, Happy Mondays and Inspiral Carpets is covered, in conjunction with the revitalisation of Manchester's image within a post-industrial context.

Once again, the tensions between City Council, the police and other authoritarian bodies is brought into play in order to examine the tensions that exist between cultures inhabiting the same space. For once, it appears, Manchester's ruling body found itself at odds with the hegemonic autocracy, and the resultant interface of oppositional dialogue is accessed as evidence of the increased urban awareness of cultural change in opposition to that of established mores.

You've Got To (Rock and) Roll With It

This chapter demonstrates that there is a clear link that can be traced from as far back as the Punk era in the formation of Oasis.

The group's cultural inheritance, via direct involvement with other bands, most notably, the Inspiral Carpets, for whom their songwriter, Noel Gallagher worked as a roady, indicates the almost incestuous lineage that Manchester bands have had with one another since the early days of Popular Music in this City.

The final part of this last chapter examines the recurrent tensions within the field of Popular Music in the City. The tensions between law and order, between community and outsiders, and in the final analysis, between questions of what constitutes 'authenticity'.

Conclusion

A brief conclusion draws the various threads and themes running through loosely together.

Chapter 2

Why Do People Join Groups?

Or, more specifically in this context, why do people join musical groups? Is it invitation, desire, accident? Is it to communicate, create, bond, or as New York Times rock critic Al Aronowitz claimed in 1978 to procreate (in a conversation with the author: "Guys join bands to get laid"). If we break the chronological scale under study into 3 approximate periods, pre-1960s, Punk and post-Punk, we can see two certain patterns emerging. Part One concerns the pre-1960s, and the Punk and post-Punk periods are dealt with in Part Two.

PART ONE

It was 20/30/40 years ago today

For several of the musicians involved in this study, their musical education began at school or home.

"I had a slight musical education. (1949/50) I was taught - I was made to suffer piano lessons as a kid ... I was about 9 years old probably."
Tosh Ryan

"I was very lucky, I went into a school when I was 10 years old called William Hulme's Grammar School and there was a phenomenal Jazz band ... you had to join what was called 'The Corps' (Army Cadet Corps) and the Corps was basically an officer training corps - and if you didn't join it you were persona non grata - you had to go and clean the school field and cut the grass and polish the whatever. But the band was ... second to none in the country. It was led by a phenomenal trombonist called Bunny Myer. Now Bunny was a musician out of his skin."
Victor Brox

Bruce Mitchell's musical start came about because his father needed a drummer for his part-time trio (his father was a schoolteacher who moonlighted as a bassist, playing weddings and such like in the Wythenshawe, Macclesfield areas in the 1950s).

> *"I always figured he wanted me to be the drummer because the first thing he taught me was when you were packing the gear away after a gig take the bass drum out separately then fill the case with what was left over from the buffet!"*
Bruce Mitchell

Tosh Ryan again:

> *"There was quite a Jazz tradition at my school (Chorlton Grammar) ... I went to clarinet and I played that at school, and then I wanted to be a saxophone player, so I took up the saxophone ... I was sacked out of there (school) before I even took my 'O' levels. At that time I'd actually started playing dance band music with small quartet/quintet things."*
Tosh Ryan

So far we have heard from people who primarily came into Pop through Jazz. What of the embryonic Beat musicians of that period, the ones who got into music principally through Lonnie Donegan and the British skiffle boom of the mid-1950s?

> *"I used to look at photographs of where people were holding their fingers while they were playing, then I tried to copy them"*
Mike Maxfield in Lawson, 1992, p15

> *"I loved guitars and the sound they made when I was a kid. I even liked going to the pictures to see cowboys playing guitars. When skiffle started that was it for me. My gran bought a guitar for me and I got it from HQ and General Supplies for 2s 6d a week. I started on skiffle stuff like 'It Takes A Worried Man' and 'Cumberland Gap' just playing at home. Then I discovered a lad called Tommy Turner at my school was into the same stuff. We used to rehearse skiffle stuff and Buddy Holly songs, but didn't do any gigs."*
Johnny Peters, *ibid*

Rockin' Radio Times

Skiffle was a powerful leveller and probably did more to instigate the 1960s Beat boom (by allowing people their first change at creating music) than the more complex nature of Jazz, be it traditional New Orleans or the more esoteric nature of West Coast and Be Bop. The influence of the first wave of Rock 'n' Roll is also vastly overrated. Its consumption when it did arrive on the radio, jukebox or in the record store is not denied. That it was embraced fervently by its devotees is not in question. What remains, however, is the question, just how much Rock 'n' Roll was there? A look at the number one best-sellers from 1955 to 1960 reveals an interesting picture (Rice, Gambaccini and Read). In 1955 'Rock Around The Clock' by Bill Haley and The Comets becomes the first ever Rock 'n' Roll record to get to number one. The other 15 number ones are the usual mid-1950s' saccharine-coated Pop shtick releases such as 'Mambo Italiano' by Rosemary Clooney, 'Unchained Melody' by Jimmy Young and 'Dreamboat' by Alma Cogan.

1956 and Bill Haley was back in the number one slot again. The only other number one Rock'n'Roll song that year (we'll discount Kaye Stars' 'Rock and Roll Waltz' which was a cash-in on the trend) was Frankie Lymon and The Teenagers 'Why Do Fools Fall In Love'.

Skiffle makes itself felt in 1957 with 2 number ones for Lonnie Donegan, 'Cumberland Gap' and 'Gamblin' Man'; Elvis had his first English number one with 'All Shook Up' and Buddy Holly and The Crickets had 'That'll Be The Day'. The dubious Guy Mitchell also got to number one for a week with 'Rock-A-Billy'. The other number ones were by the usual chart-toppers such as Tab Hunter, Paul Anka and Johnny Ray.

By 1958 for every 'Great Balls of Fire' and 'Jailhouse Rock' there were too many Perry Como, Michael Holiday and Connie Francis tunes to make any difference. The same is true for 1959 when Presley's 'One Night' or Buddy Holly's 'I Guess It Doesn't Matter Anymore' would be pushed aside by the likes of Russ Conway's 'Sidesaddle' or 'Roulette'.

What this brief incursion into the Music Week charts demonstrates is not a lack of interest in Rock 'n' Roll, but tends to indicate more clearly a lack of product available for the newly emerging British teenagers to buy. Rock 'n' Roll was played rarely on the BBC in the 1950s, an executive decision having been made to allow some to be broadcast, but in a very limited basis. For a more detailed analysis of this period, see Rob Chapman's 'Selling The 1960s'. The influence of Radio Luxembourg, while more significant, is still very limited. Plus, access to other than a family radio, usually situated in the living room, has to be taken into account in terms of physical access to the reproductive machinery (transistor radios still being some way off in the future). The music that young people heard was, on a societal level, mediated through the dominant bourgeois hegemony. But what the 1950s did see was the creation of 'scenes', that is venues, musical or otherwise, where the teenagers could be independent of the all-seeing eye of parental authority.

In relation to specificity we can now chart the emergence of two particular avenues of opportunity being created for the young musicians of Manchester in the mid to late 1950s. One led from Jazz, the other from the coffee bar and youth club. Both avenues would merge in the 1960s Beat boom, probably to go their separate ways again the 1980s, with split between guitar bands and more dance-oriented Techno progenitors. In this, our examination of the first phase of Manchester Music, we must now turn our attention to the Jazz players.

We have seen earlier in this section the essential banality of the Pop charts in the latter half of the 1950s, the moribund state of the airwaves and the rigidity of control over output on broadcast TV. As a reaction against this sections of UK youth in the late 1940s and 1950s turned for musical inspiration towards an indigenous Black American art form - Jazz.

All that Jazz

It is virtually impossible to identify any specific reason why people choose to go against the mainstream of popular entertainment forms. Why abandon the safety of Bernard Herman's BBC Northern Dance Orchestra playing a selection of Tin Pan Alley hits in favour of tracking down obscure cuts by King Oliver or Louis Armstrong? There is an air of perversity about such deliberate reactions to the norm, a missionary zeal and a whiff of the trainspotter, a delight in being different, singled out. There is also an almost spiritual emotion attached to it; bonding, being brought together by a clandestine musical taste, the participation in transcendental ritual, the shared thrill of an illicit love, the exclusivity of a superior knowledge. All these elements run through the history of our sub-cultures, from Jazz to House; distilled they become a pre-requisite of teenage rebellion, the domain of youth.

But Jazz too had its cliques, its schisms, its heretics, martyrs and saints. Far from being straightforward, Jazz was split into basically two factions, the traditionalists and modernists. United only in their rejection of contemporary Popular music and scorn for commercially successful artists, in Manchester it was principally the modernists who held sway over the music being played live in the city. A few words of explanation regarding the terms modernists and traditionalists now follows.

White dance music had assimilated Black sounds and rhythms since the early 1920s. Dance fads such as Rag and the Charleston were imported into Britain in the inter-war years to be followed by the highly sanitised White Swing of Benny Goodman and Glen Miller in the 1940s. To those in the musical 'know' however, there was a desire to get deeper into the root origins of these forms of music and enthusiastic amateurs and a handful of inquisitive musicians discovered the rich bedrock of Black music that provided the foundations of White American dance music. Steve Morris, later to be the mainswing behind the legendary Manchester music venue, Band on The Wall, was whisked away to the Cotton Club in Harlem in 1936 to play as one of the 'Little Rascals' Jazz band. These were six young lads from Ancoats in Manchester who, in their short trousers and schoolboy caps, were supposed to be a marketing sensation on the American Jazz scene. What they brought back with them was essentially more important than what they took.

In 1943 the most culturally important event of the decade occurred with the arrival of hundreds of thousands of American troops onto English shores. These troops, black and white, brought with them wholesale the trappings of American Popular Culture on a scale hitherto unimaginable. Comic books, gum, nylons and language augmented the 'Americanisation' of British Popular Culture which was already awash with Hollywood films, advertising and pulp fiction, as far as commentators like the Leavisites were concerned (Leavis, 1930). More importantly:

"American soldiers arrived in Britain equipped with 'V-discs' of swing music given away free to the GI's by the US Government."
Chambers, 1986. p 140

We will look more closely at the influence of the American invasion on Manchester later on. For the moment we will concentrate briefly on what Chambers has called, 'Reaction, revival and renewal.'

Basically I interpret this as people reacting to the commercialisation of Popular Music, and responding to it by seeking a more 'authentic' root form of that music. From reproductions of that original form, the musician, or scene, can move forward ultimately towards renewal. Unfortunately, before this can be achieved, it has to pass through a phase that Chambers terms 'the hermetic conservation of revivalism'.

It's Trad, Dad!

Authenticity then was the watchword of what came to be known as the Trad revival in the mid 1950s. For the first time the word 'Ravers' appears as a noun, to describe fans of Trad Jazz. A dress code was created, and sets of beliefs and behaviours, initiated into the sub-culture; the adoption of a patois or verbal style all went into forging the exclusivity necessary in a sub-cultural group. Part of this quest for 'authenticity' and exclusivity consisted of ignoring anything classed as 'modern' in musical terms and 'modern' could embrace anything from Jazz recordings of the 1920s to contemporary Be Bop. Ironically, the New Orleans artists the Trad fans so much admired were all more or less dead, so for live music the fans had to rely on musicians such as Ken Colyer, Humphrey Littleton, et al, White English youths playing the music of dead Black men.

"The three 'B's. That was Barber, Bilk and Ball, could sell out city halls which was a bigger deal than you'd think. We had had, was it in 1955/56, we had had like the Bill Haley tours which had all sold out in city halls, but in England you did get this sort of Trad Jazz revival which was quite dressed up."
Bruce Mitchell

The audience for Trad, however, deliberately dressed down. They adopted a kind of unique British, middle class concept of Bohemianism. George Melly remembered it in 'Owning Up'.

"... an extreme sloppiness was de rigeur, both on stage and off. The duffle coat was a cult object, sandals with socks a popular if repulsive fad, beards common and bits of battle dress, often dyed navy-blue, almost a uniform."

Melly, 1970, pp20-21

Ban the Bomb, CND and Jazz on a summer day, the first Windsor Jazz Festivals (which later metamorphosed into the Windsor Jazz and Blues, then finally - Rock Festival), Trad is generally regarded as having been a mainly student oriented pursuit, a middle class thing. At William Hulme's Grammar School the Officer Training Corps Military Band were secretly mutating into the Tech Trads Jazz Band

"Like 10 past 4 on a Monday night we'd go down to the music room and we'd pass round, we'd smoke roll-ups and we'd pass round copies of Spick n Span, and we'd play Jolly Roll Morton tunes and we'd vamp up Doris Day, Guy Mitchell tunes ..."
Victor Brox

But Trad in America was a museum piece reserved for tourist bars in Storeyville. Jazz had come a long way since the 1920s and a whole new breed of musicians had emerged from the big bands of the 1930s to play in leaner, slimmed down combos, and the music they were playing had radically altered too. Amphetamine-fuelled staccato bursts of musical virtuosity flailed round the Blues-tinged structures, laid down by rhythm sections. An alto saxophonist called Charlie Parker had come out of Kansas City to New York and revolutionised playing and to a degree, players (Russell). The music was Be-Bop (an onomatopoeic sound to resemble the instrumental solo), soon to become Modern Jazz (catch-all nomenclature that covered Be-Bop, West Coast, Cool, etc), the image was that suave cool, the hipster, a signification of style.

A Question of Style

All this was an irresistible lure to those who had seen or gone through revival, and knew there had to be something on the other side. The rigid constraints of the allegedly libertarian Trad movement and its 'hermetic conservatism' were treated with disdain by those forming the new avant-garde.

"It got a lot to do with style ... I remember going to the Albert Hall in the late 1950s when Modern Jazz was first getting a hold in this country and there were two halves to this thing - National Jazz Federation's night

- Part One was the traditional part because of the fathers - you know, Lonnie Donegan and all that - and then the second part of the night was the Modern Jazz thing. So you'd got one lot of audience coming out and another one queuing to go in and it was amazing to watch because you'd have one lot coming out with beards and duffle coats and sweaters ... really stereotypical, coming out, and then going in were all these people in smart suits ... You know it was 4 button suits with brown velvet collar, and smart American outfits - people with short haircuts all going in - so there was a definite identification in style."
Tosh Ryan

"I was keen on West Coast music, especially Gerry Mulligan ... 'Cos, you know, West Coast had an image. If you've ever seen pictures of Chet Baker when he was young, Gerry Mulligan, all those things - they had a look to them. You know, Gerry Mulligan was an interesting case to me. This guy used to hitchhike all over America with his baritone sax, but with the image, you know, the crew cut hair ... he used to carry his horn, go in jam sessions. He had relationships with all those, all the real ground-breaking Be Bop musicians ... Then when he came to Manchester (he) just reflected all that sort of stuff."
Bruce Mitchell

How did certain young people in Manchester come into contact with this genre of Jazz and the ideas and images associated with it? The answer lies 25 miles to the west of Manchester at the American Air Force base at Burtonwood. Established as a main supply depot during World War II Burtonwood became, by the 1960s, the second largest American base outside of the United States. It became an autonomous, independent outpost of American, serviced by its own P.X., schools, cinemas and radio station until nearly the end of the Cold War. Virtually a mini state within a state, the American service men who served their tours of duty there had plenty of geographical scope to broaden their horizons. During World War II they had staged what were for their time, massive dances in the aircraft hangers, to Swing and Jump bands. They were raves, to use a later phrase, held amidst the Coca Cola and parachute silk hangings of an exotic alternative culture, about which the native Britons knew little, but cared much. The end of the War created more of a diaspora of servicemen and women, people who had no particular desire to be in the military other than the fact that they had been conscripted and who brought with them their own cultural baggage from over the ocean, and who were only too delighted when people in the region asked them to open up their bag of tricks.

"What I'm trying to say is that at the time Manchester knew absolutely no limits, cos you had all the musicians that were over here for a while with the Air Force bands ... You had this great feeling for Jazz in Manchester."
Victor Brox

"... It was a massive camp - that changed dance hall music quite radically I think because you got Americans bringing albums over, you got Americans who were playing in bands at weekends, that includes dance band music, moving from dance bands to Jazz, small groups. From Jazz things developed through the late 1950s into the early 1960s, into the new Rock 'n' Roll."
Tosh Ryan

The proliferation of small venues in the 1950s meant that American musicians had a chance to play, in fact, were actively encouraged. After all, it was their mystique, their authenticity that gave credence to the fledgling avant-garde.

"... there was a drummer from there (Burtonwood) called Robbie Robinson, who had a lot of fans ... Obviously a lot of interest was in the image as well as the fact that it was more authentic if you had a Black American drummer ..."
Bruce Mitchell

Once again, the question of 'authenticity' rears its head over Jazz music!

"... even if he was crap he was right! And also the image was important ..."
Bruce Mitchell

Image became a potent signifier:

"... You know, they had great clothes ... Ivy League ... and the buttons on the jacket would be important."

Bruce Mitchell

The other main influence on Jazz musicians at this time was based in the Black ghetto area of Manchester known as Moss Side. Having passed from middle-class prosperity at the turn of the century, Moss Side slid during the Depression but still remained an area of commerce and activity. It contained everything from rows of terraced housing to Victorian mansions, but after the Second World War became an area designated as cheap housing for the newly arriving third world immigrants who came to find employment in the service industries of the U.K. As happened in other ghetto areas in England, Chapeltown in Leeds, Notting Hill in London, the West Indians and Africans who came here brought with them their own cultural practices. Amongst the most important of these, at least in relation to the musicians' history was their rather liberal approach to the archaic English licensing laws.

The club scene is examined in Chapter 4, but for now, suffice to say that the influx of immigrants to Manchester provided a fresh musical impetus:

"... at the time they were actually increasing the size of the school and we had a lot of Jamaican and Trinidadian people ... and some of these guys were great musicians and they came in and joined the band. You'd have like a West Indian bass player, a West Indian guitarist, so the music, although it was ostensibly a traditional Jazz band, its parabola were very, very, very wide ..."
Victor Brox

Several years later Victor Brox would be playing in Moss Side.

"There was only one place where they (Africans and West Indians) could get together and that was called The Nile Club and there was a big band playing at The Nile Club and that band was called the Eric Deane Orchestra and in that band you had West Indians and you had Africans. Amongst the Africans you had Fela Kuti who was playing fourth trumpet; amongst the West Indians you had Lord Kitchener who was playing string bass."
Victor Brox

Combining all these diverse cultural elements in the 1950s, the influence of USAAF personnel, African and West Indian immigration, a desire for knowledge, a desire for experience that goes beyond that of the mainstream and we can begin to find reasons for the richness of musical talent on the Mancunian Jazz scene, but something else was happening in Manchester at the time, contemporary to the adoption of suits over duffle coats and Gerry Mulligan over King Oliver, and that was the beginnings of Beat Music.

Putting on the Agony

If, what we might term, the 'trendier' or more 'cerebral' youth of Britain, were forming an attachment for an avante garde style of attitude, appreciation and creation, a more accessible hybrid of Trad was to lead even greater numbers of teenagers into another direction, Skiffle.

If Presley and Haley initiated the first stirrings of youth rebellion, then a man called Lonnie Donegan consolidated it. He popularised a relatively easy to emulate form of musical playing that derived from the rural blues of the Southern States of America (Gillett, 1970). How he transposed this into the coffee bars and clubs of Great Britain is an interesting story which we shall look at very briefly.

Donegan came from a musical family based in the north of England. His father was a violinist in the National Scottish Orchestra and Donegan too, became a professional musician. After moving to London in the early 1950s he became a guitarist/singer in the Crane River Jazz Band with Ken Colyer until settling down into the highly influential Chris Barber Band. Barber was the purist's prime mover and in the typical fashion of puritanical fervour adopted by the Trad revivalists became a fervent musicologist in the quest for truth. Both he and Donegan discovered Jazz's contemporary and partial progenitor, Blues music. Barber's proselytising for the Blues meant that with his success as a Trad player he could invite Blues musicians such as Muddy Waters to appear in concert with him on stage in England throughout the late 1950s. (They appeared together at The Free Trade Hall in Manchester in 1958.) The importance of Blues on the Manchester music scene will be discussed below.

Donegan too became a Blues enthusiast and as early as 1953 was given a featured spot in the Crane River Band playing his version of an American street corner blues style known as 'Skiffle'. This proved so popular that he carried on his featured spot when he joined Chris

Barber. Donegan's version of skiffle was a kind of anglicised folk blues played on guitar, backed by a bass and with rhythm provided by the simple expedient of thimble-covered fingers strummed across an old fashioned wash-board. The old-style train songs became a staple of skiffle, thanks to their light, fast pacing, perfectly suited to the strum and sing style of Donegan. It was a live recording by the Barber band made at the Royal Festival Hall in 1955 that unleashed the Skiffle boom on the British public (Hardy and Laing).

Donegan's section received repeated plays on the BBC Light Programme and eventually a single, 'Rock Island Line', written by Black Folk Blues artist Huddie Leadbetter was released as a single on the Decca label in late 1955. By the end of 1956 it had sold over a million copies world-wide, and for the next two years Britain went Skiffle mad.

With its simplicity of style and immediacy of impact, Skiffle opened up unheard of vistas for thousands of young people across the country. Whilst others laboured away learning chords, notation, embouchure and the other various technicalities necessary for mastering the conventional Jazz instruments, ie saxophone, trumpet, clarinet, etc, many more took their first musical steps by acquiring a guitar and learning three chords. This precise configuration would re-occur in Punk's fanzine bible 'Sniffin Glue', some 20 years later which featured a cover showing the fingering on a guitar neck and the immortal text, "This is a guitar. Here are three chords. Now form a group!"

The complexities (and expense) of a conventional four string, stand up bass were easily eliminated by the introduction of the tea-chest bass, which consisted naturally enough of a tea chest as a resonating sound box, a broom handle as neck and fret board, an a length of clothesline plucked and slapped to produce an approximation of bass notes. The final instrument, the washboard could either be acquired at the local ironmongers, or from under the household sink. Now form a group - thousands did.

In 1957 there were an estimated 3000 skiffle clubs in London alone. Bruce Welch of the Shadows started in skiffle.

"Lonnie Donegan was the unsung hero of British music - his influence was absolutely enormous and far-reaching, and he has never been given the credit he deserves."
Lawson, 1992, p5

The Beatles first incarnation was as the Quarrymen, a skiffle group playing numbers such as Donegan's 'Rock Island Line', 'Don't You Rock Me, Daddyo' and 'John Henry', plus a skiffled version of raucous, traditional scouser song, 'Maggie May' (Goldman, 1988). Skiffle was percolating through to all levels of society and could be heard in pubs, church halls, youth clubs, schoolrooms, street parties and the newly-arrived coffee bars. For many musicians of the next decade's Beat boom, skiffle was the springboard that launched them on a musical career.

"He [Donegan] was my hero. He was truly the father of British Rock and Roll. It was Lonnie Donegan who inspired everyone to buy a guitar, and he convinced them that they were able to play guitar."
John 'Butch' Mepham, *ibid*

As a fad skiffle faded almost as quickly a it had begun, but what it left behind were dozens of youngsters who, equipped originally with little more than enthusiasm, now found themselves wanting to play, and actively looking for directions into which they could channel their desires and energies. Many would give up, but a significant minority went on to pursue a career as professional musicians, for better or for worse.

PART TWO

To summarize - In the first part of this section we examined the first wave of musicians to emerge from Manchester in the 1950s. These performers went on to fill the cohorts of the Beat Boom in the 1960s and can be broadly placed in two specific camps - Those who came to Popular Music through Jazz and those who arrived there through Skiffle. I will now move on to the second wave and beyond.

"It must be true, I seen it on TV!"
(Greasy Bear, 1968)

Firstly, I would argue that there was little cultural precedent for that first wave. For whatever reason that people choose to become performers, emulation, fascination, or whatever, by the time the Beat Boom was established as a cultural phenomenon there was in place a tangible entity that was increasingly appearing on the media.

Television and radio were in some ways reflecting the events that were happening in the world of popular music, and whilst the ghettoisation of shows such as '6 - 5 Special' was still in place the whole explosion of Youth Culture was too big for the media to ignore. Consequently Beat Groups would be appearing regularly on Granada TV, championed by the legendary producer, Johnny Hamp. Liverpool and Manchester bands were receiving regular exposure on programmes such as 'Scene At Six Thirty', and the various 'What's On' style of programmes.

An interesting historical point, 'Scene At Six Thirty' was hosted for a while by Bill Grundy who, in 1976, brought the Sex Pistols to infamy on his Thames Television show, 'Today'. Hamp, at Granada, was responsible for introducing a whole succession of Manchester groups to a wider public, Freddie And The Dreamers, The Hollies, The Dakotas and Herman's Hermits are just a few of the bands who received their first television break from him. This tradition was carried on in the 1970s by Anthony H Wilson who gave airtime to the Punk/Alternative groups that emerged from the middle of the decade onwards. *See Chapter 6.*

Exposure to music on TV and radio was much more the norm for young people from the mid 1960s onwards. Technological developments such as the introduction of the transistor radio, and in their wake, the rise of Pirate broadcasting stations, meant that music began to play an increasingly significant part in young people's lives. That, coupled with the increase in teenage spending power that arose in the 1960s, created a whole new climate within Popular Culture. It would not be a falsehood to claim that there had never been anything like it before; this was a whole new ballgame.

"Do you wanna be in my gang?"
(Gary Glitter, 1973)

Role models had existed for the earlier generation of musicians, but they were generally few and far between and had to be rigorously sought out. In the 1950s several seminal figures emerged, Danny Betesh, John Mayall and Paddy McKiernan.

".... what happened is that in the late 1940s, early 1950s, the likes of Danny Betesh were, for some kind of recreation, putting on gigs. In fact the very first all nighter, thinking about it was put on by Danny out in

Macclesfield at a coffee bar called The El Rio."
Tosh Ryan.

"(At first) we didn't take Mayall seriously..... He was an encyclopaedia of all the things you wanted to know. You know that Mayall used to keep detailed inventories and if you were well in he'd give you the things you wanted to hear and he was regarded as something of an eccentric crackpot who actually didn't have any musical ability of his own, except that he was a bit of a guitar player and of course, because we all were interested in Be-Bop and all these musicians were the greatest technicians there were, we wouldn't give John much credit for his abilities. And then, when Blues, that sort of Blues thing became popular.... He had an enthusiasm for a music scene, he had a cultural enthusiasm..... When Paddy McKiernan first started bringing solo Blues artists into Manchester (he) used to promote a place like The Free Trade Hall, and (he) put American Bluesmen on and of course somebody like John Lee Hooker being announced to come to England was a very big deal, but the promoters weren't aware of what John Lee Hooker was.

And they didn't know what the right band was to put behind him because John Lee would be coming on his own. And Mayall used to knock out a lot of detailed letters to McKiernan saying that he was the only bloke who could back him because all the other musicians wouldn't realise that you don't play twelve bar blues behind John Lee Hooker. I mean, if he decides to stay on a change because he's got a particular groove on that two or four bar thing, if he decides that he's gonna stick on that change, he won't move. And of course, there were a lot of shambles. I think John Lee didn't really bother about it - like the English band behind him would do all the twelve bar changes and wonder why they weren't with him! And Mayall actually knocked out all these letters to this effect way before, as soon as it was announced. He even threatened to jump on stage at the Free Trade Hall if they didn't do the gigs right!"
Bruce Mitchell

"You can see the way Danny picked up on things from the mid 1950s onwards and set a scene going. If you follow that then it all carries on."
Tosh Ryan

Danny Betesh's love for the new music led him in the 1960s to found the legendary Kennedy Street Enterprises who represented, amongst others, Wayne Fontana, The Hollies, Herman's Hermits,

Freddie And The Dreamers, along with a host of other 1960s pop acts. In the 1970s they carried on the tradition with Hot Legs, 10cc, et al.

Paddy McKiernan promoted concerts throughout the 1950s and 1960s, turning the usually staid Free Trade Hall into an internationally renowned Rock venue. John Mayall founded The Bluesbreakers in 1961 in Manchester, before moving to London in 1964. He is now resident in Laurel Canyon in California and is still playing.

Talkin' 'bout my generation
(The Who, 1965)

Another generation of young players was emerging behind the Beat Boom, people like myself, who were too young to attend the first wave of coffee bars and clubs were looking for a way into the rapidly evolving scene. The influence of music presentation on radio and television was an important one from the early 1960s onwards, as was a growing awareness of cultural change. Every Friday tea time the words "The weekend starts here!" were beamed out across the nation as 'Ready Steady Go' was transmitted live by ITV. In relation to 'Top Of The Pops', broadcast from 1964 out of the BBC's Dickenson Road studios in Manchester,' Ready Steady Go', despite the use of Keith Fordyce as co presenter with Cathy McGowan, presented a much more 'happening' format. Fordyce only lasted one season before the show's producers realised that he didn't fit in with the rapidly emerging movement known as Mod. One only has to watch a rerun of his confrontation with The Beach Boys - "So Brian, this surfing - is it a sport or a kind of music?" to realise that here was an older Radio Luxembourg DJ who'd been tacked onto the show to lend it a kind of credence with the older viewer, which is precisely the kind of person we hoped wouldn't want to watch it.

All the way from its opening Pop Art titles superimposed over a montage of Americana and teen pursuits, 'Ready Steady Go', with its in-sight cameras and floor managers (the most famous of whom was to metamorphose in the 1970s as Gary Glitter), its heaving audience of young black and white kids always represented a gauntlet thrown in the face of the antiseptic and anodyne 'Top Of The Pops'. The naive innocence and charm of Cathy McGowan, literally plucked from the streets to be the show's presenter, was a perfect mirror of the social change that was taking place in England during the swinging sixties (Everett, 1986).

As a musical barometer 'Ready Steady Go' more than made up for the sanitised chart psychopomp that permeated the aura of the BBC's offering with 'Top Of The Pops'. Somewhere in the world of teen-broadcasting, battle lines were being drawn and 'Ready Steady Go's' constituent audience knew that something out there was happening and the best place to see it take place was on Fridays at six o clock.

Throughout its four year run 'Ready Steady Go' brooked the trend in TV pop presentation by booking acts on the criteria of taste rather than chart position and as such was responsible for introducing to the British public a succession of Black American players who would never normally have made mainstream television, Little Stevie Wonder, Otis Redding, BB King and James Brown being a few examples of the producer's choices. That these same acts would then go on to play at clubs in Manchester like 'The Twisted Wheel' the following night, says a lot about Manchester's place in the propagation of Popular Music from a diversity of ethnic origins.

Meanwhile Johnny Hamp at Granada was busy producing a succession of shows that have now gained legendary status, 'The Little Richard Special', 'The Jerry Lee Lewis Comeback Show', 'The Beatles at Granada', featuring Peter Sellers' version of *Hard Days Night*, and 'The Blues Legends' starring Muddy Waters, Sonny Terry and Brownie Maghee, and Sister Rosetta Tharpe. This was a tradition that Granada carried on into the late 1960s with their classic 'The Doors Are Open' featuring the Doors at London's Roundhouse, and 'The Stones In The Park' documentary. So for music fans in the 1960s television did supply a limited amount of extremely good material.

"Give me a child until the age of seven."

In the late 1950s in Chorlton cum Hardy, a very young Mick Hucknall sat transfixed by the television.

"He took no notice of cartoons being shown on the television, but as soon as the pop programmes came on, he sat on the floor in front of my chair, staring at the screen. I said, "Do you want to watch it?"
"Yes", he replied. "I always watch it." and he did not budge until the programme ended. He knew the names of every star, group and song on the

show. When he heard a favourite singer or song, he looked up at me and said, "I like that one," or "I like him." He sang along to the songs.... He was like a little old man."
Imre Kozaritz, in McGibbon, p 18

For musician Eddie Mooney who arrived in Manchester as a student in 1975, the television was less of an influence than radio.

"I was always interested in the Pirate stations - I was fascinated by Caroline, and I lived in Northern Ireland for a long time and you couldn't get Caroline South and Radio London you could only get at night - just like Luxembourg it kept fading away. It added to the mystique. Radio London in particular - I was fascinated by The Who and bands that were to me, like really exotic.... So it was the pirate radio stations that really got me into the idea of being in a band."
Eddie Mooney

Top Of The Pops also impressed Eddie:

"Pink Floyd, I remember seeing them on 'Top Of The Pops', all sat on cushions, and being absolutely enthralled by that footage, which I believe no longer exists."
Eddie Mooney

There were other influences at work as well.

"They fuck you up, your Mum and Dad"
Philip Larkin, Parents, (1922-1985)

Sara Cohen, writing in 'Rock Culture in Liverpool', reports that local journalists spoke of 'two waves' of Liverpool music, the first wave being the 1960s, and based around the 'Mersey Beat'. The second wave was centred around Eric's Club (run by Roger Eagle of 'Twisted Wheel' fame) in the late 1970s. She then makes an interesting observation relevant to this section:

'Many band members of the 1960s now had sons of their own who were also in bands.'
Cohen, 1991. p14
"I got into music I think, through my parents - they always used to be

singing around the house. They always seemed to be playing music, and when we were young my Dad used to sing daft songs to us and things. I always remember on holiday, Drifters tapes being played all the time, each holiday it was the Drifters... I dunno, I got into music really early for some reason."
Scott Carey, Paris Angels

"My father was a professional singer - my father was actually signed to Decca records.... I can remember the smell of the record player, the rubbery pad on the record player.... And obviously there was always music in the house and as a result I was aware of the charts and I remember my father saying, "I'll sing this one because it's in the top five."
Eddie Mooney

Scott and Eddie weren't the only ones to be influenced at home.

"When I was a kid my parents were into Tamla Motown and Rock'n'Roll. So for me it was Elvis really, he was the first icon that I had. The first time that I saw Elvis (on TV), I thought, yeah, that's who I want to be when I grow up. I didn't want just to be a musician, I wanted to be Elvis."
Clint Boon

Buying records and watching TV were the principal influences on a whole generation of young people.

"I spent a big part of my childhood impersonating him, learning the dances and everything, and that naturally got me into Rock'n'Roll.... My first album was Bill Haley And The Comets, 'Rock Around The Clock'. Bought from Woolworths. About three shillings, you know, MFP (Music For Pleasure, a budget label of the 1960s)."
Clint Boon

Then began the arduous task of learning an instrument.

Woodshedding

On January 4th 1970, a 15 year old youth named Peter McNeish wrote in his diary,

"Today I will start to learn to play the guitar."
Pete Shelley in McGartland, 1995, p13

His father had bought his brother a guitar for his tenth birthday, and armed with that, and a Beatles songbook, Pete practised along with Beatles records.

"Every day after school he would be in his room with the guitar, teaching himself how to play."
Margaret McNeish, *ibid.*

Finding the right instrument could, on occasion, be difficult.

"I tried the guitar first but it was far too difficult. Then I tried bass guitar because I thought, well it's got two strings less... Then I got one of them Casios, you know, the VL1, thirty quid it was. That was an amazing instrument at the time it came out."
Clint Boon

".... I got into music really early for some reason, I took to it well. I remember seeing the 'Great Rock & Roll Swindle', seeing Sid Vicious on the back of a motorbike singing 'C'mon Everybody'. I thought - I want to be in a band."
Scott Carey

At the age of twelve Scott got a classical guitar and began taking lessons at school, but grew bored with the teacher, who, according to Scott, always wanted him to play 'Greensleeves'. He then lost his interest in music until a programme on television.

"... the first band that really, really affected me, that I knew definitely made me go into the music business was Echo And The Bunnymen. I saw Echo And The Bunnymen on the BBC 2, live in Sefton Park and that was about 1982, so I would have been about thirteen.... I got a bass for my 15th birthday that cost £35, and a little baby amp, copy of a Precision, and at

the time, with my family saying, "Oh, it'll be just like the classical guitar. You'll give it up after a bit," I suppose that gave me the impetus to think, right, well, yeah, and I got myself into it."
Scott Carey

We can clearly see that by the mid 1960s a variety of inputs were fuelling the desires to play music - television, radio, and, in keeping with earlier years, an introduction to music at school, whether clandestine or official. It seemed at times that every secondary school in Manchester had groups forming after teaching hours. The young Johnny Marr would roam round school looking for people with equipment.

"If someone had a guitar and an amp, they were his best friend,"
Steve Cassan in Rogan, 1992, p 118

From school to the bedroom, rehearsals after classes were, and probably still are, common amongst young musicians. A member of the Paris Valentinos, Johnny Marr's first band at school, Kevin Kennedy, later to go on to fame and fortune as Curly Watts in Granada TV's 'Coronation Street', recalled,

"These were the playground years. Instead of having a gang, we had a band. It wasn't that serious at the time. We didn't play our own material but just caused a racket and had a laugh."
Kevin Kennedy, ibid p120

The Paris Valentinos did cover material ranging from Rory Gallagher numbers, through Tom Petty & The Heartbreakers, to Rod Stewart's 'Maggie May'. Under the influence of cheap cider and youthful enthusiasm they rehearsed continually, learning and practising all the time. It was the same for other young hopefuls.

"I had a friend at school who was into the same kind of music and we started a band together. He played guitar and I got the bass... I chose the bass because he'd already got the guitar and I felt some kind of empathy with bass players... So I got a bass and we started playing music in either his bedroom or my bedroom - it just used to be learning our favourite songs. Just mess about, play a bit of Jazz and things. Then we learnt chords and scales and kept on doing it."

Scott Carey

'Woodshedding' was the name given by Jazz musicians in 1930s America to the practicalities of practice. You went out back, to the woodshed where no one would bother you, and you practised your instrument until such time as you were ready to face the public. In England, from the 1950s onwards, perhaps it should have been called 'bedrooming', so often do examples of it occur. Before the invention of TEAC Portastudios, at the dead of night, some would-be pop stars recorded demo tapes.

"... he (Morrissey) sent me a tape of six songs that he'd done in his bedroom, and it was all done very quietly. He sent a little note along with it, apologising, and saying that he couldn't sing very loudly as it would disturb his mother who was in the next room."
Richard Boon

Authenticity, Adversity, and Tensions

The experiences of the people outlined above seem to indicate two patterns of emergence, those who came to music through playing, either at home or at school, and those others who were 'seduced' by the notional concept of the 'exotic other' propagated by radio and television.

There are, however, certain common factors that they all share. At a certain point musicians have to make a decision which particular genre of popular music they wish to follow, and it is at this point that we can observe 'adversity' intrude into questions of 'authenticity'.

For the early wave of young music makers who came into the professional side through tuition, there existed a 'tension' between 'straight' music and that of the forbidden - Jazz. That tension would subdivide at a later stage into another tension, this time between Modern Jazz and Trad. This underlying theme is one which we shall see recur, and my argument is that it can be reduced to a question of 'authenticity'.

"The banner of 'authentic' music has been raised several times in recent decades; in the 1940s and '50s with Trad Jazz, in the '60s with the second folk revival, and in the late '60s and early '70s with white rock's

criticisms of contemporary black music. In all these cases, white audiences rediscover yesterday's blues, 'authentic' sounds that have evaded the corruption of commerce and the city."
Chambers, 1986, p147

I would broadly agree with Chambers' assertions in the above statement, but I would also add both early 1960s White appropriation of R'n'B, and late 1970s Punk as two other genres over which the banner of 'authenticity' has been flown.

Other elements of 'authenticity' are, I argue, concerned with class, and specifically the working class, and, what was once called 'hipness', and is currently termed 'street smart'. The latter refers to an ability, or awareness of what ever cultural nuances, practices and foibles are being observed at the time. In my day it was termed being 'cool'. I shall deal with all these elements where necessary, and specifically in the final chapter.

REFERENCES

Chambers, Iain, 1986, 'Popular Culture: The Metropolitan Experience', London, Methuen & Co

Chapman, R, 1992, 'Selling The 60s', London, Routledge

Cohen, Sara, 1991, 'Rock Culture in Liverpool', Oxford, Clarendon Press

Everett, P, 1986, 'You'll Never Be 16 Again', London, BBC Publishing

Gillett, C, 1970, 'The Sound of The City', London, Sphere Books

Goldman, A, 1988, 'The Lives of John Lennon', GB, Bantam Press

Hardy, P and Laing, D, 1975, The Encyclopedia of Rock Volume 1, St Albans, Panther

Lawson, Alan, 1992, 'It Happened in Manchester', Bury St Edmunds, Multimedia

Leavis, F R, 1930, 'Mass Civilisation and Minority Culture', London, The Minority Press

McGibbon, Robin and Rob, 1993, 'Simply Mick', London, Weidenfield & Nicolson

McGartland, Tony, 1995, 'Buzzcocks: Complete History', London, Independent Music Press

Melly, George, 1970, 'Owning Up', Harmondsworth, Penguin

Rice, T, Gambaccini, P, Read, M, 1981, 'The Guinness Book of British Hit Singles', London, Grrr Books Ltd

Rogan, Johnny, 1992, 'Morrissey and Marr: The Severed Alliance', London, Omnibus Press

Russell, R, 'Bird Lives', 1972, London, Quartet Books

Sniffin' Glue, December 1976, London, Samizdat publication

TAPED INTERVIEWS

Tosh Ryan
Victor Brox
Bruce Mitchell
Clint Boon
Richard Boon
Scott Carey
Eddie Mooney

Chapter 3

Folk Music, Dylan and Onwards

The concept of there always being music in the house is familiar to me inasmuch as my mother sang to me from a very early age. From whenever I can remember she taught me by singing, what appears now to be a fairly strange eclectic mixture of old English, Scottish and Irish folk songs. 'The Mingulay Boat Song', 'The Belle Of Belfast City', 'Coulter's Candy', and 'The Raggle Taggle Gypsies' are just a few of the songs that I learned as I grew up. Her other passion, beside her family, was Blues music and she had a small but interesting collection of 78's which she updated when we got a Dansette record player in the early 1960s. As a Blues fan, with her Big Bill Broonzy, Muddy Waters and Josh White records she wasn't fazed by the British Beat Boom use of R 'n' B as source material, but she always preferred listening to the originals when she could get hold of them. This meant that I came into Rock Music from an elliptical curve that was emerging in the early 1960s, Folk Blues.

Bringing it all back home

More closely related to the Trad boom of the 1950s, Folk, with all its attendant cultural baggage, was the Purist's movement, concerned with questions of 'authenticity', 'commerciality' (or lack of), and, what can only be described as youthful zealotry. The movement, such as it was, consisted partly of older enthusiasts who had come to it via Skiffle and the Singers Clubs (more about them below). As regards Skiffle, Lonnie Donegan had started many people off on a search for the originals of his repertoire and had discovered Leadbelly, Lonnie Johnson and Big Bill Broonzy amongst others. Through them they had come to White manifestations of Folk Blues, such as Cisco Houston, Woody Guthrie and Pete Seeger.

The second part of the older contingent were more oriented towards indigenous music of the British Isles and Ireland, a position nurtured from the turn of the century when The English Folk Dance and Song Society had been founded. The EFDS was located at Cecil

Sharp House in London. Cecil Sharp and the Reverend Baring Gould were two of the principal collectors of native song in this country, travelling around the countryside on bicycle armed with cylinder recorders to preserve the rich oral tradition that they saw rapidly disappearing. Sharp also travelled to the Appalachian Mountains in America to observe and chronicle the transition of popular ballads from the old country to the new. One of the results of this was to enthuse a young musicologist called Alan Lomax, whose enthusiasm was enough to persuade the prestigious Smithsonian Institute to fund his travels across America documenting different aspects of Folk Music.

As a result of this research Lomax was able to bring to public attention many of the musicians who would be mainstays in the Folk Blues boom of the 1960s. For instance, in 1941 he stopped by Stovall's Plantation in Mississippi and recorded a young man called McKinley Morganfield. A year later when he returned McKinley had changed his name to Muddy Waters and had decided to move to Chicago where he could find enough work to become a professional musician. He did, and became one of the leading lights in starting the movement later to became Urban Blues or Chicago R 'n' B. It is not entirely unreasonable to speculate that without Lomax's intervention the young Morganfield may never have made the move and the world would have been denied one of the major influences on Popular Music that America has produced. It is also entirely possible that the Rolling Stones would have had to choose another name, having taken theirs from a Muddy Water's song.

The younger generation of Folk fans who began to emerge in the late 1950s/early 1960s, appear to have been influenced by a dissatisfaction with the overall banality of the Pop scene, with its endless retreads of tried and tested formulas, its insipid cover versions of American chart hits and crass commerciality.

" He (his father) was one of these artists who would rush to cover an American hit and you'd have maybe a dozen people who would cover this hit and only one would have the British version of the hit which would compete with the American one."
Eddie Mooney

The times they are a-changin'

The escape route from the vapidity that many saw Pop becoming was to be found in the emergence of the Folk club. Like their counterparts, the Beat clubs, a high percentage of Folk venues were to be found in the coffee bars of major cities. It was not uncommon in the early 1960s for some venues to hedge their bets and put both kinds of music on different nights. For one thing, in almost direct antithesis to the Beat clubs, Folk aficionados seemed quite happy to consume alcohol and, possibly because the participants were slightly older than Pop fans, demanded it. We must bear in mind that the coffee bar to Beat club transition was able to come about with such apparent ease because no licence was required to serve alcohol. Also, Beat, R'n'B and Pop were pitched at a slightly younger crowd, it wasn't until 1966 that the Manchester Police began to arrest people under the age of eighteen who frequented clubs, operating under obscure and arcane legislation directly mirroring the notorious LAPD curfew laws that precipitated the Sunset Strip riots of 1966/67 made famous in song by Buffalo Springfield's 'Something's Happening Here (For What It's Worth)'.

It is necessary to point out that Folk, specifically in Manchester, did not simply emerge as if from nowhere, there was a vibrant oral tradition that hadn't disappeared with the advent of radio and TV. There are various factors in the Revivalist atmosphere of the 1960s that can be clearly delineated from existing traditions and customs, all of them predating the denim capped and Dylanesque flavour of the renaissance of Folk. Perhaps the most important of these has to be the A L Lloyd inspired maintenance of the English Folk tradition throughout the 1940s and 1950s. A scion of the Communist Party of Great Britain, Bert Lloyd wielded great influence on the existing Folk scene of that period, organising festivals, holding song writing competitions and generally encouraging working class people in following what he perceived as their traditional values. It is not within the brief of this document to analyse the machinations of Lloyd, nor his penchant for mediation of texts (the same must also be said as regards Sharp and Baring Gould), suffice to say that what was classed as 'properly working class' fell under Bert Lloyd's Stalinist scrutiny, and not just in the political content of the texts, but also the aesthetic. For a further and much deeper analysis and deconstruction the reader need look no further than Dave Harker's excellent 'Fakesong' for an explanation of these rather startling machinations.

Meet the Manchester Rambler

What is apparent in Manchester is the refusal of a tradition to die. One of the finest popular songs of this century, 'Dirty Old Town', by Ewan MacColl, was written in reference to Salford, not, as I have so often heard in the past few years from younger colleagues, Dublin (no doubt this is because of the song's revival by The Pogues). If I may be permitted a brief sojourn in the field of textual analysis, 'Dirty Old Town' pleads for the demolition of Victorian Salford, "I'm gonna take a big strong axe," and demands the building of a new Jerusalem on the ashes of the old. The irony that glares with hindsight from MacColl's lyrical plea is that Salford City Council did as they were told, along with hundreds of other city councils in the 1950s and 1960s, and replaced the festering 19th Century back to backs with Corbusier inspired high rise apartments, only to meet with possibly even more opprobrium than if they had left the original buildings.

Ewan MacColl was born in Salford in 1925 into a staunchly Left Wing Working Class family, called Miller. Young James, as he was then, was brought up in the grim, twilight world of the Great Depression made infamous in literature by Walter Greenwood's classic novel of life in Salford during that period, Love On The Dole. According to MacColl, the 1930s saw the last gasp of the era of Working Class intellectualism in Salford, and over at The Worker's Arts Club in Weaste, soon to become the 'croft' in 'Dirty Old Town', the young songwriter was inspired to form a radical street theatre group which did Agit Prop style performances outside factory gates and other meeting places. They were called The Red Megaphones. It was for them that he wrote the first of many great classic songs, 'The Manchester Rambler'. This one was composed to be sung at the mass trespass of Kinder Scout, one of the largest and most successful mass demonstrations in English history, when thousands of weekend ramblers descended on the Peak District moors, which were privately owned for grouse shooting, and demanded the right to walk them.

They were met at the train station by police and gamekeepers, there were scuffles and inevitably fighting broke out, arrests were made and terms of imprisonment meted out to the trespassers. However, public opinion was on the side of the demonstrators, the right to walk in the fresh air was an important issue, and the lyrics of MacColl's song were an uplifting inspiration to many.

"He said, 'All this land is my master's'
At that I stood shaking my head.
No man has the right to own mountains
Any more than the deep ocean bed."
'The Manchester Rambler'.
Ewan MacColl, 1936

During the Second World War MacColl changed his name from James Miller. Why, has always been a cloudy issue, his critics maintain it was to avoid conscription into the armed forces, others that it was in tribute, or emulation of Scottish singer Hamish Imlach, whatever the truth we will never know and his widow, Peggy Seeger, sister of American Folk legend Pete Seeger and step-mother of Kirsty MacColl, refuses to join in the debate surrounding the naming controversy.

The Radio Ballads

What we do know and can state with certainty as regards Ewan MacColl is his influence on the English Folk revival of the 1950s and early 1960s. This came about after he met Alan Lomax at the end of the war. This was the same Alan Lomax from the Library of Congress who had recorded the young Muddy Waters in 1941, and was now in Britain recording the remnants of the oral tradition here. Lomax put MacColl in touch with Bert Lloyd and in 1951 the three of them began work on a radio series for the BBC entitled Ballads And Blues. This was a revolutionary fusion of musical styles, encompassing British Trad Jazz alongside the likes of Big Bill Broonzy and West Indian Calypso singer, Fitzroy Coleman. Programmes were recorded at venues like the Theatre Workshop, Stratford East, and the Princess Louise pub in London's High Holborn. Audience participation was directly encouraged and the dialectical theories of the Folk revival were debated.

Mention should be given briefly here to another BBC radio series that MacColl had a hand in, along with pioneering radio producer Charles Parker, The Radio Ballads series. These documentaries were groundbreaking in their use of recorded oral testimony. Prior to the Ballads series, transcriptions would have been made of the interviews given by participants, and then these would have then been read out by actors, the BBC feeling that the listening public would be put off by regional, or rough, dialects. Parker was able to persuade the programme controllers that this wasn't necessary and the programme managed to break with the tradition. Each one in the series, 'The Ballad Of John Axton' (the story of a railway man who was killed in a train crash), 'Free Born Man' (about Gypsies), 'Singing The Fishing' (the working lives of trawler men), contained songs written by MacColl. Proof of the power of his song writing abilities can be noted by the fact that several generations later these songs and others by MacColl were collected orally by singers who claimed they were generations old and came directly from the Folk tradition.

The plight of the British Songwriter (A Lament)

An emotive, influential 56 page document was published in London in 1951. Entitled, 'The American Threat To British Culture', the pamphlet opened with a critique of 'American Big Business' which the writers claimed was the shadowy institution behind the dynamics of American Mass/Popular culture. A culture, so they claimed, that was designed to inculcate in the ordinary mass of the people such things as 'dollar worship', racism, brutality and 'gangsterism'. It propagated these negative qualities through cultural commodities such as books, comics, films and music.

".... its readers were informed that those alarmingly popular US made cultural commodiites were part of a plot, part of 'a sytematic, well organised and financed attempt to impose coca-colonialisation on the British people', and then on the rest of Europe. It was, in a memorable phrase, nothing less than cultural imperialism."
Harker, 1992

'The American Threat To British Culture' was published by the Communist Party of Great Britain and was the summary of a conference held by the National Cultural Committee of the CPGB. The problems facing English music from the threat of cultural imperialism were made quite clear.

"The plight of British songwriters is so desperate that the Song Writers Guild of Great Britain have made a formal protest to the BBC against the anti-British attitude of so many well known performers and dance bands. Out of twenty of the most popular current songs, seventeen are American, one is French and two are British..... British singers repeat the identical US settings parrot-wise. British crooners ape the Americans in slurred vowels and forced inflexions. Sometimes I wonder if I'm tuned into the BBC at all...."
CPGB, 1951

The committee also noted problems with 'our own folk songs and dances'. This was despite the sterling work being undertaken by Comrade A L Lloyd and the Workers Music Association. Significantly, the committee found that the proletariat appeared to prefer 'Popular' music rather than indigenous British Folk music.

".... folksongs were 'still insufficiently known to the people'. Clearly, they would have to be 'educated' into 'their own' culture."
Harker, 1992

The process of 'education' was to be carried out by re-invigorating the native Folk tradition, and preserving it from contamination by American influences.

MacColl and Lloyd kick-started the revival into life by opening firstly, the Ballad and Blues Club in London in 1953, and then, the highly influential Singers Clubs. In 1957 MacColl claimed there were 1,500 Singers Clubs around Britain with an 11,000 strong membership. Although this might rightly be viewed a success in terms of building up a musical movement virtually from scratch, the rigid Communist Party line in dialectics concerning the style and content of what was to be sung and how it was to be sung at these venues, was not only ludicrous, but was to have tragic ramifications for the British Folk scene for years to come.

What MacColl espoused was a perverted form of what was then known as 'nationalism' and would now be termed 'political correctness'. The experiment had started so boldly.

"When Alan Lomax came along with this music that had proved popular with generations and generations, I thought, "This is what we should be exploring!"

MacColl in Denselow, 1989, p 22

In the early days MacColl had found no difficulty jumping onstage with Ken Colyer's Jazzmen and singing a Black Alabama prison song with them, but within a couple of years the traditional British Left Wing distrust of anything American had overcome his musical instincts. For MacColl, along with so many others, even, ironically from the Right, America represented Capitalism, and that equated with the Great Satan.

" I became concerned that we had a whole generation who were becoming quasi-Americans, and I felt this was absolutely monstrous! I was convinced that we had a music that was just as vigorous as anything that America had produced, and we should be pursuing some kind of national identity, not just becoming an arm of American cultural imperialism. That's the way I saw it, as a political thinker at the time, and it's still the way I see it (1987)"
ibid, p 25

How this manifested itself in the Singers Clubs in the late 1950s was in the issuing of Draconian communiqués setting down in tablets of stone what could and what could not be sung, and by whom, in their clubs. These were known as the 'policy rules' and in their crudest sense meant the following -

"If the singer was English, then the song had to be from the English tradition, if the singer were American the song had to be American, and so on"
ibid, p.26.

MacColl and Lloyd took their cultural revolution even further and a stream of 'policy rules' were issued, this time dealing with the 'style' in which a song could be sung. To many people who simply wanted to listen to good music the whole thing had gone beyond a joke. How on earth can a musicologist, or anybody else for that matter, define what is the 'true' English style? Their rigid, Stalinist approach to a particular genre of popular music very nearly strangled the Folk revival at birth. It most certainly gave rise to the problems that faced many musicians who emerged from the Folk tradition in the 1960s, accusations of 'selling out', 'lack of authenticity', etc. We need only study the unreleased Bob Dylan movie 'Eat The Document', which chronicles his ill fated 1966 electric tour with the Band to witness the legacy of the 'policy rules'.

A sequence of the footage was shot at The Free Trade Hall in Manchester in May 1966, and we can observe the varying reactions of the audience from the footage shot by D A Pennebaker in the foyer after the concert.

"Pop groups produce better rubbish than that - It was a disgrace - He should be shot!"
Concertgoer, 'Eat The Document'.

" Judas! "
Audience member, Free Trade Hall, May 1966.

Amongst Folk fans the accusation that an artist had gone 'commercial' was enough to provoke fury and outrage. What was acceptable and what was not, was to dog the development of British music for nearly a decade.

The point here is that without MacColl, even though a minority of the audience were hostile to Dylan's changes, at least they were there. His personal crusade for Folk music, pedantically Stalinistic though it appeared, actually paid off in terms of turning on a generation of souls to an indigenous musical form, and also offered them the opportunity to explore beyond those bounds.

The emergence of a young tradition

For many fans and musicians alike Folk clubs and Folk music offered avenues of exploration towards 'roots/routes' that were unavailable in the Pop and Beat clubs.

"Before this (1962) there was a lot of interest in the Blues, but the only way you could actually get it down was to join a Folk club because there were no LP records...."
Victor Brox

Manchester had two things which were important in the development of Folk music, the proximity of the Manchester Ship Canal which meant there was an already existing tradition of Shanty singing, and a moderately active Irish tradition stemming from the influx of immigrants.

There were several important Folk venues in the early 1960s, probably the most traditional in terms of MacColl and Lloyd dictum being the one based in the Manchester Sports Guild on Long Millgate. Eventually this became one of the principal Blues venues in this country, hosting performances by Little Walter, Sonny Boy Williamson and John Dunbar amongst others; this was after the purist aficionados had given up the ghost and desisted from holding back the tide of commercialisation that was engulfing them.

Harry Boardman who later went on to found the highly influential Oldham Tinkers folk group was responsible for starting off several others, most notably a club based in a pub on the Oldham Road called Help The Poor Struggler, whose landlord was Albert Pierpoint, the public executioner.

"He was the hangman who hung Ruth Ellis - And he had this amazing series of letters from Ruth Ellis.... We used to go and play there at this room above the pub. I got fired from that band by playing the banjo too fast and too stringy because he (Harry Boardman) said that... "Folk music doesn't go like that!""
Victor Brox

By 1964, a variety of venues had sprung up around Manchester catering for Folk fans. The Ladybarn Folk Club, The Crown in Oldham Street, The Pack Horse on Bridge Street, and many others These were the ones where I started my singing career, aged fourteen. Let us take a brief look at a typical evening in one of these clubs.

The Ladybarn Folk Club was situated in the basement of the Fallowfield Conservative Club, a highly unlikely venue for a hotbed of radical dissent, which the club's organiser, Paul Brown, a student at the Manchester College of Art, had to point out to people each week was run separately from the main building, a rambling Victorian pile on Wilmslow Road.

"I rented it from them. I don't think they really had any idea what was going on at first, they just thought it was a bunch of nice young people having a sing song."
Paul Brown

Which in a way it was. The audience was a mix of young Folk acolytes with a sprinkling of Old Guard traditionalists who had come up through the ranks of the Singers Clubs in the 1950s and regarded the presence of the younger, denim clad Folk crowd, with their eclectic tastes in music, as something of an intrusion into their rather safely delineated universe. Whilst debate about musical styles and 'authenticity' was sometimes heated, in the manner of the MacColl/Lloyd proclamations, Paul Brown never let that interfere with his concept of Folk.

"We had an open floor policy which meant that anybody could get up and sing anything they wanted. There was a good range of regulars who'd come and do anything ranging from unaccompanied traditional singing, to people like Paul Taylor who played Folk Blues on a steel Gibson National guitar that he'd found in a junk shop and bought for ten bob. I think, that if anything, I was much more into the newly emerging esoteric side of Folk, Dave Van Ronk, Ric Von Schmidt, Dylan of course..."
Paul Brown

This vigorous, eclectic open floor policy was more or less unique to the Ladybarn club, in the more traditionally oriented Folk venues in the centre of town innovation was less tolerated, though young English players such as Leon Rosselin and Martin Carthy were beginning to gain respect amongst the Traditionalists by dint of their obvious devotion to the accepted forms coupled with their desire to take it beyond the imposed boundaries of the Critics Club. It was, by 1964, possible to accompany oneself on the guitar without arousing too much anger from the diehards, and even to include one or two original compositions.

In the basement of the Conservative Club too the times they were a changing, and a new form of youth culture was beginning to emerge, that of the Beat.

Hanging with the Beats

Points of definition are necessary here. The term Beat to describe a particular subcultural group, was first coined by writer Jack Kerouac in 1949, and passed into popular parlance in the late 1950s. Kerouac's full term was 'Beat Generation' and referred to what he saw as a group of freewheeling, semi-mystical souls, who, bored with the conventionalities of mid twentieth century American life, sought something more than that offered by the middle class aspirations of the Eisenhower era. Despite Kerouac's protestations that the word 'Beat' actually stemmed from 'beatific' journalists and cultural pundits of the day perceived them as 'lazy', 'dirty', hedonistic pursuers of free love and drugs, in other words deadbeats.

"(Beats are).... young men who can't think straight and so hate anyone who can."
Norman Podhoretz, in Alfonso, 1992

San Francisco columnist Herb Caen introduced the derogatory phrase 'Beatnik' in an article in 1959 (quoted in ibid), caricaturing bongo playing, goatee bearded, poetry and jazz freaks. It was a term despised by the Beats themselves but nevertheless the image of the 'Beatnik' passed into popular legend and across the Atlantic.

The Chief Constable of Manchester's annual report for 1964 mentions them along with other teenage subcultural groups as habitués of coffee bars and beat clubs.

"Individuals of exaggerated dress and deportment, commonly known as mods, rockers or beatniks."
Chief Constable's Annual Report, 1964

Chief Superintendent Dingwall who compiled the Chief Constable's report is to be applauded for his perspicacity in identifying Beats so early on in the 1960s. They were an extremely small group out on the fringes of the dominant subcultures and could only be reasonably measured in terms of a handful. The interesting thing about the phenomenon of Beats is that at that stage they integrated fairly easily with the other groupings, operating independently of them yet sharing certain characteristics. They could be found in coffee bars, Beat Clubs and Folk Clubs alike. I can remember being in Saint Ives in Cornwall in 1965 and seeing signs in shop and pub windows saying "No Beats" (not, 'Beatniks', a semantic point to note), so how could a concerned member of the bourgeoisie identify a Beat?

Beats wore their hair longer than most young people of the time. We must bear in mind that I am referring to 1964/65, a period when groups like the Rolling Stones and principally The Pretty Things were the arbiters of standards in shock chic. Most Beats had longer hair than they did. Manchester Beat, Andy Stewart, had waist length hair in 1966, it had taken him three years to grow it. A certain uniform standard of clothing would be the next point of identification for our concerned shopkeeper.

By dint of poverty, the majority of Beats were the original 'dole queue cowboys', that is, if they were able to claim unemployment benefit because of their habit of having no fixed abode (in fact, all the ones that I ever came across were supplemented whatever legitimate income they came by, by begging), so clothing had to be both functional and 'current'. Ostensibly they disdained the trappings that permeated the culture of both mod and rocker, but in the long run, sartorial pride was a prerequisite of the Beat persona, but certainly not sartorial elegance. This was to come later in the metamorphosis to Hippy.

Clothes then, were cheap, and practical. Always jeans, bleached by time, the weather, or... bleach. Sandals, without socks, at any time of the year, and occasionally bare feet, again, at any time of the year. Jackets were either ex army combat jackets or full length leather, a la Bob Dylan in the 1965 documentary 'Dont Look Back'.

As these represented a considerable outgoing of expenditure it should come as little surprise for us to know that Beats very often took some form of casual employment, the majority of ones that I came across, did this by grape picking in France during the summer, thereby ensuring a relatively stress free winter living off the proceeds. One of the principal recognition factors in the Beat's wardrobe was the predilection for carrying their homes around with them, in most cases a bedroll, or rucksack. It is impossible to determine how many Beats were 'weekend soldiers' and how many were authentic, but their presence on the scene in the mid sixties was influential and culturally important, they were beyond doubt, the precursors of the Hippies and it is an area of cultural history that remains to be examined in further detail by future researchers. Suffice to say at this present time, that the socio-cultural implications generated by their existence contain deeper implications for contemporary studies of popular culture than can be covered by this particular dissertation.

In relation to the Folk revival of this period the input of the Beats was, certainly in Manchester, essential. The appellation 'Beat', although American in origin, represented in English parlance a separate accretion of cultural signifiers. In America Beats were popularly associated with Modern Jazz. Kerouac had recorded his poems to the accompaniment of Gerry Mulligan amongst others. Beat, and its inseparable connection to poetry had generated a whole genre of spin off projects. Here in England the scene evolved around much more rock oriented concepts. Although Mike Horovitz in London was busy generating the All Saints Poets, leading eventually to the Poetry Olympics with Ginsberg, Ferlinghetti and Corso at the Albert Hall in 1965, the scene in the North West still evolved around principally what Paul Brown describes as "the more esoteric side" of Folk.

From the far north, in Scotland, a trio calling themselves The Incredible String Band were recording their first album for Elektra and causing a stir on the contemporary Folk circuit. In the South Bert Jansch and John Renbourn were giving birth to an hybrid blend of Folk Blues, Jazz and contemporary acoustic guitar music and song that would contribute in no small measure to a mini revolution in English perceptions of what was possible within a modern framework. Out of Scotland, but resident in the West Country, Donovan was building up a repertoire of acoustic guitar work that would within a year take the English charts by storm, but by far the most influential figure on the English Folk scene was establishing his reputation by releasing a string of electrifying acoustic albums on the Columbia label, Bob Dylan.

Mister Tambourine Man

Dylan was beyond doubt the person who took my generation into the Folk clubs. There was, in late 1964, a vibe, that was so immeasurable that by June 1965, when he appeared at the Free Trade Hall, for the first time, an atmosphere that was beyond description. How can I begin to quantify this academically? There is no short answer. The anticipation and expectation was Messianic. Dylan had by now managed to penetrate the English Pop charts with two singles ("Times They Are A'Changin'" and 'Subterranean Homesick Blues') and 'Maggie's Farm' was about to follow. But the principal medium for dissemination of the Bob Dylan 'message' in England was the album, and hereby arose controversy. To the purists of contemporary Folk, it would not be unfair to argue that albums themselves were suspect, containing as they did, by dint of their length, messages that were not immediately 'accessible' to the proletariat. Dylan had widened the arena for debate established by the Critics Club, and indeed had played before them in London in 1964.

" I was shaken when Dylan began to make it. when I found people treated him as a serious poet!... (His work was)... puerile!"
Ewan MacColl in Denselow, 1989, p 29.

MacColl's politically jaded view of Dylan's oeuvre fortunately had little effect on the views of Mancunian music lovers; his concert in 1965 was a sell out. But Dylan had visited Manchester earlier.

First time around

In 1964 ATV Television were running a programme hosted by Sidney Carter, entitled 'Halleluyah'. Carter, had written, or adapted, the seminal tune 'Lord Of The Dance'. He played host to a variety of 'Folk' performers in a programme that went out on ATV on a Sunday evening during the 'God slot' at around six o clock on a Sunday evening.

Bob Dylan arrived with his manager Albert Grossman in Didsbury, South Manchester in mid 1964. They spent several days at a boarding house on Moorland Road whilst the programme was being recorded. A tape from the show surfaced in 1975, but was never, according to my information, turned into a bootleg. The tape shows a Dylan who was on the cusp, as it were, of his creative world. At first Dylan announces that he is going to perform a new number,

"This is an hal..ucin...atory song. It's called.... The Chimes Of Freedom...."

Dylan starts the song, but falls off his stool half way through. He attempts a fresh start.

"This is...This is... called"

The floor manager has words with Dylan. Eventually Dylan gets himself together and performs the song.
Carter approaches Dylan and speaks to him.

"We actually were rather hoping that you could do 'Blowing In The

Wind' for us. This is a religious programme(?)"
Sidney Carter

Dylan eventually performs a fairly staggering version of 'Blowing In The Wind', thanks the studio audience and then disappears. In actual fact, Dylan returned to the Parrs Wood Hotel, a pub opposite the studio where he had spent a considerable time already.

The assistant floor manager who had been given the onerous task of looking after Dylan was given an acetate copy of 'Another Side Of Bob Dylan' by Grossman, and eventually, by dint of fortune finds momentary fame in the unreleased film of the 1966 tour of Great Britain, 'Eat The Document', where Neville Kellet, for that is his name, gives his opinion of Dylan and The Band, in the foyer of the Free Trade Hall.

"Yeah, I think he was dead good like. It was a bit loud when the band came on in the second half, but, no, it was good".
Neville, 'Eat The Document', 1972.

The broad eclectic influences of the Beats and the relentless development of Bob Dylan's creative ability, his pushing of the boundaries and adoption of electric backing for his new music, combined to lead to the eventual sizing down of the Folk renaissance. One could pick and choose what one wanted to listen to, there was no need to be religiously bound up in one particular form or another of Popular music to the rejection of others. Various elements combined to bring about this perceptual change, but the principal night of catharsis took place in May 1966 at the Free Trade Hall, when Bob Dylan appeared with The Band.

A slight psychogeographic interlude

A brief word in relation to the Situationist concept of psychogeographics is necessary here. During the 1950s Guy Debord, Wolman, Chtcheglov and others, would remap the city (in their case, Paris) along emotional lines. It would begin with the 'Derive', an action, best described by Chtcheglov as a

"flow of acts and gestures, strolls and encounters.... In 1954-1955 we drifted for three or four months at a time: that's the extreme limit, the critical point."
Chtcheglov in I.S., 1964, p15

The Situationists would meet, separate, disperse around the city, then meet up again with written accounts of what they had discovered on their travels. These would be examined, argued over and from the resultant findings a new 'map' taking into account the psychogeographic findings would be posited. As in psychoanalysis, the derive, or flow of language and associations from the patient, is allowed to continue until the moment the analyst interjects by rejecting or modifying a word or phrase. The derive then transforms itself into the detournement. This was the symbolically magickal moment of spontaneous creation that the Situationists craved, the turnaround in consciousness that brought about a transformation of perception in relation to a geo-psychical space, the hidden history of a city unearthed by psychic archaeology.

"It is a turning around and a reclamation of lost meaning: a way of putting the stasis of the spectacle in motion."
Plant, 1992, p86

If cities contain areas that resonate with an aura of energy, hidden oases of cultural rumblings, then the Free Trade Hall in Manchester is certainly one of them. Originally, St Peter's Fields, an open site adjacent to the burgeoning city, it came to infamy in 1819 when a meeting at which Chartists protesting for a democratic Parliament were being addressed by reformer Henry Hunt. The Chief Constable called in the Yeomenry to disperse the crowd and led by 'Nadine Joe', a bitter opponent of the democracy movement, the cavalry charged the unarmed citizenry. Eleven men, women and children were killed and over 500 wounded.

"With Henry Hunt we'll go me boys,
With Henry Hunt we'll go.
We'll mount the cap of Liberty
In spite of Nadine Joe!"
Ballad of Peterloo, circa 1820

In an ironic commentary on the Battle of Waterloo, three years previously, the people of Manchester renamed the site Peterloo in honour of those who fell in the massacre. In 1843 a permanent brick building capable of holding six and a half thousand people was opened on the site. It was used for public meetings and performances and named the Free Trade Hall. This building was gutted during the Blitz; the present one opened in 1951, and closed its doors as a concert hall in July 1996.

Its importance in terms of Popular Culture in the latter half of the 20th Century revolves around the use of the building for concerts. It was not only the home of the Hallé Orchestra, but has been used by independent promoters for a wide variety of performers. Two concerts in particular though were of tremendous importance in shaping the musical destiny of Manchester, Bob Dylan in 1966 as mentioned above, and just over ten years later in the separate, upper concert area, known as the Lesser Free Trade Hall, The Sex Pistols. The importance of this first appearance outside London by Malcolm McLaren's Punk avatars will be examined at length in Chapter 6. For the moment, we will look at Dylan.

Fortunately for cultural historians, several documents pertaining to Dylan's appearance are extant. Firstly, 'Eat The Document', directed by Bob Dylan and Howard Alk, contains not just the foyer footage that I have already described, but extracts from the concert itself. Secondly, there is an audio tape of the first half of the evening when Dylan performed his solo set acoustically; and finally, there is a bootleg recording, erroneously known as 'Live At The Albert Hall'. Before going further I will attempt to clear up the confusion surrounding this latter item, which has now passed into legend as one of the all time great unofficial recordings ever made.

Live at the Albert Hall

Most concerts of the Dylan UK tour of 1966 were recorded by CBS. A blistering live version of 'Just Like Tom Thumb's Blues', recorded in Liverpool was issued as the B side of 'I Want You' in England in July 1966. The recording of what has come to be known as The Albert Hall bootleg emerged in America in 1970. Bizarrely, its original release sold poorly. Then, in an irony of ironies, it was bootlegged by other pirates, the sound quality being so good that degeneration was hardly noticeable. Clinton Heylin in his excellent history of bootlegging, 'The Great White Wonders', has an account of 'Alan' a mysterious Englishman who delivered the tapes to Michael O, founder of the Lemon Records Bootleg label.

"Alan wandered into our record store.... He was a very flash dressed English person walking into a hippy store, and he said he had some tapes and had no clue how to get them pressed up. So of course I said, "I do. What have you got?....."

Heylin, 1994, p 74

After much to'ing and fro'ing Michael O persuaded an increasingly paranoid Alan to let him press up the tapes and after handing them over the reluctant Englishman returned home.

Michael O estimated that he sold just under a thousand on his label before they were bootlegged themselves.

"I got all artistic on the cover, and because it was selling slow, it didn't generate the kind of money that Get Back (a Beatle's bootleg that he had put out) did, so when (Alan) got back to the States hoping for a big payoff, I had a few hundred dollars for him and some pressings. He went back to England again almost immediately."

ibid, page 76

The album went on to become one of the most consistently selling bootlegs of all time, having the accolade of being the second bootleg to appear on CD (in 1989). It is still available at outlets for this kind of product. None of this, however, helps us identify the venue of the concert. In 1979 I was interviewed by Dylan fanzine 'Barbed Wire Fence', where I stated my view drawn from personal recollection that the venue was The Free Trade Hall and not The Albert Hall. These recollections were based on my memories of certain events that took place during the concert, and also a report from the Melody Maker the week after Dylan's Albert Hall appearance where it reprinted a statement that Dylan made on stage, in full. This statement doesn't appear on the bootleg. So, for various reasons my feelings were towards a Mancunian origin for the recording. Over the years other evidence has come my way which backed up my original hunch. When I recently played the CD version for my brother-in-law who had been present at The Albert Hall in 1966, he pointed out that Dylan had played 'Ballad Of A Thin Man' accompanied by only his piano playing (this however, remains apocryphal and beyond the remit of this dissertation). On the CD he has full backing from the Band.

""Judas", "You're a liar" was not at the Albert Hall. The bootleg of Live At The Albert Hall was actually made in Manchester."
Abrams, quoted in Green, 1988, p82

By page 367 of 'Great White Wonders', Clinton Heylin refers to the Free Trade Hall as being the origin of the recordings, and finally Dylan himself makes reference to the Free Trade Hall in the booklet that accompanied his official Bootleg boxed set, released in 1991. Further evidence has now emerged to back my claim, this time by comparing reviews of the Albert Hall concert, taken from The Times issue of the 27th May 1966, and a review of the Free Trade Hall concert that comes from the Oldham Evening Chronicle of the 25th May 1966. This was a weekly paper, which would explain the time lag, the Manchester concert having taken place on the 17th May.

Nowhere in the 33 line Times review is there a mention of the Judas incident. Surely, if it had taken place at the Albert Hall it would have been reported? However, the Oldham Evening Chronicle's reporter wrote -

"When someone shouted out 'Judas!' he just calmly went to the microphone and quietly drawled, 'Ya liar'."
Oldham Evening Chronicle, 25th May 1966

Hopefully, this clears up the issue once and for all.

Sitting on a barbed wire fence

Around two thousand people packed into the Free Trade Hall that May evening in 1966. With no pun intended, the atmosphere was electric. Dylan had filled the same hall one year previously, but the intervening twelve months had seen a dramatic change in the output and style of Dylan. He had attained no less than eight chart hits in this country since March 1965 and was currently in the Top Ten with 'Rainy Day Women # 12 & 35'. All but the first one, 'The Times They Are A Changin'', had featured full Rock and Roll backing, arousing enormous controversy in conventional Folk circles.

The MacColl/Critics Club axis were apoplectic with rage at what was denounced as Dylan's commercialisation (this from a man who would earn an estimated quarter of a million pounds in royalties for a face cream advert that used his song, 'The First Time Ever I Saw Your Face'), and tempers were running high. Dylan had attracted a whole new audience for his particular type of music, Mods, Beats, Teenyboppers, and probably an equal amount of young people who had no particular constituency at all, just an avowed liking for the music. In fact, Dylan was perceived as almost messianic by a large proportion of his fans; each album eagerly received, then deconstructed and scrutinised for secret meanings; the covers decoded for clues; any minuscule scraps of information about him that appeared in the press seized upon and treated as if they were manna from on High. To the diehard Traditionalists all this adulation was yet more evidence that Dylan was a "traitor". There was an air of 'betrayal' surrounding the gig, and reports had come in that Dylan had been booed in Dublin by an Irish audience outraged at the inclusion of an electric backing band for the second half of his set. The question, of course, is how could people have failed to notice that Dylan was firmly set on playing 'electric'? The last two albums and seven singles had all been recorded that way, but somehow a group of people were bent on sabotaging the gigs under the rather bizarre misapprehension that Dylan would suddenly see the error of his ways and return to the fold.

The first half of the concert went well enough. Before Dylan took to the stage there was a buzz of apprehension as regards what appeared to be mountains of equipment. Giant speaker cabinets were set up on each side of the stage, huge Marshall amps appeared on each side of a drumkit. There was a Hammond organ with a grand piano opposite. One microphone was set at centre stage with a stool at its side. The stage darkened and there was a moment or two of silence and then a spotlight picked out the lightsuited, slight figure of Dylan entering from stage left.

The applause was reserved but warm, as Dylan tuned his acoustic guitar. Audible sighs of relief came from a section of the audience. He'd obviously decided not to play with the group after all.

The 45 minutes or so that followed were, in my opinion, magickal, Dylan performing a selection tunes old and new, with an intense fervour that was to carry on throughout the evening. Songs like 'Desolation Row' and 'It's All Over Now Baby Blue' counterpointed tunes we hadn't heard before such as 'Visions of Johanna' and 'Fourth Time Around', these would be released later in the summer when 'Blonde On Blonde' came out. What we didn't know at the time was that this would probably be the only time we'd ever hear them sung to a simple guitar and harmonica accompaniment. Dylan finished the first part of his concert with an astonishing virtuoso version of 'Mr Tambourine Man' that surpassed anything I'd ever heard before in my life, his harmonica solo transmuting into an almost timeless, ethereal crescendo of magisterial splendour. The improvisational flights of music that rang over our heads in the hall that night attained an almost cathedral like quality, shimmering and incandescent. It was one Hell of a solo.

Dylan bowed and left the stage to a much warmer and livelier reception than when he'd first appeared. The house lights came up and the audience began talking animatedly. What seemed like a host of technicians climbed all over the equipment on the stage. After about twenty minutes the stage crew disappeared and the hall lights went down again, the stage was in complete darkness as we waited for what was to follow.

A light smattering of applause greeted Dylan's return to the stage. This time he was accompanied by a group of musicians who settled themselves around the stage, tuning their instruments along with Dylan who was carrying a red starburst Fender electric guitar. After quite few moments of this tuning Dylan began strumming, and leaning forward towards the lead guitarist, brought the head of his guitar down to bring in the band. The first tune was 'Tell Me Momma', a searing electric stomper that no one had heard before. The effect I can only describe as astonishing. It was loud, louder than anything I'd ever heard before in my life. I wasn't the only one to feel knocked back in my seat by the sheer volume of Dylan and The Band in full flight. It must be borne in mind that this was in the early days of Rock concerts and Britain lagged wearily behind the Americans in utilising new technology. Several weeks later I saw The Who at a club in town and all they had(and they were a big Top Ten act by then) was the usual two column Wem PA system with a volume of 100 watts each. Dylan apparently was using a 1000 watts.

The applause at the end of 'Tell Me, Momma' was polite but tentative, it seems now on relistening to the gig that the atmosphere was a bit like a Mexican standoff, each side waiting for the other to make their move. Dylan then spoke...

"This is called I Don't Believe You, It used To go Like That But Now It Goes Like This...."

There is slight, nervous laughter from the audience, then Dylan takes off.

The Band are given a chance to solo on this song and Robbie Robertson excels himself with a hard bitten Fender break that perfectly compliments the swirling organ that follows it. At the end of the tune the applause is again polite but reserved. Dylan changed his harmonica and began to bring the Band into 'Baby Let Me Follow You Down' when the trouble started.

Just before the ensemble took off a section of the crowd began a slow handclap. Momentarily Dylan faltered but then began the riff again and off they went in to the number.

At the end, so far no one had booed Dylan, but the atmosphere was getting quite tense. Unperturbed, The Band launched into 'Just Like Tom Thumb's Blues'. In terms of energy and determination this particular song almost equals 'Like A Rolling Stone' which will come at the end of the show, but for the moment it sufficed to put Dylan firmly and irrevocably in the forefront of contemporary music. The number   shouting from the audience.

"Do a solo."

Dylan snarls into the microphone,

"I don't believe you."

One of the band replies,

"He's a liar..."

Robbie Robertson joins in with a venomous,

"He's a fuckin' liar!"

Then they smash into a hard edged, vibrant sonic boom of a reply to the hecklers in the crowd. 'Like A Rolling Stone' that night will be in my memory forever.

And so it was over. Dazed and confused we left the hall and out into the night, but for the majority of people who were there that night something significant had happened. Life would never quite be the same again. Dylan's gig heralded the demise of the Folk clubs. They didn't die over night, but within a year there were none left in central Manchester. Who wanted to be identified with people who couldn't see what was going on, who couldn't understand that it was quite alright to go and see a Rock Band one night and a Folk group another? The Traditionalists under the thumb of the Critics Club had painted themselves into an ideological and aesthetic corner that they would remain in for a long time, but for many others what they had received that night was a benediction and a direction. Music would never be the same again.

REFERENCES

Abrams, Steve quoted in Jonathon Green, 1988, 'Days In The Life', London, Heinemann

Alfonso, Barry, 1992, 'The Beat Generation' booklet accompanying Rhino Records Compilation. Santa Monica, Ca

Chief Constable's Annual Report, 1964, Manchester

Chtcheglov, August 1964, Paris, "Lettres de loin," I.S. No. 9

Communist Party of Great Britain, 1951, The American Threat to British Culture, London, Arena

Denselow, Robin, 1989, 'When The Music's Over', London, Faber & Faber

Dylan, Bob, 1996, 'Guitars Kissing and The Contemporary Fix', Sony Private Pressing CD

Harker, David, 1992, 'Bringing It All Back Home', Unpublished Typescript

Harker, David, 1985, 'Fakesong: The Manufacture of British 'Folk Song'', Milton Keynes, Open University Press

Heylin, Clinton, 1994, 'The Great White Wonders', London, Viking

Oldham Evening Chronicle, 25 May 1966

Plant, Sadie, 1992, 'The Most Radical Gesture', London, Routledge

TAPED INTERVIEWS

Victor Brox
Eddie Mooney

Chapter 4

The axe falls

Alan Lawson in his book 'It Happened in Manchester' has a partial list of over 200 Manchester clubs which featured live music during the Beat boom of the 1960s and, as he readily admits, the list is incomplete. Similarly, opening up an edition of a Friday night's Manchester Evening News and Chronicle for, say, mid-1965, you could find one-and-a-half broadside pages, or more, of club listings. Nowadays City Life magazine (the local listings magazine) is hard-pressed to fill two A4 pages with live gigs. The situation in the very early 1970s was even worse. What happened?

Too much monkey business

There are various reasons put forward depending on who you are talking to. The one common denominator in all of these is police action. Manchester had come to rival Hamburg as the Fun City of Europe. The clubs that were so popular with young people had almost as many equivalents for an older-age group. Whilst drug taking (principally amphetamines and hashish for the teenagers) was the demand in Beat clubs, alcohol and sex were the prerequisites for mature club goers. Late-night drinking in quasi/semi, or totally illegal premises is the one reason given for the police crackdown. The truth is somewhat more complex and even at this stage, 30 years later, so we are lead to believe, dangerous for several of the people willing to talk about it. There are suggestions that it involved Police corruption on a large scale and had ramifications that echoed clearly through the years, from the so-called 'Stalker Affair' (Murphy, 1991), possibly even to today's current image of 'Gunchester'. One of the results of the burgeoning Beat scene was the proliferation of legal and quasi-legal venues. Apart from the Shebeens and Blues clubs of immigrant areas such as Moss Side and Hulme (see Chapter 8) a veritable sprawl of cabaret clubs, late-night drinking dens, and pick-up points opened up in and around the city centre.

There is an apocryphal story with two or three endings extant that I have heard in Manchester and Liverpool, concerning the Kray gang of London attempting to infiltrate the lucrative night-club scene in whichever city you're told the story. In both towns there is a 'police' version of the tale, and an underworld version. I shall present them separately. All the stories take place in 1965.

Enter, the twins

The legend in the Manchester police version is that Ronnie and Reggie Kray themselves took the Euston train from London and, upon arrival at Piccadilly Station Manchester, were met by a group of large CID officers who had been tipped off that the Krays were coming to town to 'muscle in' in the legal and illegal clubs. They were informed, in no uncertain terms (hence the 'large' CID men, usually quoted as being ex-Guardsmen by police sources), that their presence was not desired in Manchester, and the disgruntled twins were put straight back on the next train to London. The Liverpool policy story is virtually identical. The underworld story is more or less the same, up to a point.

In Liverpool it was an emissary, not the Krays themselves, who was met at the station by a deputation of police and local villains. Taken away 'for a chat', he's later sent back to the Krays minus his ears which are left adorning the bar of a Liverpool drinking den. As a result, the legend has it, the twins decided to leave Liverpool out of their scheme of things, the local gangsters there being 'too hard' even for them.

The Manchester version, which has been related to me by several sources, associated with club management (all of whom have asked to remain anonymous, or have made their comments off-the-record) has the Krays arriving in Manchester and being taken away from the station by Police to the newly-built Piccadilly Hotel where a deputation of Manchester gangsters held the Krays at gunpoint and made it clear that they didn't want or need Cockney criminals muscling in on their territory. The Krays, suitably chastened, were then returned to the train station by the police and sent packing back to London.

Exit the twins and enter the bad apples

Amusing enough tales which have entered into Mancunian and

Liverpudlian folklore. Personally, I find the idea that the Krays (who were at the peak of their power in 1965/6) would be intimidated by anyone, either police or fellow criminals, highly unlikely. An interesting footnote to the alleged episode, however, can be found in West Yorkshire Police Chief Constable Colin Sampson's report into the Stalker Affair published in 1986. A substantial number of the allegations made against Manchester's Deputy Chief Constable, John Stalker, were provided by a criminal called David Burton aka David Bertelstein. In the 1960s Burton had been both a chauffeur for the Krays as well as a member of the young, but rising, Manchester criminal fraternity known as the Quality Street Gang, so we have a link, albeit tenuous, between the two groups suggesting a level of co-operation rather than antagonism.

In relation to the original question, 'where did all the clubs go?' we must now examine briefly the alleged area of police corruption.

We have already seen one (unsubstantiated, I hasten to point out) allegation of certain Central Manchester Division CID officers working in collusion with local underworld figures, i.e. the Kray anecdotes. There are other allegations from the same sources that corruption in the form of taking protection money from the clubs existed on a wide scale during the mid-1960s, and that the closure of the clubs, the refusal to renew licenses, etc., was the result of a huge shake-up of officers designed to 'morally cleanse' the Force. Before we hear from a working musician of the time, I must reiterate that all these are unsubstantiated rumours and hearsay:

"You can actually point (to the time) ... and apparently some quite important Superintendent went into a club in Cheetham Hill, run by the D--- family, and he went in at what was an after-hours period, you know, I don't know if it was 2 o'clock, or maybe it was later than that. He goes downstairs and he sees drinks being served. He says, 'What's this?' and one of the D---s runs up to him and says, 'What's the problem?' (laughs) 'Listen you guys, get out, I've made my payments this week; I've seen him right, get out'. And this was like a chance for the (new) Chief Constable to represent the fact that he'd arrived and he opposed every club license for 9 months and you can actually point to the night life in the centre of Manchester disappearing at that time, and it died for many years."
Bruce Mitchell

This, like the Krays anecdote, is a good story containing (seemingly) all the right elements: late night drinking, corrupt coppers on the take, a specific time period (early 1966), a specific name of the club owner and location, and a crusading new Chief Constable. Only there wasn't a new Chief Constable, so we must immediately treat the evidence with caution.

Speed kills

The story that I heard at the time, and was prevalent in the Mod scene in Manchester was of a different ilk yet again. It seemed at the time to go hand-in-hand with an increased uniformed police presence and drug squad activity. For instance, one early summer's evening in 1966 at the Jungfrau on Cathedral Walk, the music stopped and an announcement came over the club pa that the police were here and we had to vacate the premises. We went outside the club and gathered on the opposite side of the wall to the entrance. A police inspector then arrived and addressed us. He said that we were committing an obstruction and that we were to disperse. As we went on our way plain clothes drug squad officers picked people (all males) out of the crowd.

This pattern was repeated at venues all over the city centre. The thread of obstruction charges was used whenever young people gathered in anything like a significant number, usually a dozen or more, not just outside the clubs but in 'civilian' areas like Market Street, Manchester's main shopping area, or Shambles Square, or the area near the Kardomah Coffee House. The reason for all this hassling was given as the death by an overdose of drugs of a senior police officer's son. The details were specific.

His name was Steven Greenhalgh, he'd taken 30 black bomber duraphet capsules (a powerful enough amphetamine in just one capsule) and after complaining of feeling unwell at a Twisted Wheel all-nighter, was driven round in a car by his friend for several hours before they took him to hospital where he was pronounced dead on arrival. So here we have a story with specific names, times and places. It was common currency amongst young club-goers at the time of the crackdown and it was one which I in no way questioned for years after the events of that summer had taken place. On the whole, I would have to say that it was the principle version over and above accounts such as Bruce Mitchell's that I would at one time have cited as the definitive reason behind the club closures, principally because it was one which my contemporaries recounted with such veracity, sincerity and authenticity. Someone would have spoken to the dead boy's girlfriend another to the driver of the car. Details were added, a whole picture of the dreadful evening built up. Once again, under the scrutiny of research the story appears to be completely apocryphal.

There is no mention of the alleged incident or subsequent Coroner's inquest reports of the time, nor are there any articles in the local press. Teenage drug deaths were such a rarity in those days that it surely would have warranted coverage in the papers. Even assuming that events were left out of the press to avoid embarrassment to a police officer's family there is no way they could have failed to be recorded in the Coroner's office reports. So, reluctantly, because it had been such a strong part of my personal mythology for such a long time, I had to conclude that the story of Steve Greenhalgh's death, along with the stories of corrupt police division and gangster fiefdoms, were all complete fabrications. Or were they?

Combined with the evidence that I shall present in a moment, the sum total of the disparate parts contain certain truths: that there was a criminal element connected with certain clubs is almost an immutable law of the universe. That no police force anywhere can avoid its 'bad apples' who will look for an opportunity to exploit their elevated positions of authority is another. That the 'bad apples' and the underworld will connect at some point in their dubious careers would also appear to be a logical inevitability. That some clubs were used by teenagers as places for drug dealing and drug taking is another truism. Put all these separate elements together and we appear to have the principle reason behind the club crackdown of the mid-1960s. What came as a surprise to me when researching this section was just how early a problem had been identified and action put into operation to 'do something' about it.

Darkness closes in

The first official police reaction to the club scene in Manchester was noted in the foreword to the Chief Constable's annual report in 1964. In it the Chief Constable, J A McKay, referred to:

"the mushroom growth in recent years, of clubs licensed and unlicensed ... (with) particular reference to the problem created by the so-called 'Coffee Club'."
Chief Constable's Annual Report, 1964

So concerned was the Chief Constable that by August 1965 he had almost single-handedly generated a moral panic sufficiently large enough to warrant the passing of a special Act of Parliament allowing the police sweeping, some would say draconian, powers to deal with the problem created by the so-called 'Coffee Clubs'.

This Act of Parliament, known as the Manchester Corporation Act, 1965, will be examined later in this section. In the meantime it will be necessary to study the Chief Constable's 1965 report in some detail as it provides a fascinating glimpse into the workings of the official mind being confronted with a phenomenon that it cannot comprehend.

The section of the report with the most relevance to our study is the chapter entitled 'Social Behaviour' and its appendix 'Coffee Beat Clubs' which is a reprint of an article from 'The Police Journal' written by a Manchester Chief Superintendent, A Dingwall. Chief Constable McKay, in his foreword to the report, goes so far as to recommend the Chief Superintendent's analyses of 'the problem' and his suggestions for 'a remedy' to "all local authorities and Chief Constables throughout the country" (Chief Constable's Report, 1965) as a blueprint for securing Parliamentary legislation against what he regarded as "a public scandal" (ibid).

The Chief Constable's Report

Before deconstructing Mr Dingwall's article it is of interest that in his foreword the Chief Constable makes a one-paragraph reference to 'other clubs' by which he means adult drinking and gambling premises. From his remarks about the "much improved" (ibid) situation, using existing legislation, it is clear that the 'social problem' of Beat Clubs called for what I can only phrase as 'moral cleansing' and that he was prepared to create his own laws for bringing that about. The problems of adult clubs seem almost an irrelevance to him and are dismissed in five lines before he moves on to allow his champion, Alan Dingwall, to present his case over seven tightly-packed pages.

The report is divided into twelve sections starting with 'The Incubation Period', a fascinating, almost sociological account of the origins of popular music and its venues in post-War Britain, ranging onwards through sub-headings like 'Habitués', 'Drugs' and 'Disorder', to examples of 'Specific Cases', 'Difficulties of Action' and 'A Death'. He then offers 'A Cure' which can only be obtained by motivating 'Press and Public Opinion'. Finally he presents the Manchester Corporation Act 1965 in all its multitudinous detail and suggests that it is 'The Future'.

'Coffee Beat Clubs - The Incubation Period' looks at the rise of the Beat Clubs and shows a budding cultural historian in the making. He pinpoints the increasing affluence of teenagers in the post-War period, how they "had money to spend on record players and gramophone records". How, by "the mid-1950s, rock 'n' roll and jive captured the youth of the country" (*ibid*, p6).

"Records became big business and sales increased so that awards of the golden disc to artistes for cutting their millionth records became commonplace." (ibid)

He cites the American Forces as being responsible for the introduction of the juke box into British Coffee bars and then chronicles the growth of premises and their licensing requirements and how unscrupulous proprietors were forever on the lookout for new and improved ways for *"mulcting the teenager of his ever increasing spending money"*. (ibid) By 1961, *"Modern 'Pop' music went on from success to success until it became the principal interest of many youthful enthusiasts."* (ibid)

Owners were quick to spot the advantages to be gained by charging membership and turning their coffee bars into private clubs. No music or refreshment licence was required. The clubs were also alcohol-free so they avoided that aspect of lawful interest. From the Chief Superintendent's point of view the most worrying aspect of the unlicensed club was that they were free of direct police supervision, a warrant had to be obtained before any member of the Constabulary could gain access if the owner had originally refused them admission.

He then cites September 1963 as the date of the *"first all-*

night session" (ibid). He is probably referring to the first officially advertised one, as has been shown elsewhere, all nighters at illegal black clubs had been the norm since the mid 1950s, and white club-goers had held impromptu ones at the Shanty Clare Club in Shudehill since 1961.

Habitués and moral panics

With club owners now featuring live acts on a regular basis the clubs became more and more popular. In order to satisfy the demand more and more premises opened. And on this observational, scene-setting note, C S Dingwall moves onto identify the problems that the police had identified. In 'The Habitués' he describes the physical character of the clubs which were on the whole situated in city-centre cellars.

"Whilst in some cases efforts seem to have been made to keep the establishments clean and reasonably attractive in decor, the majority were dirty, crudely decorated with the minimum of furniture and offered only the most primitive of sanitary facilities." He added, *"All were poorly illuminated, apparently at the desire of the patrons".*
ibid, p 7

The Chief Superintendent then conveniently identifies these patrons for us: *"Individuals of exaggerated dress and deportment, commonly known as mods, rockers or beatniks."* (ibid)
He then mentions for the first time what will become one of the recurring themes in his report, that of many of the youngsters going to clubs being homeless and more-or-less living in them, *"wandered from club to club,"* *"no settled abode,"* *"slept on the premises ... even during the day time."* (ibid)
This form of moral panic has resonances that recur today with the moral panic surrounding squatters and travellers enshrined in the 1994 Criminal Justice Bill; the concept of homeless youths being a problem in society can be traced throughout modern history from the anti-begging legislation of the Tudor era, through Victorian Poor Laws and the Twentieth Century paranoia of John Major's comments on homeless youngsters being parasites. Its use as a weapon of moral outrage in 1965 should therefore, I suppose, come as no surprise

to us. Chief Superintendent Dingwall also uses the dubious moral argument that like attracts like, and so it would appear logical when we continue reading 'Coffee Beat Clubs' to discover that he informs us:

"Some of the clubs were owned and managed by persons of known criminal record and inevitably this attracted persons of similar character."
ibid

Chief Superintendent Dingwall then moves onto his next section, drugs, and once again there are few surprises in his observations about this other great moral panic of contemporary society. He starts off reassuringly enough by asserting that, while there were suspicions that drug taking was happening in the all-night clubs, its use was confined to musicians! (my exclamation). He cites the unreliability of intelligence reports received during the early club days and says that the lack of prosecutions led him to believe that the allegations of drug trafficking in clubs were being exaggerated.

Having demonstrated to the reader that he is a scrupulous officer who carefully weighs up the evidence before reaching for his conclusions, he then brings us up-to-date on the drug problem circa 1965 by devoting a whole section of his report on drug abuse to female absconders from approved school who
"wandered from club to club carrying their bedrolls and frequently sleeping on the floor. On occasion, male and female have been seen to be lying together, but there was insufficient evidence of misconduct, sexual or disorderly, to justify prosecution of the proprietors ..."
ibid

Then there is more on *"youthful persons who have been reported as missing from home by their parents"* and of youngsters having *"no settled abode"*. He then switches back to the subject of drugs and says that Police attention was increased when intelligence reports alleged that drugs were being taken on club premises. Presumably he means that drug taking was no longer confined to musicians. Mr Dingwall cites amphetamines and hashish as being the principle illegal substances being used, and concludes by making the interesting observation that
"One of the effects of hashish is to reduce the will to resist ... (and that) real concern was felt for the young people exposed to this traffic."

ibid

Homeless vagrants sapped of their wills by hashish abuse, out of their minds on amphetamines, wandering aimlessly from club to club is a potent signifier and is repeatedly drawn on in his report.

Going to a Go-Go

When Chief Superintendent Dingwall moves onto the section entitles 'Specific Cases' all his concerns (and prejudices) coalesce in vivid apocalyptic imagery. He focuses on the history of a venue known as the Beat Club situated on the ground floor of a 'dilapidated' warehouse on the now non-existent New Cannon Street. He describes it as:

"... three rooms, in which furnishings were practically non-existent, the lighting no more than a glimmer and the toilet facilities a disgrace."
ibid, p8

Proving again his argument that like attracts like, he points out that the club was opened by one Richard Ewen after his release from a five-year prison sentence (crime unspecified), and that soon -

"The club became a meeting place for young persons of doubtful characters and morals."
ibid

Worse still -

"It was a place where they found freedom from adult supervision and a place where they could stay all night and sleep if they so desired."
ibid

We now find a new addition to the report's already substantial cataloguing of moral panics, xenophobia and outright racism. We learn that Ewen sold the Club in November 1964 to Serrif Bambo - *"... a man of colour"* and that, *"there was little change in the conduct of the premises, except for the worse."* (ibid)

'Men of colour'

What, one wonders could be worse than dim lighting, inadequate sanitary facilities and a black owner? Well apparently, *"Under Bambo's ownership, it was soon noted that older women and many coloured men were frequenting the club".* (ibid)

Subsequently, and as if to prove Chief Superintendent Dingwall's suspicions and implied accusations, Bambo was charged with wounding, possession of cannabis and heroin. He fled the country while on bail.

In fact, the Chief Superintendent seems to find the links between *"men of colour"* and coffee clubs particularly noteworthy items. For example, he presents in the text the associations of will-sapping cannabis and *"white slavery"*. Two *"coloured"* men were found guilty at Manchester Crown Court of conspiring to procure a 16 year old white girl for the purposes of prostitution. The link? They were alleged to have met the unfortunate victim at the New Cosmopolitan Club. This 'evidence' and the emotive use of the phrase 'white slavery' with its myriad associations with fears of black sexuality and miscegenation was one of the Chief Constable's most important weapons in creating the highly-charged atmosphere necessary for the passing of the Corporation Act.

In the remainder of the 'Specific cases' section we are treated to even more descriptions of *"dirty and poorly furnished clubs"*, with *"dim"* lighting and *"abominable"* toilet facilities.

Enter, the Mod Squad

In 'Difficulties of Action' the report outlines the difficulties in enforcing existing legislation on the clubs, principally because:
"a police officer, in plain-clothes, on entering a club of this kind was a very conspicuous figure and no useful observations could be obtained."
ibid

So for the first time in Mancunian Police history, teenage cadets
"who were able to affect the dress and deportment of the persons frequenting coffee clubs, were specially instructed to take observations."
ibid

Chief Superintendent Dingwall claims that as a result of intelligence gathered by 'The Mod Squad' as they were known to the people who frequented the clubs (and, also incidentally pre-dating the American TV series of the same name by several years), warrants were obtained and from February 1965 onwards a number of the most notorious clubs were raided.

Ewen, who it will be remembered had sold the Beat Club to *"man of colour"* Serrif Bambo had opened up the aptly-named 40 Thieves Club on Fennel Street. Nine youngsters there were charged with possession of cannabis and/or amphetamine. On another night, the doorman and cloakroom attendant at the Cavern on Cromford Court were both found in possession of cannabis and amphetamine. Later that evening police carried out their biggest raid on a club in Sackville Street known as Heaven and Hell. In the report it gets the usual description of *"shabby and dilapidated"*. (ibid, p9)

The report describes the "raiding party" going equipped with 200 watt light bulbs to ensure they had sufficient light to search people by. The club was described as being packed nearly to capacity with 150 young persons present, and the pay-off for the massive police raid was one 15 year old female charged with possession of an amphetamine capsule, five packets of cannabis discarded on the floor and "four young persons" arrested for possession of dangerous weapons, to whit, a sheath knife, a hammer and a studded leather belt.

These figures, when added up, three drug-busts across the city centre in one night, a handful of petty weapons charges, and an awful lot of expensive police overtime and resources used up, don't appear particularly significant by today's standards. Perhaps more significantly within an historical context are the 42 female and 13 male juveniles taken to Bootle Street Police Station. None of them was guilty of any offence other than that of being under 17 years, for in those days to be in a club, even where alcohol was not served, the age limit was 18. At the station their parents were sent for:

"None of them was aware of the children's whereabouts and most of them were horrified when informed of the circumstances under which they were found."
ibid

Here is another linchpin of the Chief Constable's campaign - the threat to our children. We may ask ourselves, what 'circumstances' were they found in. It may have horrified Chief Superintendent Dingwall and Chief Constable McKay, but to a substantial portion of young Mancunians 'dim lighting' and 'inadequate sanitary facilities' did not detract from the pleasure to be gained in listening and dancing to music all night long. But the Corporation Act was not going to be passed by teenagers and to add more weight to his argument, Mr Dingwall was able to summon up the dead to aid his fight for legislation.

More moral panics

In the section headed 'A Death' innuendo vies once again with some known facts to produce a picture that could at least be clearly seen by the Chief Constable. In May 1965 an 18 year old youth died from an overdose of morphine. The link with the clubs was that, *"he had regularly frequented coffee clubs ... and was known to have slept out in some derelict property and at the Heaven and Hell Club."* (ibid) That's it. He didn't die in a club, but that he frequented them was enough.

Looking at this section now I feel that it could be argued strongly that this is where the Steven Greenhalgh story emanated. A teenage drug death linked to the heightened police activity does not appear too far fetched an hypothesis.

However, drugs, death and white slavery were the heady ingredients of the report. In his 'The Cure' Mr Dingwall addresses the question of what should be done by the authorities. Proper registration, no restriction on police entry or action, the police to decide if health and safety regulations had been breached, the police having power of veto on anybody applying for an application to run a club. The Chief Constable also added for Manchester the formation of a specialised drug squad, which was, interestingly, run in conjunction with Special Branch. A coincidence that would appear sinister during the counter-culture period of the late 1960s when drug busts were used for political information gathering. (Dickinson, 1996).

Using the media

In the penultimate section 'The Press and Public Opinion' an astute knowledge of public relations exercises vis-à-vis the media can be discovered. A concept of manipulation of public opinion by generating emotive coverage in the newspapers and on television, that belies the report's early 1960s' origins. The report states that there was already much interest in the press about the goings-on in beat clubs, particularly in relation to 'drug trafficking'. It then goes on -

"This interest was actively encouraged and interviews were readily given by the Chief Constable to press and BBC reporters ..."
Chief Constable's Annual Report, 1965, p10

These representatives of the media were given police escorts in order that they could -

"see, at first hand, evidence that the worst of these clubs had been used for drug peddling, harbouring of young prostitutes, absconders and teenage tramps ..."
ibid

Chief Superintendent Dingwall states quite clearly that the purpose of the exercise was to generate support for Corporations Act *'seeking powers of registration and control'* (ibid). He points out that as a result of the police's media campaign a series of articles *'appeared in many of the national newspapers'* (ibid) with an article in The Times on 12 May 1965, coinciding with the reading of the Bill in Parliament, being considered a particularly noteworthy coup.

A brief examination of several of these articles is of interest, particularly by going back in time to an article in The Guardian (then published in Manchester) dated 17 January 1963, with the headline 'Not everybody's cup, but these clubs are here to stay", a generally sympathetic account of the proliferation of coffee and beat clubs 'by our own reporter'.

The article praises venues for being cheap, friendly meeting places *"warm, classless, havens"*, quoting club owner Roy Williams as saying, *"We're selling space for dancing really,"* and claiming that

"there are still too few other places where a foreigner of whatever nationality can feel immediately at home, or Oxford graduates twist naturally with computer girls, or Ghanaians find that the colour of their skin is immaterial."
ibid

The article concludes with a quote from Councillor Frank Hatton, Chairman of The City Education Committee,

"I think they've provided an outlet for the interests and vitality of young people". (ibid)

Two years later, presumably as a result of the Chief Constable's media blitz, "our own Reporter' in The Guardian appeared to have significantly shifted position. Paraphrasing the Chief Constable's report the article neatly summarises the moral panic elements of Chief Superintendent Dingwall's observations:

"Generally adults are not acceptable at the clubs, but there was some evidence that prostitutes, homosexuals and thieves visited some."
Guardian, 30 June 1965

All the usual hackneyed phrases have been lifted from the report, *"teenagers reported as missing from home"*, *"absconders"*, *"drugs passed in clubs"*. *"Many of the clubs had no emergency exits"*, *"appalling standards of hygiene and lighting"* all the way down to:

"Young people sat about, and were known to lie on the floor kissing and petting. Frequently they spent the night on the club premises, many of which ran all-night sessions at the weekend, invariably attended by teenagers not only from the city, but from areas as distant as Liverpool, Sheffield and Stoke-on-Trent".
ibid

The same recipe of quasi-facts, clichés, innuendoes and indignant moral outrage appears in the Manchester Evening News:
"Teenagers can spend all night in dimmed lighting, bad ventilation and poor sanitary conditions. There have also been repeated allegations of drug trafficking and misbehaviour".
Manchester Evening News, 20 May 1965

The public relations office of Manchester City Police, displaying great acumen in terms of media opportunities, also arranged for Chief Constable McKay to appear on BBC local television in April 1965, prior to the presentation of his annual report to the Watch Committee. Once again the 'evidence' against coffee and beat clubs was presented as justification for the special act of Parliament being passed.

The final push, as it were, the culmination of the public relations exercises was the appearance by Chief Constable McKay before the Committee of the House of Commons where once again he presented Chief Superintendent Dingwall's special report as 'evidence'. It was enough to convince the MPs and in August 1965, the Manchester Corporation Bill received Royal Assent and became the Manchester Corporation Act of 1965.

Regulating the night time economy

The clause relevant to the beat scene was Section 18, subtitled 'Entertainment Clubs'. In effect, it granted the Manchester Police far-reaching powers in controlling and curtailing clubs. In essence, the fourteen paragraphs and their relevant subsections meant that no-one could own, operate or run a club without explicit police permission. The police could object to premises being registered if they felt that

"(a) the premises are not safe for the purpose having regard to their character and condition and the size and nature of the club; or

(b) the premises are not provided with satisfactory means of lighting, sanitation and ventilation; or

(c) the premises are not provided with adequate precautions against fire and satisfactory means of escape in case of fire and equipped with suitable fire-fighting appliances."

Section 18, paragraph 3, Manchester Corporation Act 1965

They (the Police) could revoke existing registration from the implementation of the Corporation Act, as of 1 January 1966, where failure to comply to any of the above was invoked as the reason. Subsequently throughout 1966 this was the principle weapon in the police anti-club arsenal. But the Act didn't just stop there.

Club owners could be prosecuted (and if the prosecution was successful, lose their licence) if their premises were used for the consumption of illegal drugs, whether the owners were aware of a crime being committed or not. This was in line with the 1964 Drugs (Prevention of Misuse) Act where the owner of any property could be charged with unlawfully allowing premises to be used for illegal drug-taking. Many quite innocent people such as landlords of private premises were taken to court as a result of this particular Act, and the Law was finally called an ass, when John Betjemen was charged with it in 1970, when a group of students were caught smoking cannabis in a cottage owned by the poet. Other commentators pointed out that theoretically if somebody was caught taking illegal drugs in the Albert Hall, the police would have to charge its owner, the Queen! The Act was duly amended in the early 1970s, too late to have made any difference to the Beat Clubs.

A further power enshrined in the Corporation Act was Section 12, paragraphs A and B, which granted the police the right to enter and search premises to ensure the clubs and the owners were complying with the other terms of the Act, and to do so without a warrant.

In the final section of the Annual Monitoring Report, entitled 'The Future', Chief Superintendent Dingwall reports on the situation just prior to the enforcement of the Corporation Act on 1 January 1966. Stating that two of the worst clubs, having seen the writing on the wall, as it were, had closed themselves down, others will close after 31 December, and that many of the remainder were making strenuous efforts to ensure they met all the requirements of Section 18.

In what the Chief Superintendent calls 'an interesting development', he states that Mr R Graham Cooke, MP, had been so alarmed by the evidence that he heard given by the Chief Constable to Parliament, that he intended to introduce Section 18 as a Private Members Bill in the next session of the House of Commons, where he would demand its adoption nationwide.

The report's penultimate paragraph concludes:

"Over a period of 12 months, much time and effort have been expended on this modern problem which has beset the city of Manchester, but our success in obtaining the necessary legislation to deal with it made it well worthwhile."

Chief Constable's Annual Report 1965, p12

The outcome

Just how 'worthwhile' was their 12 months' work? In terms of the police and the authorities' interests the answer has to be 'extremely'. Some clubs closed straight away, others struggled on. The summer of 1966 was the time of the movings on and the herdings, of being shunted around from place to place, of evenings being interrupted and music being stopped. And as 1966 gave way to 1967 only a handful of venues were left and they shied away from confrontational practices such as holding all-nighters. Some of the clubs became late night (fully licensed) supper clubs for adults, cabaret bars whose owners had seen the writing on the wall and now hoped to appeal to a different clientele, and by 1968 only two city centre venues catered exclusively for young people, The Magic Village and The Twisted Wheel. In a way, one is tempted to suggest that these two clubs were allowed to exist as symbolic outlets for teenage passions. Both clubs would be visited regularly by Fire Inspectors (they could be paid off in whiskey as I witnessed myself on several occasions) and the Drug Squad (they could not be paid off, but their potential for trouble could be circumvented by a flashing lightbulb warning system). Both lasted longer that the others, but eventually the Village closed when its leading light Roger Eagle decided to pack his bags and go into independent concert promotion in Liverpool. The Twisted Wheel followed the 'adult' route and became Placemate's Disco, but the infrastructure of fans and DJs transposed themselves and their passion for Northern Soul, to a new venue that became a Mecca for all-night freaks, Wigan Casino.

Tearing out the heart of the city

Another contributory factor in the demise of the beat clubs was the Corporation's strategy for a modernised city centre, a kind of 'slash and burn' policy that would see a vast tract of side roads leading off Market Street, including Cromford Court, home of the Manchester Cavern, The Jigsaw and The Magic Village, and Brown Street, billed as Manchester's very own Carnaby Street, a riot of clothes shops and record stores, pulled down and sold off to the P & O Ferry Company for redevelopment as a high rise, Arndale Shopping Centre. The only reminder of the good times that were is a small corner of the Arndale's de-personalised, concrete mezzanine has been christened Cromford Court. Like the subterranean medieval street that lies buried under Cathedral Walk the catacombed cellars of long-forgotten beat clubs await excavation by archaeologists of the future.

In conclusion, one question remains unanswered - why did Chief Constable McKay take such exception to the coffee and beat clubs of Manchester that he felt the need to have a special Act of Parliament passed to deal with the problem? Perhaps the answer lies in the memory of a former Chief Inspector who served under McKay until his retirement from the Force in 1967:

"He (McKay) was a very sad little man. He just couldn't abide the idea of anybody having any fun."

James G Lee

Before closing this chapter completely, it is worth looking at 1966 in a wider socio-historical context. In terms of the tensions existing between what we may call 'youth' sub-cultures and 'authority'. The fact that it took an Act of Parliament to shut down a thriving arena of cultural practice is even more remarkable for the fact that there was no backlash. No organised opposition at all, in fact.

I have already mentioned the Los Angeles Sunset Strip riots as the reaction to police policy and the enforcement of a 'youth curfew' in the United States. In Holland, after a savage attack on 'longhairs' in the Dam Square area, by Dutch marines, an attack that left many injured and led to some of the worst rioting that Amsterdam had seen since the war, a political movement was created from the turmoil. The Provos, an abbreviated version of 'Provokateers', emerged in 1966 with a remarkably coordinated series of Anarcho-Situationist inspired campaigns, or 'provocations'. These included, mass 'cough ins' where they blocked the city centre in protest at car pollution; attacking a Royal Wedding, the German bridegroom had been in the SS; and their campaign to have the police turned into social workers. (Davidson, 1976; Nuttall, 1968; Stansill and Mairowitz, 1971)

What is probably the most surprising thing about the Provos, was the shock that awaited voters in Amsterdam when it came to local council elections. The Provos polled enough votes to elect five city councillors. They all immediately resigned, were then persuaded to take back their seats, but did it on a strictly rotational basis. Their next action was to disband Provo.

What happened next is a story unto itself, and not within my remit to cover here, but what we have seen, is that repression need not necessarily result in success for the authorities. Provo, and the next movement to follow them in Holland, Kabouter, were able to galvanize disaffected parties, and through democratic procedure, change local government policy. The smoking of cannabis in specially designated areas, for instance, was allowed. Council money for 'arts' centres, in actuality, slightly more adult oriented versions of youth clubs such as the (in)famous Paradiso, and Melkweg, was provided. Dutch youth mobilised and brought in the changes despite the fact that the legal voting age was still set at 21.

In Manchester, there was no such radicalisation. There was no opposition, organised or otherwise. Actually, very few people knew what was going on. Even to this very day, it is hard to meet many people who have become subsequently aware of the police and the council's action at that time. This is also borne out when researching for further information as regards the Act, or, any comparable piece of legislation against youth culture, up until Graham Bright's The Entertainments (Increased Penalty) Bill 1989/90 which did provoke a reaction amongst young people that has, and is, being documented elsewhere.

Academic research into regulation of the nightime economy is still in its infancy, and although work is being pursued in various institutions such as the Manchester Institute of Popular Culture, I have been unable to discover any relating to the period in question, either on a local, national, or international level. Further more, other than issues of 'moral panic', and a reading of oppositional meanings in Punk, the research field lies barren.

Shank's, 'Music Making In Austin Texas', has accounts of various police actions precipitated by musical events, eg a performance at Raul's Club by embryonic Punk rockers, The Huns.

"During the song 'Eat Death, Scum', City of Austin police officer Steve Bridgewater entered the club, ostensibly answering a noise complaint..... In the middle of the song, Tolstead (the lead singer) spotted Bridgewater, pointed his finger at him and, improvising a new line, chanted, "I hate you, I hate you." Slowly, Bridgewater made his way through the crowd, approaching the stage as if drawn there by Tolstead's pointing finger. Tolstead continued to chant, "I hate you. Eat Death Scum," at the police officer, while Bridgewater stood two feet away from the singer, leaning in closer towards him.... The singer grabbed the microphone with his left hand and shouted over the PA, "Start a riot! Start a riot!"..... "
Shank, 1994, pp 107-8

Tolstead and six other persons were arrested in the resulting melee, and Tolstead was found guilty three weeks later of disorderly conduct. Shanks does not report on the sentence Tolstead received, but does go on to say that Raul's remained a centre of opposition to perceived performances and stayed open for at least the next three years. In fact, Austin, particularly after the formation of the Austin Music Advisory Committee, in 1983, would appear to be a model of virtue in the promotion and maintenance of contemporary music.

Music making, music playing and promotion have always been considered an 'outside' activity. Whilst we have plenty of studies relating to the deviancy of subcultures, particularly 'youth', oriented ones, i.e. Willis', 'Learning To Labour', or Hebdige's, 'Subculture - The Meaning Of Style', to name but two, in terms of regulation of musician's activities, it is much harder to fine anything concrete, or even more than arbitrarily covered by research. Hopefully, legislation and regulation will be areas given closer scrutiny by researchers into Popular Music, as there is much to be gained from a closely detailed study of the responses of authority to this supposed 'outlaw' occupation.

REFERENCES

Chief Constable's Annual Report, 1964, Manchester

Chief Constable's Annual Report, 1965, Manchester

Davidson, S, 1976, 'The Penguin Book of Political Comics', Amsterdam, Van Gennep BV

Dickinson, Bob, 1996, 'Imprinting the Sticks', M Phil Manchester Metropolitan University

The Guardian, 17 January 1963

The Guardian, 30 June 1965

Manchester Corporation Act, 1965

Manchester Evening News, 20 May 1965

Murphy, David, 1991, 'The Stalker Affair and the Press', London, Unwin

Nuttall, Jeff, 1968, 'Bomb Culture', London, MacGibbon & Kee Ltd

The Sampson Report, 1986, HMSO,

Shank, Barry, 1994, 'Dissonant Identities', Hanover, USA, Wesleyan University Press

Tansill, P and Mairowitz, D Z, Eds, 1971, 'Bamn, Outline Manifestos and Ephemera 1965-70', London, Penguin Books

TAPED INTERVIEWS

Bruce Mitchell

Chapter 5

Music Force

The steady decline in live music in Manchester's clubs, brought about by police pressure and Parliamentary legislation, led to a depressing period for the area's professional musicians. This brought around changes in the City's night time economy, and the late 1960s saw the demise of the Beat Club and the rise of cabaret and disco, aided and assisted by the construction of new demographic groupings of late-night revellers.

The rise of the Cabaret club

The majority of people attending Beat Clubs in the mid 1960s were in the 16 to 20 year age range. Put simply, by 1970 they had grown up and had become 'young adults'. The era was one of full employment, more or less. In spite of the influences of the 'swinging' 1960s, the social pressures of an earlier age coerced, pressurised or programmed young adults into marriage and the adoption of the usual bourgeois trappings of domesticity. Whilst access to Further and Higher education existed it was still an area denied to many, whether by choice or circumstance. Leisure activities were dependent on market forces and choice was becoming limited by economic and technological factors.

Club managers and owners were nothing if not pragmatic and seized upon loopholes and opportunities as they arose, and it was through these that Manchester experienced a mini-renaissance in its nightlife, creating something of a detrimental effect on jobbing musicians.

This rebirth went in two directions. Firstly the rise of the cabaret/supper clubs, The Princess, Mr Smiths and The Riverboat being just several examples. These were establishments run along very simple lines; they catered for an 'adult' audience, that is, for people over the age of twenty one. 'Smart dress' was obligatory. An evening's entertainment would consist of a comic or two, and a singer backed by a small combo. Simple meals were on offer and this sees the beginning of the 'chicken in a basket' circuit. They were cheap venues with a veneer of sophistication. In effect they were a continuation of the more up-market Workingmen's Clubs of the 1960s such as The Golden Garter in Wythenshawe, which in its prime offered an astonishing variety of top, world class acts, performers like Shirley Bassey, Tony Bennett and Diana Ross (post Supremes). The demands of these top acts though had taken their toll and effective rationalisation of finances was called for.

"So you'd have an act for ten quid. Tarby for instance. Jimmy Tarbuck (a Liverpool comic) you could have for a fiver - (Goes into dialect) - "I get a hundred quid a week now" So I said, "Go and get your hundred quid a week, I'm paying a fiver" ....And one of the first acts we got (when moving into the big league) we really copped for it. It was Shirley Bassey and she said "Alright, I want a penthouse at the Piccadilly," which was the best hotel in Manchester, " a white Rolls Royce, a chauffeur, my own dressing room and no eating or drinking during the act".... And Batley (a Yorkshire variety club that actually managed to coax Frank Sinatra to England) did it for her and all the others came, Frankie Howard and said "Close the bar, no eating", and that killed it"
Benny Van Den Burg, Club Manager.

The older generation of musicians who had started out, or were principally associated with the Beat boom had to adapt to survive. Pete Hughes, drummer with pop group The Chuckles remembers,

"And we tried to do cabaret clubs, just a way of earning money really. Nobody had their hearts in it at all. Eventually we just split up and I went to work in cabaret clubs... I could sight read and that."
Pete Hughes

In the early 1970s many of the cabaret clubs discovered another way of making money, gambling. They became casinos overnight.

"Any fool could put in a roulette wheel, there was no legislation. It was a licence to print money"
Bernard Manning, Club owner and comedian.

The rise and fall of the casinos in Manchester, whilst a fascinating story in its own account, is beyond the remit of this book.

Suffice to say that the cabaret clubs metamorphosed into gambling joints, or didn't, as their owners' fancy took them, until finally police action cracked down on them in the late 1970s. There was, however, another way for the clubs to survive, one that was much more worrying to practising musicians - Disco.

Let's go down the disco

Disco, or more correctly 'discotheque' meaning 'a library of records' had existed for three decades before its popularisation in the 1970s as a genre. In England, Jimmy Savile claims the distinction of being its inventor at his Plaza lunchtime dance sessions in Manchester in the very early 1960s ...

"Jimmy Saville must take the credit for being the first DJ to use the old shellac and vinyl - In the Plaza. It was 6d (six old pence, just over two and a half new pence) - Nobody knew Jimmy - His photograph was over the door, but everybody thought Karl Van Verden was the boss - And Jimmy said, "I can't afford the bands, same old problem - I'm going to play gramophone records, bring your own sandwiches".
Benny Van Den Burg

... though it can be traced back, in its modern pop music state to the Whisky A Go Go in Paris in the mid 1950s. If one is referring to disco as being a place where entertainment is provided solely by the use of recorded music without recourse to a live group, then the appellation 'disco' must surely go back to the Second World War and the mass dances in American aircraft hangers where the music was relayed through giant PAs to the jitterbug dancing crowds. However, the situation in Manchester in the early 1970s (and indeed throughout the country as a whole) refers to the use by club owners of recorded music provided simply by a DJ. What followed in America, rapidly adopted by their European counterparts, was the creation of a whole separate subculture related to the disco phenomenon, linked to the adoption of dress codes and mannerisms inspired by Disco music and films such as 'Saturday Night Fever'. In Manchester it was linked to two things, economics and technology. In terms of economics, Benny Van Den Burg explains how he saw it as a club manager.

"... we talked to Takis who ran the Rowntree Group (of clubs) Discos - and George (Takis) was making a bomb. The DJs worked for nothing. The DJs would work for just the birds and the booze. And from the day we went disco we were ten grand a week better off"
Benny Van Den Burg

From the musician's point of view, however, Tosh Ryan presents a different perspective.

"... there was a lull in the business - you know, like bands would have worked right through the 60s solidly, six nights a week - and suddenly that had totally dried up. That went. Because things happened. You know, discotheques, the technology for playing records became better, the sound systems were better. It was cheaper to have a DJ. So the bands weren't working as much"
Tosh Ryan

Trying to keep things alive

But there did exist an albeitly small circuit of venues for local rock musicians to play in, the colleges and universities. The situation was certainly a far cry from the halcyon days of the 1960s, but a door was still left open for the handful of bands who were struggling to survive. The major problem was one of celebrity status, the groups that the Social Secretaries were booking for their college venues were the ones promoted by the big London agencies, Chrysalis, Virgin, etc, and these bands tended to be ones who had record contracts with the majors. Very often a Social Secretary would book a package that was on tour, and this represented a great problem if one was to try and include a local band on the lineup. There was simply no space in the scheme of things for a local band.

When the Magic Village closed in 1969 the principal outlet for 'underground' music in the independent sphere went with it and the promotion of alternative acts fell squarely in the lap of the universities. The main problem for them was usually financial, but some venues such as UMIST went out of their way to promote gigs that passed into legend. One allnighter there culminated with The Pink Floyd playing at dawn on the green facing the Students' Union (a uniquely rainless night). An equally awe-inspiring gig that I played on was headlined by Canned Heat and also featuring Fleetwood Mac, Country Joe McDonald and The Edgar Broughton Band. Still, the problem remained for up and coming musicians of where they could play to earn their dues as it were. Record contracts only existed in London and London had the stranglehold on the bread and butter work of touring.

Put basically, in order to succeed you had to go to London and play, but that could only come about if you lived in London, and few had the inclination let alone the necessary finances to be able to make the transition.

The golden era of the 1960s had well and truly disappeared for the beat groups, and the early 1970s was a depressing period all round for the local music scene. The forces of two catalytic events which occurred around this time, however, combined to radically change the shape of the Manchester scene. These were the occupation of the former College of Music building on Deva Street by Manchester University student rebels, and the founding of a musician's co-operative called Music Force.

Early days at The Squat

The first of these, the occupation of a building about to be demolished by the University authorities to create another car park, was significant in that local bands were active in the sit-in that saved the space. Gigs were held throughout the occupation on a rolling basis, virtually nightly. Despite the electricity to the old Victorian edifice being cut off, a ramshackle system of bootleg cables and generators ensured that the music stayed on throughout the weeks of negotiations that took place over the building's future. Eventually, and perhaps rather surprisingly, the student's won and The Squat as it became known was born. Providing an annexe to the main Students' Union building on Oxford Road, The Squat rapidly became a 1970s version of the Alternative Society's Arts Labs, a cultural meeting place and activities centre that in a far-reaching moment of radical hysteria was opened to all as a rehearsal and performance space, complete with concert hall, capacity 300, dressing rooms, cafe bar and cavernous cellars ideal for rehearsing music. As a venue it was much used by The Albertos throughout the 1970s and saw the first ever performance by The Albertos as a musical group (with a trio of girl backing singers called The Lillettes) and the world premiere of Sleak, the Snuff Rock musical, not to mention gigs by a variety of up and coming bands who would later become international stars. Tony Moon in Sounds reviewed the embryonic Joy Division:

"There is a gig tonight at The Squat, be there! The Squat is an ancient Colditz type building just outside the centre of Manchester. It's an all purpose gig, tonight it's the turn of Warsaw to play their sixth gig and the Worst to play their second. Next week it's a jumble sale....Soon Warsaw are on. They have slightly better gear than The Worst and, since they've done a couple more gigs, are a bit tighter. Tony Tabac is on drums....he only joined a few weeks ago, Peter Hook is on bass/plastic cap, Barney Rubble is on guitar and Ian Curtis is the voice. Lotsa action and jumping in the air...to...'Tension', 'The Kill'....."
Sounds, 1977

The Squat was active from 1971 to 1981, when it did eventually become a car park, and in that decade it played host to all sorts of activities other than music. For a time, activities at The Squat were co-ordinated by Colin Bell, who would later become manager of The Tom Robinson Band. Several newly-written plays were premiered there, and comedians such as Rik Mayall and Ben Elton got their first comedy break. As such it was one of the few venues in Manchester to offer a platform for all performing artists, particularly rock musicians who would normally have been denied a chance to perfect their live, on stage shows. In a way, it represented the multi-media experiments of the 1960s and as such was possibly an anachronism filled with part student, part hippy idealism, but its importance in terms of its contribution to the Manchester music scene must not be overlooked. Now let us move on and examine the second factor in the renaissance of Manchester music - Music Force.

Get things moving with Music Force

To state that Music Force was probably the most single important event in the development of Manchester music would arguably not be an understatement. The connotative ripples that emerge from this socialist-based musicians' co-operative still lap on the shores of contemporary music. (Middles, 1996) Without Music

Force there would have been no Rabid Records, without Rabid there would have been no Factory Records, without Factory there would have been no Haçienda, no 1988 Summer of Love. The effect of Punk on Manchester would be impossible to speculate on; no Morrisey, no Stone Roses, no Oasis. Music Force was the principal reason why these events happened and its history is outlined here.

In 1971, The Squat had just opened and any attempt to construct a musical philosophy to go with its rambling anarcho infrastructure was stymied from its inception by the very freedoms inherent within that infrastucture. Essentially, although it represented a triumph in the face of bourgeois sensibilities, its working code of conduct was heavily influenced by whatever political machinations were behind the day to day running of the bureaucratically top heavy Students' Union. At the end of the day, they paid the running costs and no matter how exciting the concept of social revolution within The Squat's constitution the Union moved slowly as one would expect of those who paid the bills. Ultimately, one gig does not a summer make, and for Manchester musicians the lack of working venues in their home town had reached such a peak of simmering resentment and frustration that it was obvious that something had to be done. Here was a city with a rapidly growing population of young people, the Babyboomers of the 1950s, and the rapidly growing student intake, and they were all looking for something more than regular visits to the Free Trade Hall and concerts by touring American artists. If ever there was a time when venues could be opened and exploited then this was it.

What must also be borne in mind was the fact that a whole new generation of players were ready to take the stage, together with their constituent audience. People who had been too young to attend the Beat clubs in the mid 1960s were ready to go out and participate in the rituals of deviancy and transgression. By the heyday of Punk, which for the sake of argument I will date as 1977, there were even more of these disenfranchised young souls ready and waiting in the wings for a movement that would carry them beyond the bounds of the acceptable and mediocre. For the moment however, let us concentrate on the victims of mail order cheese cloth shirts and split knee loons, that characterised the early 1970s, a lost generation, who relied for their information about what was happening from the pages of the rock press with its London oriented schemata, and the ever present veneration and beatification of transatlantic personas and cultural whims.

As has been mentioned before, the stranglehold of the South was dominant within the rock ideology of the early 1970s, but two places began to actively oppose the dominant hegemony, Liverpool and Manchester. It is interesting to note that these were the two principal theatres of action during the early years of the Beat boom and therefore it is not too surprising that they represented the main channels of resistance in the early 1970s. It could be argued that they were resentful of the emphasis, even stranglehold, that London saw as its rightful position within the world of Rock music.

It is most definitely worthy of note that in the UK the only two areas of opposition to London came from these two North Western psycho-geographical regions. I have been unable to find in my research any comparable movements from other areas, such as Birmingham, Bristol, Cardiff, Dublin or Edinburgh. This contradicts the claim by Music Force that alternative musical organisations were springing up nationwide. If any others were created, their lifespan was very short lived indeed, and no record survives.

In 1972 an article entitled 'Music Force Versus The Slit' appeared in the Melody Maker. Written at the behest of muso-journalist Chris Welch, it was penned by Manchester Blues stalwart Victor Brox. Basically it was Victor having a gripe about the dominance of London in the world of music, but it struck a chord in his home town and a meeting at the Bier Kellar off Piccadilly in Manchester city centre was arranged. The original article was very heavily biased towards a working class theme, but essentially it was a clarion call to arms for musicians to defend their rights, form working co-operatives, and control their own destinies. As such, it was inspired to some degree by equally scathing attacks by former Liverpool Scene frontman and guitarist Mike Evans, founder of the Musicians Liberation Front, which operated for a short time as a co-operative on Merseyside. Victor put out the call and the musicians responded.

"And we hired The Bier Kellar in Manchester and I got everybody down; it was packed out. And I read my article, I said right, I want you to vote now unequivocally.

I want an absolute vote positive with - I don't even want one person voting against it - I want it absolutely unanimous - So that we can put it into The Melody Maker as like the charter of the new north west, working

class, radical musicians against the establishment."
Victor Brox

"It [Victor's] was a real schoolmasterly performance. I think I nodded half way through it..... I was the General Secretary. Victor was the Chairman. It was formed as a properly constituted organisation."
Bruce Mitchell

The prime movers of Music Force at its inception were Bruce Mitchell, Tosh Ryan and Victor Brox. A plumber named Gordon became the treasurer and a token £1.00 fee was charged at meetings to set up a kitty so that the dream of a musicians' collective could be financed.

"It was a sort of alternative musicians' union for hip modern groups who had nothing to do whatsoever with the establishment at all, but wanted to go out and play and could actually do live gigs."
Victor Brox

There is no doubt that a political imperative stood at the back of the Music Force idea, though its importance to individual members varied quite dramatically from the romanticism of Victor's brand of William Morris, Craft Movement style of socialism -

"...we'd done a very successful series of music things for the Socialist Labour League...... the complete history of the working class revolt, working class gaining of rights for working class people all over the British Isles, with the Taff Valley Railroad, with the Chartism from Manchester, with the great march from the north east, you know, the Jarrow March."
Victor Brox

- through to Tosh Ryan's more committed adherence to Communism -

"It was great. And there were lots of lemons in there (Music Force) who hadn't a clue what was going on and behind it all in my thinking there was a political structure developing that could be quite useful. No-one else saw it like that I don't think - I think Victor might have done vaguely - Bruce certainly didn't."
Tosh Ryan

"It was a left-wing climate. Tosh was a noisy Marxist. It just had a left-wing kind of feel. And various union type people - There was a whole infrastucture of people who knew one another and who were known to these various left-wing groups. I think it was Corin Redgrave came along and addressed one of the Bier Kellar meetings."
Bruce Mitchell

Whatever the political agenda behind the origins of Music Force, the imperative remained the desire to work. As a result of the initial meetings, the adoption of a constitution and its flirtation with the Socialist Labour League, Music Force found itself with a pool of talent ranging from musicians, to roadies, to artists and graphic designers, all ready, willing and able to work. The question was, how to go about it. The late Martin Hannett, aka Zero, remembered in an interview for the Music Force magazine, The Hot Flash, in 1975.

"Supplied with a suitably idealistic constitution, about 80 - 90 members, a little money from an initial £1 contribution, and a crude sketch of the route to the top we set about the brain numbing task of promoting a surly, incoherent mass of local talent encompassing a huge spectrum of skills. Any kind of music, equipment hire, transport, poster printing, all these operations were conducted with a kind of guerrilla consciousness, and a peculiar nihilism reminiscent of a Japanese suicide squad."
Martin Hannett, 1975

Getting up and running

The first task was to set up an office from which inroads could be made in terms of acting as an agency for the disparate group of people composing the membership of Music Force, and establishing a series of venues for gig promotion. The first office was in Bruce Mitchell's flat in Chorlton-cum-Hardy and from there contacts were made with Mike Evans' Music Liberation Front, and like minded agents and promoters around the country, people who had in some way retained the idealistic Hippy alternative mentality of the 1960s, people who operated outside of the traditional areas of the music establishment.

The radical element within the University Students' Union, the ones who had been the mainstay in saving the Squat from demolition, were intrigued by the idea of Music Force and voted to give them office space in another building due for demolition, 100 Oxford Road. This formally grand Georgian building, up until the 1960s home to Quilligotti's Imported Marbles, had been allowed to go derelict by the University authorities who planned to turn the Georgian terrace into yet another car park.

"We acquired it via the Student Union. It was the Student Union officially opened the building. It was a derelict building and we started it until other people joined in...And Grass Roots (Manchester's premiere radical bookshop during the 1970s) moved in there as well."
Bruce Mitchell

Taking up occupancy in February 1973, the dedicated stalwarts of Music Force soon found their dedication stretched to the limit as they struggled with the problems of working in a fairly primitive environment. When Quilligotti's had left the building all the amenities had been stripped out. Within a short space of time local ne'er-do-wells from Chorlton-on-Medlock had stripped the lead from the roof and no doubt had they been given enough time would have taken the tiles too. The ground floor exterior was boarded up with corrugated iron sheets.

It was, all in all, a fairly dismal place from which to start an enterprise such as Music Force, but the co-op members set to with a will and made the place habitable. Electricity and phone lines were restored fairly quickly, but I can remember quite clearly the ancient Victorian toilet and sink being places to avoid wherever possible. Music Force took over the front ground floor, the office overlooking Oxford Road being the nerve-centre. This is where the desk and phone line were. Rooms behind, off the corridor, were used as storage for PA equipment and the rapidly expanding store of posters for rock concerts with their accompanying buckets of paste and brushes. Slowly but steadily Music Force as a working entity came into being.

Booking out bands

"These venues were set up (Music Force gigs in and around Manchester that we shall examine later) - bands were working - but it was limited because you were in one area, so it became an exchange system between

*us and the Music Liberation outfit in Liverpool.... and someone else was
running something in Birmingham and Bristol - so there was a network....
because a lot of these were bands who had worked in the 60s who weren't
working anymore and they had PA systems and they had vans and they
had equipment so you had a resource pool."*
Tosh Ryan

In those early days in 1973 radical political involvement was
still high on the Music Force agenda and packages of bands were
supplied at cost for fund raising events. Amongst the organisations
that benefited from this were Frelimo, SLL, PPU and CND. At Easter
in 1973 The Victor Brox Blues Train, The Spyder Mike King Band, The
United Mates of Hysteria and an embryonic, non musical Albertos,
piled into a rag tag collection of vans and drove north to Clydeside,
Red Clydeside as it was affectionately known then, to perform
all weekend at CND's major anti Polaris demo. Fortunately the
Glaswegian welcome was warmer than the weather.

The Council laid on spartan accommodation in school
halls along with free food in exchange for which the musicians
and entertainers performed at a succession of Council venues
throughout the weekend. Nobody was paid. There was an unspoken
understanding of the importance of doing these gigs for free. There
was a camaraderie and sense of common purpose about performing
at them, and it cannot be denied that it helped spread the name and
ideals of Music Force to quite a wide audience. The Hot Flash, Music
Force's in-house publication, mentions John Hoylane in Let It Rock,
and Penny Bosworth in the Melody Maker writing articles about the
co-operative.

By the summer of 1973 the agency had become more active too
and began to expand.

*"There has always been a strong sense of injustice at Music Force
about agent's practice of virtually stuffing their own supports (acts) down
the throats of college secs, and the market came under strong pressure from
us."*
Hannett, ibid

Music Force reacted to the London agencies' stranglehold on
the national music scene by doing direct mail shots at every Social
Secretary in the country. The fliers that arrived through the post

carried details of all the groups available through Music Force and details of other services that were available. Amongst the bands represented by them were Spyder Mike King, Dhyani, Wally, Victor Brox Blues Train, Hamilton Grey and Iron Maiden. Nor were the smaller venues neglected; pubs and clubs that were known to promote music were also placed on the mailing list, and by 1974 Music Force acts were being booked regularly at a variety of venues across the country. Although the major zone of operations was mainly in an area bounded by Stoke-on-Trent, north up to Lancaster, and as far east as Leeds and Bradford, Music Force sustained bookings for their acts as far south as Bedford.

Promotion

As early as 1972 when Music Force was first formed the concept of promoting gigs in Manchester was mooted. Initially a series of fund raising benefits were held at the Houldsworth Hall on Deansgate in the centre of the city. In 1930s this building had also been used for recording the Halle Orchestra and, as such, has its own interesting musical history. Originally exploited in the late 1960s for musical purposes by Roger Eagle, this venue, an old Methodist meeting place, was popular with audiences and performers alike. It was a large cavernous space with a capacity of around 600, and under Eagle's auspices had played host to an array of alternative rock acts. Big Brother and the Holding Company, Country Joe and The Fish were two of the headliners he promoted there before moving to much larger premises at the Liverpool Stadium, where the groundwork was laid for the opening of the legendary Eric's Club.

The Music Force benefits held in the Houldsworth Hall appear in retrospect to have much of the stamp of '1960s happenings' about them. Ad hoc ensembles of musicians would free-form their way through meandering bursts of what is still known as Modern Jazz. More rock oriented outfits such as The Shape Of The Rain, Greasy Bear and Victor Brox would perform on the main stage, while poets like John Cooper Clarke, and Zen anarchists like Hari Odin And The Thunderers, plied their trade around the confines of the hall, staging bizarre game shows such as Beat The Guru, where "only one spiritual leader can score enough karma to become top god!" They were interesting events and also financially successful ones, unlike

Music Force's other centre of town fundraiser, Mr Smiths, a cabaret/ nightclub off Princess Street.

This venue was made available to Music Force by an agent who had it block booked for Sunday evenings. What had looked like a good idea at the time turned into a financial albatross. Music Force suddenly found themselves having to pay the Sunday night rental on a gig that nobody wanted to go to. As Martin Hannett recalled events in 1975 -

".... it almost all went over the edge as the community of musicians not directly involved in the day to day round of booking/publicising and trying to balance the books began to forget to support us....we watched helplessly as a steady stream of bright new recording talent struggled against the dense apathy of an almost empty niterry (sic)"
Hannett, ibid

Brushing aside the setbacks of the early days, Music Force continued to search for regular venues in which to promote new talent. Eventually, by 1974, they had established a small circuit of gigs in the South Manchester area that proved extremely popular with the public and provided a modest regular income for the co-operative. They were Squires in Didsbury Village, The Midland on Burton Road and The Lloyds in Chorlton. Squires and The Lloyds tended towards a 'progressive' musical policy, whilst The Midland had a regular Rockabilly clientele, though every Tuesday night boasted "a West Coast disco" with live music from a band called Bread and Roses. On Saturday nights it was Teds all the way; 200 sweating greasers from all over the place 'bopping' to Kid Cadillac's disco and enjoying bands like The Flying Saucers. These live gigs were more accessible and enjoyable than going to places like the Free Trade Hall, beer and dancing being to the fore rather than queuing and listening. In effect, what was happening at these places was the groundwork being laid for the punk phenomenon that was to come in a couple of years time.

"We opened up nights on a regular basis. If they didn't make money it didn't really matter because it was like priming a pump - other gigs came in, we started picking up university gigs and stuff like that."
Bruce Mitchell

What had started as an attempt to assert autonomy for musicians, built within a framework of clearly defined socialist principles now began to defy common practice associated with these forms of utopian idealism and become a success.

Making things happen

100 Oxford Road was finally scheduled for demolition and the ever acquiescent Students' Union happily moved Music Force into another occupied block, Waterloo Place. This was another architecturally superb Georgian terrace fronting onto Oxford Road, situated right next to Manchester Museum and only a hundred yards stroll from the main Student Union building and The Squat. In passing, it is worthy of note that this row of now highly desirable buildings is still standing, the radical students having at least been successful in preventing one part of Manchester's architectural heritage from having been obliterated by the insatiable need of the University for car park space.

Ensconced in their new, moderately salubrious surroundings, the building not only had functioning central heating, but a white Rastafarian vegetarian restaurant, Music Force carried on consolidating its position in the local music scene, and was now able to offer a wide variety of services to the co-op members on its rosters. Apart from headlining or support acts these included, PA hire, theatre lighting rigs, van hire via Thompson and Thompson Trucking (run by former Alberto's roady, Dimitri Grilliopolus), artwork and poster design and printing, and Music Force's foray into publishing, a music magazine called The Hot Flash. A fully comprehensive equipment outlet was available, franchises having been struck with JBLX Quad and Altec. But perhaps most importantly for musicians looking to subsidise their income from a spot of light manual labour was the Music Force flyposting service.

"I would claim the credit, I would call it a flyposting bureau. As far as the venues were connected with one another, they had a ... they wanted to get posters up, and if you got posters for three gigs to put up and you charged whatever per poster. Obviously it would earn money because you wouldn't be going around putting one concert up, you'd be putting up posters for three concerts. You'd put a pile of posters up and that would earn money.

And we started doing it for the record companies. After I'd done it for maybe a year and a half, because I'd made quite a few quid out of that, by the time it got to maybe its second year I was fed up being covered in Solvite."
Bruce Mitchell

Sticking around with Superfly

The importance of flyposting in terms of the history of Popular Music in this country cannot be overestimated. Its place within the realms of Popular Culture as an entity of its own is borne out by the numerous publications devoted to its development. Historically it is an indissoluble imperative in tracing the advancement of capitalism. From examining 19th Century billboards for Music Hall and Variety we can psycho-geographically trace the growth of a counter-culture, a culture that was all but subsumed by the encroachment of the blessed curse of the 20th Century, cinema and Hollywood in particular. In terms of Popular Music we can follow the spoor that has been left by the flyposter.

"We used to hire a civic hall for the evening. We'd arrive and put up a sign outside that said - 'Tonight - A Beat Group - 2/6d' We always sold out"
Roger Eagle

Rock music has continually been denied access to the more mainstream outlets of advertising because of its nature being culturally unacceptable, or because of financial constraints. Hence, it has had to develop its own methods of circumventing the stranglehold of contemporary media practices. Flyposting has become the 'telephone tree', beloved of anthropologists, aiding and abetting the word of mouth on the street in its propagation of 'hip' and acceptable artists, enhancing the inaccessibility of new and challenging artists.

By flyposting, I am not referring only to billboards or posters, which have become the lingua franca of the flyposting world, but also the A3 and/or A4, photocopied flyers for a gig held somewhere, sometime, by someone. Typically they are the felt tipped psychedelic handouts that wind up pasted to the poles of traffic lights or utility junction boxes. These are the transmitters of Laswell referred to in his theory of sender and receiver. (Fiske, 1982) In a sense, ultimately they become the 'samizdats' of an underground of deviancy, forever propositioning 'straight' society with their promises of an hedonistic utopia, "Free for nurses before 10 o'Clock" - "Blow Your Mind At The Carwash" - "Flesh - Let It All Hang Out" - etc. Fly-posters became one of the best means of advertising gigs that would have been hitherto unnoticed.

Drawing heavily on the flyposting success of the counter culture in San Francisco, English Rock music entrepeneurs were quick to emulate the resounding success of the Bay Area. By the late 1960s posters by artists such as Martin Sharp and The Fool had moved over into the display cabinets of Athena poster shops and were being transmogrified onto the walls of bedsitters with an ease that would have astonished luminaries such as Blake or even Warhol. Radio advertising was out of the question, financially prohibitive and also, possibly failing to find the target audience. The same can be said about the placement of advertisements in the Manchester Evening News which at the time was not widely read by young people. In fact, this publication lived up to the paraphrasing of its own advertising slogan, "A friend dropping in", which was altered by the local underground cognoscenti to "A Fiend Dropping In".

Ultimately, the only way to ensure success in filling a venue was to rely on the tried and tested power of flyposting. The right geographical areas could be covered, ie the main arterial routes into the city, principally those that carried heavy student traffic, and also coverage of the right areas of the city in terms of what kind of audience you were looking for as a promoter. Situating flyposters was also influenced by what you could stick them on. Urban redevelopment provided a plethora of temporary hoardings. Some long established walls were available, though in the years to come these would eventually end up as a bone of contention, not only with the local council who made concerted attempts to eradicate fly-posting, but between rival flyposting gangs. By 1994 such rivalry had led to assaults and, in 1995, a fatal shooting at a prime flyposting site opposite UMIST. However, the flyposting wars had started long before these events took place.

At first, flyposting was Bruce Mitchell's area, his fiefdom within the Music Force structure. Later, as his drum-playing commitments with the Albertos grew larger, the task of papering the blank spaces of Manchester fell more and more on Tosh Ryan's shoulders. Under

Bruce's auspices the areas being postered grew, almost unnoticed, and the fly-posting had spread far and beyond the geographical confines of Manchester or even Greater Manchester. Stoke, Birmingham and even Newcastle were target areas for the ever expanding group of Music Force workers.

Co-ordinated flyposting on a national level had hitherto been unimaginable. Prior to 1974 all Rock concert promotion posters had been the business of the interestingly named, Terry The Pill, a London businessman. People were nervous that they might be encroaching on his territory, but as things transpired he was quite content to stick to London and eventually an amicable agreement was reached.

"We were the first to formalise it outside of London. Terry (The Pill) used to send me posters and I remember John Curd (One of the main Alternative music promoters in the country) being very surprised...... he'd also find new sites and let Terry know about them.... And we did a similar thing y'know, we were into it and we found new sites and we'd let Terry know and there was a funny kind of gangster thing about it, but it was alright so long as you communicated."
Bruce Mitchell

Throughout 1975 and 1976 Tosh Ryan consolidated the hold Bruce had gained on the poster circuit and an unofficial sub company of Music Force called Superfly came into being.

"And he (Tosh) was the only person who had the right sort of energy to do something with it. Y'know he had enormous physical energy and drive....Tosh took it to an enormous business within nine months."
Bruce Mitchell

"...I developed it into a massive business, and it all just went haywire."
Tosh Ryan

In Music Force publicity material published in 1975, Martin Hannett estimated the number of posters being pasted by Superfly at approximately 1,000 per week. In logistical terms, a 1,000 a week was a formidable figure, and the business required an enormous amount of organisation, time and people.

Thus the flyposting scene in the mid 1970s had become a large, financially successful enterprise and, being outside legitmacy, it was bound, sooner or later, to attract the attention of unsavoury characters. Tosh and Music Force abdicated from the independent music publicity world sometime in 1977, due to a variety of factors. The emergence of Rabid Records certainly was one and threats from underworld elements who wanted to muscle in on the scene was another. For a while it was continued in Manchester by two brothers from Wythenshawe, Vinnie and Terry Faal, who were to branch out into group management with Punk band Slaughter And The Dogs.

However, old habits die hard. Before ending the Music Force flyposting saga, it is worth illustrating that you can take the boy out of the Solvite but you can't take the Solvite out of the boy. In 1977, when the Albertos were appearing at the Royal Court Theatre in London with their hit show Sleak, Bruce Mitchell and Les Prior couldn't resist handling the London flyposting for the show. This wouldn't have been so bad had not Les then developed a liking for using aerosol graffiti to publicise the show. It finally became evident that things had gone too far when in the middle of one performance a posse of CID arrived and carted Bruce away for questioning. It transpired that a person, or persons unknown, had spray-canned the legend "Snuff Rock Lives" all over the front of the Old Bailey in their zeal, no doubt as fans of the Snuff rock show. Fortunately no charges were laid and the show carried on.

Moving into publishing

In 1974 Music Force branched out into publishing with the launch of a magazine called The Hot Flash. Gracing its masthead was the legend "Dedicated To Music". Its editorial policy stated,

"Welcome to The Hot Flash a local paper dedicated to music. Hotflash will be a monthly publication, and will not be ruled by a rigid policy, but tempered by suggestions (clean ones) and contributions from anyone who wishes to contact us.

We have no permanent staff, all articles and reviews have been contributed by a small core of people who care about music in the North West......It is intended that the mag will not be inward looking, or parochial; we're interested as much in the National scene as the local one, so expect material on both name bands and emerging bands of local origin"

The Hot Flash editorial, 1974

The Hot Flash is definitely pre Punk. In style, issues 1 to 4 are typical IBM Golfball, cut and paste, off set litho, fairly standard for the era. However, after issue 5 it underwent serious design changes and for the next six issues, until its demise in October 1975, a more rigorous editorial policy was adopted. Music Force, and Martin Hannet in particular, exercised much more input in the running of the magazine. Going on the contents and appearance of the early issues, it would appear that The Hot Flash was aiming for the Zig Zag magazine market, but it failed to attain the remarkable standard set by that particular legendary publication.

"This guy came along and said he wanted to do something. Glyn Hazelden. He just came into the office and he just wanted some help and a bit of money and we gave him something very modest like 50 quid or a 100 quid and within five days this was happening."
Bruce Mitchell

What exactly was happening looks, with hindsight, to be not a lot, but placed within a socio-historical context, on the whole, The Hot Flash was at the very least a bold attempt to break away from the London stranglehold on Popular Music. All the music press, with the exception of Zig Zag (which had lost much of its early energy and enthusiasm anyway), was produced in London. Here was a new magazine that declared its North Western roots, but did it live up to the claims made in that first editorial?

Inside a Hot Flash

There is a reasonably varied mix inside The Hot Flash's pages. Apart from the co-ordinator's address (no fascist hegemonic posturing here with titles like 'editor') two other dead letter drops are given for those who may not be able to afford a stamp. These are the Music Force address on Oxford Road and Probe Records in Liverpool. Throughout the magazine's life the input from the Liverpool based Music Liberation Front is quite strong, with regular contributions from Mike Evans and Albie Donnelly in particular. In the first issue Mike Evans has a kind of Fantasy radio station concept, as we would view it now, in which he suggests formats and content for an ideal commercial radio station. As Mike actually had an hour a week at the time on Liverpool's Radio City, whether this was actually a real life fantasy or something which came to fruition remains a mystery to this day as the station never kept tapes of his shows. In it he suggests a running order for a salute to 1950s comedy classic Rock tracks such as 'Little Egypt' by The Coasters and Stan Freberg's version of 'Heartbreak Hotel'. As an article, it is interesting, and it would be hard to accuse it of parochialism.

Glyn Hazelden writes an appreciative article about Albie Donnelly's anarcho comedy rock band, Supercharge, a Liverpool band who were just about to sign to Virgin. Mel Akers contributes a piece on Liverpool and Manchester entitled 'Local Band Scene' which is a fairly depressing item that appears to announce that a local band scene virtually doesn't exist. He mentions two Liverpool groups, Strife and Medium Theatre, and two Manchester ones, Spyder Mike King and Kraken, then rather mournfully announces that Kraken have broken up anyway. This is not a happy article.

There is a piece reprinted from the local radical newspaper Mole Express about the Women's Rock Band, an organisation that grew out of the Women's Liberation Movement with the avowed aim of addressing sexism within the rock business.

"Most 'pop' and 'rock' music is totally sexist; it treats women as sex objects or supports in the lyrics a very conservative and conventional view of woman's position - love and marriage, the family, etc. One way round this is for the band to write their own material... and a manifesto, which will include a critique of the whole pop/rock business"
The Hot Flash #1

The article continues with a prescient announcement apropos punk,

"Playing together as a band has helped them to recognise the political force of music, something the male left has ignored as marginal. If a cultural revolt does start and bands refuse to recognise any separations between the audience and themselves, its original impetus will come from bands like the Women's Rock Band who have the support of their sisters in the movement and are totally involved as part of the movement."
The Hot Flash #1

Page two sports an interview with Lynard Skynard, that Glyn Hazelden had somehow managed to gain at the Free Trade Hall when the band were appearing there. Interestingly, on the same page is an early cartoon by the soon to be feted Ray Lowry, now a regular contributor to The Observer newspaper, but perhaps more popularly recognised as an essential Punk laureate in graphic form on the pages of the NME during the late 1970s.

Live reviews from the pages of the first edition of The Hot Flash contain features on Golden Earring, Kevin Ayers and the Pink Floyd, all of whom are reviewed performing at Liverpool venues.

The record review section of The Hot Flash could in no way be accused of being parochial by dint of the fact that none of the local bands mentioned in the issue, or, in point of fact, at all, had releases out at the time. It's the standard mid 1970s blend of Americana, hold over and retro. The J Geils Band, Bachman Turner Overdrive, Deep Purple, Pretty Things, Steppenwolf, Jethro Tull, Fleetwood Mac. None of the reviews are even slightly critical, probably because the reviewers didn't want to alienate the record companies who would send them free copies if they published favourable reviews. The air of hushed reverence that greets a release from the J Geils Band is sad, not to say obsequious.

An indication of Music Force's input into The Hot Flash is most likely indicated by the centre pages being given over to a feature on the Albertos. This isn't even an article, in terms of having been written by a journalist. The whole two pages are a surrealist rambling spoof on conventional Rock business biographies, accompanied by a black and white picture of the group involved in an S and M male orgy. The metatext is a bizarre collection of warped signifiers couched in a pseudo Rolling Stone magazine portentousness with an unhealthy overload of creeping cynicism. Of note also is the inclusion of stage crew as integral members of the band, including Elliot Rashman, also called by the article, Billy The Yid, who later went on to find fame and fortune as manager of Mick Hucknall and Simply Red.

To summarise, although issue #1 of The Hot Flash graphically isn't the greatest thing to look at, basically it carried out the intentions laid down in its inaugural editorial.

"I only ever saw Glyn two or three times in my life. When he first came and said he wanted to do this and we said yeah you should do it and we encouraged him with whatever he needed. Maybe we paid the print costs

and his enthusiasm made up for everything else."
Bruce Mitchell

By Issue 3, however, the aims and objectives as regards Issue 1's editorial appeared to have gone slightly awry. Only one page of the whole issue is given over to anything remotely North West and that consists of a piece by Mike Evans on Liverpool's Deaf School, later to become winners of Melody Maker's Band Of The Year 1976, and a feature on another Liverpool group, Medium Theatre, by contributor Jim Fendean. There's also a live review of Supercharge later in the issue, but as regards coverage of any other Manchester or regional music this particular issue of The Hot Flash doesn't appear to live up to the magazine's original intentions. There's an exhaustive, two page account of the career of Deep Purple that has actually been painstakingly hand written in that curious spidery style so beloved of DIY rock chroniclers such as John Tobler, half italic, half Baroque curlicue. A feature by Glyn Hazelden on an archetypal mid 1970s Rock band called Babe Ruth in which he predicts great things for the future.

"The addition of Steve (Gurl, "who recently left Wild Turkey") has made subtle improvements in the band's overall sound.... and since he is playing six keyboards onstage, there is obviously more scope than the original use of piano only."
The Hot Flash 3#

There's a rather good account of The Beach Boys aborted Smile album which rather interestingly for the time in which it was written doesn't propagate the myth that Brian Wilson had destroyed the master tapes. This is followed by an article by Spencer Leigh in which he names his ten favourite Bob Dylan tracks, one of those indulgent, masturbatory articles that makes the demise of the magazine an obvious inevitability. The item says nothing new and goes nowhere in particular.

Added to all this is a review of the post Buddy Holly career of The Crickets and a fairly humourous piece by John Cornelius about how to start a band that's guaranteed to fail! And the inevitable two pages of the latest vinyl releases, which in this particular issue consisted of artists such as the Royal Philharmonic's version of Tubular Bells, Mahavishnu Orchestra, Joe Walsh and ELO, etc.

In retrospect it certainly appears that Issue Three and the aspirations of the Music Force collective had somehow lost their way, and this is a feeling that is consolidated by looking at Issue 4. Articles on The Grateful Dead, Foghat, Captain Beefheart, Kiss and Leonard Cohen provide the main texts of the magazine. There is however a sign of imminent change. Martin Hannett contributed, or more correctly, published a kind of Music Force Annual Monitoring Report, which is the only item in the whole thing to remind us of where it had all originally come from, and then, near the back of Issue 4 is a letter from Glyn Hazelden announcing his retirement to America and that from now on The Hot Flash will be edited, significant change from that of co-ordinator, by Martin Hannett.

"As you have noticed - we've changed. New cover, new layout, new staff."
Editorial, The Hot Flash July 1975 (From then on, no issue numbers were used.)

The magazine was certainly impressively different in style. The days of amateurish, IBM golfball, cut and paste were now a thing of the past. In its place was a fairly slickly produced magazine that could have held its own on a newsstand along with the small but fertile world of come and go rock mags. Three colour gradation, justified margins, columns, 'proper' graphics, immaculate typography and commissioned photographs instead of pictures 'borrowed' from the NME. In terms of its appearance, The Hot Flash had come of age.

The people responsible for this change were Martin Hannett, classed as Associate Editor, not Editor as Glyn Hazelden had put it in his farewell note, Tony Cassidy as editor, and Les Thompson as Art Director.

A momentary digression is called for here to look at the remarkably incestuous nature of Manchester.

The Hot Flash - Phase Two

As The Hot Flash was relaunched from the new Music Force premises at 178 Oxford Road Manchester, another publication called The New Manchester Review was being created upstairs. Brainchild of one Andrew Jaspan, this publication was more in the style of a Time

Out, come What's On type of magazine, it was to last approximately five years, folding in January 1980, and amongst its staff it boasted cartoonist Ray Lowry, and Art Director, Les Thompson. These two went over with Jaspan in 1981 into the short lived Flash, a creditable attempt to create a radical newspaper for Manchester that unfortunately failed to find the funding necessary to establish its chances of survival. Andrew Jaspan subsequently became editor of The Observer, and appointed Ray Lowry cartoonist on the editorial page. However, back to the history of The Hot Flash.

"From a variety of pressures - commercial, artistic, historical - ROCK MUSIC has lost a lot of the cultural dynamism that steamhammered the 60's and early 70's. ROCK CHANGED SOCIETY..... Now, far too often, the music squeaks in falsetto for a decaying aristocracy of greasy management and gilded superstars, or mumbles incoherently to cloistered coteries of musicians and self appointed experts jealously guarding their exclusivity....."
ibid

With the undoubted value of hindsight, the screaming vortex of anger against the music establishment evident in this Music Force polemic indicates that clearly, as early as 1975, the groundwork for not just a radical, but more of a cataclysmic upheaval within Popular Music was in place already. Punk Rock was a revolution waiting to happen.

"So where does The Hot Flash come in? We believe it's time to open up a window and let some air into the room; to demystify the scene, bridge the gulf between audience and performers, and have some laughs along the way."
ibid

This concept of demystification and eradication of perceptual gulfs between sender and receiver, punter and player became an overriding mainstay of Punk philosophy. What is interesting to note is that we have already had a call for this fundamental change in the perception of audience, player relationships called for by the Women's Rock Band in Issue 1 of The Hot Flash. It was an item of concern for a long time before attempts were made to codify change in the unwritten manifesto that became Punk sensibility.

"A music paper does not have to be a superficial fanzine, or an obscure jerk off. A music paper does not have to be either intelligent, or entertaining - it can be both. We are not afraid of looking outside the strictly musical for our material, and into all the social and cultural areas that either lean down on the music and influence it, or feed off music for their energy and ideas."

ibid

So the semi-official Music Force organ had once again nailed its colours to the mast and stated firmly that its intentions were now to embrace Popular Culture as a whole and as a legitimate manifestation of a desire to bring about change in society. How then did it go about this in the pages of its magazine?

Tony Cassidy contributed part one of an ongoing series entitled Rock Culture and Anarchy, paraphrasing Matthew Arnold's influential 19th Century essay, but looking sympathetically at the possibilities inherent within the adoption of classical anarchy within the music business. The basic thrust of his argument was that the spontaneity of Popular Music was anarchistic in its origins and was integral to any definition of Popular Culture. That these anarchic manifestations were then mediated or appropriated by Capitalist enterprises was not necessarily an inevitability, rather it was a rubric to be challenged.

What we have here, again predates McLaren Punk sensibilities, and as will be shown as we progress through our examination of the later issues of The Hot Flash, reflects an anger that existed throughout the land, an anger that was waiting to be harnessed. What becomes surprising is the sudden change in the pages of the magazine from the almost air of hushed reverence that crept throughout the texts of the Hazelden co-ordinated issues, to the joyfully irreverent and more than somewhat 'fed up' attitude of the later contributors.

These signify a definitive sea change in the hitherto vapid sensitivities of English, and dare we say it, international music aficionados. It is also highly significant in that it demonstrates that the theory of the passive participants in the world of Popular music is an invalid one. Here are active participants in the Ritual. Within the pages of this issue of The Hot Flash is ample evidence of the dissatisfaction felt by a contemporary group of young people. They did not idly follow the changes that were about to take place within the world of Popular Music, in a sense we can argue that they defined those changes that were in the air.

Another example that demonstrates the dissatisfaction within the Collective can be found in an article written by Peter Everett who was a producer for BBC Radio in Manchester. Called 'Flash From The Past' it clearly demonstrates the dilemma of pre Punk as it was being experienced by the public. In this case the particular form in which dissatisfaction has manifested itself was in what the French were terming at the time Retro, a retreat into the past to find a form of entertainment that was more vibrant or vital. Everett's article was about the Classic Rock n' Roll revival that was taking place at the Midland pub in South Manchester. What the article shows is that a significant number of young people were rejecting the material such as appears on the review pages of The Hot Flash and were in a conscious way choosing to pick from the culturally rich fields of the past.

Other indicators of the change in sensibilities are an attack on record pricing by Spencer Leigh, an attack that is both informative and amusing.

"Let's have a look at some of the rip offs and we'll start with Elton John's Greatest Hits. For a start, this album only contains ten standard length tracks. By no means are all his hits represented (Step Into Christmas and The Bitch Is Back)... In short, there was no lack of suitable material and yet the bitch certainly is back as the album retails at £2 . 99 or 30 pence a track. The original singles cost 50 pence or 25 pence a track so the album is more expensive than the initial singles...... However the number of tracks is really only half the story as we should consider playing time. Most albums clock in at around 35 to 40 minutes. Pye's Golden Hour offers just that....

I've been trying to discover what are the shortest albums on the market and I defy the reader to top these:

1. Paradise Hawaiian Style. (Elvis Presley) 21 minutes 46 seconds.

2. Original Golden Hits Vol 3. (Jerry Lee Lewis) 24 minutes 12 seconds.

3. The Best Of Tim Hardin. (Tim Hardin) 25 minutes 12 seconds.

Side one of the Presley clocks in at 10 minutes 15 seconds, which is only three minutes more playing time than Richard Harris' single MacArthur Park... "

ibid

Other indicators of the imminent changes about to burst on the music scene is the inclusion of a highly irreverent gossip page, pitching its attacks at the pretensions and foibles of the contemporary Rock scene.

" Interesting politics.... during Roy Harper tour - a large comprehensive light system had been hired for the concerts which included Jerome Rinson's band 'Headstone' as the support act, but the Roy Harper contingent would allow only very limited use of the lights for the 2nd band. The result was a very dim ' Headstone ' set and an extremely bright Roy Harper set. Nice one Roy"
ibid

In keeping with its newly declared line on covering aspects of popular culture The Hot Flash also contained film and book reviews, which by the penultimate issue, The Hot Flash September 1975, had broadened out to include features on Lenny Bruce and Contact Theatre Company along with Part Two of Rock Culture and Anarchy; a massive three page feature on Gene Vincent, a comprehensive guide to recording facilities in Manchester, another three page feature on proto Punk local band Gyro, who in true Punk to come style named their band after the Social Security cheque payment one received if one were on the dole, and whose picture spread showed the group engaged in a fight with the audience, again predating the Sex Pistol's Nashville pub massacre by almost a year.

"Gyro are inadequates, they are the kind of people who in these turbid times attract the attention of well wishers and others, who, freed from the responsibility of performing a useful function in society like to be entertained by helping lame ducks, the socially inept and so called inadequate..... They represent young people, who though formally enfranchised and supplied with the wherewithal to join the game of the consumer, somehow know that society is laughing behind their backs.... This is today's sound of the city - the crunch of bone and the calico ripping squelch of the switchblade. The agony of a stolen guitar and rough justice in dimly lit carparks."
The Hot Flash, September 1975

Dole queue rock indeed. By the time Punk Rock had clearly manifested itself in 1977 Gyro were long gone, keyboard player Dave Tomlinson changed his name to Formula and played with Howard

Devoto's Magazine, Paul Young and Ian Wilson went on to form the distinctly unpunk Sad Cafe, and guitarist Chris Gill went back to his Moss Side roots playing Ska and Bluebeat in the distinctive cross over band Cairo, this time predating the Coventry Two Tone explosion.

Perhaps the most significant thing about the September issue is the inclusion on the editorial page of a large picture of a grinning Martin Hannett sat cross legged on the Music Force office table. Underneath this is an obtuse, confused editorial stating that Martin has temporarily taken over the editor's reins from Tony Cassidy.

Portrait of an invisible girl

Martin Hannett was born in 1948 in North Manchester and by his late teens was one of the growing number of young, local musicians who had talent but no particular outlet for it. After a spell as a student at UMIST in the late 1960s, the turn of the decade found him more interested in the technical side of music rather than the playing. Despite his virtuoso ability on the bass guitar Martin was ultimately a rather shy performer who preferred to operate from the sidelines. For an example of his virtuosity you only have to listen to his playing and arranging on many of the recordings he was responsible for throughout his career, perhaps the highlight being his incandescent swooping, double tracked bass on 'Sleepwalk' by John Cooper Clarke (Columbia Records 1979).

"Martin wanted to be involved (in Music Force) when we got to here (100 Oxford Road), he started wanting to be involved. We had to call some sort of meeting and formally propose him (a lot of people didn't want him) and the thing is I really wanted it because Martin was good company and he was into it and there would be somebody else on the phone."
Bruce Mitchell

Martin took up residency in the office in late 1973 and fast became an integral part of the Music Force operation. By 1975 Bruce Mitchell was almost totally committed to working full time with the Albertos, Victor Brox was undergoing a metamorphosis into a Manchester Education Committee's Music Service stalwart, and Tosh Ryan was building up the Superfly flyposting service, leaving

Martin pretty much in control of things at the new premises at 178 Oxford Road. After initially "just hanging out" -

"He started out doing something called GB Audio which comes from Greasy Bear.... And then Martin started retailing equipment that he could get from an old friend of his down at Quad (Amplifier manufacturers). It was more a revenue thing, y'know, finding equipment suppliers for the Student Unions (and local musicians)."

Bruce Mitchell

When The Hot Flash started under the auspices of Glyn Hazelden, Martin sold advertising as well as placing ads for his/ Music Force's electronic services. As has been noted already his involvement in the magazine became more central and complex, seeing out two previous 'editors' until the September issue where the reader finally gets a look at one of the personalities behind Music Force. But by now Music Force itself as a workers collective had more or less had its day.

In the bunker - the final days of Music Force

"Music Force stopped as far as I'm concerned when they rejected me! - I thought they'd all be fully behind me in putting this piece against the London record companies - against the established agents that were all from London that were all against the Northern scene and stuff like that.... I said, right, fuck you. I don't want nothing more to do with it. And I bowed out. Now later that all became the Oxford Road show. It became Rabid, and Factory and the Albertos, and all kinds of stuff. I mean, I became London based because I couldn't believe my friends in the North - it was like somebody's gone - I couldn't believe it you know. But they'd done it."
Victor Brox

Despite Victor's initial dismay at the turn of events regarding Music Force he didn't stay in London for very long and he returned in 1975. Given Martin's interest in music technology it was more or less inevitable that sooner or later Music Force would begin to offer recording facilities.

"One of the first things in the manifesto of Music Force was that we should at all levels of the business be independent of the monopolies and the idea was we would create our own studio. We would actually have our own label, we would put our own music out you know. And that never really came about through Music Force. Music Force began to collapse and all these other various aspects of it began to develop individually."
Tosh Ryan

Tosh and Bruce have slightly differing recollections about how Martin got into music production.

"The first recordings came in - I've got a feeling the first one was a Belt and Braces Theatre Company did an EP and Martin got the gig producing it."
Bruce Mitchell

"Martin got asked to produce something for a band called Afro Express from Stoke on Trent I think they were - and they were selling buckets of albums out in Nigeria and they'd done a particular album that related very much to the end of Ramadan for some reason. And we found out how to do it all from that. Martin went to the studio and recorded them, found out how you got the records pressed, how you got labels done, how you got the sleeves done, and even how you exported them out of the country. And that was quite a major learning process, and from that his appetite was fairly whetted by then."
Tosh Ryan

Whether it was Belt and Braces or Afro Express that Martin was first involved in recording may remain a mystery for the foreseeable future, what is more certain is that in the autumn of 1976 Howard Devoto and Pete Shelley, from a newly formed Manchester group, Buzzcocks, came into the Music Force office. They wanted to make a record and that record was to be entitled 'Spiral Scratch'

"... Martin was by that time the sort of, the right generation to be relating to the next lot of musicians, which were the punk musicians."
Bruce Mitchell

The fact that Music Force was now being run virtually single-handedly by Martin coupled with his increasing interest in the newly developing music scene, and recording, meant that the demise of Music Force was now only a matter of moments away. Historically it was time to wind it down and start something fresh, and the idea that Tosh and Martin came up with was to start their own record label.

"He was always interested in that bit. ... And his interest in recording and you know, quality in all that side of things was always of great interest to him, and of course he had friends with similar interests. He was from something like a technical background."
Bruce Mitchell

And so, in early 1977, Music Force quietly dissolved itself, and with money salted away from their flyposting operation Tosh and Martin moved to an old grocery shop premises in a Back street of Withington in South Manchester, called Cotton Lane and started up Rabid Records.

In academic terms there is no analysis of Music Force in existence. Despite the fact that the 1970s were a culturally active period, research carried out in the formative years before Punk reflects a discipline that is in its infancy. Post Punk studies into Popular Music, whilst strong on theoretical approaches, appear to shy away from an historical basis for research, centering more on issues of 'meaning', or 'readings' of texts. These texts may be cased in flesh or trapped on vinyl, but considering the importance of the formation of a musician's co-operative, and how it affected the lives and practices of a considerable number of people, not to mention the legacy of autonomy that it provided for the next generation of musicians, that musicologists have so far overlooked Music Force demonstrates a weakness in the field.

Works that have included an outline of the situation prior to 1977, such as Dave Laing's 'One Chord Wonders' have tended to cover, by dint of their brief, the national situation, and include within their remit the dissatisfaction felt by members of the music community. Echoes of The Hot Flash editorial of the July 1975 issue are to be found in the opening chapter of 'One Chord Wonders' in a quote provided by my former manager, Pete Jenner.

"The big show will vanish.... I think the political thing is a possibility. I'm thinking of someone who's 16, who's going to start saying, "Look, all

this stuff these bands do with these huge PA's and lights, that's not where it's at. It's down to the people. And I'm going to get out my acoustic guitar and sing revolutionary songs in pubs, working men's clubs and factories."
Laing, 1986, p6

Laing also supplies an interesting overview of a genre of musical style called 'Pub Rock', which again, reflects much of the dissatisfaction felt by the Music Force members. Pub Rock bands, such as Doctor Feelgood and Brinsley Schwartz, tended to operate in a London based milieu where there was a circuit of venues in public houses, catering for this 'back to the roots' movement.

"(Pub Rock is) something like the old R'n'B circuit, small places where you get some feedback and a bit of magic in the air."
Nick Lowe quoted in ibid, p 7

To conclude, the only area where comparable research is being carried out is in the anthropological side of musicology, e.g. Konstantin Economou's 'Making Music Work', which is a study of young people in a Swedish youth club, forming bands and playing music, Sara Cohen's 'Rock Culture in Liverpool' and Finnegan's 'The Hidden Musicians', are studies that have approached the direct, lived experience of music makers. However, these are, if the authors will forgive me, 'snapshots' rather than a long term historical overview.

We also have Shank's 'Dissonant Identities', which is an invaluable 'look' into the cultural practices of Texan musicians. However, entrepeneurial enterprises such as those propogated by the Austin Chamber of Commerce and its relationship with contemporary musicians, have to be viewed in light of capitalist constructs, whereas Music Force was initially conceived as a far left, radical exercise.

REFERENCES

Cohen, S, 1991, 'Rock Culture in Liverpool, Oxford, Clarendon Press

Eagle, Roger, 1979, in conversation with the author

Economou, Konstantin, 1994. 'Making Music Work', Sweden, Linkoping University

Evans, Mike, 1974, The Hot Flash No 1

Everett, Peter, July 1975, The Hot Flash

Finnegan, R, 1989, 'The Hidden Musicians: Music-Making in an English Town', Cambridge, Cambridge

Fiske, John, 1982, 'Introduction to Communication Studies', London, Methuen & Co

Hannett, Martin, 1975, in The Hot Flash No 4

Hazelden, Glyn, 1974, The Hot Flash No 1

The Hot Flash, 1974, No 1

The Hot Flash, 1975, No 3

The Hot Flash, 1975, No 4

The Hot Flash, July 1975

The Hot Flash, September 1975

The Hot Flash, October 1975

Laing, Dave, 1985, 'One Chord Wonders - Power and Meaning in Punk Rock, Milton Keynes, Open University Press

Leigh, Spencer, July 1975, The Hot Flash

Manning, Bernard, July 1995, in conversation with the author

Melody Maker, April 1972

Middles, Mick, 1996, 'From Joy Division to New Order - The Factory Story', London, Virgin

Shank, B, 1994, 'Dissonant Identities', New England, Wesleyan University Press

Sounds November 1977

TAPED INTERVIEWS

Victor Brox
Pete Hughes
Bruce Mitchell
Tosh Ryan
Benny Van Den Burg

Chapter 6

The Anti-Christ comes to Manchester

"..... when I read the review (Sex Pistols at the Nashville) and June 4th came, I thought I must check this out. It was an eye opener and a road to Damascus conversion."
Jon The Postman

More re-mapping of the city along emotional lines

Another startlingly important Situationist style psychogeographic event that took place at the Free Trade Hall, or more correctly, the Lesser Free Trade Hall, a small seated concert area upstairs from the main hall, was the appearance of the Sex Pistols on the Friday 4th June 1976. This event, combined with a return concert on the 20th July, created a revolution within Manchester music that was to have consequences that went far beyond the geographical confines of the North West. The concert unleashed an energy that had been lying dormant and moribund within a generation of younger musicians and would ultimately lead to not just the Madchester scene, but would also exert a tremendous influence on international Popular music as a whole. This is a not a statement made lightly; in the same way that the Dylan 1966 gig liberated a large number of people in the city from the limitations that had been imposed by the social strictures of taste or style, so too, the Sex Pistols appearance in Manchester that summer turned on a group of youngsters to the possibilities of 'doing it themselves'.

From Punk came a whole group of performers who, one way or another, wrought changes on a world scale. Without this 'road to Damascus' type conversion mentioned by so many people who were in the audience at the Lesser Free Trade Hall, there could conceivably have never been House Music, or certainly not in its present form. An appropriate signifier of House was New Order's Blue Monday (from a riff by Gerry and the Holograms). Peter Hook and Bernard Sumner from New Order were there. Also present for the Sex Pistols was a young Steven Morrissey, who would go on to form The Smiths with

Johnny Marr, before going solo. Anthony H Wilson, then a young Granada TV reporter who would go on to found Factory Records, and Howard Devoto and Pete Shelley from the proto- Buzzcocks who promoted both events were also there.

Shelley and Devoto were both students at Bolton Institute of Technology. Prior to their 'awakening' by the Sex Pistols they had flirted with the idea of forming a group. Howard remembers putting an ad up on the college noticeboard looking for musicians. It contained the codeword 'Sister Ray' which was the title of a tune by New York proto- Punk rockers The Velvet Underground.

".... I do remember mentioning 'Sister Ray', or something like that, and I'm almost certain it would have had something by the Stooges in it as I was rather into 'Funhouse' at the time, and a few other names had probably been conjured with, and the model, as much as anything was Iggy Pop because that music sounded so simple, his vocal range was very much like mine.... I was going to college and seeing the usual bands you would have seen on the circuit then, and really getting bored with them. Not just bored - frustrated and angry with people for not thrilling me."
Howard Devoto

"Did you see this NME review of this band called the Sex Pistols? Wasn't that great? Well, I've rung the NME and it seems they're playing (in London) this weekend and I'm coming down with a friend and you're putting us up"
Howard Trafford to Richard Boon, February 1976. (Sublime Catalogue, p 10)

The three young men were more than impressed.

"We saw them on the Friday and Saturday and they were great and inspirational and blah blah blah and my life was ruined."
Richard Boon (ibid)

Howard and his friend Pete McNeish returned to Bolton where they were both students at B.I.T., and immediately set about the dual task of getting a group together and promoting the Pistols. According to Richard Boon their first act within days of returning was to change their names to Devoto and Shelley respectively. Pete MacNeish took the name he would have had had he been born a girl.

Howard Trafford's change of name was inspired by a story told to him by his philosophy tutor concerning a bus driver in Cambridge who's name was Devoto.

"My life changed the moment I saw the Sex Pistols. I immediately got caught up in trying to make things happen. Suddenly there was a direction, something I passionately wanted to be involved in. It was amazingly heady. I'd said to Malcolm, "Do you want to come and play at my college?" and he said, "If you can set it up we'll do it." I tried to persuade the Student's Union to put them on, but they wouldn't go for it. Not because of their reputation, just that they'd never heard of them."
Howard Devoto (Savage, 1991, p 174)

Howard and Pete came up with the name Buzzcocks from a review of Rock Follies in a copy of Time Out magazine published the week of the mythical Sex Pistols gig, that ended, "get a buzz, cock" and even though they were still in an embryonic stage in their development, having very few numbers and even less musicians, decided that the best way to get a gig for themselves would be to promote the Sex Pistols so they could play with them as the support act.

"Someone told me about this little hall above the Free Trade Hall. I got it for the fourth of June."
Howard Devoto (ibid, p 175)

Howard was determined to make the gig a major event. Bruce Mitchell remembers him calling in at the Music Force office.

"I met Howard Devoto going in there. He was trying to hunt down a film of the New York Dolls and it was said there wasn't any and I knew there was one from when they'd done something like The Old Grey Whistle Test. Howard wanted to show it at the Lesser Free Trade Hall gig...."
Bruce Mitchell

The New York Dolls connection is of major importance. Malcolm McLaren of course had managed the band in its final incarnation and in a sense was trying to recreate something of their persona with the Pistols. (Heylin, 1992) That they mutated beyond simple pastiche is a credit to both him and the four members of the band. However, the connection was crucial in the early stages in giving audiences a kind of handle they could get a grip on in terms of identifying something that was entirely new to them. Other East Coast American bands also figured in the equation.

"Well, that was one of the reasons we'd gone to London because they played a Stooges number, and it was an immediate reference point. Nobody else played the Stooges and suddenly here was this band, and we'd been fumbling around trying to play a couple of numbers off Raw Power, and suddenly here was this group doing it, and they said they were into chaos and wow! the Sex Pistols! The very name!"
Howard Devoto

"I read a review of them in the NME back in February 1976, which was the first time I'd heard them mentioned. It said that they played a version of No Fun by The Stooges and me being a big fan of theirs since about 1969/70 thought I've got to check this out. Because my favourite bands prior to Punk had been the proto-Punk bands, Velvet Underground, Flaming Groovies, MC5, etc."
Jon The Postman

Morrissey too was drawn to the Lesser Free Trade Hall by the comparison with American 'garage' bands as his letter to NME displays. I reproduce it in full because it sums up the attitude of a time quite perfectly.

"I pen this epistle after witnessing the infamous Sex Pistols 'in concert' at the Manchester Lesser Free Trade Hall. The bumptious Pistols in jumble sale attire had those few that attended dancing in the isles despite their discordant music and barely audible audacious lyrics, and they were called back for two encores. The Pistols boast having no inspiration from the New York/Manhattan rock scene, yet their set includes 'I'm Not Your Stepping Stone' a number believed to have been done to perfection by the Heartbreakers on any sleazy New York night, and the Pistols' vocalist/ exhibitionist Johnny Rotten's attitude and self asserted "love us or leave us approach can be compared to both Iggy Pop and David JoHansen in their heyday.

Not to mention the fact that the Pistols' manager is the legendary Malcolm McLaren who has had close connections with the New York Dolls. The Sex Pistols are very New York and it's nice to see that the British

have produced a band capable of producing the atmosphere created by the NY Dolls and their many imitators even though it may be too late. I'd love to see the Pistols make it. Maybe then they'll be able to afford some clothes which don't look as though they've been slept in."
Morrissey (NME, June 27th 1976)

In the Melody Maker he broadened his scope slightly,
"I attended the Sex Pistols onslaught at the Manchester Lesser Free Trade Hall out of curiosity, and although they have no manners and don't use their instruments in the traditional way, they should make it for their enthusiasm alone.... Musically, like many newcomers to this field, they owe a lot to the New York Dolls and, of course, to the Stooges.... I think that their audacious lyrics and discordant music will not hold their heads above water when their followers tire of torn jumpers and safety pins."
Morrissey   (Melody Maker, June 26th 1976)

The gig itself

The 4th June gig was advertised in the Manchester Evening News and also by an A2 sheet folded into four. Admission was 50 pence and approximately 75 people turned up. They arrived to find Peter Street teaming with armed police. Any thoughts that the police were there to welcome the Sex Pistols was soon dispelled, there had been an armed robbery on a jewellers shop on King Street close by. Malcolm McLaren took the opportunity to hustle the passersby; after all, wasn't this the perfect example of the Spectacle in action in Situationist terms?

"As the doors were getting ready to open, I was in the box office taking the money: Malcolm was in the street saying to people, 'Come on in there's a great band from London, you know, they're going to be famous. Roll up! Roll up!'"
Pete Shelley (Savage, 1991, p175)

Buzzcocks had to defer their premiere gig because of a lack of musicians, but they did gain a bass guitarist that night who would go on to become a full time band member. McLaren had overheard Devoto telling Shelley that a bass guitarist had phoned to say he would turn up to meet them. The musician who called never turned up, but outside the venue a young man stood waiting.

"There was this guy standing on the steps, saying he was waiting for somebody, he probably said he was waiting for a guitarist. So Malcolm said, "Oh, you're a bass guitarist?" "Yeah." Malcolm said, "Oh, they're in there," and brought him inside to the box office and said to me, "Here's your bass guitarist." And there was the bemused Steve Diggle with collar length hair. It was a real Brian Rix farce. So I said, "While you're here come and see this group." And he liked it, and so we said, "We've got a band, we're not dissimilar," and we made arrangements."
Pete Shelley (ibid)

Inside the hall memories differ about the support act.

"There was a support group from Blackburn, and their hair swept off the stage."
Morrissey (ibid)

"The first one was a group called Solstice. Friends of Dave Bentley and Gaz Callender of The Drones. They were awful. They did a cover of Nantucket Sleighride. They came from Eccles."
Jon The Postman

Despite the support act, by the time the Sex Pistols were ready to take the stage the small but enthusiastic audience was geared up for something special. Fortunately, yet again a tape of the concert survives so we can get some idea of the flavour of the gig.

They opened with one of their own compositions called 'Satellite', a tune written to describe the boredom of life in a satellite town of London. The PA is loud enough but the clarity of John Lydon's vocals leaves a lot to be desired. However, the reaction of the audience at the end of the song is positive. Stylistically the Pistols are light years away from the throngs of groups who would emerge in a year's time. If anything they are a proto-power chord band, and the influence of Glen Matlock's solid grounding bass is evident throughout the performance. 'Pushing And Shoving' and 'Lazy Sod' follow on. Again the audience reaction is positive. There are shouts of encouragement form the crowd along with healthy applause. Lydon stays quiet between the numbers. Then into a rip roaring version of The Monkees' 'I'm Not Your Stepping Stone'

After another power chord rendition of one of their own compositions, 'I Wanna Be Me', the audience are still very enthusiastic and people are shouting encouragement to the band. Steve Jones doesn't quite understand, and assumes that they're being heckled. "If you don't like it - Fuck off out of it!" he shouts at the crowd, which launches the group into a cover version of the Small Faces 'Watcha Gonna Do About It'. Lydon transmutes the purity of Love that permeates the original tune, with a scathingly vitriolic opening line that sums up the new Punk attitude -

"I want you to know that I hate you baby, I want you to know I don't care!"

There's no problem here understanding the lyrics. The statement is quite clear and the clarity of the PA is fine. Just like Dylan ten years earlier you can almost hear the audience being blown back into their seats by the power of the performance.

With hardly a break for breath the Sex Pistols launch into another cover version, this time The Who's 'Substitute'. Again it's a blistering aural assault, full of power and conviction. Lydon's vocals aren't perfect but there's an energy and aggression present that is direct in its message. The audience are applauding and shouting when the song grinds to a halt.

With the last number of the official set Lydon finally speaks to the crowd.

"This is called 'Va - Cunt'"

He draws out the words making them into a provocative obscenity. 'Pretty Vacant ' of course will become the Pistols third single. Here in Manchester it's already at full tilt, an anthemic rallying cry for the disaffected youth of 70's Britain. 'Vacant' finishes the set but the crowd won't let the Pistols go. For a first performance in an unknown city the power of both the playing and the audience's reaction is quite remarkable, there's a sustained period of clapping and foot stomping that eventually brings the Pistols back on stage. A member of the audience, probably going on the hype present in the media, or maybe he actually feels like it, shouts out:

"This is a load of bollocks!"

He's immediately put down by other members of the audience before any of the Pistols can get a word in.

"He's a wanker!".

The Pistols then performed rousing versions of 'Problems' and 'No Fun' by the Stooges. By the time they finally left the stage their conquest of Manchester was complete.

Aftermath (Part one)

For many present that night, life would never be the same again.

"We decided we'd have a go, so I went out the next day and bought a 35 quid bass guitar from Johnny Roadhouse, which I've still got but I've no idea where the bloody hell it is!"
Peter Hook

This is exactly what I had done after Dylan's Free Trade Hall gig.

By the time of the 20th July concert there was a significant buzz going around the music scene in Manchester. Howard Devoto had become a one man Pistols promo organization, sending tapes of three of the band's numbers to anybody he thought might be useful in getting them the recognition and publicity he thought they deserved. A flyer had been produced to promote the gig, half hand lettered and half stencilled. This time the price had gone up to £1. and two groups were billed to support, Slaughter And The Dogs and at last, Buzzcocks.

The most significant factor in the gig as far as the Sex Pistols legend is concerned is that it was to be the first time they ever played 'Anarchy In The UK' in public. In terms of Manchester, the evening meant much more.

"It brought all sorts of people out of the woodwork, people thought they were left alone in their rooms with their obsessions. They began to meet: they were saying to each other, " Didn't I see you last month?" A

pocket size community was forming as a result."
Richard Boon (Savage, 1991, p 198)

A young woman called Linda Mulvey was also there that night. The effect on her was such that subsequently she changed her name to Linder and dropped the Mulvey altogether.

"I was in South Manchester Cemetery sketching one day, I walked out and there was this van parked outside saying, 'Malcolm McLaren presents the Sex Pistols'. It was the names: McLaren sounded all tartan, and tartan with sex and guns. When we got there (the Lesser Free Trade Hall), I just knew that something strange was going to happen that night. These people looked so separate: not threatening at all, just fascinating. It was a shimmery night: all energy and light."
Linder (ibid)

Linder worked in close collaboration with Richard Boon, journalist Jon Savage, Malcolm Garrett and other graphic artists of the Manchester Punk era, and as such was responsible for popularizing the photomontage style much in evidence in the early output of New Hormones. In later years she would form her own band Ludus and become court photographer to Morrissey.

The impact of those two Sex Pistols' gigs on Manchester and its music scene can never be overestimated. Anthony H Wilson who was present at the Pistols was so overwhelmed by Punk that the second series of his Granada TV Rock show, 'So It Goes' changed direction dramatically. In its first incarnation it had been typically reflective of the prevailing moribund atmosphere within the music scene. He'd tried hard to make a challenging production, but apart from a few cosmetic touches the show essentially relied on the established names and format, the kind of people you would read about in Music Force's The Hot Flash. Then suddenly, it was as if a floodgate was opened. There was a new music and it was demanding to be heard.

Wilson premiered the Pistols nationally on 'So It Goes' in September 1976, performing 'Anarchy In The UK'. The furore the screening generated was, however, at this time confined to the musical audience. The infamous Today programme wouldn't happen until December 2nd, prior to this most of the anti Punk flak was taking place within the confines of the music press. Post the Grundy debacle, the debate about Punk would become a national issue fuelled by the tabloids, in mid-summer 1976 the battle lines that were being drawn related principally to questions of 'can Punks play'? a turgid musical argument, the flames of which would be fanned merrily by Sniffin Glue's (the first Punk fanzine) wonderfully iconoclastic cover featuring a drawing of the finger positions for three chords on a guitar neck and the immortal admonition, "This is a chord... This is another.... this is a third - Now form a band!"

However, all this was to take place after the gig. That night the ideological framework of Punk, as it was to be in Manchester, as elsewhere, was becoming solidified.

"Ain't bin to no music school!"

"... it was primarily a working class audience. Not many students which is one reason I don't go to too many gigs nowadays (1995). Primarily intelligent working class, the in- between generation who just missed out on being hippies."

Jon The Postman

There was a lot of rhetoric about Punk and the working classes, not least in texts such as Dick Hebdige's 'Subculture - The Meaning Of Style', an examination of the Punk phenomenon which first appeared in 1979. Using a Marxist analysis, Hebdige draws comparisons with earlier working class youth movements such as Teddyboys and Mods.

His basic argument is that Punk was a working class reaction against a variety of factors. The truth of the matter is six of one and half a dozen of the other (see Chapter 10 for a more fully developed argument about this). Whilst class played a part in the formation of the Punk movement it was principally in a downwardly mobile form, people deliberately taking on the persona of working classdom. This is exemplified in the rendition of song lyrics during performance and recording. Howard Devoto, in retrospect, expressed dissatisfaction with his "Mickey Mouse, fake cockney..." accent, as he describes it.

Stylistically we can see a logical progression in accents on English recordings that become evident on Punk tunes. They emanate principally from Glitter type recordings of the early 1970s performers such as Steve Harley and Cockney Rebel, Bryan Ferry and David Bowie. If we wanted to become completist about this we would have to go further back and cite examples by people such as Syd Barrett and some recordings by Stevie Marriott and of course Adam Faith and Tommy Steele.

It is my contention that the majority of Punk musicians were middle class, adopting a working class pose for the duration of their involvement in the movement. Having said this, there is no denying the fact that a number of significant persons to do with the Punk world came from working class origins.

"... we always felt a little bit left out of the scene because I always thought it was very middle class whereas we (Joy Division/New Order) were very working class."
Peter Hook

At the second Sex Pistols gig these class contradictions were very evident in the attitude of the support groups.

" [Slaughter And The Dogs] are well outside the boundaries being drawn by the Pistols."
John Ingham's review, Sounds, 25th July 1976.

Beyond any shadow of a doubt, Slaughter And The Dogs were as working class as you could come. Born and brought up on the huge, sprawling Wythenshawe council estate in South Manchester, they came into music purely out of a desire to play because they felt no one at the time was offering them anything musically. Admittedly inspired to a large degree by Mick Ronson and David Bowie, their musical form developed into a Ramonesque proto-Punk thrashing that was nurtured by playing to their young Wythenshawe fans in the local pubs and youth clubs of the area. They were literally Punks but didn't know it because nobody had come up with the term yet. When Punk arrived they were almost burnt out already. There wasn't one of them over nineteen.

"They were a bit more football terrace. It was arrogant, so we kept our distance..."
Pete Shelley (Savage, 1991, p199)

Whatever the origins of the performers, the adoption of a 'class' stance was an integral part of the Punk mythology (Home 1995). It was the symbolic rejection of a middle class world incarnate. Values were turned upside down and the classic codes of teenage rebellion re-enacted for a new generation.

A question of style

It is hard now to imagine how the battle for the right of men to have long hair was so hard fought throughout the 1960s. 'Letting your freak flag fly' was a principal mode of expression. Boys were expelled from school, men lost their jobs. At my school the legal length was one inch over the collar. Mine presented a problem for the school authorities because it grew out in an Afro style rather than down, as in 'long'. As it never went over my collar, only out and up, the battle over its state went on until I finished school in 1967.

The shock generated by the prison haircuts forced on the three defendants in the Oz trial has been well documented. Enforced shearing became one of society's ways of ritualized punishment. But slowly, what had started out as an act of rebellion as much as a fashion statement, became absorbed into the dominant hegemony. Long hair, by 1976, had become de rigeur. One only has to watch archive footage of a football or cricket match from the period to see just how far long hair had now become accepted. Worse still, it was no longer a 'youth' thing. It was not unusual to find fathers with long hair styles. In truth, it no longer had the same shock, or recognition value that it once had. Long hair had become commonplace.

Punk was to change all that. After seeing the Sex Pistols at the Lesser Free Trade Hall,

"I went and chopped all mine off. But I'd been doing that for years. I used to go down to the UMIST disco and get so fed up of seeing all this long hair. I used to get drunk and go home and chop mine off."
Jon The Postman

Pete Shelley, upon meeting bassist -to- be Steve Diggle, at the same gig, commented,

"And there was the bemused Steve Diggle, with collar length hair."
Pete Shelley (Savage, 1991, p 175)

It is essential to note here that short hair as a form of protest was not something specific to Punk. As early as 1968, what Hebdige calls 'hard mods' had broken away from the traditional Mod scene and started off what was eventually to metamorphose into Skinhead. Originally, cropped hair and its attendant fashion accessories of Doc Martens, Cromby coats, Ben Sherman shirts and braces, were sported in emulation of West Indian youths. By some strange quirk of fate this brief flirtation with multi racialism metamorphosed at the end of the 1960s into the prototype of the neo-fascist Skinhead movement, and despite several attempts over the decades to seize back the original initiative, (see for instance, the Redskins of GLC fame), the Skinhead movement has to this day retained its right wing ideological stance. The situation at the time of Punk was the same. For a moment the Skins seemed to have embraced the mutant Anarchist philosophy espoused by the McLarenesque Situationist inspired Punk movement, but within a very short space of time, these real working class provocateurs had resumed their infatuation with Nazi iconography and rhetoric, despite overtures by groups such as Sham 69, and retreated into their musical bunker accompanied by Oi bands like Screwdriver.

However, for some in 1976, the act of cutting one's hair and being involved in music was seen and perceived as a demonstrably radical act. It was an act that placed you firmly within specific musical and, it could be argued, social parameters. You had made not just a choice but had also laid down the gauntlet. Hair length was not simply a matter of aesthetics.

In terms of style there are significant regional differences in Punk. London, so it seemed to observers at the time, was obsessed with fashion. This is not so surprising when we remember that the prime mover behind the original London Punk scene was Malcolm McLaren, who did after all own a boutique with Vivienne Westwood. Lurking at the back of people's minds was always the feeling that somehow Punk was simply part of a greater scheme in order to sell more clothes.

"You didn't need bondage trousers and spikey hair to be a Punk in Manchester, it was more a question of your attitude. Everybody got their clothes from the Salvation Army or antique clothes markets. Coming to London to see the Ramones in June, I was astounded at how fashion oriented it was. It was more home made in Manchester: people aren't as

cool there as they are in London. There, everyone is on the guest list; in Manchester you get dressed up, you go out to have fun, and you get wild."
Malcolm Garrett (Savage, 1991, p 405)

There was undoubtedly a certain kind of Oxfam chic connected with the Manchester scene, understandable when one considers the fact that there was no offshoot of Sex, McLaren and Westwood's boutique in the north west. Nor were the music papers offering mail order bondage trousers as yet. 1976 was still the time of adverts for cheese cloth shirts and split knee loons, Hippy was still alive and well in the world of commerce, so for the average kid who was into the newly emerging Punk movement, in terms of fashion, anything went.

"I was at art school in Rochdale, and one of the lads there was Phil Diggle, and we all knew that his brother was in this band that was just starting up, called Buzzcocks. I mean, Punk wasn't even called Punk at that stage, but we were already buying our clothes from Oxfam and places like that. We used to go out and buy black blazers and paint the collars white and the pocket flaps white, then put big splashes of white paint down the back, and that was our look ..."
Clint Boon

This basically, certainly here in Manchester, meant a rejection of forms that had gone before, for instance, flared trousers. Parallels were back. Drainpipes were in. There was a complete rejection of the flared trouser because it stood for everything that Punks hated musically, i.e. the old order. Flares were worn by the dinosaurs of rock and that was sufficient to condemn them. It is hard to get across now the opprobrium in which wearers of flares were held by the up and coming sentinels of the new music. And yet if we look at the famous photograph of Buzzcocks, by Phil Mason, taken in the summer of 1976 certainly John Maher and possibly Steve Diggle are wearing flares. However, we must bear in mind that these were early days of the Punk movement and stylistically the battle lines had not yet been drawn sufficiently. Also, in the Manchester area, if you were attempting to change your wardrobe and you were a sixteen year old youth, money was, to coin a phrase, too tight to mention. That's why second hand became the order of the day especially here in the North West. Pete Shelley has his own particular view on why the area developed so dramatically differently than London.

"There was a difference between us and the London scene because the London scene was more record company driven - So it was only occasionally when people made forays up into Manchester to see what was happening in the grim north, that, you know, there was any interest from London.... It was a bit like Australia, you know, the animals had a chance to develop in their own peculiar ways, untainted by what was happening in the rest of the world."
Pete Shelley (BBC TV, 1995)

I feel that it is most certainly true that geographical and financial constraints were the principal forces governing the development of style in Manchester. Economic constraint can be as effective as political constraint in leading to a kind of samizdat/ underground consciousness in terms of aesthetic development. The more you repress the greater the fight back against repression. This resistance is carried out on many levels and here with Punk we see a coming together of many of the talents that had either yet to germinate or had been buried, coming to fruition.

" I think the thing to avoid was rigid stereotypical definitions... No bin liners and safety pins, because that was something that closed off the possibilities. All that potential was snuffed out by the Anarchy Tour. Because when it was over - it was over. There were all these bands and stuff, but they all sounded the same and they went through the same motions and they just didn't get it."
Richard Boon

A whole scene going - Punk emerges in Manchester

By the autumn of 1976 the "disparate isolates" of Richard Boon's memories were indeed "coming out of the woodwork". Inspired by the Sex Pistols and basking in the warmth of communal feeling generated by tribal spirit or at the least a mutual recognition, the nascent Punk movement in Manchester began to find its feet.

"They (Mick Hucknall and friends) were buzzing when they came home that night. Suddenly they realized you didn't have to be in a band

that copied the Rolling Stones. Punk was the most important musical fad that I turned them on to. If they hadn't gone to see the concert that night, they might have carried on playing 'All Right Now' and 'Satisfaction'".
    Ian Moss (McGibbon and McGibbon, 1993, p76)

"As a kind of "thank you" from Malcolm McLaren Buzzcocks started playing gigs with the Sex Pistols and by dint of this became prime leaders in the Punk scene. Richard Boon graduated from his Fine Art course at Reading University and moved to Manchester. Within weeks, almost by default he had become the Buzzcock's manager. True to the Punk ethos he had absolutely no experience whatsoever.
    "No one was equipped or experienced, so I drifted into independent artiste and label management"
    Richard Boon (Rogan, 1992, p82)

"There was definitely something waiting to happen.... There were all these frustrated 19, 20, 21 year olds who'd missed out on the late 60's era and had to make something happen. Then followed this amazing period of creativity with people forming bands overnight."
    Jon The Postman

"History was burning up. Every second a palpable threat to being, a serried, serious hazard to health and becoming a spur to action!"
    Richard Boon (Savage, 1991, p296)

With precious little money but ample enthusiasm Richard began to promote gigs in Manchester. Taking a leaf out of Music Force's handbook to independent promotion, the Houldsworth Hall on Deansgate was hired for a one off featuring Eater, infamous in the tabloids for having a fourteen year old drummer, Dee Generate. An early, pre-Punk venue, The Ranch on Dale Street in the centre of town was utilised. Prior to the Pistols the disparate crowd that hung out there were very much in the Bowie/Roxy mould.

"People were throwing in all these ideas, it wasn't only the freedom to make the music you wanted, but it was also that other people with other ideas were coming in. It was like going to college. People were being Bohemian rather than trying to conform. During that time, gay bars were the places where you could go and be outlandish with your dress and be beaten up. It was about that time that I started going to The Ranch, a gay

bar, two or three times a week. Everyone used to drink Carlsberg Special out of the bottle with a straw. It was a very bisexual time really: a lot of the clientele was under age boys but them there were a lot of girls there. It was almost like a youth club with alcohol."

Pete Shelley (Savage, 1991, p 298)

In August 1976 Buzzcocks put on two gigs there and the proto Punks came, events were judged a success, all that was needed was regular Punk venue.

This came about in the unlikely environs of Collyhurst, at a Heavy Metal venue that was set in a converted cinema. The area was run down to say the least, and had, at the time, a reputation for violence that would only be superseded in the 1980s by Moss Side. At one time in the early 1980s aggrieved residents woke up to find the area had been sealed off by a joint army/police operation (the participants were fully armed). The Chief Constable James Anderton explained to worried councillors that it was merely an anti terrorist exercise and that residents should not be unduly alarmed by the sight of armoured personnel carriers in their streets. What they made of the roadblocks and machine gun posts is left to conjecture. However, in 1976 the venue, known as the Electric Circus, was a prime site for a Punk gig.

It wasn't until April 1977 that the Electric Circus put on regular Punk gigs on a Sunday night. Up to that point it was used for occasional concerts, just enough, however, for it to gain a national reputation as a home for Punk music. The gig that established it being when it played host to the famous Anarchy Tour consisting of The Clash, Johnny Thunder And The Heartbreakers and the Sex Pistols on Thursday 9th December in 1976.

Thirteen out of the nineteen dates on the tour were cancelled by City Councils, vice chancellors or worried managements. This was all as a direct result of the fallout from the Sex Pistols appearance on Thames Television's 'Today' programme and their verbal spat with presenter Bill Grundy. This was picked up on by the tabloids who then orchestrated a moral panic outrage over the group and anything to do with Punk Rock. Those gigs that did honour their contracts to allow the groups to play ran the risk of having their licenses revoked by the authorities. Several promoters were threatened with action by the police. For once the Manchester City Council didn't appear to have any united policy on the subject, nor did the police object to the concert going ahead. Richard Boon admitted later to fearing that the whole scene might be crushed by the authorities.

"By late 1976 the tabloids suggest that there's a whole scene going, ready or not. Bill Grundy. Anarchy Tour. Gobbing. Pogo. This thing had better be documented, we say, perhaps as the end - or only - result."
Richard Boon (Sublime Catalogue, p10)

Upon their arrival in Manchester the Pistols were refused admission to two hotels. Every performance from now on was quite rightly described by Jon Savage as a 'spectacle'. They took the stage that night as if in a daze, but still the Mancunian audience loved them. Word of mouth had promoted the band amongst young people, and since their last appearance in July quite a few members of their audience had made steps towards starting up their own bands. The Punks were emerging from the shelters and the atmosphere of change was electric.

"That night was just a riot, there were so many football fans and lunatics throwing bottles from the tops of the flats. It was really heavy, a horrible night. Punk had been completely underground until Grundy; after that it was completely over the top. There were so many Punks getting battered."
Peter Hook, (Savage, 1991, p274)

For others it was a continuation of the 'Road to Damascus' story.

'We went down and it was a quid to get in. I think the Buzzcocks came on first, then Johnny Thunder And The Heartbreakers. The Clash, and then the Sex Pistols. A quid to get in or that.... And that night I thought, I could actually do that, because they're kids like me... So, from that moment on I knew that was seriously what I wanted to do. So I do credit that night as a turning point in my life.'
Clint Boon

Stiff Kittens go Warsaw

It was that night that the embryonic Joy Division got their first write up in a national music paper.

"These sentiments (that the Pistols were great) were echoed by most every kid I spoke to - they were certainly all in the process of forming bands. Stiff Kittens (Hooky, Terry Wroey and Bernard, who has the final word) being the most grotesque offering."
Pete Silverton (Sounds, December 19th, 1976)

Bernard and Peter Hook it will be remembered had been inspired by the Pistols at the Lesser Free Trade Hall to go out and buy equipment and start a group. Stiff Kittens was their first incarnation. The name was inspired by a phrase they'd overheard a girl called Louise use at Richard Boon and Howard Devoto's rented house in Salford. She came down one morning and told everyone that the upstairs room was full of 'stiff kittens'. Her cat's offspring had all died overnight. It seemed like a good name at the time..... The embryonic Joy Division became acquainted with Buzzcocks through Richard Boon.

"Ian Curtis had just got back from this festival in France where the Damned and Iggy had played, and this bloke approached us and started chatting and I asked him what the festival had been like, and he said, " who are you?" and that's how I got to know Ian Curtis, and he was saying how he was trying to get a band together and he had some mates and they used to spend all their time together in a pub in Salford talking about getting a band together and I used to say to them, "Do something! Do something!, we'll put you on with us." And they didn't have a name...."
Richard Boon

It was at the Electric Circus that Peter Hook met Ian Curtis for the first time.

"He had a jacket with "Hate" written on the back. I thought I should talk to him."
Peter Hook

The Stiff Kittens spent the new year rehearsing over the Black Swan pub in Salford.

"We were just learning to play really. At the time it was just, "Aw,

we're doing it". We just couldn't believe it. Really, we didn't think about it. It was just great to be doing it. None of us had ever been in a group before".
    Ian Curtis (Johnson, 1984, p12)

    Richard Boon who was doing the booking at the Electric Circus for that night, invited them to come along and play on a bill with Buzzcocks, John Cooper Clarke, Penetration and Jon The Postman. When the band arrived they told Richard, "We're 'Warsaw", taking the name from a David Bowie track, "Warszawa".

    "(We chose it) simply because it's a nothing sort of a name. We didn't wish to be called 'the' somebody."
    Bernard Albrecht (ibid)

    Why did Richard Boon book a band that had never played before?

    "Warsaw was booked because it was very important to have another Manchester band for a Manchester audience, because there were so few. There was a governing policy behind Buzzcock's dates that they would try to galvanize something - hype a scene before there was one."
    Richard Boon (ibid)

Destabilisation

    This, Buzzcocks did again and again, putting on as support, The Fall, The Worst, The Drones, and many others during their early career. The underground ethos of Hippy, so generally despised by the Punk movement was never more clearly displayed here in Buzzcocks musical policy than anywhere else. What began building up was a scene. This was more than music.

    "The reason that Manchester happened was that they had undisputed talent in a number of fields, the music, the management, the journalists, designers and photographers. The media were very supportive: the New Manchester Review and Granada's What's On. There was a professional infrastructure, but it was so small that it was like a village community, You felt you were in control."

Malcolm Garrett (Savage, 1991, p406)

"Local activity was seen to be important and was more commonplace although still open to the same mutations as in London. The Drones had been like the Bay City Rollers. They were operating on the media definitions: these were the shapes to throw and they threw them. It was pretty thoughtless. But there were also groups like The Fall beginning and Warsaw, the group that was to become Joy Division - also tacky and captivated by the media interpretations of Punk."
Richard Boon (ibid)

"Our first concert was supporting Buzzcocks in May: playing wasn't important, getting up and making a noise was. The playing would just come. It was incredibly naive, but that is what you gathered from the Pistols. The air you gave off was the important thing: how you had the cheek to get up onstage I don't know, but everybody was in the same boat so they weren't bothered."
Peter Hook (ibid)

Jon The Postman became a Punk legend in Manchester on the strength of his eccentric *a capella* performances. He played at the Electric Circus that night principally because he was the people's choice.

"April 1977 was the first time I got on stage at the Band On The Wall. New Manchester Review Benefit night . It was the Buzzcocks on a Monday night and I'd had a lot to drink and was inspired to do an a capella *version of Louie Louie, probably because it was one of my favourite garage band tracks from the sixties. And for some reason it appeared to go down rather well. I suppose I was taking the Punk ethos to the extreme - anyone can have a go. Before Punk it was like you had to have a double degree in music. It was a liberation for someone like me who was totally unmusical but wanted to have a go."*
Jon The Postman

Newcomers in the village - new kids on the block

"The impression I had of Manchester was that it was a village, and looking at it as an outsider, the elder statesmen of the village treated these

incomers with suspicion - if not hostility for a while. It takes time when you move into any village to be nodded at in the corner shop, recognised at the bar - It (the Manchester music scene) did seem to have played itself out. Whatever had been going on was ready to be taken over and something had to be revived and kept going and be renewed. I mean, this is where you lived."
Richard Boon

The above comments by Richard Boon reflect some of the problems that the newly emerging Punk scene in Manchester had to face. Confronted by a distinctly hostile media campaign, generated in no small part by Malcolm McLaren and the Sex Pistol's antics on the Thames TV 'Tonight' show, this hostility also washed over into the pages of the music press. In papers such as Sounds and NME the debate generally revolved around the 'can they/can't they play' argument. After Buzzcock's debut TV appearance on Granada's What's On in April 1977 an anguished viewer wrote to Anthony H Wilson the show's presenter and said that as a musician who had been 'practising and playing' the guitar for ten years he was outraged that airtime had been given to these hopeless amateurs who couldn't play properly. This was a view held to a large extent by the musical community in Manchester. It was not, however, one that would last for long. It is interesting to note here however, that one of Manchester's post-Punk superstars, Johnny Marr, who would form The Smiths with Morrissey, spent the summer of 1977 studiously ignoring the Punk phenomenon.

"Punk rock was regarded with disdain by Maher (the original spelling of his name), who saw three chord minimalism as no substitute for the rich pursuit of virtuosity. At a time when many of his contemporaries were glorifying the chaotic screechings of a disenfranchised youth culture, Johnny was earnestly leafing through the back pages of rock n' roll history."
Johnny Rogan (Rogan, 1992, p 119)

Marr/Maher was more an exception though. Punk was providing a new generation of young people with the direction in which they wanted to travel. Howard Devoto had established the beginnings of a scene with Pete Shelley, a scene which Richard Boon was to act as 'facilitator' too in his capacity as the band's manager.

"It felt very important at the time to put Manchester back on the map. There was some gig at the Squat where a very primitive Fall were playing... and we went along to check out their form and they were doing 'Industrial Estate' and it was just garage, and they were really good so we tried to help them along - took them along if we got a gig where they fitted the budget - and we'd do the occasional gig in London and it seemed important to bring somebody along with you. We began to realise that substantially there was something happening in the provinces, keeping the flame, passing the torch."
Richard Boon

As more and more contacts with other bands and promoters were created the 'exchange system' of gigs became a viable, working alternative to the established Agency/London axis so despised by the Music Force co-operative.

"... there was a tour which kicked off at the Lyceum (in London) with Cabaret Voltaire. They sent me a tape and I liked it and I phoned them up and said we're doing a gig in London, can you make it, and they said yes. The Gang Of Four from Leeds sent me a cassette and I phoned them up. We had John Cooper Clarke - and it was a great package show. It had lots of different kinds of music, and it captured the spirit of adventure that was in the music, I would say."
Richard Boon

Spiral Scratch

On Tuesday the 28th December 1976 Buzzcocks set in motion an event that was to revolutionize the record industry in this country. They went into Indigo Studios in Manchester and recorded four tracks that they released in the new year as an EP entitled Spiral Scratch.

" There were no record labels up in Manchester then, it's a question of ambition. A lot of people in our situation would have realised, hey, there's something happening here. But we had some sort of wherewithal, which made us borrow money from Pete's dad, book a recording studio and have records made."
Howard Devoto (Savage, 1991, p296)

The release of Spiral Scratch has to be viewed on several levels. It ushered in the age of independent recording that was to lead to the eventual formation of Rough Trade Records and The Cartel distribution service. It stated firmly and clearly that you didn't have to rely on the majors in order to achieve success. It was done on a shoestring budget with homemade sleeve and a kind of devil may care, fatalistic approach to its eventual outcome that was tempered by a naive, yet crusader like zeal regarding its message. Prior to Spiral Scratch there were a handful of 'indies' in the UK, mainly handling ethnic, or 'specialist' recordings. Its basic message to the established musical community was, "here we are and we've something to say".

Buzzcocks had already recorded an albums worth of material at Revolution Studios in Cheadle, with engineer Andy MacPherson. It had been done for a cost of £45 and took four hours. Everything was recorded 'live' with no overdubs. Called Time's Up, these recordings were eventually released in 1991 on the Document label. Why the band decided it was necessary to go into the studio in December isn't clear.

"Well, we'd done these demo's or whatever you call them at Revolution Studios. Quite why we decided to re-record them I don't know, and why we felt... I mean, Martin (Hannett) was the only person we knew who called himself a record producer.."
Howard Devoto

Martin and Howard had met at the building which housed Music Force and the editorial offices of the New Manchester Review, where Howard did the gig listings for the magazine. With Martin's desire to become more involved in the production side of the music business it is hardly of any surprise that he got himself involved in the early stages of Buzzcocks by stressing his role as a producer. Another link is provided here by Susannah O'Hara, Martin's long suffering girlfriend who had got Buzzcocks various gigs through what was left of the Music Force Agency and had forged a link of sorts between the old and the new worlds of the Manchester music scene. Another important factor was Martin's connections to the London music establishment.

"... Martin might have had some expertise with cutting, and Richard or Pete's memory is that the reason Spiral Scratch was cut at Phonogram,

or pressed at Phonogram, was part of some deal that Martin had. He was doing something else there at the time."
Howard Devoto

Boon and Buzzcocks were to use the Music Force/New Manchester Review postal address for their company New Hormones until they were able to move to their own premises at 50 Newton Street later in 1977. By talking to Martin and Tosh, Richard and Howard had worked out that the cutting and pressing costs for an EP would work out at around £500. Pete Shelley's father started the ball rolling by lending the band £250 from his Friendly Society account. This was to lead to an article in the NME, written by Paul Morley, of whom more will be said later, that had the headline, "Teen rebel scores £250 from dad."

The rest of the money came from two sources: Sue Cooper, an old friend of Richard's who was living in Brighton while studying at university provided £100 from her parental grant contribution towards her course. Sue would later drop out of university and move to Manchester as a member of the New Hormones office team, and Dave Sowden, another friend of Richard who had gainful employment in London as a school teacher and was able to provide the rest of the money towards putting out the record. New Hormones ordered 1000 copies of the disc. They needed to sell 600 to break even.

With the release date scheduled for the 29th of January the next step was to get the sleeve ready. On a Friday two weeks before Spiral Scratch was due to hit the shops Richard took the band out to Piccadilly Gardens in the centre of Manchester, and armed with a Polaroid camera he took the cover shot of the group huddled around a statue of Robert Peel.

"There was a feeling amongst the group and myself that the record could illustrate part of the 'do it yourself', xerox/cultural polemic that had been generated. I took the cover picture on the step of some statue in Manchester Piccadilly with a Polaroid, which was a joke: a very Walter Benjamin, art - in - the - age - of mechanical - reproduction sort of a joke. It was instant replay."
Richard Boon (Savage, 1991, p296)

"My absurdist response to what one knew was coming - in the

wake of all that tabloid reductionism - the cut n' paste unthinking xerox collage of imminent fanzinery - this had to be spare and clean, avoid that trash clutter, which missed and wasn't the point - to jape on the means of production itself (hey, a Polaroid goes through the same mechanical transfer process for film/plate-making and printing as anything else, but it propagandises access, a by now/then mystical yardstick for the tack onslaught you could see coming);"
Richard Boon (Sublime Catalogue, p10)

On the reverse side of the sleeve were all the relevant recording details, equipment used, overdubs involved, etc. It was an almost guerrilla act of insurrection designed to demistify the recording process that had by the late 1970s become, as it were, part of an invisible priesthood, available to only those who knew, or had passed the initiation test. This demystifying process that was initiated by Buzzcocks is responsible for significant and major changes in people's perceptions of the recording world. For musicians, whether they came from Manchester or anywhere else, Spiral Scratch was a liberation.

"It seemed very important to me to note what you did, and the back of the sleeve had an archway. It has a Malevitch white cross on a white background.... I was very into minimalism, I liked it. When I painted it was an academic thing and I just wanted white on white, or black and white. And we couldn't afford colour...."
Richard Boon

As with the eventually released 'Time's Up' all the recording details were printed on the back of the sleeve.

"What was put on the back was true - I sang the vocals live, and we did one overdub on a couple of them. It took about three hours with another two for mixing."
Howard Devoto (Savage, 1991, p296)

With a minimalist hint of ambiance added by producer Martin Hannett the four tracks on Spiral Scratch, 'Breakdown', 'Time's Up', 'Boredom', and 'Friends Of Mine', become the perfect snapshot of late 70's youth, Devoto's lyrics the perfect counterpoint for Shelley's power chord tunes.

"*I'd been in these sub-Heavy Metal bands before, so really Punk evolved from sub- Heavy Metal played badly. That's what it was, fast riffs and singing over the top.*"
Pete Shelley (ibid, p297)

"*I thought Howard's lyrics were really funny. The period of Buzzcocks with Howard was difficult for people to digest because there was a lot of confusion about the ideas. The humour in Punk has been lost: 'Boredom' was satire, taking the piss out of the whole scene. It was deceptive. Boredom had been a feeling in currency by the time it became a word in currency.*"
Richard Boon (ibid)

What set 'Boredom' even more apart musically was the guitar break in the middle. It's important to place the guitar break in an historical context. At this point in time, and still, to major degree, nowadays, the guitar group's dominant format of musical virtuosity is the lead break where the soloist is given a chance to excel, improvise, or dominate. The guitar break has become the leit motif of the Rock age. The elevation of soloists to deified status was, and is, one of the major factors in contemporary music making. We have before us the examples of Eric Clapton, Eddie Van Halen, Jimmy Page, Richie Blackmore, etc, etc. Punk music rightly identified this deification as one of the principle problems of Rock music; in 1976 it had reached a grandiose and elevated status out of all proportion to the actuality of the content. The guitar God dominated. Whole shows were built around the sturm und drang of the blistering licks peeled off electric Fender guitars. It was to the boredom induced by this virtuoso playing that Pete Shelley responded in his guitar break for 'Boredom'.

The break consists of the same two note pattern repeated frantically over and over again, 66 times before, slithering off into a final modulated seventh that leads back into the chord structure. In rehearsal the lead break had started off as a joke.

"*I just played the two notes and we fell about laughing, so we kept it in.*"
Pete Shelley (ibid)

For the period in which it was recorded the solo was a direct slap in the face of contemporary Rock. It was also a joke that went over the heads of many who heard Spiral Scratch, even some of those who were obliquely associated with it.

"The engineers wouldn't take it seriously, they were laughing at us. They just didn't get it. They didn't get the group...... they just thought it was this noise."
Richard Boon

Another point about the so called 'musical ineptness' of the solo is that it is actually extremely difficult to play. To hold onto, and maintain just two notes at that speed for that period of time requires a lot more than basic skill. It requires a perfect sense of timing and rhythm and an ability to resist the temptation to extemporise. For a simple joke it possesses much more than the sum of its parts.

Aftermath (Part two)

With the tracks recorded and the sleeves printed the group and Richard waited for the arrival of the pressings. These were delivered to Lower Broughton Road in Salford in early January and every one of the thousand copies was painstakingly bagged and quality controlled by them, ready for release on the 29th of January.

"We checked each and everyone of them for scratches and stuff."
Pete Shelley (McGartland, 1995, p 38)

A leaflet was inserted into every copy -
"This is almost certainly going to be a limited edition release, there won't be much advertising."

Crossing their fingers in the hope that they would sell the 600 copies needed to cover their costs, the band toasted the success of their debut release by drinking two bottles of cheap Spanish wine.

"It was meant to be very spontaneous, like a snapshot of what was happening at that time. It was just something to show your grandkids."
Pete Shelley (ibid)

All 1,000 copies of Spiral Scratch were sold out in four days. As Geoff Travis of Rough Trade put it:

"It was the first independent record that people really wanted. We must have ordered hundreds of them, and it was that which got us thinking we should become distributors."
Geoff Travis (Savage, 1991, p297)

By July 1977, with Buzzcocks signed to UA, Spiral Scratch was finally 'retired' from repressing. The record had sold over 16000 copies and its impact on the music industry had been enormous. Melody Maker reviewed it by saying -

"This is fast, sparse, intense and red hot with the living spirit and emotion of rock and roll."
McGartland, 1995, p39

With the release of Spiral Scratch, Buzzcocks had shown the way for the legions of independent releases that were to follow over the next decade and beyond. As Jon Savage notes in Savage, Jon, England's Dreaming,

"From the New Year, Rough Trade became a centre for small labels, Reggae pre-releases, and fanzines. Perhaps most importantly, the Buzzcocks' record struck a permanent blow for regionalism.... By 1977, both Liverpool and Manchester had small but active musical communities that were proud of their autonomy, and Spiral Scratch cemented this; here was a record, produced and manufactured by a local group, which had as big an impact as any that came out of London."
Savage, 1991, p298

All of this however, was hard to see from where Buzzcocks were standing. While the rest of the group may have been optimistic Howard Devoto wasn't so sure, and on February 11th 1977, after 11 gigs with the band he resigned.

"One (reason) was about finishing my college course, or at least giving it a reasonable shot after so many bloody years doing this whole educational lark. Another reason was the feeling that the band was going nowhere - we were in Manchester, people from record companies or for that

matter anyone else just didn't come to Manchester. We simply didn't have people knocking on the door or turning up at gigs. In addition, the key thing that really changed everything was Spiral Scratch coming out. We had a thousand pressed and were worried if we were going to sell enough copies to pay back everyone we had borrowed money from. The unexpected success of that record really pushed things up into top gear. Finally, there was always a part of me that wasn't too enthusiastic about there being so much Punk rock music, suddenly it was everywhere. If I had felt it had been going somewhere, I probably would have thought somewhat differently about the whole thing."
Howard Devoto (McGartland, 1995, p40)

Pete Shelley put it more succinctly -
"When we started the group he just wanted to know what it was like being a rock star. Once he found out, he just left."
ibid

Howard didn't withdraw from the music scene altogether. He would pop up here and there at Buzzcocks' gigs, and six months later he set about forming another band, Magazine, which got a record deal with Virgin and scored several chart hits including 'Shot By Both Sides' and 'Sweet Heart Contract'.

Buzzcocks continued to build on the success of their independent release and bided their time before signing up with a major label, United Artists. Bookings, however, were beginning to become easier to get, and there was still the 'underground' reciprocal circuit, which saw them supporting The Clash on some of their 'White Riot Tour' in the spring of 1977.

"All these promoters like John Curd who'd sneered at the Punk thing went out and promoted 15 date tours where the group basically went out and got spat at. That was another tabloid invention. Basically it had started with people frothing up their beer bottles and spraying the stage, but they read about gobbing and the audience went along and gobbed because they'd nothing else to do."
Richard Boon

Eventually Buzzcocks would become internationally famous.

Another music in a different kitchen

The impact of Punk on the younger generation of Mancunians was beginning to be felt. The old Music Force venues had by now long folded, but a new wave of entrepreneurs were now ready to start promoting at a variety of venues around the city. By the summer of 1977 the Manchester music scene had exploded with regular gigs being established at The Oaks, a public house with a large functions room in an annexe, on Barlow Moor Road, opposite Southern Cemetery; The Squat, gaining a new lease of life as a regular venue; the Electric Circus, the Elizabethan Ballroom at Belle Vue, and Rafters in the centre of town. The Band On The Wall began to establish itself as a prime site for new music and the University and college circuit was, as always, operating normally as a training ground for new acts.

What Music Force had been founded for had finally become a reality. But where was Music Force? The organisation had, as we have seen in the separate chapter, dissipated in various directions, but Tosh and Martin were now equipped and ready to go in a new direction, and that was to become an independent record label. Tosh had accrued the necessary finances through the flyposting enterprise initiated by Bruce Mitchell to buy the old shop premises in Withington, and Martin Hannett had been busy learning the tricks of the trade as a record producer. Both of them by now had enough contacts in the record industry to handle problems like pressing and distribution without too many mistakes being made. As regards acting as an agency, however, after their move from Oxford Road, that side of things fell completely into abeyance.

Tosh and Martin founded Rabid Records form the ashes of Music Force and Rabid's first release was Slaughter And The Dogs 'Cranked Up Really High', in May 1977. It remains a seminal Punk release, unusual and effective, as so many of the Rabid releases were to be. It sold enough copies to keep Martin and Tosh interested in the possibilities of the label.

Meanwhile, other bands were emerging from the crucible of Greater Manchester. Stiff Kittens had become Warsaw, and in January 1978 would re-emerge as Joy Division. In keeping with Richard Boon's exhortation to them to play they were booked to appear at the final nights of the Electric Circus which was finally being closed down due to pressure from the Fire Brigade and the local police. On the liner notes to a live Electric Circus album, Paul Morley bad the gig a fond farewell -

"If you didn't get drunk for the first time or make an utter fool of yourself or dance without inhibitions or make your first acquaintance with illegal substances or spew up at regular intervals during an evening or French kiss with someone of your own sex or fall asleep for hours on end or...... then you weren't really a part of the Electric Circus Club..."
Paul Morley, 1978

"The last night of the Electric Circus was so bad: we really had to fight to get on. The Drone's wouldn't let us into the building. The next night was the Buzzcocks, and Richard Boon had told us we could play and then on the night mysteriously changed his mind. In the end Ian just had a blue fit at him."
Peter Hook

Anyway, Joy Division appeared that night, and, looking at the size of the bill, it's remarkable they were able to find the space for them; The Fall, Jon The Postman, Buzzcocks, Magazine (the first appearance of Howard Devoto's new band), Rip Off, John Cooper Clarke, The Prefects, The Worst and Manicured Noise, all shared the stage that night.

A week later I went to see Joy Division perform at Salford Technical College. I went along with Martin Hannett who was impressed enough to want to record them for Rabid.

"And Martin said to me in 1977, we should put this out... their first single, their first EP - It was called 'Ideal For Living'... and I looked at the cover that they'd got and I said "No. I'm not having anything to do with that, it's neo-Nazi" and Martin said, "It doesn't matter. It's the dance music of the eighties!"
Tosh Ryan

The Nazi connection with Joy Division/New Order, is unfortunate in that they never had any conscious idea of the demons they were invoking by their choice of names. It is necessary here to state that they never had any Fascist or Nazi connections as far as I was aware at the time, or since. Joy Division was the title of a lurid S/M novel about concentration camp prostitutes, but was chosen more

154

for Punk style shock value and Ian Curtis' choice of reading material than anything else. It is on a par with the Velvet Underground, which was a pulp publication looking at the New York S/M scene. New Order sprang from a newspaper headline referring to the Pol Pot regime in Kampuchea, not, yet another Nazi connection, though throughout the 1980s critics would continually refer to theses so called 'connections' as if they were evidence of some sort of Factory Records conspiracy, or design.

But Warsaw/Joy Division were about to make it big nationally -

"One day we were nothing and the next day we had like... I mean it's the way that Madchester did it with the other Manchester bands... There was a scene then. There was this huge explosion of the Punk phenomenon, an audience that was willing to give any group a chance, which I don't think there is now... but then, if it was a Punk night, and it was a group you knew, everyone would go, you'd get 200/300 people."
Peter Hook

"It was definitely an inspiration. You felt you were with kindred spirits, you weren't alone in the world - you and your small group of friends in Manchester."
Jon The Postman

Jon, who really was a postman, actually released three LPs. His basic format was to arrive at a gig, see who was performing and then see if he could recruit a scratch band from people he knew in the audience, or who might be performing. At a suitable point they would be ushered on stage and then Jon would lurch into his standard repertoire of Louie Louie. In fact his first LP there are two versions of Louie Louie, one of which is 23 minutes long. Jon performed outside of Manchester on quite a few occasions, playing with Buzzcocks, The Worst and The Fall. The ultimate accolade for this rather eccentric, as he would no doubt agree, performer was at the final night of the Electric Circus when Pete Shelley introduced him in the following way -

"That's it from us, but the favourite of all Manchester, the one guy who never appears on the bill but is always there - Jon The Postman, step forward - This is your life!"

Pete Shelley (McGartland, 1995, p45)

Jon represents the absolute true spirit of the Punk ethos. As such he fits in perfectly with the unwritten manifesto of the New Hormones and Richard Boon camp. As Punk became something that the music business could manipulate, and the true energy was diverted and destroyed, the final word on Punk in Manchester should be left to this stalwart of the whole scene, who was there at the first Sex Pistols gig and who was there at the end of the Electric Circus -

"Well, the destruct mechanism was built into it from the start. There was so much energy and so much outpouring that it couldn't be sustained. It was like.... It was like - Burning up in glory...."
Jon The Postman

Punk appeared to generate a certain amount of excitement within academic circles and it was not before long that attempts to analyse it began to appear. The most successful, in terms of initial acceptance and subsequent shelf life, has been Hebdige's 'Subculture: The Meaning Of Style'. It is, however, a text riddled with inaccuracies, written from an outsider's theoretical persective, attempting an analysis of class oriented youth movements through a Marxist, semiotic microscope.

Since its publication Hebdige himself has acknowledged some of the book's shortcomings, particularly in relation to his failure to address the topic of women and subculture. To this I would also add, that for a work ostensibly examining style, the author has restricted himself to the conventional London-centric view of Punk fashion, and appears to have been unaware at the time of writing that each region had its own styles dictated by economic necessity rather than design czars.

Dave Laing's, 'One Chord Wonders', published six years later is a well argued and well observed study of Punk music, though I find his argument that Slaughter And The Dogs had given themselves that name because it defied taboos on death and violence (see 'Naming' Chapter 2), amusing. They had named themselves in honour of two David Bowie tracks, 'Slaughter On 5th Avenue' and 'Diamond Dogs'. This same misunderstanding over Slaughter And The Dog's name is also to be found in Simon Warner's 'Rockspeak! The Language Of Rock And Pop', where he attributes it to 'a canine obsession'.

On page xi of his introduction, Laing makes the persuasive observation,

"Unlike nearly every other youth subculture (the Teds, Mods, Skinheads, etc.) punk began as music and punks themselves began as music fans and performers. In every other case, the youth subcultures adopted an already existing type of music"
Laing, 1985, p xi

As has already been noted by Home, 1995, Laing, in his attempts to reach an analysis of Punk lyrics, tends to lend them more credence than they actually deserve. On the whole, however, despite 'One Chord Wonder's' Londoncentricism, it remains, by and large, a reasonable analysis.

REFERENCES

BBC Television, 1995, 'England's Dreaming'

Hebdige, D, 1979, 'Subculture The Meaning of Style', London, Methuen & Co

Heylin, Clinton, 1992, 'From The Velvets to the Voidoids', London, Penguin

Home, Stewart, 1995, 'Cranked Up Really High', Exeter, Code X

Johnson, Mark, 1984, 'An Ideal For Living', London, Proteus Books

Laing, Dave, 1985, 'One Chord Wonders - Power and Meaning in Punk Rock, Milton Keynes, Open University Press

McGartland, Tony, 1995, 'Buzzcocks - The Complete History', London, Independent Music Press

McGibbon, Robin and McGibbon, Rob, 1993, 'Simply Mick',

London, Weidenfeld & Nicholson

Melody Maker, June 26th 1976

Morley, Paul, 1978, Liner Notes - 'Live At The Electric Circus', Virgin Records

NME, June 27th 1976

Rogan, Johnny, 1991, 'Morrissey & Marr - The Severed Alliance', London, Omnibus Press

Savage, Jon, 1991, 'England's Dreaming - Sex Pistols and Punk Rock', London, Faber & Faber

Sounds, 25th July 1976

Sounds, 19th December 1976

Sublime, 1992, Manchester Music and Design 1976-1992, Manchester, Cornerhouse Publishing

Thames TV, 1976, 'Tonight' 1st December

Warner, Simon, 1996, 'Rockspeak! The Language Of Rock And Pop', UK, Blandford

TAPED INTERVIEWS

Richard Boon
Howard Devoto
Peter Hook
Bruce Mitchell
Jon The Postman

Chapter 7
Post punk operatives

At the beginning of 1976 there were a handful of groups in Manchester. By 1980, the International Discography Of The New Wave, a compendium compiled by B George and Martha Defoe, listed over seventy groups from the area that had made records, many of them on their own labels. In addition there were many more in existence that hadn't recorded, but were playing the many venues that had sprung up after the initial Punk explosion. Viewed from any angle, these are remarkable figures.

Punk became the great provider for a new generation of musicians and young people who felt a need to become involved in what was perceived as an alternative to the dinosaur world of the established music industry. The world of Punk would act as a springboard, not just to music making and recording, but also to other areas of the business, such as design, journalism, distribution and management.

For local musicians it was an opportunity to develop, through playing live, and, eventually, if all went well, to record. For a brief moment in time it seemed as if everybody was doing it.

Establishing the new

Peter Hook of New Order recalls song writing for the early Joy Division -

"... We more or less went straight into doing originals. One of the very first songs that we did, the first songs on the demo, Cigars N Stuff, we wrote really early on... I'm always a staunch believer in that you shouldn't be taught something, if you are taught you can't have a really unique style cos you're always learning and borrowing."
Peter Hook

One of the significant articles of faith of that immediate post Punk era was the sheer originality of the material; almost without exception, the seventy three recorded bands of that period produced brand new tunes for performance and release. It was an explosion fueled by a combination of elements, a thirst for fame, an ability to create, the increased availability of cheap recording time, and the enduring, wonderful naiveté of the arrogance of youth.

"I played through a bass amplifier with all the treble off. It didn't sound brilliant but it was good enough for those early sessions. Mick (Hucknall) would have the outline of a song and we'd work through it as a threesome. He and Moey (Neil Moss) wrote very basic bass lines and it was up to me to provide some flair. When Moey and I left the house, Mick would work on the song and finish it by the next rehearsal. We'd practice it one more time and it would be done. After that it was simply a question of what the drummer should play, and where there should be a break. We would have a completed song after just three rehearsals at the most."
Mark Reeder in McGibbon and McGibbon, 1993, p 89

To aid the creative process band members were likely to be introduced to musical influences they had never heard before.

"Ian (Curtis) was like our mentor in a way because he was the one, he had all the records. Me and Bernard basically just listened to Deep Purple and Led Zeppelin because that was the fashion you went through, that was the fashion through the music papers, whereas Ian had a real underground thing with American music. He was listening to The Doors and he was listening to the Velvet Underground, and it was like an education. You'd just sit there and he'd bring these records in and say "listen to this" and we'd go, "Oh my God!"
Peter Hook

Occasionally, Ian's 'underground thing with American music' could have its drawbacks.

"... we wrote a track on Ideal For Living which goes (sings bass part) and every one said it sounded just like The Doors, but me and Bernard had never heard The Doors, ever. Ian had, but he thought it was such a good track that he thought we should use it, so he didn't say anything about it. When we listened to The Doors we found out that it was a complete copy of The Doors, so there is a synchronicity about these things. A coincidentality (sic). But he was the one who sat us down and educated us to a whole new world of music. He had much more grounding in music if you like, whereas we didn't. It was a good cocktail."

Peter Hook

In bedsits and bedrooms across Manchester, fueled by inspiration, alcohol and that old musician's standby, amphetamine, a vast repertoire of songs were created. 'Snap It Around', 'Voice In The Dark', 'Who Is Innocent?' 'What Do I Get?' All different, all original. From Eric Random's one-man electronic band, with tracks like 'Dow Chemical Company' and 'Shidoo', to the speed charged frenzy of Mark E Smith and The Fall's 'Totally Wired'. From the inspired mania of Chris Sievey and The Freshies' 'I'm In Love With The Girl On A Certain Mega Store Checkout Desk', to the anarcho-feminism of Linder's Ludus, so beloved by Morrissey, with her proto Riot Grrils cuts like 'Witch's Kitchen', 'Mother's Hour', and 'Box', by 1980, Manchester was firmly on the musical map and the London based pop press referred deferentially to 'the Manchester music scene'.

Waxing the tracks - Studios and Recording

It was Buzzcocks who had shown the way. 'Spiral Scratch' was a clear signal to groups, not just in England, but around the world, that it was possible to put out your own records independently of the major companies. By 1981 this message had been received and clearly understood. The International Discography Of The New Wave, published in 1982, lists nearly 2000 independent labels in the UK alone. This is a massive figure that demonstrates the enthusiasm and enterprise of the New Wave scene, and briefly, for a moment, it was a figure that had the majors worried. What must be borne in mind however, is that the overwhelming majority of these Indie, as they came to be known, labels, rarely existed beyond one release.

Indie labels occupy a position in popular music similar to that of vanity publishing in the literary world. But each one represents the hopes and aspirations of individuals who felt a compelling need to go on record, as it were, with a statement about life, or themselves within a society that was careering fast forwards into the turbulence of the 1980s. The legacy that they have left in present day Britain is their recognition as a genre, with their own charts and distributors, and a succession of A and R (artist and recording = basically, music business talent scouts) personnel from the majors plundering the latest talents to add to their mainstream label listings.

The birth of 'Indie'

All of the current crop of 'Britpop' bands, Oasis (Mancunians), Blur (Essex), Pulp (Sheffield), etc, have come from the Indie world, and if we consider that as a genre it has now been in existence for twenty years, it is not unreasonable to assume that it will continue for as long as Popular Music provides the anthems that drive Britain's subcultural youth groupings.

It was, then, at the tail end of the 1970s that this particular aspect of the music world was established, and it was through developments in recording technology and easier access and availability that musicians got the chance to record.

A short history of sound

The mechanics of recording history are already well documented, but worthy of a recap. (Edward R Kelly, 'From Craft To Art: The Case Of Sound Mixers And Popular Music' 1979) Even in 1967 when artists such as the Beatles and Brian Wilson were taking the art of studio recording to unparalleled heights with such masterpieces as Sgt Pepper and Pet Sounds, the equipment they were working on was scandalously primitive. The late 1960s were the days of improvisational recording. EMI's studio at Abbey Road, while equipped with the most up to date recording technology available, was not up to the task of coping with the multi-textural layers of sound that the Beatles needed. Technology had only gone so far as the four-track machine. In order to record more than simply four separate pieces of instrumentation, ie bass, guitar, drums and vocals, any subsequent additions had to be 'bounced', that is bunched together on one of the four separate tracks.

A producer might therefore put bass and drums together on one track, rhythm guitar and backing vocals on another, keyboards and vocals on another, etc. It was a time consuming process that restricted the final product from possessing total aural clarity. You couldn't bring up one of the instruments at a specific point in the recording without bringing up all the others that were on the track as well. When the Beatles complained to George Martin at the frustration they felt by being restricted this way, he came up with the brilliant, if now with hindsight, logical answer, simply join two four track machines together and make eight.

The manufacturers were very quickly off the mark in developing this innovation, and soon companies such as Westlake and TEAC were assembling studios that increased overnight from four track to eight, and then by 1970, 24 track studios were in operation. Obviously, these studios were vastly expensive to build and maintain. The legendary Strawberry Studios in Stockport, owned by Godley and Creme, two of Manchester's most spectacularly successful pop artists, fronting such bands as 10cc and Hotlegs, opened in 1968. The interior of the control room had been acoustically designed by audio engineers from Westlake.

When I recorded there in 1970 I was more than suitably impressed with the walls. Whereas every other studio I had been in, including Phillip's state-of-the-art Marble Arch studio, and EMI's Abbey Road studio, had been content to use cork tiles in their control rooms, these were layered in a mixture of Californian pine and a particular kind of stone that had been quarried off a cliff face in Colorado. Apparently, only this stone would absorb sound in the specific way that the audio engineers deemed acoustically correct.

The sheer expanse of mixing desks in all these studios, complete with sliding faders and EQ balancing knobs, flashing lights and VU meters, was daunting for anyone except a trained engineer. There was an almost mystical air about the whole procedure, a kind of freemasonry that guaranteed its exclusivity to all except the initiated. Studios in the 1970s were an off-putting affair.

Things were about to change, however, with the introduction of microchip technology to the world of recording. Around the middle of the 1970s reasonably priced, compact domestic recording systems were arriving on the market. For the more professionally-minded home studio enthusiast, old four track machines being dumped by the big studios also became available at a reasonable cost. By the end of the 1970s anybody with £500 to spare could have their own studio. It was to these enthusiasts that the New Wave musicians turned.

And a day in the studio will cost?

Glancing through copies of 'City Fun', the Mancunian New Wave fanzine, gives us the opportunity to analyse what potential outlay a group would need to invest in 1980 to record some tracks.

I say 'some' because the time involved would depend on the artist. Twilight Studios were offering "4 track - all day - £24". Decibelle in Rusholme had an eight track on offer, plus rehearsal rooms. They were charging the average for recording which overall works out at around £10/12 per hour. For an eight track, in Manchester, that would have been about right. There was a sliding-scale charge depending on how many hours you wanted to book, and the more facilities a studio had on offer, ie noise gates, compressors, harmonisers, etc, the more it could charge for use. The overall average that bands would try and work to was generally a minimum of two tracks and a maximum of four in a day, and a day would reasonably consist of approximately eight hours. The Albertos recorded, mixed and cut their Snuff Rock EP for Stiff Records in 12 hours, which would probably be about average for the time.

"It was then that I realised why studios have big monitors - To make you think that it sounds great. Then when you get it home it's the most disappointing feeling in your life. That's something you learn."
Peter Hook

"(Tosh Ryan) He had an office near the university at the time, if I remember rightly, and I remember I was walking past one day and somebody said, "Do you know, there's a bloke in there who releases records?" And again, totally naive, I thought, "I'll go in and talk to them". ... I just walked straight in and said, "I want to make a record". And Tosh Ryan sort of looked at me and said, "Have you got any studio tapes?" I said, "Well, how do you get them?" So he said, "Well go and make some up first and we'll see what we can do".
Eddie Mooney

Such was the level of expertise with which many of the new crop of musicians entered the studio.

"You get sort of hoodwinked by studio engineers. We recorded Ideal For Living and I remember it was the most exciting moment in my life when I picked the record up and put it on my little Dansette. And that was the most disappointing thing in my life when I heard the flaming thing!"
Peter Hook

The man behind the shades

Despite all the enthusiasm of the New Wave they needed guidance in terms of production and control. It was to producers like Martin Hannett that people turned.

"I then met a bloke who became a well known producer called Martin Hannett - I can remember being completely horrified because he met me at Owens Park and he had, I think it was a French Renault car, this French type car, and, again, totally naive, I knew nothing about drugs. I just couldn't understand why he was smoking what to me looked like very long roll ups, and the journey.... was one of the most frightening car journeys of my life."
Eddie Mooney

Martin Hannett was fast establishing a reputation for being one of the top producers in the country. At the time Eddie Mooney was being taken for a ride by him, Martin was beginning to set out on a career which would, over the next ten years, see him producing artists such as John Cooper Clarke, Jilted John, Orchestral Manoeuvres In The Dark, U2, Happy Mondays and New Order. But just like Buzzcocks, who discovered that Martin's arrangement for them to get Spiral Scratch cut at Phonogram was because he had a deal going down with that particular company as regards some equipment, Joy Division found working with Martin was on occasion not for the reason they thought it was.

"The band commented privately to Ramballi (a journalist for Sounds), not without humour, that they were in the studio more for Hannett to play with some new digital equipment than to record."
Johnson, 1984, p 38

Whatever, Martin Hannett's blend of neo-psychedelic Spectorism became the sound of the 1980s and his death due to heart failure in 1990, just as he was undergoing a renaissance, robbed the Manchester music scene of one of its greatest talents. Once recorded, however, the next problem was to get onto one of the independent record labels.

"... we did get some tapes done at a local studio called Smile, which was in Sale, run by a bloke called Steve Foley. And we turned up at Tosh's

house... and this other student called Graham Fellowes turned up with this tape, and his stage name was Jilted John, and I remember Tosh saying at the time, and there were other people there, and again, looking back, they were probably stoned although I didn't understand that at the time. He said we've only got enough money for one record, so it's going to be one of you two. And he played our tape first and he said, " Oh, that's interesting, very strange, yeah, I like it." and he said, "Right, what have you got?" to this Graham and he played that Jilted John record (Gordon Is A Moron) that became a hit record, and I said, "You'll never get anywhere with that, it's crap".... Anyway, Graham Fellowes who did this tape, went on to have a silver disc from it so I was in a fit of pique and my ego was hurt and we went off and did sessions for Piccadilly (Radio) and all this kind of thing, and we eventually got involved with Tony Davidson who was running a label called TJM Records."
Eddie Mooney

"There again, you know, when we got Rob (Gretton, Joy Division's manager), Rob had a much more, you know, because he was older, he had a much more mature outlook. He could actually say to us, 'well let's get someone good'. We thought anybody who had a studio was good. We never thought of that. He'd go out searching and he got it remastered for us. It was that thing of you need some one a little more mature to manage you, you know.... We were only kids, twenty, twenty one. We were so into the playing side of it we never paid attention to the technical side and you forget how important the two were."
Peter Hook

The next important question is, how were the labels that followed on from New Hormones initiated? What cultural processes were set in motion that led to the immunisation of so many companies, short lived as the majority of them were?

Anthony Wilson and the world of Factory Records

Anthony H Wilson, founder of the internationally famous Factory Records, beyond doubt the best known of all the Manchester independent labels, and by far the most successful, was persuaded into it by his accountant.

"... I went round to see my accountant in Prestwich, who said to me, "Tony, I have bus drivers coming in to me who earn better money than you do." I said, "Yeah, well, that's life isn't it?" and he said, "My daughter tells me that every band you put on television, when you put them on, no one's heard of them. Then, six months later they're the biggest thing since sliced bread... Is that true?" I said yes. He said, "Well' there's a lot of money in that. For God's sake, why don't you do something with it?"
Anthony Wilson

Anthony Wilson had been, up that point, a lone crusader for music on the local television station, Granada. Born in Salford in 1950, he went from Salford Grammar School to Cambridge University. After graduation he spent two years at ITN in London before moving back up North to take up a position as a reporter/ presenter for Granada. Whilst working on Granada Reports, the local news magazine, he was offered an extra slot fronting a once weekly arts roundup called 'What's On'. Stamping the show with his own idiosyncratic blend of hip irreverence 'What's On' soon became highly popular with young people throughout the North West, but Wilson found himself at odds with his peers in the media.

"... I didn't go to the Stables Bar (Granada's main watering hole) and live that strange metropolitan lifestyle that they lived. I wanted to find some way for me to live in the world I wanted to live in, which was the Rock'n'Roll world. I loved my day job, being in TV and as a journalist, but I wanted my culture, and I chanced upon a bunch of people who were doing music and drugs, which was a group called The Albertos, and that crowd in Didsbury, Dougie James and Sad Cafe, those people.
"So it gets to about 1975 and I've got my own little arts programme on Granada, and being inserted as it were, into the south Manchester music scene... and it was first and second generation hippies. I was a third generation hippy, I suppose, but I was attracted to the fact that here was a bit of culture, and I kind of got involved in that on a personal basis, and at the same time I would put bands like the Albertos on television..."
Anthony Wilson

The ITV companies were always on the lookout for a competitor to the BBC's long running, highly rated 'Top Of The Pops', and Granada saw in 'What's On' the germ of a potentially promising music series. In November 1975 a pilot show called 'So It Goes' was recorded and given the go-ahead for production in the New Year.

"... I suppose the strange thing was that we invented 'So It Goes' as a comedy programme with Clive James.... and the reason we did that was because in late 75 there was no music worth listening to. I mean, people don't realise - They keep going on about an early 70s revival and it was a desert, a complete fucking desert ..."
Anthony Wilson

By the time the first series went into production in the spring of 1976, Wilson was becoming aware of the imminent changes about to take place within the music scene. Howard Devoto's one man Sex Pistols promotion campaign had alerted him to the avatars of Punk, and their forthcoming gig at the Lesser Free Trade Hall on June 2nd. Just prior to that, on May 15th, Martin Hannett took him to a club in Stockport called The Garage where they saw Slaughter And The Dogs, who Hannett was interested in producing.

"I think I was on acid actually, in Stockport, and saw Slaughter And The Dogs, who were a bit Bowiesque. All wearing dresses and that kind of stuff. All a bit interesting and peculiar. And then on the 2nd of June I went to the famous first Sex Pistols performance at the Lesser Free Trade Hall, and like everybody else my jaw was stuck open and I raced into Granada the next day and said we've got to put these people on!"
Anthony Wilson

You can't say "Fuck" on TV

Despite the severe misgivings of the Granada executives 'So It Goes' became the first TV programme in this country to present the Sex Pistols actually performing live. They premiered 'Anarchy In The UK', and went three and a half minutes over their allotted time, causing mayhem in the control booth. History had been made, but whether the executives knew it or not we can never know for certain. They did, however, commission another series to be recorded in 1977.

In between series, Wilson filled the musical slots of 'What's On' with proponents of the rapidly emerging Punk scene, Buzzcocks, Slaughter And The Dogs, Elvis Costello, and many others, received their first break on Granada TV. An audience was being created to inhabit the alternative realm of Punk. A constituency had been established. But with the exception of 'So It Goes' and 'What's On', both personally handled by Wilson himself, and fuelled by his ideas on culture and art, the rest of the British televisual media only approached Punk from the level of a moral panic.

"'So It Goes' came back and I spent the whole of the summer of '77 dying a million deaths waiting for someone else to put these fuckers on television, and, of course, no one else did it because a man called Michael Appleton ...... controlled BBC music, and had this theory that technique was important."
Anthony Wilson

By December 1977 Mike Scott, the Programme Controller at Granada cancelled the show after a row over a performance by Iggy Pop, filmed at the Manchester Apollo. At the climax of the number the Detroit singer used the word "fuck" once. Wilson and his director fought long and hard for the words inclusion. It was on the record version and was arguably artistically integral to the song's construction. When the programme was aired the offending word was obscured by the simple device of mixing the crowd's roar over the top of it. Scott felt that enough was enough and saw the row as part of an ongoing problem with the show. Punk was not yet acceptable and Granada's apparent championing of the cause of chaos could no longer be tolerated.

"I get told, "That's it. That's it. You're going back to doing 'Granada Reports'. You're going back to doing straight television. You can do anything you want, straight stuff - This crap's over."... but basically I wasn't doing it anymore and I felt sad."
Anthony Wilson

Wilson's removal from the contemporary rock scene left a void in his life.

"I remember spending a lot of my time at university doing the mediaeval mystery plays. Not because they in themselves were that interesting, but because the way to understand, the way to artistically critique that period of culture is the same way you deal with pop music.

Because that too, was arguably the last popular art form where all the members of the community, from the richest to the poorest would get the same depth of experience from the play.... Now I was removed from this (music) culture. After having had this miraculous period from 75 to 78, when I actually knew these people - I actually met Elvis Costello, I talked about life to Malcolm McLaren. It was so exciting, and suddenly all that was going to be over, and I thought, I'd love to stay in touch... I'd love to stay involved."
Anthony Wilson

Initiating FAC1

On the 24th January 1978, he got a telephone call from Alan Erasmus, a young Mancunian actor who was managing a band called Flashback. There had been a coup d'etat, and Erasmus had been fired from managing the group, which had split up, leaving him with two musicians, rhythm guitarist Dave Rowbotham, later known as Cowboy Dave of the Happy Mondays, and the original guitarist with Simply Red. Succumbing to heroin addiction, he was found axed to death in 1992, so far no one has been convicted of his murder. The other musician was drummer Chris Joyce, who also played with Simply Red, and who went on to own Planet Studios in Manchester.

"I said, 'Alan, let's start managing these two kids. I'll join with you, we'll build a band around them and fuck those old dickheads. You and me will build a band with Dave and Chris...' And that was my motivation, and that was why the company was called 'The Movement of the 24th January', and it's still the name of our publishing company. That was my motivation. That's what led me, the desire to remain artistically and socially within that culture. To start managing, not even a band, two people, and really, everything since then, like Topsy, it just grew. A series of let's do this, let's do that. We began managing a band and we put the band together, we did this, and then you have to have somewhere to do that, and so forth..."
Anthony Wilson

Erasmus and Wilson recruited Vinnie Reilly, lead guitarist from Rabid label band Ed Banger And The Nosebleeds, and former Albertos bass player, Tony Bowers (who also went on to join Simply

Red). Dipping into 'Leaving The 20th Century', a kind of Situationist guide book, published in 1974 by Free Fall Press, they appropriated the name, The Durutti Column, from a chapter entitled 'The Return Of The Durutti Column'. This, in itself, had been appropriated by the Situationists from a military campaign that took place during the Spanish Civil War, when a relief column of Anarchists under Buenavatura Durutti had marched to save Madrid from the Fascists.

Thus began the Factory labels oft-cited relationship with Situationism, a relationship that would lead in the 1980s to the opening of Factory's world renowned Haçienda Club, which hosted an international conference on Situationism in January 1996. Before examining the rise of the Factory label, it is worth looking briefly at the effect Situationism has had on Wilson and the Factory ethos. Whilst denying that it was anything more than a grab bag for ideas, its importance was enough for Wilson to cite it as one of the reasons for the label's eventual demise.

"... That culture. That complex, ridiculous culture of the late sixties, where you were both an Anarchist and a Marxist at the same time. If you add Anarchism and Marxism together, then add my own Catholicism, you get a ridiculous mix of attitudes, and Situationism being the most important element of the second one, Anarchism, it just led one to approach it (music) in a very different way. The idea that you didn't want to treat music like a product, you didn't market, you didn't advertise, you didn't do any of that stuff. Which was the first thing - Not marketing was great marketing..... All those theories, that mixture of Marxism and Anarchism, Situationism and Catholicism, were all in the background and led to all those wacky things. In fact, they led fifteen years later to Factory's demise, in the sense that we hadn't realised that if we had no contracts with our groups at least you owned the back catalogue because you'd paid for the recording of them. Therefore, in our back catalogue would have been an inherent value of half a million or a million pounds, which meant we could have saved ourselves when we got into difficulty in the early nineties. It was precisely the appearance at a meeting of this one page letter, signed by me, in blood, in 1979, that says 'we don't own the music, the musicians own the music, blah, blah.' Which meant there was no inherent value in Factory. It meant we would have to go into receivership, so that Polygram could fuck us over completely. I have never regretted that, in the sense that it is what we were...... I have to say that I think Factory's concept from day one, has always been, do what you want, and Factory's overriding

characteristic is willfulness, and willfulness seems to me to be a simplified version of Situationism."
Anthony Wilson

While the Durutti Column rehearsed in an old scout hut in Didsbury, Wilson and Erasmus began searching for a venue to promote their band in. They rejected as 'boring' the already established venues such as Rafters and Band On The Wall, and at the suggestion of Erasmus went to take a look at the Russell Club in Hulme. This run down, inner-city area of Manchester had yet to gain its reputation as a haunt for drug running and shooting, but even in the late 1970's it was not an area most people would have thought of for setting up a rock venue. Surrounded by the infamous high rises known as the 'Crescents', mugging and petty crime were rife in the locality, unemployment was high, but the savage cuts of the Thatcher years had yet to be inflicted. All in all, there was still some semblance, or vestiges, of a community in place.

The Russell Club was a squat, boxlike building situated just off Royce Road, and was owned at the time, by an interesting Mancunian underworld character who went by the name of Dom Tonay ("Don"). The Don's business interests were not solely confined to clubland, scrap metal and used car trading were also amongst his many pursuits, and there were several allegations of unorthodox business practices involving violence, made against him. After meeting him, he agreed to Wilson and Erasmus taking over a club on a Friday night. They would take the door money, he would get the bar proceeds. (Middles, 1996)

"We went away and we thought about it, and we thought, since we're taking one Friday why don't we take four Fridays? We've got loads of mates who had bands, there were lots of wonderful bands around then. We thought, why don't we do a few? Then we thought, if we're doing four Friday nights why not give it a name? - And it was Mr Erasmus, walking down the road, the two of us were walking down the street, probably in March. and Alan saw a sign saying 'Factory Clearance', completely un-Warholesque, and he said, 'Why not call it Factory?' and that seemed like a good idea."
Anthony Wilson

The four Friday nights at the Factory were highly successful. The musical friends that were booked consisted of Cabaret Voltaire from Sheffield, Big in Japan from Liverpool and Jilted John and Joy Division from Manchester. Rather like Richard Boon's retro package shows with Buzzcocks, there was a deliberate policy to create a buzz, to include acts that , though diametrically opposed musically and stylistically, operated within a certain frame of reference that would communicate itself to a certain audience. Another scene was being launched.

Along the way, Wilson recruited the talented young designer Peter Saville, to produce a poster for the events. This was the beginning of the close association between Factory and the designer that has lasted for over twenty years. The original Factory poster became Fac 1. in the record label's eccentric catalogue of 'non marketed product', establishing the label's reputation for 'arty' coolness. Saville has gone on over the last twenty years to win many design awards for his work, and Factory, with their minute attention to design detail have promoted many emerging trends in the design and architecture world. Their club, the Haçienda, and Dry Bar on Oldham Street, both designed by Ben Kelly, have won architectural awards, and label designs for their Factory product repeatedly broke barriers in terms of technological and artistic innovation.

Going on record

Wilson views the Factory Club as the beginning of the Factory record label. Being aware of the pioneering work done by Tosh Ryan and Martin Hannett at Rabid, and Richard Boon at New Hormones, Wilson was noticing the changes taking place within the world of the Indies. Originally approached by Roger Eagle, who was, by then, living and working in Liverpool, running the highly successful Eric's Club, to put out a dual Manchester/Liverpool EP, and to become an A and R person for Eric's Records, a fateful encounter with LSD the night before the meeting, led him to different ideas.

"I'd taken some illegal substances and gone over to see my drummer, Chris Joyce. And he had, over in the corner of the room, a Santana 'Abraxas' album from Singapore, or somewhere. This typical far eastern album ... in those days you'd print your UK/American glossy sleeve on tissue paper, then cover it, seal it with some kind of crappy piece of plastic. Just messing with this record I was fascinated by how the thing felt. So I drove over to

Liverpool thinking, great. If you're going to put out a four band sampler, which Roger and I were planning to do... why don't we do a double seven inch, because nobody's done a double seven inch since the Beatles' Magical Mystery Tour. So I get there and we spend three hours arguing about doing an ordinary twelve inch single in a bag, or, what I wanted to do. I'd already figured out a way of sealing the paper and plastic and stuff. We disagreed about this for three hours, quite pleasantly. I got back in my car, drove back down the M62, and thought, 'Fuck it! We can do it ourselves.'"
Anthony Wilson

Some confusion has arisen over the years as to exactly how the first Factory record was funded. We can now put the record straight.

"My mother had left me some money, not a lot, but enough to do this... She left me ten thousand actually. The money that came back (from the EP) paid for 'Unknown Pleasures' (Joy Division)."
Anthony Wilson

During recording, The Durutti Column broke up as a foursome (they are still going as of 1996, with Vinnie Reilly assisted by the Albertos former drummer, Bruce Mitchell), due to arguments with Wilson and Erasmus over producing. The majority of the band wanted Albertos sound engineer Laurie Latham, Wilson and Erasmus wanted Martin Hannett.

Wilson had been doing research into what the function of an indie label was, and in the year his research had taken him, the basic fundamentals of the operation had changed significantly.

"I remember interviewing Tosh Ryan about Rabid when he signed Jilted John to EMI. I remember saying, 'Why are you signing the bands up to majors? Isn't the independent thing supposed to be against the system?' He said, 'Tony, you're living in the past. That's like three months ago.' And if you think about it, The Clash had gone to CBS, McLaren had made his name about signing to anybody on God's earth. The Buzzcocks had gone to United Artists, and really, no one had seen independent labels as....? ...? As being any kind of war against the majors.... Because this system was there, if you managed a band, you could, in some way or another, put out a record by your band, get a kind of a buzz going, and the buzz that would get going would then get your band signed to a major. That's what everyone was doing. Putting their band's records out, getting them hot, and then getting

them signed up.... The question I'd asked Tosh Ryan in 77, I wouldn't have asked in 78."

Anthony Wilson

Whatever the situation, as regards Indie releases was, The first Factory release came out on the 24th December 1978. This is a preview that was published by the NME.

"Manchester noise nightclub The Factory, a welcome rock venue, soon takes the inevitable next step from staging to recording. Incorporating the diversity of Rough Trade Records with the sharply eclectic marketing processes of New Hormones, Factory Records is run by actor/tramp Alan Erasmus and graphic designer Peter Saville. With the ever-enthusiastic Tony 'So It Goes' Wilson inevitably involved, it will release an attractive double EP sampler of acts and artistes who have appeared at the club over the last few months.

"The EP (Fac 2) includes three tracks from the abandoned comic John Dowie, produced by CP Lee; two pieces from Cabaret Voltaire's cult cassette, produced by themselves; two songs from Joy Division, produced by Martin Zero; and a couple of fascinating dub psychedelia exercises from Durutti Column, produced by Zero with Laurie Latham.

"A devious sampler out to both seduce and introduce, its packaging is both thoughtful and unusual, its implications exciting. It is provisionally set for mid-December release, priced an irresistible £1.50.

"Future Factory Records projects remain endearingly vague; Fac 3 (Fac 1 was the original Factory venue poster, designed by Saville) look set to be a 12 inch disco single from the Tiller Boys, but internal confusion has temporarily shelved that. Factory has expressed interest in The Distractions, The Negatives, and current musician's favourites Manicured Noise (ask Vic Godard, the Banshees, Wire what they think of M. Noise - politely of course).

"Send Factory Records your cassette: The Factory, Hulme, Manchester. Let's all take risks this Christmas!"

Paul Morley, NME, December 2nd, 1978.

Within two months the double EP had shifted 5,000 copies and Factory were in profit to the tune of £87. Despite the fact that the Durutti Column appeared to have collapsed, they would later re-emerge as a two piece, Erasmus and Wilson were pleased at the response to the debut recording. Single releases by Orchestral

Manoeuvres In The Dark and A Certain Ratio would follow later in the year, plus singles by X-O-Dus, an English Reggae band, and The Distractions, plus Joy Division's debut album, Unknown Pleasures. Wilson had learnt the lesson of independent releasing off Tosh Ryan, but how closely was it followed?

"Then we started to put more records out to get bands known. We found this band from Liverpool that no one wanted to know, called Orchestral Manoeuvres In The Dark. Put a record out for them, then put out a record for A Certain Ratio, who were a Manchester band. The first single got lots of interest, blah blah. I had meetings with Phonogram, I had meetings with Virgin Dindisc, and in the end they went off with them. We'd done our job well, set up for the next ones to do, and went along like that."
Anthony Wilson

The initial idea had been for Factory to act as a facilitator for their acts, to release a disc that would get them exposure which would allow them to create a buzz which would lead to the group negotiating a deal with a major label. In this sense, the Indies were virtually acting as talent scouts for the music industry. This attitude was to change however, with Joy Division and their first LP, Unknown Pleasures.

Integrity and Control

"It was Mister Gretton (Joy Division's manager) who turned to me and said, 'Before we go to Warner Brothers and Genetic, why don't we do our first album with you?' Far from jumping at him, I went, 'Are you sure?'"
Anthony Wilson

It is both interesting and informative to study the early recording career of Joy Division. By charting their progress from early demos to album releases we can begin to discern a model that in some senses confirms, and yet, in others, denies the standards of post-Punk operatives. In essence, they remained with Factory, almost exclusively, throughout their subsequent careers, deliberately avoiding the paths taken by their contemporaries. Until Factory's demise in 1992, when they signed to London Records, they, and their manager Rob Gretton, stuck rigidly to the original independent label ethos, an ethos that, in retrospect, now appears to be very Hippy in its intentions.

The band had gone into Pennine Sound Studios as early as July 1977, when they were still called Warsaw, and cut four tracks. These would later emerge as a bootleg. They returned to Pennine in December of that year, and cut another four track EP, 'An Ideal For Living', this time through the auspices of T J Davidson, who promised to pay the costs and arrange the distribution. The band, however, were unhappy at the sound quality and it wasn't released until June 1978, by which time the band had renamed themselves Joy Division.

A major development in their recording career took place in early May 1978 when the band were given the opportunity to cut an album. Ian Curtis had visited the RCA office in Manchester looking for Iggy Pop posters and had struck up a relationship with Derek Branwood, the company's north west promotions manager. Curtis gave Branwood a pre-release of 'An Ideal For Living' which the promotions manager had sent to head office in London, but the response had been negative. Branwood's assistant Richard Searling went scouting for other directions in which to steer the group's career and came up with the unlikely figure of John Anderson. I say, unlikely, because Anderson's career so far was exclusively concerned with Soul music.

He was head of Northern Soul label Grapevine Records, and was partner to Bernie Bennick with whom he had produced Soul records in Miami. Anderson and Searling felt that Joy Division had potential and agreed to finance an album which they would place with a major label for them. Accordingly, they went into Arrow Studios on the 1st May 1978, and upon emerging several days later they signed a recording contract with Anderson and Searling. What must be borne in mind here is that Rob Gretton had yet to enter the picture as their manager. This was a deal done by the group themselves and would lead inevitably to some chaos, some confusion and a small amount of acrimony. The recording contract was lifted from a standard RCA copy and, as such, was fairly straightforward. The problem lay with the publishing contract which was American in origin, and, while it may have reflected what was usual practice for an American label signing an unknown band, did not reflect the changes that the British music industry was undergoing as a result of the Punk invasion of the business. The band took the contract to Richard Boon who told them to seek the advice of a lawyer.

Further complications arose when Anderson mixed the tracks and added synthesiser onto several of them. They felt that their original Punk sound had been diluted by the additions and it would harm their credibility. Anderson and Searling agreed to shelve the album and use the tracks as a bargaining point with RCA. The irony, of course, is that within a year Joy Division would become famous for being in the forefront of the use of synthsisers on recordings, however, that comes later.

It was around this time that Rob Gretton entered the picture. Manager of The Panik, Rob had been impressed by Joy Division when he saw them performing at the Stiff Records challenge at Rafters earlier in the year. Invited to a band meeting by Bernard Sumner, just after they'd signed the contract, Rob, whom it was unanimously agreed should become their new manager, left himself out of negotiations, waiting to see how it panned out.

Waiting would last for a long time, however. As with all things to do with the conventional music industry, these things took time. Not for the majors, snap decisions, spur of the moment choices dictated by excitement or what have you, were the preserve of the indies. The band continued to gig, and were picked by Richard Boon to appear at the first Factory night at the Russell Club. It was here that Anthony Wilson's original impressions of the idealistic young group were confirmed and his interest in recording them, or at least in having something to do with them were kindled.

In June, Joy Division put out 'An Ideal For Living' on their own Enigma label. They pressed up 5000 copies and then discovered that there was already a label with the same name. The fold out poster contained in the sleeve was to lead to further trouble when people accused it of containing pro-Nazi imagery (a photo of a small Jewish boy from the Warsaw Ghetto being held at gunpoint by a Waffen SS trooper, and other Hitler Youth style imagery was included in the design), again, unconscious use by Sumner who had thought the images were potent but in terms of disaffected youth.

The RCA deal came to a head in August 1978 when Derek Everett from the company agreed to put out one album with the label then having an option for renewal of the contract if sales warranted it. Joy Division and their new manager were less than impressed. Several weeks later Gretton phoned John Anderson and laid out the band's terms. They wanted £10,000 advance and 15% of the royalties. Anderson, who had so far put all his own money into the project terminated the telephone call by telling Gretton to, "Fuck off!"

Within a week Anderson had received a letter from a solicitor acting for Joy Divivsion telling him that the American style publishing contract was invalid under British law and that any attempt to release the album in order to recoup losses on outlay would meet with an immediate injunction and that Anderson and Searling would be sued. The album was now effectively dead.

An agreement was worked out whereby the band could buy back the tapes for £1000, a price which actually left the original two investors with a working loss of £350, but they were so fed up by now of the whole thing that a couple of weeks later they were prepared to accept a cheque for £850 in exchange for the tapes. The RCA deal now being over, Gretton set about looking for another label.

This is where Martin Hannett began to play a part in the fortunes of Joy Division. They had decided to re-release 'An Ideal For Living' as a 12 inch EP, as opposed to an ordinary 7 inch. There was a resultant improvement in sound quality and it came to the attention of Martin who was by now becoming established as house producer at Rabid Records. He persuaded Tosh Ryan to distribute the EP through their resources, and a relationship between Martin and the band was formed.

In October they went back to Pennine and recorded their contribution to the Factory Sampler EP, this time with Hannett producing the session. Though he annoyed them by mixing the tracks in their absence, against group instructions, the band felt pleased with the results. The EP, which emerged on Christmas Eve 1978, was a huge critical success.

At this point in their career, Joy Division were rapidly becoming established as names to watch out for on the alternative circuit. Gretton's rejection of the RCA offer and his subsequent search for 'a deal' would lead to one more false start before finalising with Factory. The final false start went by the name of the 'Genetic demos'.

The genetic demos

"What happened then was that the record (the Factory Sampler) was a success, we started getting interest from people like Martin Rushent (a producer from London who had started his own label in association with Radar, a subsidiary of WEA), so we did a few demos with him, and then by dealing with Martin Rushent who was so much different to Martin Hannett, more upfront than laid back, or whatever, we were introduced to the business side of it, and you know, compromising, and doing your music, tailoring your music, which we weren't really into..."
Peter Hook

Then there was the business angle -

"... They offered us £40,000 to sign to Genetic in 78, or 79. And that was so unbelievable for us that we just went like that - Phew! - Once we actually sat down and thought about it, sort of summed it up, how much we were actually loosing by doing that and how easy it was to get hold of Wilson and how much he was into the music. That was all he was interested in, not the financial or a marketing side of it. I think Rob felt we were going to lose the purity of it, and basically, after we talked to Rushent, after we talked about signing for five LP's and stuff, and there was Tony Wilson saying, "Oh, whenever you get a tune, come in and we'll record it. It seemed patently obvious to us that was the way you should do it."
Peter Hook

Even at that point, in 1978, while the negotiations with Rushent were going on, Joy Division still hadn't given up their day jobs. They had seen how Buzzcocks had negotiated what amounted to financial security from United Artists and they were looking for a similar deal. Why then, the question almost asks itself, did they decide to go with Factory, when they could have got a £40,000 advance from Genetic?

They've got control ...

"When we made Unknown Pleasures it was a fantastic LP and it went down fantastically. You earned money straight away because you were on a deal where you were on 50/50. It meant that we could survive on 10,000 LPs, whereas Souxie And The Banshees who'd signed (to a major) could

only survive on selling 100,000 LP's. So they obviously had to tailor their whole way of doing things and their whole attitude to selling 100,000, whereas we didn't. I mean, we were lucky the way we were successful, we could grow at our own pace. I think that shows in the music. We didn't have to make any compromises, they didn't put any pressure on us to do our second LP very quickly, and it's unusual I now know, for the second LP to be better than the first, and I think Unknown Pleasures is better for that reason that we didn't have those pressures on us."
Peter Hook

So, was Joy Division's decision to go with Factory governed by artistic or economic reasoning?

"It was an artistic one (choice) and freedom and control.... The thing we liked about Tony was, his whole point was in taking a chance. But then again, that comes down to the strength of the Manchester music scene ..."
Peter Hook

"I asked Rob how much it ('Unknown Pleasures') was going to cost and he said 'Six grand', which was a lie. Martin (Hannett) and he lied to me - it cost about twelve grand. What I didn't realise was that Rob had had the idea that we got the money from the first Factory Sampler... If this actually worked, and you can't find out with an album until you actually release it; if this works like this, then I could do this absolutely free with my band, because Tony's got all these wacky ideas about no contracts, no ownership, and at the same time, not have to get a train and go to London and talk to assholes... And that was what was in the back of Gretton's mind... I didn't know that at all... By the time Unknown Pleasures was out, and the rest of it, we were an independent label that didn't want to lose our bands, etc, etc... And that was the final cultural change."
Anthony Wilson

So, accident, or design? Or artistic caprice? Whatever the answer it was story that was happening around the country at the turn of the decade. For once, artists were working in unison with management, and although these breakthroughs would be gradually rolled back during the 1980s as the ubiquitous music business reasserted itself as the dominant partner in musical relationships, certain significant shifts in the relationship structure would make themselves more obvious in the years to come.

REFERENCES

DeFoe, B George and Martha, 1982, 'The International Discography Of The New Wave', London, Omnibus Press

Johnson, Mark, 1984, 'An Ideal For Living', London, Proteus Books

Kelly, Edward R, 1979, 'From Craft To Art: The Case Of Sound Mixers And Popular Music', in Frith, Simon and Goodwin, Andrew (Eds), 1990, 'On Record', London, Routledge

McGibbon, Robin and McGibbon, Rob, 1993, 'Simply Mick', London, Weidenfeld & Nicholson

Middles, Mick, 1996, 'From Joy Division to New Order - The Factory Story', London, Virgin

Morley, Paul, NME, December 2nd, 1978

TAPED INTERVIEWS

Peter Hook
Eddie Mooney
Tosh Ryan
Anthony H Wilson

Chapter 8

Fun in the Heart of the City

In psychogeographic terms, the emotional remapping of the city began in earnest in the early 1960s, with the advent of the coffee bars and Beat clubs. Unconsciously following the Situationist concept of 'the Drift', groups of teenagers would wander the streets and 'scenes' would be established in an abstract, almost casual way, very often depending on that old, indefinable Sixties standby - 'the vibe'.

After hours

Venues were amorphous and constantly shifting. Centres that catered for specific musical tastes began to emerge as identifiable genres came into being. One venue in particular, The Twisted Wheel, started its life in the late 1950s on Brazennose Street, just off Albert Square, as a coffee bar called The Left Wing. The Twisted Wheel is still remembered today for the culture that arose from it.

"It was a big caff - it was just a nice idea because it was a meeting place for CND, and you know, emerging radical groups... Readers, writers, it was a bit of a pseudo intellectual place. They started to put on late night gigs on Saturdays, in fact, all nighters. But it was drink free, it was foolish to take bottles and that... And people used to play there. You know, you'd get Ronnie Scott and Phil Seaman - London Jazz players - Joe Palin...."
Tosh Ryan

The first legal all nighter had been held in 1961.

"... The first club that I remember was a place on Shudehill called the Shanty Clare Club, and it was run by an Armenian guy called Eddie Sharuto and it was a dead small club. You know, during the day it was just a drinking club, and at night it was like a few prostitutes and that. And we took it over for the first all nighter and it was a massive sell out. That would be about 1961... There was a night when Dizzy Gillespie was playing in

Manchester. In fact, it was 1961 because it was around about the time I was 21 - My 21st birthday - Ernie Garside who was the promoter... said I could get Dizzy to come down and have a play, and so he got him down to this club. So, like word got about that Dizzy would be playing and it was packed. And that was like the first Jazz all nighter. That ran for quite a few months and then I got a bit sick of it, and there was a move..."
Tosh Ryan

Nights down at the Wheel

The move was to The Left Wing, which as music began to take over from the coffee bar function, saw a change of name to the Twisted Wheel, and also a change of ownership, and, eventually, relocation to Whitworth Street over on the other side of town.

"Yeah. It was actually run by a guy called Andy Capp. Andrew Capp. He eventually opened that French restaurant in Rusholme, L'Auberge De France. And when that (the club) got taken over eventually by the two brothers - The Abaddi brothers - the most popular night there was the Monday night. The Monday R'n'B night, which was Roger's night"
Tosh Ryan

Prior to the advent of the coffee bar clubs, the axis of late night playing was centred around the Moss Side area of the city. It was a scene that had developed in the 1940s and 1950s.

"... There were a number of Shebeen (slang for illegal drinking clubs) all nighters that had been popping up all over, especially in Moss Side... They were like cellars that had been turned over to drink and records... There was the Nile, there was The Capitol Club, which was above the Capitol Garage. There was The Blue Lagoon, which Mister Salaal had. There was the famous one down in the cellar below The Nile - The Reno - and a lot of these places were actually taken over by Jazz promoters on Sunday afternoons, Sunday nights, midweek - You know, taken over for specific clubs".
Tosh Ryan

The introduction of legal all nighters carried the trade back into the centre of town, and a whole new culture grew from the proliferation of clubs that catered for teenagers who wanted to spend their free time dancing, or listening to music in the converted cellars and warehouses of the city centre. For musicians, sometimes playing two, or three gigs a night, the abundance of work could present problems of logistics in terms of how to stay awake. This was overcome by the illicit use of amphetamine.

"... You know, you could actually buy things over counters. You could buy quite powerful amphetamines called Keludine, which was a slimming aid, and you'd buy them in a phial of 25 tablets, and each tablet would have 25 mg of amphetamine which was like five times stronger than a Dexadrine, so they were good value. You'd get them for like, 5 shillings, five old shillings, you'd get 25 tablets. So they were very apparent. They (the authorities) began to realise and they took them off the market, so everyone started buying the inhalers called Benzedrex which were pure Benzadrine, again amphetamines. It was like wadding, like some sort of cardboard, soaked in the stuff, and you'd eat it and it would be foul, but it kept you going for days and days. That was widespread in all nighters."
Tosh Ryan

And so, fuelled by amphetamine and enthusiasm, scenes began to emerge. For those who preferred more mainstream Pop, clubs like the Jungfrau and the Oasis presented a wide, and occasionally bewildering, variety of acts - The Beatles and Rolling Stones played there in their early days, local acts such as Freddie And The Dreamers and The Hollies had residencies in several city centre clubs, but just like the followers of Folk were beginning to diversify, so too were Pop fans. For those who sought something different from the mainstream, the arrival of Black American music in this country in the form of R'nB and its derivative, Soul, catered for their Mod outlook.

Roger Eagle and urban rhythms

For those with a penchant for R 'n' B and Soul, The Twisted Wheel began its rise to supremacy as a nationally reknowned gig, principally under the auspices of its DJ/booker Roger Eagle. He arrived in Manchester after a stint in the RAF, in the early 1960s and quickly established himself as a force to be reckoned with in terms of musical knowledge and energy. It was Roger who, almost singlehandedly, created what came to be known as 'Northern Soul', through his devotion to spreading the word, or rather, music, of a wide variety of previously unheard of Black American artists such as Screaming Jay Hawkins and Ramsey Lewis. Mancunian musician's love of Blues and R 'n' B can be traced back to the early 1950s with John Mayall, who had inherited his father's passion for that style of music, and his urgent letters to Paddy MacKiernan (see Chapter 2, pp 41-42), regarding Muddy Waters' appearances at the Free Trade Hall. Then there were those like Bruce Mitchell and Tosh Ryan who fell into it through the influence of Jazz. Then there was Victor Brox.

"Because we wanted to do something that was contrary to MerseyBeat, so we picked up all the Soul hits and we got them first and we did them first. There were only two bands in the north that did Soul hits. One was Georgie Fame and The Blue Flames, and one was The Victor Brox Blues Train, and between us we did the entire lot. But because we had Jacob MacNab (a Rastafarian percussionist) in the band we wanted to do Reggae, and we used to do Prince Buster and all those kind of guys, early Ska and Bluebeat... I remember, we used to do an alternate residency with a band called Herman's Hermits... And like, all the West Indians used to come to our gigs and all the MerseyBeat people used to go to his gigs... It was a totally different scene..."
Victor Brox

Owing to the difficulties in getting American musicians over to England, and also because of the rapidly expanding interest in R'n'B espoused by musicians in this country, Roger Eagle would regularly book English acts that fitted the bill. Performers such as The Graham Bond Quartet, Jimmy Powell And The Dimensions, Manfred Mann, and the Cyril Davis All Stars featuring Long John Baldry, were regular players at The Twisted Wheel, alongside homegrown stalwarts like John Mayall's Bluesbreakers, The Victor Brox Blues Train and Georgie Fame And The Blue Flames. Manchester, and The Twisted Wheel in particular, began to gain a national reputation by the early to mid 1960s.

"My uncle was really into the Blues and he used to come up from Cornwall and hang out with Victor Brox, John Mayall and Alexis Korner - they used to go to all the clubs".
Andy Harris

In fact, Manchester had become such a lucrative market for the new wave of performers that bands such as Alexis Korner's Blues Incorporated and Graham Bond actually had flats in town because they spent so much time in the area. (Shapiro, 1992)

All these musicians contributed to the rich, active and vibrant nightlife that had come to dominate Mancunian youth culture, but, as we have seen in Chapter 4, all this was to be sadly curtailed by the machinations of the police and the City Council. By 1968 only a handful of clubs were left in operation, Roger Eagle's the Magic Village, and the recently relocated Twisted Wheel.

The Magic Village came to be

The Magic Village was the Hippy equivalent of The Twisted Wheel. Situated in the tangle of alley ways that threaded their meandering route between Market Street and Cannon Street, this Cromford Court basement, was originally called The Jigsaw. In 1965/ 1966 I managed to see The Who, Martha Reeves And The Vandellas, Percy Sledge and many others inside the black painted cellars of The Jigsaw. It was a classic example of all the Council; were trying to ban.

Roger Eagle managed to persuade the owners to let him run it as a 'Progressive' music venue in 1968, and it joined the small, but active legion of clubs around the country catering for the upsurge in Psychedelic, or, Underground music. With a lightshow focused on its cramped playing area the venue played host to a whole gamut of performers ranging from the Third Ear Band to The Pink Floyd, Jethro Tull to perennial favourites, The Edgar Broughton Band. It also served as a proving ground for the handful of local musicians who became the second generation of Manchester groups, though there were fewer than had emerged earlier, in the Beat boom.

The Magic Village was Manchester's first permanent 'Underground' venue. Prior to 1968 there had been sporadic promotions at the College of Art, promoted by Paul Brown (late of the Ladybarn Folk Club) and Jim McRitchie, who were members of two neo-psychedelic bands, Black Silk Frog and Five Paper Fantasy. These two outfits were avant garde performance art activists as much as players, and had been banned from holding 'Happenings' at the Art School after a series of events entitled Radio Albania, one evening of which culminated in the seemingly real castration of a 'drunken straight' in the audience. The full technical facilities of the art department had been utilised to create a casting of a blood filled rubber penis which had been hacked off the 'punter' by an allegedly irate female student. The woman in question, Penny Henry, later went on to manage The Haçienda in the 1980s.

Aside from these Happenings, the only other regular Psychedelic venue in Manchester was one evening a week at the Blue Note Club on Gore Street, near Piccadilly Station, run by myself as a chance to gain exposure for the first proper band I had been in, Jacko Ogg And The Head People. The band was formed in 1966, immediately after I had seen Bob Dylan at the Free Trade Hall. The next day (May 18th), I went to A1 Music Centre and bought a Fender Cow Horn bass and a 30 watt amp. The idea had always been there, and electrification was an inevitability that was precipitated by the Dylan gig. Along with a colleague from school, Mike King, we set about rehearsing without a drummer.

The music that we started playing in the middle of 1966 was cover versions of Paul Butterfield Blues Band material and various odds and sods from the rapidly expanding repertoire of 'weird' music that was beginning to emerge from the States. My cousin, who was in the Royal Navy, was often in San Francisco and would bring back, throughout that period, a variety of albums by artists as diverse as Frank Zappa, Love and the Doors. These were a major inspiration on the direction that Jacko Ogg took in the early months. By the autumn of 1966 we had gained a drummer, and for weeks we coaxed him into doing a drum solo during our version of the Who's 'The Ox'. By chance his father was present when we finally performed it at the Bluebell pub in Denton, to a completely uncomprehending audience. His father immediately made him leave the group, accusing us of playing 'drug songs'.

His replacement came about in a most peculiar fashion. We used to rehearse at the top of a house in Didsbury, south Manchester. The next door attic was occupied by Tosh Ryan and his family. Several days earlier I had been to a jumble sale and bought an antique, full length Royal Flying Corps leather coat for the princely sum of two shillings and sixpence. Tosh asked us if we were interested in someone he knew, Bruce Mitchell, a drummer who had played with John Mayall. In exchange for Bruce's phone number, I gave him the leather coat.

Jacko Ogg and The Head People, ie Mike King, Bruce Mitchell

and me, performed its first gig at Chorlton-on-Medlock Town Hall (now part of the Manchester Metropolitan University) at a benefit for CND. We were the first band in Manchester to use a light show, which was in fact, out of focus slides of the Blackpool illuminations with somebody's hand waved up and down in front of the lens. By 1967 we had worked out the use of glass slides with oils and revolving filters, and we had also gained a fourth musician, a guy called Les, who played rhythm guitar. In fact, the actual reason that we had him in the band was because we had got the Tuesday nights at the Blue Note Club and wanted to expand our horizons musically. Les was also the North of England junior bag pipe champion. A typical evening at the club would culminate in a 'Freak Out' when the band would play a version of the Beatles' 'Baby You're A Rich Man', with Les on lead bagpipes. At the finale of the number, the guitars would be left on feedback, and Bruce, who was dressed in a gorilla suit, would let off maroons and smoke bombs in the audience, as Dave Backhouse, who ran the lightshow, would ride his Lambretta through the crowd.

Jacko Ogg inevitably slipped into musical oblivion, but not before overtures had been made by the English representative of Buddah Records (Captain Beefheart's label). The next logical step was to enter the world of Roger Eagle and The Magic Village.

By the time of the opening of the Magic Village, Jacko Ogg had mutated into a close harmony duo called Greasy Bear, a name given to us by Eagle, that came from combining two Jefferson Airplane song titles, 'Bear Melt' and 'Greasy Heart'. What became of The Magic Village, in the fullness of time, is that the audience went their own way. Drug Squad pressure certainly exerted a strong influence on the denizens of the Village, and led to a disenchantment with going to town. Day, or night, there was always a police presence at the turn of the decade, looking for, in particular, long hairs to hassle. This was well before the repeal of the iniquitous 'Suss' Laws.

In Manchester, these 'search on suspicion' Laws were applied less in a racist sense, as they were in London, but on a much more cultural level. Society was beginning to enter the time of the Angry Brigade outrages, and the 'Counterculture', such as it was in England at the time, was a prime target for the forces of Law and Order. By the time The Magic Village had closed, the tightening of Society's grip on the Underground, vis a vis, the Oz trial, It busts, and sundry other prosecutions against book importers, etc, was beginning to be felt in a myriad of other forms of repression. The resultant dearth of live music outlets in the city is detailed in other chapters, as is the rise of Music Force, and its attempts to rejuvenate the night time economy. With the changes wrought by Punk rock and the New Wave, described in Chapter 6, the revitalisation of the Manchester music scene takes place. By 1980 the Manchester music scene had a cultural identity and a pride in an embryonic form. Now, at the turn of the decade, the people were drifting the streets once again, in order to create a 'heart of the city', whether it be in physical, or metaphorical terms. The 'Drifting', where, before in the Seventies, had been aimless, now had at least, a certain direction. Though there would never be again, the sheer multiplicity of gigs, that had been around in the 1960s, for the Rock 'n' Roll footsoldiers of the 1980s, there was at last a soul in the heart of the city.

Chronicling the changes

City Fun was a post Punk guide to the rapidly evolving Manchester scene. It was founded and edited by Andy Zero, and went through several incarnations. Started towards the end of 1979, the fanzine City Fun is in some ways a successor to Hot Flash. In other ways it was a follow-on from Shytalk, an earlier Manchester Punk fanzine, but overall City Fun was an entity unto itself. At first deliberately down market, this Xeroxed round-up of a whole scene going on. It was Samizdat style, cocking a snoot at the big guns from London, such as the NME and Sounds; IBM typeset, often hand-written and with occasional mimeographed inserts, City Life's rough and ready attitude perfectly reflects the state of the Manchester music scene at the turn of the 1970s. Reviews of gigs and releases vie for space with methamphetamine ramblings of poets and people with a grudge. Snippets of news, fed to the local zine by local bands on their way up, and down, jostle for space with anecdotes about... what?

"Did you know that in America, for every cop killed by a civilian 4 civilians are killed by cops. With 60 deaths a year of people held in custody in the UK it sounds almost as bad here." (sic)
City Fun No15

Fragments of fiction from the pen of Jeff Noon, who in the 1990s would become an internationally reknowned Science Fiction author, sat uncomfortably beside reviews of sundry gigs by correspondents going under the (I presume) pseudonym of 'Mr R Sohl'.

City Fun harked back to the good old days of the 1960s when street sellers were recruited to push copies on the Queen's highway, a right that was fought for by the anarchistically-inclined in Manchester (Dickinson, 1996). Only one site in the entire city area, outside Central Library, was deemed by the police to be a legal selling point. Anywhere else and you were liable to be arrested and charged with vagrancy. Sellers of Oz and It, and the local Underground magazines like Grass Eye and Mole Express often found themselves in Bootle Street Police station while calls to civil libertarian lawyers were made. Finally, the right to sell anywhere in the City centre was grudgingly allowed, as long as you didn't constitute an obstruction. City Fun sellers made life a bit easier for themselves by restricting their outlets to gigs, but the principle of earning money by direct selling was there, just as it had been in the 1960s.

"Do you want an instant approach to complete strangers?

"Ever thought of selling City Fun?

"We are looking for street and gig sellers anywhere and everywhere.

"What does it involve? - We will deliver or send copies to you (sic) doorstep once a fortnight, you sell them: to friends, at gigs, on a street corner, or ask a local shop: how you sell them is up to you. When we bring the next issue you give us the money from the copies you've sold, and any unsold copies. If you want it, you're welcome to the 3 1/2p a copy that the shops take. It can also be a good way of getting into gigs for nothing (I'm selling City Fun. Is it alright if I come in?) Not everywhere says yes, but most places do if you're polite about it.

"Selling City Fun isn't all sweetness and light - but neither is it drudgery and darkness....

"Write in or phone...."
Backpage ad, City Fun, Vol 2, No 5

What significant differences are there between City Fun and Music Force's The Hot Flash? The main one would be that The Hot Flash would not have been out of place in Nottingham, or Taunton. In its early days, The Hot Flash styled itself as a national publication;

City Fun, on the other hand, is totally and unashamedly parochial. This time, however, there is a pride, or tangible aura of cultural identity within a geographic space, one that recognises itself for its strengths in unity, and thankfully, retains an ability not to take itself too seriously.

The layout of City Fun, whilst cut and paste like Hot Flash, is a lot less professional looking. It would not be unfair to suggest that this is possibly part affectation, in keeping with the Punk ethos of Sniffing Glue, etc. Some articles have obviously been typed up, or hand written elsewhere and then sent in for inclusion. There are even adverts for concerts, promoted by Wise Moves, that have been very badly hand lettered underneath the venues' printed logos. In the earlier issues there are headings which appear to have been mainly done with hand stencils, and contributors often have their own signatures appended to their by-lines. One aspect of City Fun, however, that is shared with Hot Flash, is the appearance of cartoons by Ray Lowry.

A nationally read local magazine

Despite its parochialism, or possibly because of it, City Fun was popular in other parts of the country. The same impetus that had inspired Punk rock independent distribution was now being applied to fanzine and alternative publications. Through the auspices of Rough Trade, whose founder/ manager, Geoff Travis, had in turn been inspired by Buzzcock's Spiral Scratch, City Fun was given nationwide distribution. Just why this idiosyncratic local newsletter appealed to a geographically wide audience can only be surmised at. Perhaps it was the paper's apparent sincerity and no nonsense approach to the subject matter in hand? I would maintain that it was recognition of the City as an entity in its own right, with its own cultural identity and practices that was being acknowledged on a national scale by the newly developing generation of music fans across the country. The concept of the 'Manchester scene' in the consciousness of the nation's youth began to coalesce as it began to be referred to in the national music press. The idea of the Manchester scene would come to prominence in the international media later in the 1980s with the Time Magazine led onslaught of 'Madchester' articles, and yet again in the mid 1990s with the triumph of Oasis on the Britpop scene.

The scale of national distribution is reflected in the Gig Guide section of City Fun, Issue No 23, lists not just the usual Manchester venues such as Band On The Wall and The Cyprus Tavern, but the Distractions and the Members playing at The Stagecoach Pub, Dumfries-shire, Holly And The Italians at The Boat Club, Nottingham, UK Subs at the Cambridge Corn Exchange, and the Cure at Mountford Hall, Liverpool. There are more. The Gig Guide section was a free service, so presumably the entries had been supplied by either the bands or the promoters. What is significant is that whoever put them in felt it appropriate to do so because they would be read by the right audience geographically. In terms of City Fun's content, however, with the exception of the inclusion of some reviews from Liverpool and Merseyside (shades of Hot Flash) the features and articles are almost wholly concerned with what's happening in Manchester, and not necessarily simply with the music scene.

With a vengeance

"Did you know...... that the biggest private arms warehouse in Europe is situated here in Manchester?

"This one building contains enough equipment to furnish quite a sizeable army and it's not just antiquated old war - surplus small arms either, it also contains modern gear such as anti-tank missiles and other such sophisticated stuff that the Government ASSURES us, is developed 'solely' for the 'legitimate' security forces, and is NEVER made available to private dealers, or allowed to end up in 'trouble spots'.

"........ The firm in question is INTERARMS. Its premises are situated at the extreme end of the Mancunian Way......... They're extremely unlikely to let you in, although they did once let the telly in far a very cagey and obviously contrived and edgy 'look round'. Just what would happen if you DID try to get in, we don't know. You'd probably meet with a slight 'misadventure' under the wheels of some unmarked official vehicle or something."

Steed, City Fun No 23

"BUSES. You will have noticed that the bus fares have gone up again. Manchester has the most expensive buses in the country & less & less passengers as a result - leading to more fare increases. Sheffield subsidises

its buses. It has the cheapest in Britain and is increasing its passengers."
Hand written, City Fun, No15.

Other articles deal with the frustration of life on the dole, cafes
in the Arndale centre, and other minutiae of teen angst.

Let us now turn our attention to how City Fun dealt with the
Manchester music scene.

"DON'T LOOK AT MY HAIR STYLE- IT MIGHT FALL OVER." Gig review, City Fun, Vol 2, No5.

Ostensibly, fanzines are, by their very nature, just that -
magazines written by fans of a particular genre of music. As such,
there is usually a lack of criticism, but a great deal of enthusiasm.
Fanzines originated in part as devices to propagate and disseminate
information about specific entities, be they cult films, train spotting,
or Rock music. One of the singular differences about City Fun was
its healthy scepticism and general New Wave distrust of people or
bands who were perceived to be in the process of selling out. Here
we can spot echoes of the debate around accusations of Bob Dylan's
'commercialisation' in the 1960s, or the debates surrounding
'authenticity' in Jazz circles in the 1950s. City Fun was never afraid
to bite the hand from which it fed.

*"As the years move on..... the establishment no longer oppresses 'new'
music instead it realises its 'commercial' potential: what is marketable?
Did you buy the Police? Nice... wasn't it? Gary Numan? Squeeze? Blondie?
The Jags? Nice isn't it? The Clash storm America and London's Calling
for dollars. I must say!! The Buzzcocks are trying hard (can I have your
autograph - Mr New Wave star). WHAT IS THIS SHITE.*

*"1980 YOU HAVE ARRIVED. Have you made it?? Did you get what
you want??? Hassle did you? Made out? Huh? But they're so natural....
my friends became celebrities - You chose it, they sold it.... Did you like my
bowler hat?? It's not for sale and will you FUCK OFF."*
Andy Zero, City Fun, No 15

"THE BUZZCOCKS WENT LIMP.
*"The Buzzcocks were fucking terrible. Appalling. All vestiges of
everything I'd ever seen or liked in them had gone. They were a shambles.*
"The songs sound tired, and, for the most part, were played without

the slightest degree of conviction. Their set still contains songs that are now three and a half years old - Two years ago they were complaining they were sick of them they're still sick of them. Now what kind of a groove is that, eh?.... Entertainment? Maybe, but it's a pretty fucking perverse form of entertainment...."
Review of Buzzcocks, City Fun, Vol 2, No7

The magazine also contained positive reviews of up and coming local bands that retained the fervour of the heady days of fandom, movingly inept pieces that reverberate with all the excitement of the true fan.

"Before, death warmed up; after, a million dollars. I'm probably preaching to the converted, but the Distractions must be one of the world's best, say, dozen pop groups. If you don't have the Irresistible Urge to shake a leg when they are on stage, you're either stone deaf or in urgent need of the Samaritans. Electrifyingly strong, compulsive songs are dynamically performed...."
Matt Snow, City Fun, No10

Inevitably this kind of factionalism, or heroically truthful journalism, depending on your perspective, was bound to invoke a backlash. Things came to a head somewhere around 7th February 1980 when Factory Records staged a benefit for City Fun featuring Joy Division, A Certain Ratio and other bands from the label's roster. Andy Zero chose to run a negative review of the event that stated that Section 25, and A Certain Ratio shared a remarkable musical similarity to Joy Division. Factory, and Anthony Wilson in particular, went to war over the piece, writing a rebuttal (which was published in full), and removing City Fun from the Factory mailing list. The centre pages of Issue 23 are devoted to the fall out.

"Dear City Fun,
"Now we know the reasons for the Factory having written off City Fun, I still wonder what they hope to achieve by this gesture, such a reaction is hardly going to help to improve C/F. Obviously a none too good (though hardly vicious) review in the paper of already established groups isn't going to effect record sales or the band's popularity, so why the ridiculous over reaction on the part of Factory Records?
Love,

Kerry A Huish"
City Fun, No23

"Dear Mr. Zero and colleagues.....
"On my last visit to the Factory I was fortunate enough to obtain a copy of your organ and what a load of juvenile drivel it is! The reprint of the City Fun Benefit confirmed what Tony Wilson said about third rate journalism....
"My next complaint is levelled at you Mr. Zero. O.K. so you wrote about J.D., A.C.R. before the London papers came up with them. I should bloody well think so too!... that's partly what you're in the business for!! You're very lucky to have such a crop of talented bands in the M/CR area, and you can help us Londoners out by bringing them to our attention..........
Yours Sincerely,
Andy Hooper"
(ibid)

Controversy of this kind, plus a number of other issues concerning the style and content of the paper, led to a meeting of concerned parties, amongst them Cath Carroll and Liz Naylor, Jon Savage, Bob Dickinson and Andy Zero. The first incarnation of City Fun was terminated with Number 25, and Volume 2 was embarked on from that point onwards. The magazine was given a style overhaul consisting of a much more professional typography and layout. Much of the anarchic approach of, not just the contents, but the ethos of the early issues, disappeared too. Regular public meetings were still held, where any readers interested enough could turn up and express an opinion about how the magazine was shaping up.

"EDITORIAL.
"CITY FUN MAGAZINE is run by a board of people. Once a month the board meetings will be open to anyone who wishes to come along with their views/suggestions/criticisms."
City Fun, Vol 2, No5

In Volume 1, there is a mimeographed insert containing various bits of information, gig guide, credits, etc. It also has an account of their finances. I reproduce it in full -
Cash:- £53.00

Neil owes:- £3.00
Total   £58.00
DEBT to printers £60.00
Balance: minus £2.00
City Fun, insert. No15. (sic)

Volume 2, Number 7, has a whole page devoted to carefully detailed and itemised accounts, calls for readers to attend meetings, all openness and glasnost, yet overall the impression is that whilst it may have become tighter, City Fun was in someway more exclusive, less approachable.

Benefiting from the input of a regular tribe of writers, several of whom would go on to impressive future careers, eg Cath Carroll with NME (Middles, 1996), Bob Dickinson with Granada TV, then BBC Radio, Jon Savage as a writer. The actual contents of the magazine maintained a consistently high standard of writing. In terms of championing the new bands from the local scene, City Fun had originally been designed with that in mind and never did it jettison that purpose.

From its inception in 1979 to its eventual decline and demise in 1983, City Fun fulfilled a unique function in chronicling an exciting and new phase in the development of the City's musical culture. It offered more than the listings magazine, New Manchester Review, which had started in 1975 and was around until 1980. NMR's remit of what's on was too broad to cover the rapidly expanding music scene too closely. Its successor, City Life, wouldn't begin publishing until 1983, by which time the initial phase of the Manchester music scene was temporarily in abeyance, undergoing a period of regrouping before the big push that was to come later in the decade.

Another reason for the importance of City Fun was its effect on helping to create an identity for the musical side of the city. The fact that it was distributed nationally and yet remained so parochial and 'true to its roots' was a major factor in consolidating the gains that had been made in terms of Independent recording and distribution. It helped keep alive the idea that performers didn't have to go to London to 'make it'. Its healthy irreverence also served as a useful reminder to those up-and-coming bands that were emerging from the Manchester area not to lose sight of their origins.

Fuck Art - Let's dance

"We decided to open a club. Gretton has always wanted a club, and we'd earned a bit of money and we thought what a good idea to reinvest some in the city... Anyway, we built this discotheque - club - nightmare... God... When we started Factory I used to give everybody a copy of 'Leaving The 20th Century'. I bought about ten of them. And we thought, we've got to think of a name for the club. Gretton's sat there one night at home and pulled out this book, scanned through the first few pages and said, "Why don't we call it The Haçienda?"
Anthony H. Wilson

Clubs can be opened and clubs can be built, but ultimately, it's down to the public whether they are a success or not. Throughout the 45 years outlined in this work there have been as many failures as success, some of them spectacular both in their luck or even ineptness.

It has always been down to the public to decide where they want to spend their time and money. Of course, a certain degree of capitalist manipulation has fostered new developments, but quite often in the Manchester story there have been venues opened up purely for the fun of it. For every Hard Rock (an ill-fated branch of the seventies Rock chain that hosted gigs by luminaries such as Lou Reed and David Bowie before metamorphosing into a Texas Hardware DIY store at Old Trafford) there have been a succession of smaller gigs, promoted by enthusiasts. In a sense, these have acted almost like missionary churches, spreading the word. Many of them can be perceived as beacons, shining their light out of the back alleys of the City centre, attracting young people by the messages contained therein. It was certainly missionary zeal that enthused Richard Boon to put on various nights at the Electric Circus and Rafters during the heady days of Punk. The same can be said of various other entrepreneurs and their venues throughout the whole period under study. Rafters, Devilles, The Tropicana, Fagins, the Three Coins, The Magic Village. The list is endless.

A common denominator in all of them is that people went there for the music, be it House, Psychedelia, Indie, Punk or Pop. These clubs become temples of worship. Tribal identification is cemented there, initiation rites carried out. It is not too out of left field to suggest that gigs fulfil a function of ritual that is otherwise missing within our society, and musicians in some way adopt the priesthood in the ritualised archana that has become the ceremony of performance in our time. Sexuality and mysticism are mixed together in the repetitive beat of Popular Music.

Young people gather together for whatever purpose, in semi darkness, concentration centred on the Shamanic figure of the singer or the DJ. All these elements add up to more than a simple night out. Here is a transubstantiation of base metal into gold. Inside these clubs are stories of power and meaning, of signs and symbols, of communion and transcendence. The rites of passage involved in the process of attending these rituals lead from youth to adulthood. Sometimes the journey is a hard one, and for many, the journey may mean nothing at all, but for a significant number of participants, most notably the musicians, at the end, the journey itself has become the goal.

The drift goes on forever

It sometimes feels that there has never been anywhere else than The Haçienda, and that dedicated as it is to the concept of DJ Culture, all the bands who have emerged from Manchester since The Haçienda opened, did so from out of some sort of limbo. Of course, this is far too simplistic a view. Whilst it is true that The Haçienda has been one of the dominant signifiers of the Manchester Scene for over a decade, other venues have thrived as well.

The Band On The Wall has continued to operate as a live music gig for over fifty years. Revitalised by the diminutive Steve Morris in the 1970s, it rapidly established itself as a prime cross-over club, hosting a variety of musical styles on a regular basis. Dub nights, Latin nights, R'n'B and Indie, have all received Band On The Wall promotion. By not over stretching itself financially by booking acts that were too expensive, the club's reputation grew to the point where musicians clamoured to play there. It was a gig with a close relationship to the Musicians Union, and as a result there was never any question of the artists being 'burned', as happened so often at other venues.

Another major factor in Band On The Wall's success was the installation Of an in-house PA, which meant that there was a consistency of sound reproduction, no matter who was playing. It also meant that groups need only bring their backline equipment, guitar amplifiers and drums. This brought the venue in line with practices of major venues around the world.

Another venue that has consciously promoted Mancunian music is The Boardwalk on Little Peter Street. Opened in the mid 1980s, it has consistently provided a stage for new talent. In the early days, Saturday nights promoted by Nathan McGough and Dave Haslam, under the banner of 'Workhard', played a significant role in cementing the City's musical identity, presenting groups such as The Man From Delmonte, Dub Sex, The Waltones, and dozens more.

In more recent years, two other outstanding City centre clubs have opened their doors to a live music policy, La Republica (formerly PJ Bells), and The Roadhouse. There are, or either, have been, many more live music venues in action over the last fifteen years, allowing the discerning punter a multiplicity of choices in their quest for the musical fix. The city has been traversed time and time again, the psychogeographic emphasis shifting and mutating from the East side to the West side, North, South, and back again as the mood has changed. Live gig promotion has always been like that, evangelical fervour and word of mouth 'buzz' counting for more than mere advertising in the psychodrama enacted within the city streets.

When two cultures clash

As has already been noted elsewhere in this work, musical movements within youth culture have often occupied a polarised position within a mega world of tensions. Scenes have co-existed side by side, but have been mutually exclusive, and the principal arena of diversity has forever been the occupation of spaces against the wishes of Authority. We saw in 'The Axe Falls', how Government legislation was used to crush the burgeoning Beat club scene, and before moving on to look at the tensions within Youth Culture itself, and the reception of Popular Music movements therein, we shall now look at developments in the regulation of the night time economy since then.

Armed with their draconian powers the City licensing magistrates continued to exert total control over the dispensation of club licences. For working musicians, this hardly mattered as the early 1970s were dominated by discotheques, and there were very few local bands emerging anywhere in the country. The arrival on the scene of Music Force demonstrates the problems that existed for promoting gigs. Music Force were generally confined to operating in public houses that had a dance and music licence attached to their standard drinking licence, for instance, the Midland, or the Old Grey Mare, in Didsbury. When these venues became popular on the South Manchester music circuit the police took action to halt them.

Instead of going to the magistrates, they told the landlords of the pubs in question that if they carried on hosting Music Force evenings they could be liable to be charged with allowing their premises to be used for taking drugs, and therefore they would lose not only their licence but their livelihoods as well, because no brewery would employ anybody with a criminal record. The point to be noted here is, that to the best of my knowledge, despite frequent visits form the drug squad, nobody was ever arrested at a Music Force promotion, for anything, let alone drug taking or dealing. I can testify as an eyewitness that I was present at a pub function room in Didsbury when the drug squad threatened the landlord that they would 'break him' if he carried on allowing us to use the premises for music nights. Needless to say, he closed us down at once.

The emergence of Punk, and the need for a more centralised club base saw the hiring of existing venues for perhaps one night a week. Rafters, The Electric Circus, De Villes, etc, were all functioning as venues when the movement broke, and all were utilised. In the centre of the City, the attitude of the police seemed to be slightly more tolerant, despite the seemingly provocative stance of the new music and its adherents. Perhaps it was felt that the fans would be easier to control if allowed access to certain places. This had certainly been the case in the 1960s when the Magic Village and The Twisted Wheel had been allowed to stay open when all the other gigs were closed down.

One venue, however, paid the price for providing a stage for Punk - The Electric Circus. After the Sex Pistols had played there on the ill fated Anarchy Tour, there were ructions at a Council meeting. The Manchester Evening News was bombarded with letters of complaint about the group being allowed to appear in Manchester and Chief Constable James Anderton promised an urgent enquiry. It will come as no surprise to learn that the converted cinema became the object of much attention by the police and fire brigade, who eventually forced its closure in October 1977.

Music events at Student Unions were, on the whole, immune from police pressure throughout the whole period of the 1970s. Right up to the present day they continue to contribute much to the City's musical identity by providing opportunities for local musicians to play. Throughout the 1970s, the Squat was probably the most consistently available and approachable gig in all of the Greater Manchester area. The Poly Socials nights too, began to develop a healthy reputation for promotions. The line up for just one week in 1982 included the following - Bow Wow Wow, Generation X, Wah Heat, Gary Glitter and Roy Wood's Helicopters.

Looking at the overall scene during the period 1980/1982, we can easily detect that the initial enthusiasm for Punk and New Wave had waned. Band On The Wall, and Rafters would appear to be the only regular gigs in the City centre, though mention must be made of The Gallery and The Cyprus Tavern, both of which would come and go as regular venues.

The Haçienda must be built

In 1982, Factory opened The Haçienda, and in their own way ushered in a new era. Originally it was a live music venue, and although The Haçienda still promotes live bands, its reputation internationally is principally that of a dance club. It certainly championed the rise of House in its early days in this country. Hip Hop, Electro Dub, Salsa and Funk were also on the menu, and gradually the Hac's dance nights became (in)famous all over the world. The dance vibe though, was spreading rapidly throughout British Youth Culture and a bewildering array of alternative venues sprang up in Manchester specifically to cater for the new movement. This new movement led in turn to the creation of a new moral panic, in the form of concern about drug abuse.

The tabloid press were quick to jump on the bandwagon when 16 year old Claire Leighton died in The Haçienda after taking the drug Ecstasy, in 1989. 'Acid House' music was identified as the 'enemy' by the press and the authorities. It was an opportunity that the police had been waiting for, and they initiated an action called 'Operation Clubwatch', in which plain clothes officers mingled with the crowds in Manchester clubs. All this has remarkable echoes of the 1965 'Mod Squad' infiltration of the Beat Clubs initiated by

Chief Superintendent Dingwall. In 1990 a new piece of legislation was passed nationally, that gave the Greater Manchester Police the powers they needed to launch an all out assault on the new clubs: the Licensing Act, 1988.

"This gave the police greater discretionary powers to object to the granting of licences to nightclubs by local magistrates, who were themselves empowered to revoke licences at any time during their currency. Licensing hearings were to be more frequent so that the Justices of the Peace who sat in on the sessions would have more opportunity to revoke licences than they had before the Act came into force."
Savage, 1992, p 73

As soon as the requisite legislation was in place, the police swooped and opposed the licences of several Manchester dance clubs, amongst them, Konspiracy, which had overtaken The Haçienda as the place most popular with young Manchester clubbers (Champion, 1990). In December 1990, Konspiracy's licence was revoked. In February, the police turned their attention to The Haçienda.

What happened next is of critical significance to our understanding of the changing face of local British politics. From 1966 onwards, Manchester City Council appear to have been content with allowing the police to get on with their job and heeding their advice when it came to the issuing of licences. This time, a relatively young, moderately Left-wing City Council felt that enough was enough, and reacted accordingly.

"... both Manchester's Lord Mayor and the Labour leader of the city council, Graham Stringer, had written letters (to the Court) in support of the club's aims and status. Graham Stringer had, in fact, written saying that The Haçienda made a 'significant contribution to active use of the city centre core', actively helping the government's own policy of regenerating the inner city through 'arts and entertainment'."
ibid

This is an extremely significant development in the relationship between the authorities and the music world. Prior to this there was very little support for musical ventures, with the honourable exception of allowing the use of parks and facilities for the Anti Nazi

League concerts in the late 1970s, and the odd, free concert in Platt Fields and elsewhere during the 1980s. Here, at last, was unequivocal support for Manchester music... or, more cynically, a successful Mancunian business enterprise. Other cities, in other countries, had been much faster at noticing the opportunities that arose by collaboration with their local music scenes, instead of tacitly watching their destruction.

Music making in Austin, Texas

In Austin Texas, as early as 1982, an academic called Phyllis Krantzman had written a Masters thesis on 'The Impact Of The Music Entertainment Industry On Austin Texas', a paper which broadly, argued the case for musicians being an integral part of the economic fabric of the city of Austin. An integral part that should be sustained by investment.

Ernie Gammadge of the Austin chapter of the Texas Music Association, took on board Krantzman's findings and initiated a dialogue with the Austin Chamber of Commerce. By 1984 this had developed into a relationship, the Chamber viewing music as an opportunity for increasing tourism in their area. They labelled it, "an opportunity economy". Eventually, an organisation called, the Austin Music Advisory Committee (AMAC), was formed.

"There are four necessary ingredients to a full fledged music industry. Every industry has to have its own research and development function. We have that in spades. It's the clubs and the musicians, the songwriters. But all industries also have to have a production function, distribution, and marketing, and finally, the point of sale, where you reach the consumer with the product......"
Shank, 1994, p 205

Another area where Austin was ahead of Manchester was in seeking links with the New Music Seminar, an entity that came into life in 1980 through the auspices of Mark Josephson's Rockpool organisation. This was an informal attempt to co-ordinate all the various 'alternative', New Wave and Post Punk, independent outfits, by a holding a day long session of panels and workshops in New York. This became so successful that by 1990, the New Music

Seminar was drawing thousands of applications from music business representatives each year. The Austin branch of AMAC held the first of their South By South West alternative music business seminars in 1987. By 1990 there were two thousand registrants at the AMAC convention.

Meanwhile, back in Manchester, too much tension

While Austin's local authorities supported Popular Music vigorously since the early 1980s, Manchester City Council has been a latecomer in this field. By 1995, Manchester was hosting its fourth 'In The City' international music convention. Organised in response to the New York New Music Seminar (Middles, 1996), In The City has rightly become internationally reknowned and since its start in 1992 has justifiably been supported by Manchester City Council, amongst others. However, in 1996, after a brief period of acrimony in 1995, when the failure to secure late night licences for a variety of In The City venues soured relationships between the organising body and the council, In The City has moved to Dublin, for their 1996 conference at least. This represents a significant loss to the city of Manchester and highlights the fact that tension between authority and youth oriented cultures still prevail.

It must be acknowledged that, while the Haçienda retained its licence in 1990, and the council has adopted a much more positive attitude towards the thriving music and alternative culture that exists in the city, problems still remain with the police and Justices (see above). Many tensions have existed over the past forty five years; they have not always involved outside agencies, but they have been generated within the cultural community itself. The impetus of tension lies in the generation of youth factionalism, which revolves around questions of authenticity. In post modernist terms these various forms of youth allegiances to particular cultural practices would be described as an inevitable reflection of the fragmentation of society.

The phenomenon of forming and splitting, as it were, has been around probably for ever, one ancient example being the 'Blues' and the 'Greens' of Byzantine charioteer following (Graves, 1938). In more recent times various cultural theoreticians have attempted to analyse why cultural groupings diversify into sub-cultural groupings. Probably the most influential would be Dick Hebdige and his 'Subculture - The Meaning Of Style'. Published in 1979, this was an attempt to deconstruct Punk by adopting a semiological model. (See Chapters 6 and 10)

REFERENCES

Champion, Sarah, 1991, 'And God Created Manchester', Manchester, Wordsmith

City Fun, 1980, No 10, Manchester

City Fun, 1980, No15, Manchester

City Fun, 1980 No 23, Manchester

City Fun, 1981, Volume 2, No 5, Manchester

City Fun, 1981, Volume 2, No 7, Manchester

Dickinson, Bob, 1996, 'Imprinting the Sticks', M Phil Manchester Metropolitan University

Graves, Robert, 1938, 'Count Belisarius', Harmondsworth, Middlesex, Penguin Books

Krantzman, Phyllis, 1983 'The Impact Of The Music Entertainment Industry On Austin Texas', Master's Thesis, University of Texas at Austin

Middles, Mick, 1996, 'From Joy Division to New Order - The Factory Story', London, Virgin

Savage, 1992, 'The Haçienda Must Be Built', London, IMP Publishing

Shank, B, 1994, 'Dissonant Identities', New England, Wesleyan University Press

Shapiro, Harry, 1992, 'Graham Bond: The Mighty Shadow', London, Guinness Publishing

TAPED INTERVIEWS

Victor Brox
Andy Harris
Tosh Ryan
Anthony Wilson

Chapter 9

Madchester and Scallydelia

A layperson at the time, who didn't live in the City, could be forgiven for thinking that nothing much happened in Manchester between 1980 and 1988. The rock music media affair with the city was confined to reviews of the so-called 'Manchester Miserablists', or 'young men with minds as narrow as their ties', a popular misconception deemed to have been the archetype of bands on the Factory label. Nothing, of course, could be further from the truth.

The emergence of The Smiths and Simply Red on an international level are two of the most high profile examples of 'a scene that wouldn't go away', and it was also a period that saw the birth of James, The Stone Roses and The Happy Mondays, amongst many others that we shall be looking at later in this Chapter. However, the early 1980s was a moribund period for Popular Music across the UK. The drive and enthusiasm of Punk and New Wave had given way to the manufactured aesthetic of New Romanticism and the synthesiser oriented pop of Culture Club and Depeche Mode. On a national level music appeared to be slipping back instead of moving forward.

When in Hulme, do as the Humans do

Psychogeographically, Hulme is of great significance in the history of Manchester music in the 1980s. Situated just over half a mile away from the City centre, Hulme is the inner city nightmare of urban planning writ large. The pleasant, if primitive, terraces were demolished in the 1960s to make way for a brave new world of walkways in the skies, elongated crescent high rises, and other Corbusier-inspired horrors of modern architecture. The red brick slum of the 1960s had given way to a concrete slum. It quickly gained a reputation for lawlessness, drug dealing and prostitution, mugging and random violence. The City Council, in one of their periodic attempts to do something about it, began moving out the original residents and offering space in the 'dwelling units' to young people at a premium rate. Many students from the Polytechnic just across the road moved in with other young people who had settled there because of the area's cheap housing costs and close proximity to the City centre.

By the early 1980s, Hulme was beginning to gain a new identity, albeit a schizophrenic one. Students graduated and stayed on; some started small business, others worked in town, most were on the dole. These newcomers mingled uneasily with the older residents, but a partial truce of sorts existed between the thieves, cider drinkers, musos, nouveau proloteriat and the law-abiding habituees. Hulme was becoming a crucible into which poured the raw elements of change.

Before the opening of The Cornerhouse in 1985, Manchester's only Arts cinema was the Aaben in Hulme. Situated opposite a pub called The Grey Parrot, it was frequented by patrons from all over the Manchester area. Its scheduled programming was very similar to the legendary Scala Cinema in London's Kings Cross, everything from Kurosawa to Warhol, and hoping that your car would still be there when you came out merely added to the frisson of going to see a film.

Music was catered for at the PSV Club, aka the Carribean Club, aka the Russell Club, aka the Factory and at The Bull's Head, where Elvis impersonator, Big Jim White, held court once a week. Add to that the impromptu Rent Parties, shebeens, Blues clubs (West Indian illegal drinking dens) and sound systems, and the dynamics of Hulme night life begin to emerge. This cultural hodge podge of Dub, Psychobilly, Raincoat and Rock gelled and coalesced into an identifiable 'scene' in the early 1980s. It may have been Hell living in Hulme, but it was happening.

Prior to all this, the main psychic centre for musicians had been the South Manchester Didsbury/West Didsbury axis. The slightly run down Victorian mansions of this leafy, tree lined suburb perfectly reflected the laid-back, pre-Punk era. It was more dope than amphetamines. Town was a car or a bus ride away; in Hulme you actually felt you were in the heart of the City, even if you had to cross a major dual carriageway to get there. Hulme throbbed, while Didsbury gently sighed, music had changed and the next generation of players were finding their own scene.

Surfin' in Locustland

'... if you live in Hulme you are seven times more likely to commit suicide; 31 times more likely to be the victim of crime; 41 times more likely to be murdered.'
Champion, 1991, p 34

Despite the above statistics, and living in the shadow of Morrissey and the Smiths burgeoning fame (and imagery), the Hulmeites produced a large number of groups in the space of a very short time. Hulme had become a sounding board and a laboratory for new talent. There was no definable genre of style that could be pinned down; it was an eclectic mix of musical tastes that reflected the rich cultural diversity of its participants. Hulme even had its own studio, Jamie Nicholson's eight track, Kitchen. Hulme produced the Inca Babies, who earned the sobriquet, 'Manc Cramps' for their Beefheart, Link Wray blend of Goth, Punk and Psychobilly. There was Big Ed And His Rockin Rattlesnakes, The Slum Turkeys, Skol Bandeleros, Dub Sex, Ruthless Rap Assassins, Kiss AMC, Tools You Can Trust, who offered a post-industrial noise manufactured out of trash cans, fire extinguishers, and corrugated iron ripped off the windows of boarded up buildings. All these and more practised their trade in the crescents of Hulme, keeping the faith on cassette-only releases and Indie labels that came and went like the glimpses of sun that occasionally filtered through the clouds over Hulme.

Although in psychogeographical terms we can identify Hulme as being an epicentre of the 'Drift' in the period leading up to the mid 1980s, it was towards the centre of town that the people looked for the temples of performance. Hulme was the creative melting pot, but town was still the foundry.

Expansion and reclamation

The cultural importance of these performers is that they kept the flame of Mancunian music flickering through the years leading up to the explosion that was waiting to happen. Throughout the 1980s the student body in Manchester was increasing year by year, until in 1989 the campus was the second largest in Europe. Manchester was rapidly becoming a young person's city, and the leisure and pleasure industries were not slow to notice the increased numbers and increased cash that was seeping into the nightime economy. The Haçienda had led the way in showing that clubs didn't have to be dingy cellars, that people liked style and a certain amount of comfort when they went out.

More clubs were opening, more bars and shops, more live music was being played. What happened next was that other people began to notice that something was happening in Manchester, the music press were continually taken aback by the sheer number of bands that came from the city. Reporters were sent down to find out what was going on, and articles started appearing that carried the signifying label, 'the Manchester scene'. It wasn't long before the arrival of new drugs and new circumstances would find the world beating a path to Manchester in order to find out what was going on.

Hit the north

In 1986, the NME produced an audio cassette, entitled C86, which can be used as a convenient date for the start of the 'acknowledged' Manchester scene. A sampler of Indie bands, it featured such Manchester acts as Miaow, Big Flame, The Bodines and A Witness. Another significant event in the progression of the music scene was the opening of the Boardwalk, or more properly, the Saturday night gigs promoted by Nathan McGough and Dave Haslam, under the name of Workhard. This was a live night to showcase newly emerging talent. Smart programming enabled the discerning punter to move on from the Boardwalk to the Haçienda after the groups had stopped playing. It was a hit.

"We went into the Boardwalk as fans from the week it opened".
Clint Boon

Clint Boon, organist and songwriter with the Inspiral Carpets was one of the main movers on the 'Madchester' scene.

"I was spending a lot of time watching the American bands that were coming over here. There was a movement then called the Paisley Underground. It was bands like REM, Green On Red, Longriders, Rainparade, True West... and I used to go watching these bands at The Gallery, or The Boardwalk. And at a local level, people like the Bodines

were pretty happening then. Then there were a lot of bands that didn't break through like T'Challa Grid, Judge Happiness, who became The Mock Turtles. It was a good scene but I don't think it was as thriving as it is now.... At the time, it was all the C86... It was jingle jangle music, which was very nice, but it wasn't very inspiring..... It was, in some ways, quite a mediocre scene."
Clint Boon

As someone who had come from the Punk movement, Clint Boon obviously has a personal view of the mid 1980s music. Also, the music that Inspiral Carpets were perfecting was, in a lot of ways, removed from what one might describe as the quintessential Manchester sound.

"We were like this psychedelic band from the North of Manchester, with mad haircuts and crappy shirts.... Well, mad shirts and crappy haircuts. We were making this noise that was very aggressive and very dirty, shouting and loud organ and that, and no one else was doing anything like that.... We were like a Punk band with an organ. That's all we were, but we had the psychedelic imagery."
Clint Boon

Other musicians were watching the changes as well.

"I remember seeing The Happy Mondays with New Order in 1985, and at the time, United had just won this match and were through to the FA Cup Final, so everybody was out celebrating because being from Manchester you're born with one team. So we saw the The Happy Mondays and we thought they were pretty, pretty strange...."
Scott Carey

The Happy Mondays were a strange crew with decidedly unorthodox views.

"With the release of their legendary, aptly titled Freaky Dancing single and later the classic Tart Tart, things became clearer. This lot were just a bunch of dragged up, drug taking nutters, badly dressed in trainers and T-shirts. A band who couldn't play, fronted by a man who couldn't sing.
"'In them days, I didn't really give a toss," Shaun himself admitted to

213

Mandi James, "Nothing took more than two minutes. I never liked the first album, I wasn't interested working at it. The music was second, even third. It was more like us lot having a good time which counted.'"
Champion, 1991, p106

All this is heavily redolent of the Punk ethos and attitude to performance and production.

"Ever got the feeling you've been had?.... "
Johnny Rotten, 1977

"The amplified voice can be seen to provide a comparable object for identification to that of the screen image of the film hero or heroine. In addition, the musicality of the process is crucial to this sense of perfection and coherence: singing can make a voice extraordinary in a way that everyday speech cannot (though heightened, dramatic speech can - an important point for Punk)."
Laing, 1985, p 54

"Mick's voice is just another instrument, man."
Andrew Loog Oldham, 1966

'By repositioning and recontextualizing commodities, by subverting their conventional uses and inventing new ones, the subcultural stylist...... opens up the world of objects to new and covertly oppositional readings."
Hebdige, 1979, p 102

"If You Don't Want To Fuck Me - Fuck Off"
Wayne County & The Electric Chairs

This assertive, devil-may-care attitude, belies the apparent professionalism of the recorded output of both The Happy Mondays and Shaun Ryder's most recent group, Black Grape. The carefully studded arrogance and born-again masculinity of contemporary bands such as Oasis will be studied in the final chapter, though this is an appropriate point to delineate its inception.

Scallydelia

'Scally' is a shortened form of 'scallywag', an early 19th Century, American word for scoundrel, or n'er do well. In its long form it entered popular English usage in the early 20th Century, and was shortened in the Liverpool area in the 1960s. There its use was derogatory. In the 1980s however, it became common parlance amongst young people in Manchester, and, as is the way with these things, assumed other, more subtle meanings. It came to imply a particular kind of youth who was 'sussed', or smart, street wise, and a follower of the next new wave of bands that were emerging. The 'Delia' tag, completing the phrase, was a pointer to the quasi-psychedelic sound of people like The Stone Roses and Happy Mondays, and also to the explosion of colour generated by new fashions in clothing that accompanied the music. It also, no doubt, refers to the resurgence in the popularity of mind altering hallucinogenics such as Ecstasy and LSD. The phrase, according to Sarah Champion, was originated by Greg O'Keeffe of Hulme band Big Flame.

> *"As a matter of historical trivia, it was Greg who first coined the word 'scallydelic' in a drunken brawl at The Boardwalk, in September 1989."*
> Champion, 1991, p 43

Scally fans bought the whole package. From the baggy Joe Bloggs pants, through to the pastel coloured trainers. A new hybrid accent, part Wythenshawe council estate, part hard core Salfordian insinuated its nasally twang into the Mancunian psyche. This was a scene that was totally dedicated to having fun, and being a 'lad' was part of that fun. As if twenty years of feminism had never happened, women became 'birds' again, and gender became a significant aspect of the 'new tribalism'. Angela McRobbie and Jenny Gerber had already covered elements of this cultural phenomenon in their 'Girls And Subcultures' paper, published in 'Resistance Through Rituals' (1975), where they studied the absence of girls from Popular Culture research. Women, for them, had become, invisible.

Dave Laing, in 'One Chord Wonders', pointed out the significant changes that Punk as a discourse offered all genders.

> *"Within Punk rock as a musical genre, gender representations did not offer such a dismally reactionary picture (as mainstream rock). Punk's*

deliberate refusal of romance as a theme for songs meant that it could avoid one of the most potent sites of gender stereotyping......." (What, we may wonder, are we then to make of songs like Buzzcocks' 'Ever Fallen In Love With Someone?*)

Laing, 1985, p125

As if taking McRobbie and Gerber to heart, Pauline Murray, formerly of Penetration, had a backing band formed by Martin Hannett and other Manchester musical luminaries. She called them The Invisible Girls.

It is an historical point to be made here, that in Manchester in the late 1980s and to this day, women occupied highly prominent positions within the musical and 'alternative' infrastructures. Paula Greenwood ran Playtime Records and still does; Penny Henry and Ellie Gray were assistant manager and manager of the Haçienda; Mandi James and Sarah Champion both emerged as writers for national papers and magazines, such as NME and The Face. Many other notable women are fashion and graphic designers, artists and artisans.

How two women reacted to the Happy Mondays' inclusion of a picture of a naked woman on the inner sleeve of 'Bummed', is to be found in Sarah Champion's book 'And God Created Manchester':

"Vivacious pop-hack Penny Anderson, manager of Dub Sex, seethed in City Life. "I'm not annoyed: not outraged, just irritated. Not at the sight of nudity, no, not at that, but I don't need to gratuitously observe anyone else's. Look here little boys - and I mean all of you - if you want to build up your wrist muscles do it in the privacy of your own home, not your design offices...." Fellow NME journo, Mandi James agrees. "There's no point in being dewy eyed. Shaun Ryder can't sing, they're a sloppy unit, and their attitude towards women sucks. They're sexist wankers!..."

Champion, 1991, p109

As we shall see later, it is from this climate that Oasis emerged.

The Summer of Love

1988 was the year of Acid House, the gigantic explosion of hedonism and energy, when drugs and music fused once again to create a cultural phenomenon that, in turn would lead to another media generated moral panic. As it was a genre that excluded live musicians more than employed them, and saw the rise to prominence of what we now call DJ Culture, I intend only to examine it briefly. Dave Haslam was a DJ at The Haçienda.

"The vibe was so intense, the club so packed, the music just so pure, fresh and mind blowing; DJ-ing at the Haçienda in 1988, 1989 and 1990 was fantastic. It was an unmediated experience. It didn't feel secondhand, it wasn't forced, it had no models, it wasn't faked, it wasn't ritualistic, it was immediate. This was Madchester. Nobody was excluded; shop assistants, secretaries, dole-ites, plasterers, thieves, students. I felt at the centre of the pop world, that's one thing, but better still was that I felt in the middle of a huge explosion of energy. Everybody danced; on the stairs, on the stage, on the balcony, and at the bar. They danced in the cloakroom queue. For all I know, they were dancing in the street outside."
Haslam, 1995

"It was a pure fucking amazing sight. Took me a year to get to grips with it. Wished I was 18 again.... a Mancunian generation Hell bent on hedonism and hooked on a lifestyle as self-assured and self - possessed as it is anti-liberal... White working class terrace sub-culture indulging in casual drug taking on a scale not seen since their parents did it twenty years before."
Spinoza, 1989

'Acid' or 'House' had grown out of a variety of disco-oriented sounds emanating from a variety of club cultures. Some say Chicago, some say New York, others say that it was a fusion of Euro-Beat influences such as Kraftwerk and New Order, mixed with Hi -Energy, Gay, Black dance music. Others contend that it was born in Ibiza and brought back to this country as Balearic Beat. DJs began to assume the role of the performer and some, like the Haçienda's Mike Pickering, through remixes, and then graduating onto songwriting, would eventually become the musicians of the 1990s - Pickering, of course, with his internationally successful, M People. Other Manchester musicians who have gone this route include 808 State and A Man Called Gerald. Before moving on to examine the influence of House on local musicians, let us look briefly at what went wrong with this supercharged, high octane pursuit.

Acieed! Acieed! Acieed!!!!

"Back in January 1988, however, London Records had successfully launched acid house as a genre on the coattails of drug-oriented potential for scandal. The sleeve notes to 'The House Sound Of Chicago Vol 111: Acid Tracks' described the new music as "drug induced," "psychedelic," "sky high," " and "ecstatic," and concluded with a prediction of moral panic....."

Thornton in Ross & Rose, 1994, p182

It didn't take long for the British tabloid media to pick up on the drug references, that were quite clearly outlined for all to see. According to Sarah Champion, The Sun ran headlines such as the following.

"Evil Of Ecstasy" - "Acid House Horror" - "Girl 21 Drops Dead At Acid Disco Party" - "Hell Of Acid Kids: Pushers laugh as teenagers see terror of bad trip boy".
Champion, 1991, p112

The resultant backlash wasn't long in coming. MP Graham Bright moved The Entertainments (Increased Penalty) Bill 1989/90. Steve Redhead, Lecturer in Law and Popular Culture at the then, Manchester Polytechnic, and author of 'The End Of The Century Party' commented

"The bill will criminalise a whole section of youth culture. They're jumping on the anti-acid house bandwagon because it's hedonism. Why should young people have a good time, when the country has hit hard times, when the economy is on the decline and everyone else is in trouble?"
ibid, p118

We have already seen how the legislation affected Manchester clubs, some closed and others weathered the storm by adopting a high profile anti-drugs policy, but it wasn't just clubs that fell foul of the law.

Another phenomenon of the acid house scene was known as the Rave. Basically these were semi-legal, or totally illegal gatherings in disused warehouses, or other empty buildings, where sound systems and DJs swooped in for all nighters. The ubiquitous all nighters, while technically legal in Manchester clubs, are seldom promoted owing to the curtailment of the drinks licence, generally at 2 am. Therefore Raves, which don't rely on alcohol sales, became the perfect places to get away from it all and party.

Another historical point of reference here, is the revival of the word 'Raver' to describe an habitué of these affairs. In the 1950s, a Raver was a Trad Jazz fan, usually described as being dressed in a duffle coat, wearing sandals, and being a member of CND. In some ways, the original Ravers were a precursor of the Beats (see Chapter 3).

At its inception, House, Acid, Rave, call it what you will, operated as a genuine underground phenomenon, there was a cult snobbery about it, an exclusivity that goes with all things new, and like all things new, it would soon become just another product. When D Mob entered the charts at number 20 with 'Pump Up The Bitter' with its accompanying chant of "Acieed! Acieed!" genuine Ravers were mortified. There are parallel echoes of how the Hippies felt when The Flowerpot Men got into the charts with 'Let's Go To San Francisco', Nehru jackets went on sale at Lewis's in 1967 and the Smurfs' versions of all the chart toppers they can cover. Once again, the circular history of Pop revolves full circle.

Other commentators found similar acts of indiscriminate synchronicity.

"I looked at House as being a new sort of Punk. For that generation, it was their Punk......At the time everybody was clubbing it, you see. If you were really into the Stone Roses, you didn't necessarily get a band together. You'd go out to the Haçienda and drop an E, and it was like, weird. Going back to the Punk days, it was like when Punk and Reggae became locked together. What happened with the Baggy scene and Rave music was that the two forces became intrinsically linked because they were part of the same lifestyle."
Clint Boon

But, blessed with the hindsight of Post-Modernity, other people at the time, while acknowledging the 'Indieness' of the Punk scene, were aware of the pitfalls of teenage rebellion.

"Punk was too much like Rock'n'Roll and they knew how to deal with it," Mike Pickering commented to Andy Spinoza. "They don't know how to handle this. It's gone underground again.... it appears to be very easy to make, but if you've not got a feeling - soul, for want of a better word - you'll fall flat on your face."
Champion, 1991, p113

The same old unease about the 'new music' was expressed by musicians from an earlier generation, just as it had been during the Punk revolution. Even the same old, "can they/can't they" play arguments were trotted out. Perhaps the strongest argument of the working musician was the one that the more DJs there were playing records, the less likelihood there was of there being a space for a live band. This was precisely the situation that had faced Mancunian musicians in the early 1970s. A situation that led directly to the formation of Music Force, and indirectly to the beginnings of Punk and the New Wave in Manchester. Other contemporary musicians, like Tim Booth of James, were even more forthright in their condemnation of House.

"Rap and House may have a big following, but so did Hitler." He later clarified his position in a rant to NME letters page. "NME is trying to give House fans the status of valiant revolutionaries surrounded by the conservative forces of oppression. Well, I'm sorry, but this state only exists in the heads of a few far out minds. It sounds like some Punks I knew who enjoyed the feeling of persecution because it made them feel important. Why on earth should they? We have seen so many fashions in music over the past few years, we should be used to it by now.

"I am not impressed by any movement that seems to be based squarely on a drug. God knows, we've seen it before. It's nothing new, just a repeated cycle. We've seen acid casualties in the 60s, amphetamine burn outs from the 70s, and no doubt we will see the full effects of ecstasy on another generation. I believe, one day you will regret your advice to the non-believers in the church of House...."
ibid

"Hang the DJ! Hang the DJ! Hang the DJ!"

The view from Dave Haslam's perspective was also interesting. He called it 'Punk versus Funk', and perceived it as a generational problem. In our terms, what Haslam is articulating, is the continuation of the battle, if it can be called that, between the Mods and Rockers, the Trads and the Modernists in the world of Jazz, the Folk purists and the Electric movement in the mid 1960s, all the way through to the arrival of House in the late 1980s.

"The Punk against Funk battle was fought all through the early part of the Eighties in the music papers and in the clubs. For instance, the two dominant club nights in Manchester in the couple of years up to 1986 were Goth nights and Black dance nights. Goth music was an obvious evolution from Punk and Goth nights were miserable affairs featuring hours of Spear Of Destiny, The Cramps, and 'Should I Stay Or Should I Go' by the Clash. The busiest club night at the Haçienda up to 1985, incidentally, was The End on Tuesday nights; "No Funk Night" it was billed as (an echo, perhaps, of the 'anti-disco-discos' at Liverpool's famous Punk club, Eric's, in 1977)"
Haslam, 1995

Dave Haslam is one of the most successful DJs to have emerged from the Manchester circuit and was in a unique position to observe the transition from 'miserable' to 'euphoric'. He started the Haçienda Temperance and Wilde nights, has had his own record label and magazine, and observed, indeed helped build, the whole Manchester/Madchester scene. He had this to say about the generational gap between Punk and Funk -

"At the Temperance Club I was witnessing the bridging of the biggest gulf in music; the one between dance fans and the rock fans. The breech may have begun in the late 1960s (I actually identify it much earlier) when white youth took to lying in fields listening to guitar solos rather than to crowd into basement clubs for rhythm heavy soul or r'n'b. I've always maintained that it was a generational thing. The punk generation had always considered Punk to be a reaction against dinosaur rock acts like ELP or Pink Floyd, but shared rock's traditional disdain for disco music. Punk was an excluding movement, despite a nod towards Reggae, it sneered at anything outside its values..... Those whose mindset was formed during

that era - among whom I would include Morrissey and Tony Wilson - found it hard, or even impossible to see any positive values in dance music..... My Thursday nights at the end of 1987 were still mixing and mashing the genres; if Morrissey couldn't cope with the idea of The Smiths back to back with Public Enemy, I found that the ordinary Indie fans could. It was then that I knew the old Punk generation had had its day; in August 1987.... I suggested in NME that "Happy Mondays are turning the phrase '24 hour party people' into a slogan for a generation, and you're recommended to join them.""
Haslam, 1995

I want to examine these oppositional trends more fully in the final Chapter, so for the moment, we will continue looking at the Madchester scene.

The news and TV crews that flocked to Manchester in 1988, did so to witness, what?

A scene that had burst beyond the usual bounds and conventions that one normally associates with musical movements. They came, at first, to witness a 'happy scene', as reflected by the resurgence in Smiley faces and similar Hippy paraphernalia that flowed out of centres like the alternative markets in the Corn Exchange and Affleck's Palace. They visited the record stores like Eastern Bloc that stocked the hits that made the scene go round, and they went to the clubs where it all happened, not quite 24 hours a day, but 'if you closed your eyes for long enough it felt like it'.

"I think it was the most colourful music scene that I'd ever seen. I wasn't in San Francisco in the 60s, but I think what we got in Manchester in the late 80s early 90s was as colourful as that, and the vibe..... I was the man who was living it 24 hours a day. The phone would be going, people celebrating what I was doing, or what they were doing. It was like one day you'd be doing an interview on TV, the next you'd be doing a gig in Belgium, the next day you were shopping at Affleck's Palace. And it was like, colour, colour, colour, all the time. To me it was like what I'd seen on the telly about the 60s scene... Like the Small Faces shopping in Carnaby Street... Madchester to me was colour, and it was flowers, all that kind of thing."
Clint Boon

As with all scenes though, even Madchester, at least in its media inspired incarnation, was bound to fade.

"Subsequently, I think the people who got on it a bit late lost out, and that was an education for me. Because seeing what happened to the Paris Angels, Mock Turtles, the Farm to some extent, bands that kind of saw what was happening and restyled themselves to get in on it lost out. And they were my friends... Northside, a great example.... A lot of other people were like, oh, this is what's happening, we've got to get a funky drummer, and I've got to talk like this (does nasal twang) 'cos that's what Shaun's doing, and we were never like that... I just think that with any scene that the people who help start it, the people who build the foundations for it are the ones who come out of it with respect."
Clint Boon

Shortly after the gloss had faded on Madchester, an older musician had this to say,

'You cannot look back, you have to look forward. And we're not looking forward into digital stuff - we're looking forward into people who'll go on stage and play their fucking arses off .... I mean, we've got to have the best possible people that will go all over the world and shit on people from Los Angeles. Not because we actually want to do that! but because our expertise will be that much sharper, our humour will be that much more inviolate - our music will be that much more creative..... Manchester is not a progenitor, it's a next generation. It's like the differance between Athens in the Greek world and Alexandria in the Hellenistic world. Alexandria changed the face of the entire planet - Liverpool changed England. Manchester could change the world.'
Victor Brox

REFERENCES

Champion, Sarah, 1991, 'And God Created Manchester', Manchester, Wordsmith

Happy Mondays, 1988, 'Bummed', FACD 220, Factory Records, Manchester

Haslam, Dave, 1995, 'Reading Pop', Unpublished Manuscript

Hebdige, D, 1979, 'Subculture The Meaning of Style', London, Methuen & Co

Laing, Dave, 1985, 'One Chord Wonders - Power and Meaning in Punk Rock, Milton Keynes, Open University Press

McRobbie, Angela and Gerber, Jenny, 1975, 'Girls And Subcultures' paper, published in Hall, Stuart & Jefferson, Tony, 'Resistance Through Rituals', 1975, London, Harper Collins

Oldham, Andrew Loog, on Eamonn Andrews chat show, ATV, 1966

Spinoza, Andy, City Life, August 1989

Thornton, Sarah, 'Moral Panics', in Ross, Andrew & Rose, Tricia (Eds),1994, 'Microphone Fiends', London, Routledge

Wayne County & The Electric Chairs, EP 'Blatantly Offensive' on Safe Records, 1978

TAPED INTERVIEWS

Clint Boon
Victor Brox
Scott Carey

Chapter 10

You've got to (rock and) roll with it

My fundamental underlying subtext has been concerned with tensions generated from within, and without, the musical culture of a city. By bringing the history up to 1995 we can examine the career of a group that reflect those tensions in a variety of ways. The band are the phenomenally successful Oasis who emerged in 1993 from the Burnage council estate in South Manchester. By the end of 1995 they were poised on the brink of international stardom. They have managed to achieve this status by seizing the zeitgeist, a zeitgeist made up of contradictions and conflict, so redolent of our post-modern age. How they rose to this position in such a short time will be examined in a moment.

Where have all the flowers gone?

After the initial euphoria of the 'Madchester' scene had died down, and the media crews packed their flight cases and gone their own ways, Manchester appeared, once again, to slip back into that state of hiatus that had followed the Punk/New Wave explosion at the end of the 1970s. But just as the seemingly fallow period of the early 1980s was deceptive, in that it became a period of retrenchment and experiment that produced internationally renowned artists such as Morrissey and the Smiths, as well as Simply Red, the Manchester music scene didn't disappear in the early 1990s. Although the international spotlight of publicity was no longer focused on the city, the cultural imperative to produce and play music in no way waned.

"What happened in Manchester was, the face went away, but the scene remained. It didn't become a ghost town. It carried on being a hotbed of musical talent. It's a cliché, I know, but it always has been and it always will be. I do believe you could cut off the rest of the world. You could have an industry just based around Manchester music and you wouldn't notice."

Clint Boon

"Welcome to the 90s. Do your own thing, do it to extreme and get rich/happy. Enterprise culture becomes more than a numbers game disguising dole figures. Instead of a nation of shop keepers we became a nation of T-shirt sellers and musicians.... The unthinkable has become reality. From now on anything is possible. The authorities might clamp down on hedonism, but so what? The Manchester music explosion of the late 80s will continue to boom into the next century."
Champion, 1991, p143

So predicted Sarah Champion at the turn of the decade. What she had failed to predict, and no one saw it coming, was the sudden increase in gangland 'turf -wars'.

Broadly speaking, the clubs survived the latest round of government clampdowns. What became harder to survive was the rise in gun culture that spawned the nickname, 'Gunchester', an ironic comment on the happier days of 'Madchester'. On the 30th January 1991, the Haçienda closed its doors for three months, driven to do so by firearms related incidents. The management felt that they could no longer guarantee the safety of staff.

'When he left the club this year, the Haçienda's head doorman Roger Kennedy forecast that, "Closing the Haçienda is not the answer - you simply knock the problem on somewhere else." He was right. Now the club's gangland headache has largely evaporated, the gangs plague other, lower-profile venues, whose employees are finding it wise to keep the free champagne flowing all night."
Spinoza, 1991

With articles in the national press brought about by a spate of shootings, Manchester's music industry was almost subsumed by the ghoulish interpolation of what was actually happening. With shootings taking place on an almost daily basis the only outcome was an inevitable media feeding frenzy. What eventually passed unnoticed by the press, was a ceasefire, brokered by the gang leaders in early 1994. As an event this was deemed 'un-newsworthy'. The ceasefire by no means solved Manchester's gangster problem, but it did go a long way towards revitalising the City's night time culture and economy which had already been riven by a mini-depression in the national music industry.

> *"Pop In Crisis*
> *What have these bands in common?*
> *Paris Angels* The Adventure Babies* The Durutti Column* The Mock Turtles* Urban Cookie* Intastella* Chapter And The Verse* World Of Twist* Omar* The Railway Children* MC BUZZ B* Distant Cousins* The Fall* Northside* MC Tunes* Ruthless Rap Assassins & many others.....*"

City Life, 4-18 February 1993

The above question was printed on the front cover of City Life, issue number 221. The answer was that they were all Manchester bands, and that they had all lost their recording contracts after the honeymoon with Madchester was over. The article inside, by Chris Sharratt and entitled, 'Pop Goes The Music Business', goes a long way in throwing light on the financial machinations of the music industry.

> ' *"One thing I can tell you," says Jeff Clark-Meads, Director of Communications at the British Phonographic Institute (BPI). "It's tough out there at the moment." "How tough?" "Tougher than it has been since the last recession 10 years ago."*
> ibid, p 12

A significant fall in consumer spending power, plus a change of style in leisure-wares, meant computer games such as Sega and Nintendo were cornering the market, hitherto occupied by record sales, in a manner no-one had foreseen or predicted. The conglomerates were cutting back ferociously, and company accountants didn't stop at dumping groups, middle management were getting the chop too.

> *"There's a lot of scared people in the music business and they're panicking," says Saffron Smith, co-manager of The Fall, who recently left Phonogram having given the label three Top 30 LPs...... When MCA made Intastella's A&R man redundant, the band lost an important ally. And someone on their side was just what the band needed. After three singles, one LP and no hit, it was deemed they had failed to deliver...... "It*

got to the point where the American or Japanese division would look at the balance sheet and say, 'God you've spent x number of pounds on these and you haven't got anything back'," says Caroline Elleray, manager of both *Intastella and World Of Twist, who were also dropped last year..... "*
ibid

The article ends on a generally negative level, but does offer what must have appeared at the time to be a slight, up beat note, with the following comments.

"... It's a business. If you don't sell enough records quick enough, you get the push. The days of the million pound deal and extravagant pop star lifestyles are largely over. Austerity is all the rage. Can anything good come out of it all? Maybe. As the majors pull back from throwing large sums of money at new bands, the smaller independent labels might get a look in."
ibid

In one sense Chris Sharratt was right. In the same way that independents acted as a testing ground for new bands in the aftermath of Punk, now they were to act for the 'leaner, fitter' majors, by performing the function previously carried out by A&R persons. That is, discover, and nurture new talent, which is then passed over to the majors for broader exploitation.

"Most of the Indies have got backing from the majors now. They bought into them."
Clint Boon

However, Chris Sharratt's comments about extravagant pop star lifestyles falling by the way side in the new, austere music world, will certainly have to be re-examined in light of Oasis.

What's the Story (Morning Glory)?

Chocolate brown Rolls Royces, matching mopeds as Christmas gifts, beautiful female, film star lovers, self confessed bouts of drug and drink bingeing, public brawling and ostentatious displays of wealth, Rock finally comes home, or at least in a fairly full circle. As if nothing had happened socially, or culturally since the hey days of

The Beatles, Oasis have managed in three years to reverse decades of change.

They carry within their very beings the essence of the tensions that are the highlights of the sub-text. They are the personification of the 'new lad', the antithesis of the 'new male'. Arrogant, brash, stoned and unrepentant, they have alluded to the press that their background carries more than a suggestion of criminality, that housebreaking was a hobby before music took control of them. Who are they?

Basically they are five young Mancunian males, two of whom are brothers, one of which is the songwriting powerhouse behind their output, Noel Gallagher. They are at the forefront of a fairly recently concocted genre - Britpop.

Britpop is a retro form of guitar band sound, that carries with it compelling echoes of the height of British Beat group music from the 1960s. Melodic and basically structured, critics have detected influences encompassing The Small Faces, The Kinks and the Beatles in the new, post-modern music of Britpop bands such as Blur, Supergrass, Pulp and Oasis. It emanated from within the world of Indie, and rapidly gained commercial success. Within the space of several years the Britpop bands have attained a position of chart dominance in this country, making them an economic and cultural force to be reckoned with. It is possible to argue that an element of their success is due in some ways as a reaction against the essentially 'faceless' musicians who produce Techno or House records. Here, at last, is something young people can identify with.

"(During Madchester) You didn't have to be in a band. Coming up to the present day, Oasis have caused people to definitely want to be in a band with guitars and to want to play in Manchester.!"
Clint Boon

There is a quintessential 'Englishness' about the textual content of the Britpop bands that harkens back to the Golden Days of the Beat Boom, and songs like 'Waterloo Sunset', or 'Ithchycoo Park'. The fashion style too, certainly with several of the modern groups, goes back to the 'hip' coolness of the Beatles around the time of 'Revolver'. Others, it must be pointed out, have eschewed that look in favour of a polyester version of 1970s pre-Punk. The look(s), blended with the sound, are the major signifiers of Britpop.

Come together

Before examining the tensions I have claimed are inherent within the micro-culture of Oasis, let us briefly study their career.

Generally speaking, groups are not the sum of their parts. More often than not, one, or possibly two members, will supply the drive and energy that propels the unit forward. In the case of Oasis the driving force is songwriter Noel, brother of lead singer Liam Gallagher.

It wouldn't be far from the truth to claim that Noel Gallagher is a man with a mission, that almost from the outset he had but one single purpose, and that purpose was to make it as a Rock 'n' Roll star. In order to further that end he put himself through various processes that we can only liken to that of a Rock 'n' Roll university course. Success did not come overnight, it came after several years diligent studying of the 'business' and all that that entails.

As so many others had done before him, Noel Gallagher started off as a child, watching groups on Top Of The Pops and listening to his mother's record collection. It is worth noting here that the Gallagher brothers are another example of what we might call, the Manchester/Irish connection. The brothers, like so many other Manchester musicians are the first and second generation children born to Irish immigrants in this country. This 'Irishness' is something which is worthy of a far more detailed study than I can provide here, but if we look at the genealogical roots of many local artists over the years it certainly appears to have been some considerable factor in their chosen profession, worth trying to quantify. The two leading lights of The Smiths, Steven Patrick Morrissey, and lead guitarist Johnny Marr, were both first generation Irish.

"The Mahers (the original spelling) were a musical family with a strong interest in Country and Western music. During the early sixties, Jim Reeves was extremely popular in Eirean communities and there was a strong Country and Irish boom, headed by Big Tom And The Mainliners, Larry Cunningham and The Mighty Avons and numerous others. Carrick-on-Suir's Clancy Brothers and their sinewy Armagh banjoist Tommy Makem, had returned triumphant from America, where Bob Dylan had sat at their feet. The Clancys..... undoubtedly popularized some of Ireland's great 'lost' music and focused attention on the work of such important traditionalists as Zozimus, Patrick Joyce, Thomas Moore, PJ McCall,

Ethna Carbury, Seosamh Oh Eanaigh aka Seamus Ennis.

> *"Johnny recalls several childhood summers in Kildare where the music flowed like Guinness and his guitar playing uncle sang traditional ballads mixed with pop hits of the day."*
> Rogan, 1992, pp 113/114

Other musicians of Irish descent include Freddie Garrity and Bernie Dwyer of Freddie And The Dreamers, Martin Hannett, Tony Bowers of Albertos and Simply Red, Shaun Ryder, and myself, among many others. I'm by no means arguing that it is a prerequisite of becoming a Manchester musician, but there do appear to be strong links between music and the Irish community, and the Gallagher brothers are no exception.

In the mid 1980s, a teenage Noel followed a very similar route to that taken by Johnny Marr: football and music, two traditional escapes for working class youth, as noted by Sarah Cohen -

> *"It might sound cliche'd but it cannot be denied that being in a band was seen by many, whether employed or unemployed, to be a 'way out' of their current situation, 'a way out of the jungle', as some have phrased it."*
> Cohen, 1991, p 3

> *"Paul Bardsley, one-time vocalist with Manchester's Molly Half Head - a band who were supported by Oasis in their early days - and presently between bands, remembers jamming with Noel Gallagher 'when Mike Tyson came on the scene, I think it was '85 or '86. There was a lot of kids who played football together in Burnage and me and Noel were in that gang, we'd play guitar and sing a little bit, we had a stupid name, it was Fantasy Chicken And The Amateurs'."*
> City Life, 17 April-1 May 1996, p10

By 1987, Noel had found a job working as a watchman for the Gas Board at their Little Peter Street depot, which, by one of those fateful coincidences, was just down the road from The Boardwalk Club. It was also around the time that Nathan McGough and Dave Haslam were starting up their Saturday night live music promotions, the beginning of the Madchester scene, in fact. It was here that Noel began his first formal relationship with the music world. He became a big fan of the Inspiral Carpets, who at that point were at the early

231

stage of their career and had just released 'The Planecrash' EP on Paula Greenwood's Playtime Records. Then their singer decided to leave.

"... the singer decided he was doing one (leaving). At this stage the press were really going for us, we were going to be the next big band, etc. The singer decided he didn't want to risk it. He had a job stacking pallets, or whatever in Oldham; he was ready to get married; he had a mortgage to think of. He didn't want to take the risk of us spending two or three years developing..... so we started auditioning singers. At this stage we'd picked up Noel. He was a fan, and he followed us around to all the gigs. He had a broken leg, his leg was in plaster, he was on crutches."
Clint Boon

It was 1988, and Noel was about to embark on the career in music that he had always wanted. However, it wasn't to turn out quite as he'd expected.

"We auditioned him on the night of the Lockerbie plane crash... He came down to Ashton, to the Mill, the little studio I had at the time, and sang some of our songs, slagged some of the lyrics off. He made enough of an impression, but he sings like me, and we wanted a crooner.... We said to Noel, 'Do you want to be a roady? Because we know you can sing, we've heard your tapes'. He was doing stuff at home on a four track, stuff that he'd written. 'You don't sing the style that we want - Do you want to be a roady?' And he said, 'Yeah, no problem'."
Clint Boon

Noel found himself working alongside the Inspirals, who were soon to become one of the fastest rising groups within the Madchester firmament.

"Each release sold more and more, and by the time we did 'Move' it got to number 41 in the charts, which was pretty amazing for a total Indie label with no major backing, which is what most of the Indie labels have now, pots of money behind them. At that time we were just five lads in an office in Manchester, and the manager, paying ourselves a tenner a week to cover bus fares and that, and we got to 41 in the charts. So what happened is that all the majors were like taking us out and we had the pick of the crop basically.... We had this classic scene of every record company in the world

chasing us for a deal.... So we played this game of being courted...."
Clint Boon

The Inspirals rapidly brokered a deal with Mute Records, which enabled them to develop along the lines that Clint Boon saw as being essential for an up and coming band. It was a relationship that was to last until into the 1990s, when they felt the need for a change of direction. Back then, in 1988/89, they were on the verge of international stardom, and Noel Gallagher was on board, firmly ensconced as one of the crew.

"Noel started then as our roady. Tom's (their new singer, picked up from local band 'Too Much Texas') first recording with us was the 'Joe' record produced by 808 State, and that was Noel's first time in a studio ever in the world. He was helping us out in the studio and learning how to be a roady and that... From then on, that was it, Noel was right in there with the band."
Clint Boon

Being 'right there with the band' was to prove an invaluable lesson to the young Noel Gallagher. Quickly, he began to develop into a personality in his own right.

"When people say he was your roady, he was more than that. He put a lot into it in terms of style and cosmic vibes man! I personally took to him a lot and really enjoyed having him around... For a long time, me and him shared rooms when we were on tour, until when we got bigger and we started travelling around separately. Not for political reasons... (he was the roady)... he travelled with the gear..... Noel learnt the trade of being a roady and did it very well. He used to get fan-mail for being a roady."
Clint Boon

On the road with the Inspirals, Noel honed and perfected his guitar playing and musical techniques.

"We knew that he could do the music, we could see it when we were sound checking. He was a brilliant guitarist.... He was learning the keyboards. He'd borrow my synth off me. He could drum... We used to discuss with Noel what his next band was going to be. He made no secret of the fact that he was going to go out and do it on his own."

Clint Boon

Noel also astutely gathered information about the music business.

"There were no secrets. He knew everything that we were doing. We did 'Top Of The Pops', he'd come round and see it all, what the pluggers were doing, the way that the industry worked. How much you could get for publishing, etc. He was in on all the meetings, he saw it all.

"On another level, songwriting. He'd sit in with us. I remember regularly we'd come back from rehearsals and give him practice tapes of the stuff we'd been doing, and he'd sit and talk about songs that we'd written... Those were all ways that he learnt the industry."
Clint Boon

Creation

Creation Records, run by Alan McGee, was the independent label that finally signed up Oasis. How did Alan McGee arrive at a decision that was to catapult Creation and Oasis into a mutually symbiotic partnership that would make them one of the biggest groups in the world, and one of the most respected labels?

"A friend of McGee's, Nathan McGough, once manager of Happy Mondays and presently part of the East West Records A & R squad, recalls: 'Alan is always euphoric about every band he signs. He rang me after the gig, and said "Have you heard of Oasis?", I said, "yes", and he said, "Well, I've just signed them and they're going to be the next Beatles." My response was 'You say that about every band you sign', and he replied, "Yeah, but this time, I really mean it"."
City Life, 1-16 May 1996, p 13

McGee found a five piece band that had already got the basic mainstay of their catalogue ready for auction. He witnessed a gig they did at King Tut's Wah Wah Club, in Glasgow, on May 18th 1993.

"We got there and Noel said, "We're on tonight" and the manager said "Sorry mate, no you're not", Noel said, "I've sorted it out with one of

my friends, that's not on." Noel had a little word in his ear saying, "Look,
there's fifteen of us here. If you wanna kick us out it's going to kick off."
Basically the manager said, "I'll give you a fifteen minute slot, but you'll
have to go on first", so they went on, and there was only about six people
in."
Tony French, ibid

McGee signed them on the strength of that performance and a
copy of their demo tape.
Noel, however, hadn't simply come into a group blindly.
Originally they were called Rain, and had featured his brother Liam
on vocals, before they changed their name to Oasis.

"'Rain were fucking crap,' remembers (Paul) the eldest and equally
candid Gallagher brother. 'When Liam joined, the name was changed to
Oasis straight away, it was taken from the Swindon Oasis which was a
venue in Swindon'."
Paul Gallagher, City Life, 17 April - 2 May 1996, p11

This familial account belies the generally apocryphal memory
of where the band acquired their name, that it came from Oasis, a
shop in the City centre that sold trainers.
Noel had returned from tour with the Inspiral Carpets at
Christmas 1992, and found that his position with the band was no
longer required. A variety of factors were at work here in his dismissal,
but it is most likely Noel's increasing drug habit.

"It wasn't something we could accommodate anymore really," says
Boon. *"I mean, we all loved him, he was part of the brotherhood and stuff,*
but we couldn't handle it. It was a very amicable split. It's probably the best
thing that ever happened to him.
"It was hard, he was a friend, someone we had always gotten on with.
And it was on the eve of us going to America. He did have something else to
focus on though, and we gave him a golden handshake, a really big golden
handshake. We felt bad about it, but we really didn't lose a lot of sleep over
it."
Clint Boon, City Life, 1-16 May 1996, p12

Noel had received a fairly large wage as an Inspiral Carpet's
roady, around £500 per week, and he took as a golden handshake

something in the region of £5,000. We must also bear in mind that it wasn't just a financial reward that he took away with him. Aside from learning the ins and outs of the music business from his association with Clint Boon, he also developed an association with Inspiral's monitor engineer, Mark Coyle, who went on to co-produce the first four Oasis singles. When Noel came back from a 1991 tour with the Inspirals he found brother Liam singing with Rain. Noel's immediate response was to talk about becoming their manager. His next response was to come on board as the mainstay.

Noel decided to take immediate control of the band, which at the time consisted of Liam Gallagher on vocals, Bonehead on guitar, Tony McCarroll on drums and Guigsy on bass. He joined as guitarist, songwriter and immediately began to push them into the direction he envisaged.

They moved into rehearsal rooms on Little Peter Street and began working out six nights a week. Just before Christmas 1991 they made their first demo recording.

"When Oasis played their first gig with Noel at The Boardwalk in January 1992, 'The first song they played was 'Columbia', which was an instrumental,' says Paul Gallagher. Even back then, Noel was shrewd enough to claim the songwriting credit. Martin Fisher, who also worked for the Inspirals at the same time as Noel, recalls, 'Even at the beginning Noel was saying the only reason he was doing this (Oasis) was to get in there and make as much money as possible and leave some really good tunes behind'."

City Life, 17 April - 2 May 1996, p11

As to whether the elder Gallagher will 'leave some really good tunes behind', only time will tell. With regard to his making money, Noel Gallagher's personal wealth is currently estimated at around £7 million and rising.

This was achieved by applying all the lessons learnt as the Inspiral Carpets roady; learning the techniques of writing and recording, the machinations of management negotiation, the intricacies of contractual law. All these elements combined to further Noel Gallagher's assault on Popular Music and dreams of stardom. Considering the position that he and Oasis have reached within three years, he has been eminently successful.

Too tense - hyping the uptight vibe

In 1995 the press began to hype a so-called 'war' between two of the top Britpop bands, Blur and Oasis. The conjecture at the time was, which group would reach number one in the charts first? Both bands were releasing singles at the same time, Blur's 'Country House', and Oasis's 'Roll With It'. The resultant battle for chart position even became the subject of conjecture on ITN's national 'News At Ten', and BBC Radio Four's news bulletins. Both bands were at the time vying for the prestigious Mercury Music Award for their respective albums, so, as far as the media were concerned, some kind of stand off was inevitable.

The resultant column inches and air space, whilst bearing in mind the essential shallowness of the whole enterprise, does allow us opportunity to examine the contradictions and tensions inherent within Oasis as a group, and to a degree, Manchester music as a whole. The exercise enabled much of what had preceded it over the previous twenty five years to surface in a way which is invaluable to the cultural historian.

Awopbopaloobopaeebygum!

More or less as a direct result of the success of Madchester, one of the main tenets of Britpop was 'authenticity' within the music world. What constitutes this 'authenticity' is slightly harder to quantify, but would certainly include the following - a working class pedigree, a retro-guitar sound, being 'street smart', and an aura of 'new laddishness'. In the media 'battle of the bands' this basically boiled down to North versus South, and is a magnified legacy of the Thatcher years in terms of employment and recession.

"A working class hero is something to be"

We shall look at definitions of 'working class' first. In his conclusion to 'One Chord Wonders', Dave Laing presents an interesting analysis of the claim that Punk was a predominantly working class movement.

"The most widespread view of punk's relationship to class is typified

by this statement: 'British punk grew up in the late 1970s among young working class people at a time when the country faced severe economic problems.' (John Shepherd, 'Sociomusicological Analysis of Popular Musics', in R. Middleton and D. Horn ((eds)) Popular Music A Yearbook, 1981 - 84.) As an assertion about the class origins of punk musicians this can be shown to be inaccurate."

Laing, 1985, p 121

Laing then follows this with a table which presents a comparison between the membership of 1960s Beat groups and late 1970s Punk groups that demonstrates quite clearly that a sizeable minority of both groups in the sample came from other areas than working class. This is quite similar to the argument that I make in Chapter 5. With Laing's Beat group findings in mind, it is amusing when one gets the opportunity, to observe the vocal changes that Mick Jagger went through in order to obtain the more fashionable cockney drawl that he has affected since the late 1960s. Up to that point he used a moderated BBC 'classless' accent which more clearly demonstrated his background origins.

Class, however, became a potent signifier in the Rock world throughout the decades, and the situation is no less so today. Dick Hebdige, in 'Subculture - The Meaning Of Style', sees Punk as progression of working class youth movements preceded by Teddy Boys, Mods and Skinheads. His book, however, contains inaccuracies -

"Dreadlocks, the long plaited hair worn by some Rastafarians, were originally intended to reproduce the 'ethnic' look of some East African tribes."

Hebdige, 1979, p143

Firstly, dreadlocks are not plaited. They are matted clumps of hair, left uncombed to grow 'naturally', and they are most certainly not intended to look like the hair style of 'some East African tribes'. They are left uncombed and uncut following instructive exhortations in the Bible to neither comb nor cut the hair. Interestingly, there was a fundamentalist Christian group in the Rochdale area of North West England in the 19th century who practised the same thing. Nor, like Rastafarians, would they eat pork, or work on the Sabbath (Saturday). Chief Constable James Anderton was a grandson of one of the sect.

Several more errors in Hebdige relate to forms of dancing which he claims were popular in the Punk movement, the 'Highrise' and the 'Bailey', neither of which I ever saw practised anywhere throughout the British Isles at any Punk gig. His views on style, which I have commented on elsewhere, remain Londoncentric. In light of these factual inaccuracies I would argue that his views on the class basis of Punk must also be taken with a pinch of salt.

None of this however, detracts from the observation that certain people have perceived Popular Music to be a 'class' thing, indeed, have manufactured it in light of this desire. It resolutely remains above arguments of this sort, in a purely analytical way, whilst remaining part and parcel of the packaging of pop. The fan's chance to mix with a 'bit of rough', as it were, without getting their hands soiled, and that, now, is the way that pop presents Oasis, as something that is about as real as 'Coronation Street'.

In comparison to Blur, Oasis are the real working class Macoy. With their exaggerated Thames Estuary English and lyrical fascination with the underbelly of Southern life, see the 'Parklife' video for a visual exposition of this particular fetish, Damon Albarn's schmoozing with the lower classes is thrown into much sharper relief. It comes as no surprise to learn that his family are comfortably well off professionals, involved in the arts. Noel and Liam's mum still refuses to leave her council estate semi for a luxury mansion.

From Joe Meek's middle class fumblings with his teenage protégés, to John Lennon's 'Working Class Hero', pop has had a fascination with the working classes that just won't go away. In this, it has myriad echoes of the Folk revival and Bert Lloyd and Ewan MacColl's CPGB dictums and rhetoric on 'authenticity'. Perhaps it is something to do with the 'sound'?

Cranked up really high!

One of the main areas of disagreement between music fans at any moment throughout the history of Popular Music is the dislike one fan has for another's choice of music. This has been a cultural battleground for longer than this book covers, but we need only look at the distinctions drawn by TW Adorno and the Frankfurt School, in his pioneering, if dismissive studies of Popular Music, such as those included in 'The Culture Industry', and 'On Popular Music'.

(Adorno and Horkheimer, 1977) In these, and other works, Adorno posited the theory that all Popular Music served to do was operate as part of the capitalist machine's attempts to undermine the workers endeavours to enrich their lives by enslaving them to the lowest common denominator - the repetitive beat of Popular Music. This basically boiled down to an argument over the relative merits of 'High Art' versus 'Low Art', Adorno coming down heavily for the former.

From the mid 1950s onwards the culturally dominant form of Popular Music has tended to be guitar oriented. The Beat combo has stylistically changed very little over the decades. There have been fads that seemed to auger changes, such as synthesizer rock in the 1980s, but until the technological breakthroughs provided by midi-sampling in the late 1980s and the arrival of Techno and House, the virtual stranglehold of the guitar sound held sway over the shape of the sound of popular music.

Many commentators on Popular Music, as well as performers, were disturbed by the trend they saw coming in the clubs in the mid 1980s. They viewed the rise of House in much the same way their predecessors had when Disco became a major force in the early 1970s.

"I remember Morrissey coming one evening (to the Haçienda) and settling himself down in the DJ box. I was all fired up; I pulled out that classic electro track 'Hip Hop, Be Bop (Don't Stop)' by Man Parrish. "Remember this?" I yelled to him. He didn't of course, and he didn't seem impressed. I didn't see why he wouldn't like the records I play; after all, I liked the songs he sang. Who knows what could have happened if I'd managed to turn him on that night? Imagine if he'd gone round to Johnny Marr's the next day and said, "I heard this great record last night, all drum machines, no guitars, no lyrics. Sack this gloomy rockabilly tinged balladeering, we're going hip hop". It was not to be."
Dave Haslam

It is an interesting cultural conundrum that Madchester's principally guitar oriented sound emerged from the sweat lodges of House. Nationally, its success furthered the industry's interest in Indie as a whole, and subsequently, when Madchester faded, the retro-guitar resurgence had a cultural platform from which to operate. Historically, guitars and pop go together in the minds of most people, and the symbiotic relationship between the two has fused into one image, one vision, one set of signifiers that can be read as one more facet of 'authenticity'. This 'coming together' is clearly demonstrated in the seemingly endless flow of guitar bands that have emerged since the success of Oasis. It is a trend we have seen being repeated since The Shadows, since the Beatles, all the way through bands inspired by the Sex Pistols, like Buzzcocks and Joy Division, and now Oasis.

Street Smart

Street smart is an extended concept that goes beyond mere fashion statements. It implies a knowledgability, a 'sussed' awareness of urban living. Possession of it allows an individual to steer their way through the psychogeographic map of the inner city and its environs with an ability that displays more than a passing acquaintenceship with the morals and codes of subcultural urban living. Historically, we can locate modern origins of street smart in the 1940s concept of 'cool' and 'hip' in relation to Jazz fans. Going even further back, we could even possibly link it to the Decadents of the late Victorian era, or further back still to the Regency Dandy.

Where did you get that jacket/pants/video?

Again, it has allusions towards a working class sensibility, and therefore an implied 'authenticity', but 'street smart' is an aura that is developed, not genetic. In the perceived media battle between Blur and Oasis, Oasis 'have it', while Blur are seen as having more of an 'arty' persona, a legacy of the art school genre of British music. Their use of Damian Hirst to direct the 'Country House' video would be seen as confirmation of this. Juxtaposing Oasis's 'Wonderwall' video with 'Country House' we can identify a fascinating class reversal. Hirst and Albarn chose to populate their video with 'Page 3' girls, scantily dressed in provocative clothing. Generally this would be perceived as 'working class'. Oasis, on the other hand, chose to decorate the set for their number with languid, sultry 'supermodels', acting more as ornaments than as fetishized objects of male desire. Oasis were being 'smart', Blur were being 'clever'.

Fashion too plays its usual significant role in the identifiable image of street smart. A characteristic that it shares with the Mod look of the 1960s is the apparent casualness of the image. On the whole, Britpop's look and feel is relaxed, but this is an illusion. Behind the carefully studied dishabille lies an intricate coding implying infinite planning. The dominant trend, as of the mid 1990s, would appear to be the hooded top, casual slacks and trainers, but there are also strong retro elements at work in the fashion choices. In terms of hair styles for males, this too has undergone a return to the forward brushed, mid-length look of middle period Beatles.

At present, these particular types of clothing are the ones worn by fans of the groups, or, and this is the interesting point, are the groups wearing the same fashions as the fans? As in all things tribal, identification with one's subcultural group is essential for survival. (Amit-Talai and Wulff, 1995) Clear recognition provides comfort, security, and above all - exclusivity.

Exclusivity is a principal component of street smart, especially in terms of the type of music listened to by the 'tribe'. The 'sound' is integral to the 'look'. The two go hand in hand, it is an unwritten law that they are inseparable. Hebdige has argued in 'Subculture - The Meaning Of Style' that Punk music was deliberately exclusive, both within its rituals and its content. During the early days of Soul and R'n'B at the Twisted Wheel and other Manchester clubs, Roger Eagle and the other DJs would carry round with them boxes of 'scratchouts'. These were singles that had come from America. If they proved popular on the dance floor the DJs would scratch out the labels so no-one could identify them and therefore would be unable to buy them to play at other venues. Dave Haslam has recently told me that this has become common practice again, this time with remixes of House tracks: DJs asserting the right to exclusivity of property.

There have been many studies of style and subcultures, so there seems little reason to go over the ground again here. Suffice it to say that 'hipness' has always equated with fashion at the forefront of (sub)cultural movements. Being street smart means having the right look and the right attitude at the right time. Hangin' with the movers is an indispensable requirement of 'authenticity'.

Birds, Booze and Brawling

We now reach the penultimate equation of 'authenticity' - New Laddishness.

"Come on over here baby - I'm gonna teach your pussy to whistle!"
Bo Diddley

Or maybe, not so new.....
The culture of excess has always been associated with Popular Music. Musicians have by dint of necessity inhabited the twilight world of the criminal. As far back as the Blues we find the dead and the debauched littering the ground. Robert Johnson, murdered by a jealous rival. Sam Cooke gunned down in a motel room. Parker, Joplin, Hendrix, Jones, Morrison, Hannett, Cobain, Vicious, the list can go on and on. Each example, however, merely adds to the mystique of 'authenticity', and there is insufficient reason at present to add even more to it. To argue that excess went away as Popular Music grew older in years would be naive to say the least, but there is a disturbing element within the persona's of Oasis in particular, that has worrying cultural resonances, and that element revolves around the cult of 'new lad'.

Exemplified within the pages of new lad journals such as 'GQ' and 'Loaded', and proudly presented on television in shows such as the BBC's 'Men Behaving Badly' and Granada's imaginatively titled 'The Lads', the retro-male sensibility is once again to the fore.

The carefully nurtured 1980s image of the 'new man', rebirthed into the liberal consciousness by books such as Robert Bly's, 'Iron John', is rapidly giving way to the new sensibility of postmodern 'Alfie's', which was, as is the way with these things, merely a reworking of the Casanova/Don Juan myth, anyway. Suddenly it is alright to get drunk, stoned and screw anything, and if you want to fight about it, so much the better.

Some cultural commentators have observed that the phenomenon is a reaction to the last twenty-five years of Feminism, that young men feel threatened by the advances that women have made in the emancipation stakes, and that it is an inevitable consequence. Others have noted that the return of the macho male, the lager swilling lout, is a misnomer, that they never went away in the first place.

There is some truth to both viewpoints. There is a questing for cultural identity amongst young people, there always has been. Young males, in particular, may be attracted to the image of excess as portrayed by Oasis. Heavy Metal fans have been doing the same thing for generations with their cultural icons. What is most interesting is the attraction that appears to be felt by so many young women for the phenomenon. This is a question that will have to be answered by those whose interests lie in the discipline of psychology and behavioural science, suffice to say that it does exist.

Get your kit off for the lads!

As I observed in Chapter 9, Scallydelia, Oasis weren't the first Manchester band to trade off the macho image. Stone Roses did, and Happy Mondays were at the forefront with their inclusion of a picture of a naked woman on a record sleeve and general 'yob' behaviour.

"May 87. In the furthest alcove of The International Club, two ropey blokes were chatting.

'Men's nipples....' slurred one, turning to the girls at the next table, '...don't you find them attractive? Sexy?' A mad glint in his eye, he persisted, 'Men's nipples, don't you find them erotic?'

The girls stared back, speechless at this novel chat up line. The other guy smirked. 'What do you think of the Stone Roses?' he drawled, giving his mate a poke in the ribs.

'Errrm....well, they're better than that band Inspiral Carpets.' Laughter.

'Don't you know who we are?' Blank stares. 'We're the Stone Roses!' 'Oh....'

"... The nipple obsessed one was Reni, a minor league Keith Moon. The girls were Manc plugger Alison Martin and yours truly!"
Champion, 1991, p123

Food fights in restaurants, trashing their former record labels offices, were part and parcel of the Stone Roses universe. Shaun Ryder of Happy Mondays specialised in narcotic events.

".... I've stopped taking E. Last time I did, I was the last one out of the

warehouse. Didn't know where I was. I had a load of E in my pockets 'cos I was selling them then. I put about ten in my mouth to get out and they all melted. Sent me potty and I ended up having a heart attack on Oxford Road, collapsing and ending up in BUPA. Took me three weeks to recover. I couldn't move one side of my body. Totally cabbaged!"
Shaun Ryder in Champion, 1991, p106

It is arguable that, to some, this kind of behaviour is perceived as working class. We know this to be a nonsense, but never the less, our society is one that prefers to believe that loutish hedonism is somehow confined to the lower classes. It is this view that would see the new laddishness of present day performers adding to the area of 'authenticity' outlined above. As I hope I have demonstrated, it is neither a new, nor particularly young form of behaviour. That it is male, and in some ways central to the core myths of rock is undeniable.

We have now reached the final stage of our analysis - the North South divide.

AND GOD CREATED MANCHESTER
(T-shirt slogan) 1989

A social tension of sorts has always existed between the North and the South, with the former invariably portrayed as 'grim' and industrial, while the latter was seen as more affluent and aloof. Lovable, but stupid, gormless and cheerful was the popular conception of Northeners supplied by a steady stream of comics such as George Formby and Rob Wilton. These were set up against cheeky cockney chappies, like Max Miller, or wideboy spiv types such as Arthur English and Sid Field. Archetypes and stereotypes abounded in the world of popular entertainment. This is the reality from which many of the perceptions of regionalism sprang. All Scots were skinflints, all Scousers were scallys, all Mancunians were daft. Whatever the regional variations present in Popular Culture, one idea held sway - that London was the centre of the world.

Blur versus Oasis highlighted a situation that has been present in Popular Music since before 1977, that of the Londoncentric view of the musical universe as envisaged by the music media and the industry. We saw in Chapter 5, 'Music Force', how prior to that point there was a general resentment at the stranglehold exerted by London based managers and agencies, but very little could be done about it. No matter where a band came from in England, the perceived wisdom was that in order to achieve success they would have to move to London. This immutable law was thrown into slight disarray by several successful groups. For example, Lindisfarne in Newcastle, and more importantly by 10cc in Manchester, who by choosing to set up the infrastructure of their business in the City, were managed by the highly successful Mancunian management agency, Kennedy Street Enterprises. The internationally reknowned Strawberry Studio in Stockport was built by 10CC, and a precedent that many other people would follow in later years was set.

In 1977, Richard Boon and Buzzcocks, with their deliberate policy of encouraging regionalism in terms of Punk creativity, unleashed a deluge of independent recordings that were to seize the imagination of musicians all over the world. Post 1977, you no longer had to go to London in order to make it. You could do it from your own living room.

By the end of the 1980s, London was generally seen as lagging behind in the world of youth culture. It had been transformed into a kind of vast heritage centre that continued to live off past glories instead of leading the way in innovation and creativity. Perhaps that is all it ever did, acted as a sponge that soaked up and drew in the talents of artists and performers from the regions, buoyed and sustained by its reputation rather than its reality. In the 1960s it had been seriously challenged by the Merseybeat boom, but the reality of that situation was that the musical infrastructure in place in Liverpool at the time was insufficient to keep the musicians interested in staying there. Much the same could be said of the Manchester Beat musicians who emerged at the same period. For better or for worse, London was the place to go to, but by the Madchester boom, as a result of Punk and New Wave, people were no longer interested in moving.

"It's (Manchester) fascinating. That's why I'll always live here. I'm convinced that in thirty years time it'll still be the centre of the music world. Not in terms of the industry, but in terms of the creativity. I could have moved to Dallas several times in the last five years... (but here)... In the space of a couple of hours I can have a meeting with Granada and get a theme tune under my belt; I can walk across town and speak to a potential

manager; I can go and see a band rehearse that I'm going to produce that night. I've got such a close network of contacts in Manchester that it'd be just silly to walk away from it...."
Clint Boon

The final element in the 'authenticity' of Oasis, and to a degree, the Manchester scene as a whole, is now finally in place. Its very 'Northernness'. It's no longer cloth caps and whippets, but Fenders and cagoules. Not factory chimneys but a leaner, fitter Factory Too, the Haçienda as international youth venue of choice, and no longer Hammersmith Palais. Pete Waterman has brought his studio and label to Manchester, the onus of broadcasting by Radio One from Manchester is increasing year by year. The success of 'In The City' has seen thousands of industry luminaries visiting Manchester for a week long series of talks and workshops. It is impossible to predict what the situation will be like in five, let alone, ten years time. Perhaps everything will have gone full circle and the scene will have shifted elsewhere. Whatever, Manchester will still be here and so will its musical community, and they will, as always, still be producing music.

"As a fan of music who was totally unknown, I completely enjoyed Manchester. As a pop star I completely enjoyed it, and now, as a father of two kids who lives on the outskirts of Manchester I still love it. I could have moved anywhere in the world but this is my home."
Clint Boon

REFERENCES

Adorno, T W and Horkheimer, M, 1977, 'The culture industry: enlightenment as mass deception; in Curran, J, Gurevitch, M and Woollacott, J (Eds), 1977, 'Mass Communication and Society', London, Edward Arnold

Amit-Talai, Vered and Wulff, Helena (Eds), 1995, 'Youth Cultures - A Cross-Cultural Perspective', London, Routledge

Champion, Sarah, 1991, 'And God Created Manchester',

Manchester, Wordsmith

City Life, 4-18 Feb 1993, Issue 221

City Life, 17 April - 2 May 1996, Issue 303

City Life, 1-16 May 1996, Issue 304

Cohen, S, 1991, 'Rock Culture in Liverpool, Oxford, Clarendon Press

Communist Party of Great Britain, 1951, The American Threat to British Culture, London, Arena

Haslam, Dave, 1995, 'Reading Pop', Unpublished Manuscript

Hebdige, D, 1979, 'Subculture The Meaning of Style', London, Methuen & Co

Laing, Dave, 1985, 'One Chord Wonders - Power and Meaning in Punk Rock, Milton Keynes, Open University Press

Rogan, Johnny, 1992, 'Morrissey and Marr: The Severed Alliance', London, Omnibus Press

Spinoza, Andy, The Face, August 1991

TAPED INTERVIEWS

Clint Boon

Chapter 11

Conclusion

As an essentially historical work there is no underlying or central argument in this book, though the notation of certain themes and trends have emerged in the course of its completion. These have related to the tensions inherent within our society concerning youth-inspired culture and authority, and the tensions inherent within sub-cultures regarding questions of authenticity. Two other topics that came to light were what I would call 'the almost incestuous lineage of Manchester bands' and the influence of Manchester on the economics of the record industry vis a vis independent labels.

Regarding the tensions between youth culture and authority, these have been clearly linked with the impetus of changes in the musical scene in Manchester. From the destruction of the Beat Clubs in 1966 to the restrictive legislation of the 1990s, the oppositional tactics of local and national agencies have failed so far to curtail the activities of music makers in Manchester. Arguably musicians continue to be creative in the face of direct opposition from those in power, whether it be parents, police or any other authoritative figure. This has been clearly delineated.

There are recurrent themes in terms of authenticity. These are related to identity of class, style and 'street credibility'. These elements have been at the centre of discourse since the 1950s, and I have shown their progression from that period through to the present day. Arguably, the developments in authenticity and identity in our Post Modern society are signifying reaction giving way to interaction, and authority to empowerment.

It was not the aim of this work to explore issues of the 'local' or 'regional'. It is not an history of Manchester, but of Mancunians. It is not situated economically or sociologically. I have simply followed a notational path, letting people tell their own stories with my overlaid comments concerning contemporary events that appeared to me to draw their stories together. Similarly, I can draw no conclusions about 'regional'. It is referred to briefly at the end in terms of the media's obsession with the North/South divide, but if Manchester is different from everywhere else I can draw no conclusions about what makes it so. However, there have been lots of reasons offered by the interviewees, ranging from the obtuse: '...it must be something to do with the water ...' (Peter Hook) to the competitive: '... we've got to have the best possible people that will go all over the world and shit on people from Los Angeles' (Victor Brox), and to the media's interpretation of regionalism: 'It felt very important at the time to put Manchester back on the map.' (Richard Boon).

Appendix 1

Interviewee Profiles

The following have been quoted at length:

Clint Boon
Founder member of Indie chart toppers Inspiral Carpets. After a highly successful international career, Clint is making a solo album as well as writing music for television.

Richard Boon
Richard was manager of Mancunian Punk band Buzzcocks, and self styled 'label supremo' of New Hormones Records. He lives in London with his family.

Victor Brox
Multi talented veteran of the British Blues scene, Victor has played with everybody. He currently lives in France, but returns to play in Manchester frequently.

Scott Carey
Scott started his musical career in the Inspiral Carpets and then went on to play bass with the Paris Angels, who were signed to Virgin Records. He is between bands at the time of writing.

Howard Devoto
(nee, Trafford) Howard was the person responsible for bringing the Sex Pistols to Manchester. He then formed Buzzcocks with Pete Shelley, left and formed Magazine. He is a photographic librarian in London.

Andy Harris
Andy Harris moved to Manchester from Cornwall. He is the studio manager at Salford University, and plays keyboards with Italian Love Party who had a single on Factory Too.

Peter Hook
Founder member of Joy Division, which became New Order, Factory Records' most successful act. Currently working solo.

Peter Hughes
Peter was the drummer with The Chuckles, a moderately successful Manchester Beat group. He retired from the music business in the 1970s, and now lives in North Manchester with his family.

Jon The Postman
Jon became legendary during the Punk era for his rousing renditions of 'Louie Louie'. He made two albums, moved to San Francisco, came back and is now a record dealer.

Bruce Mitchell
Bruce started playing drums in the mid 1950s. Along the way he played with Victor Brox, Greasy Bear, The Albertos, and is currently drummer with The Durutti Column.

Eddie Mooney
Eddie came from Northern Ireland to attend University in Manchester. Was on TJM Records as Eddie Mooney and The Grave. Now plays with The Dakotas, Billy J Kramer's former backing group.

Tosh Ryan
Sax player in the Victor Brox Blues Train, Tosh was a founder member of Music Force, the musician's collective. He then started Rabid Records with Martin Hannett. He now runs the Basement Video Project.

Benny Van Den Burg
Was manager of several clubs in Manchester throughout the 1960s and 1970s. He now owns an independent video production company.

Anthony H Wilson
Salford born TV personality who founded Factory Records. He now runs Factory Too and is a partner in the Haçienda.

Manchester Groups 1950 - 1995

The following list is not exhaustive; I am sure there are many others.
Apologies to those not included.

10cc
1234 Five, The
262
4 Mosts, The
42nd Street
48 Chairs
808 State
A Certain Ratio
A Guy Called Gerald
A Witness
Abstracts, The
Accident on the East Lancs
Addicts, The
Admirals, The
Adventure Babies
Advisers, The
Alan la Pellay
Albertos Y Lost Trios Paranoias
All Stars, The
Alone
Angels, The
Anglias, The
Aniseed
Anne Brent
Antares, The
Antones, The
Apples, The
Aqua
Art Nouveau
Astorians, The

Astrals, The
Astronoughts, The
Atlanta Roots, The
Atlantics, The
Audioweb
Avalons, The
Avengers, The
Aztecs, The
B Fab UK
Baby Suicide
Backbeats
Backdoor Men, The
Balmains, The
Bandit Queen
Bandwagon
Barbarians with Prince Khan, The
Bardots, The
Barons, The
Barry James and the Strangers
Barry Langtree and the Lancastrians
Barry Vaughan and the Horizons
Beachcombers, The
Bearjacks, The
Beat Messengers, The
Beat Squad, The
Beatbelles, The
Beatfenders, The
Beathovens, The
Beatmakers, the
Beatrice
Beatvendors, The
Bed
Bee Gees
Bees Knees, The
Beetaab Sangeet
Berry Pickers, The
Bet Lynch's Legs
Big Beat Boys, The
Big Block 454
Big Ed and His Rockin Rattlesnakes

Big Flame
Big Jim White - Elvis in Mind
Bill Bowes and the Arrows
Bill Leslie and the Alleycats
Billy and the Impacts
Billy Dee and the Deacons
Biting Tongues
Black
Black Beats, The
Black Grape
Black Orchids, The
Black Silk Frog
Black Stan's Blues Band
Black Velvets, The
Blackberris, The
Blackcurrants, The
Blackjacks, The
Blackouts, The
Blah Blah Blah
Blue Angels, The
Blue Diamonds, The
Blue Orchids
Blues Syndicate, The
Bluetones, The
Bobbins, The
Bobby and the Benders
Bobby Brown and the Barons
Bobby Christian and the Avalons
Bobby Dell and the Dellstars
Bobby Laine and the Confederates
Bobby Sampson and the Giants
Bodines,The
Bodysnatchers, The
Bong
Boom Boom
Boothill Footappers
Bounce Mouse
Bo-Weevils, The
Boys, The
Bread and Roses

Breather
Brenda's Boyfriend
Brent Wade and the Wanderers
Bridgebeats, The
Brokers, The
Brownsville Jug Band, The
Brubaker
Bruce Haris and the Kingpins
Bruce Harris and the Cavaliers
Brutas Men, The
Brystals, The
Buccaneers, The
Buddies, The
Buddy Britten and the Regents
Bunny Baker Eight, The
Burning Hunks of Love
Buttons, The
Buzzcocks
Cadillac and the Playboys
Cairo
Cake Shop Device
Cameo 5, The
Camerians, The
Canto Five, The
Carl Mann and the Candymen
Carmel
Carol Kay and the Dynachords
Carrovelles, The
Carsons, The
Cartwrights, The
Cathy La Creme
Cavaliers, The
C-Charts
Centurions, The
Chads, The
Challengers, The
Chameleons
Champion Frannie Eubanks
Chancellors, The
Changing Times, The

Chaperones, The
Chapters, The
Chariots, The
Charlie Parkers
Chasers, The
Cheeba
Cheetahs, The
Cheryl Laine and the Renegades
Cheshire Cats, The
Chessmen, The
Cheynes, The
Chez Vandell and the Ravens
Chick Graham and the Coasters
Chondells, The
Chorltons, The
Chris Nava Combo
Chris Ryan the the Strangers
Christine and the Norsemen
Chucaburrra
Chuckles, The
Citadels, The
Citizens, The
Citrons, The
Classics, The
Clearways, The
Cliff Bowes and the Arrows
Cliff Gale and the Jangles
Clint and the Chordettes
Clive Prince and the Vampires
Coasters with Phil Corbett, The
Coasters, The
Cock 'A' Hoops
Col Kennedy and the Presidents
Collegians, The
Colorados, The
Colours Out Of Time
Commanchees, The
Commancheros, The
Con Brios, The
Concords, The

Condours, The
Confederates, The
Connoisseurs, The
Contours, The
Contrasts, The
Cool Hands, The
Cops 'n Robbers
Corals, The
Coronets, The
Corvettes Combo, The
Corvettes, The
Cosmos
Cossacks, The
Cotten Singers
Counterfeits, The
Country beats, The
Country Gentlemen, The
Cow Freaks, The
Craig Davies
Crazy Heavy
Creepers, The
Cresants, The
Crescents, The
Cresters with Malcolm Clarke & Richard Harding, The
Crispy Ambulance
Crusaders, The
Crush
Curious Yellows, The
Curt's Creatures
Cyclones, The
Cymerons, The
D J Smith and the Moon-Rakers
Dae Shirley and the Raunchys
Dakotas, The
Daltons, The
Damien Shrub, The
Danny and the Democrats
Danny and the Demons
Danny and the Dominators
Danny Havoc and the Ventures

Danny Lee and the Dominoes
Danny Marshall and the Lawmen
Danny Moran
Dappers, The
Dark Lagoons, The
Darling Buds
Dauphin Street Six, The
Dave and the Midnights
Dave Barlow and the Knights
Dave Baron and the Chariots
Dave Beatty Rock Group
Dave Curtis and the Tremors
Dave Howard and the Boys
Dave Lee and the Bostons
Dave Plum and the Stones
Dave Prentice and the Paiges
Dave Storm and the Crestas
Dawnbreakers, The
Dean Stanley and the 4Ds
Dean West and the Hellions
Dean West and the Vantells
Debrettes, The
Dee and the Lindmen
Dee Jays with Johnny Dee
Defenders,The
Defiants, The
Deke Bonner and the Tremors
Deke Rivers and the Big 3
Deke Rivers and the Big Sound
Deke Wess and the Jaguars
Del Barry and the Downbeats
Del Raymond and the Estelles
Del Renos, The
Dell Stars, The
Delmont Four, The
Deltas, The
Deltones with Tony Laine, The
Deltones, The
Demokrats, The
Demolition Crew, The

Demons, The
Dene and the Citizens
Dene and the Deltones
Denny and the Witchdoctors
Denny Seyton and the Sabres
Derrick and the Falcons
Desert Wolves
Detroits, The
Deviators, The
Dharmas, The
Dhyani
Diablos, The
Diagram Bros
Dicky Newman and the Crusaders
Dictators, The
Die Kunst
Digerreedoos, The
Diplomats, The
Dislocation Dance
Distant Cousins
Distractions
Dolly Mixtures, The
Dolphins, The
Dominant Four, The
Dominators, The
Don Curtis and the Coasters
Don Lane and the Secrets
Don Sands and the Stylos
Donna Day and the Knights
DOSE
Dougie James Soultrain
Dowlands, The
Dr Pill and the Purple Hearts
Dramers, The
Dreadnauts, The
Drifting Hearts, the
Drive In Rock
Drones
Dru Harvey and the Jokers
Drumbeats, The

Dub Sex
Dumb
Durutti Column
Dustbinmen, The
Dymonds, The
Dynachords with Carole Kay, The
Dynachorts, The
Dynamic Delltones, The
Earl Duke and the Shabooms
East West Coast
Easterhouse
Echoes with Paul Keen, The
Echoes, The
Ed Banger and the Nosebleeds
Eddie and the Cymarrons
Eddie Marton and the Sabres
Eddie Mooney and Grave
Eddie Sheron and the Stormbeats
Eddie Sheron and the Tremillos
Edward Barton
Eight Silverhead
Electronic
Electrons, The
Eli Ryan
Elkie Brooks
Elti-Fits
Emperors of Rhythm, The
Emperors, The
En Signs, The
Eric Lee and the Four Aces
Eric Random
Erkey Grant and the Tonettes
Estelles, The
Eve Lorraine and the Chaperones
Exile Three, The
Exiles, The
Exit 21
Exuberants, The
Fab Spellbinders, The
Factotums, The

Fairies, The
Falcons Mk II, The
Falcons, The
Fall, The
Fallover 24
Fangers, The
Fantoms, The
Fast Breeder
Fast Cars
Fauves, The
Federals, The
Feelgoods with Phil J Corbett, The
Fenders, The
Firing Squad, The
Fish On A Stick
Five Go Off To Play Guitar
Five Paper Fantasy
Five Statesmen, The
Flash
Flashback
Fleece
FOC
Followers, The
Fontanas, The
Footappers, The
Foreign Press
Forresters with Little John, The
Fortune Tellers, The
Four Just Men, The
Four Plus One, The
Fourtones with Ricky Young, The
Frank and the Trendsetters
Frank Kelly and the Hunters
Frank Lees Four
Frank Sidebottom
Frankenstein and the Monsters
Frantic Elevators
Frantic Four, The
Frantic Grange Suited Twisters, The
Fred and the Flintstone Five

Freddie and the Dreamers
French, The
Fresh Vibes
Freshies
FT Index
Fugitives, The
Gabrielle's Wish
Gags
Galaxies, The
Gambelers, The
Garbotalks
Gary Rodgers and the Vampires
Gay and the Guys
Gay Animals
Gay Dogs, The
Gee South and the Blue Cats
Gemini Zent
Generations, The
Genius Beat
George Borowski
George Sugden XI, The
Gerry and the Holograms
Gerry Burns and the Invaders
Gerry de Ville and the City Kings
Gerry Wilde and the Wildcats
Ghosts, The
Giants, The
Gin House
Glass, The
Glowing Embers, The
God
God's Gift
God's Sister Helen
Godley and Creme
Going Red
Golden Apples, The
Gonks, The
Good Guys
Gordon The Moron
Graduates, The

Grant Tracey and the Sunsets
Greasy Bear
Great Leap Forward
Great Tornado, The
Green
Gremlins, The
Grow Up
Guy Les Trio, The
Gyro
Habits, The
Hagan and the Henchmen
Hammers, the
Happy Mondays
Harbour Lights, The
Hari Odin and Thunderers
Harlem Spirit
Harvey's Rabbit
Hazelbelles, The
Heartbeats with Mark Byrne, The
Heartbeats, The
Helene and the Kinsmen
Hellions with the Unknown, the
Hellions, The
Henchmen, The
Herman's Hermits
Hessians, The
Hey Day
Hi Five, The
Hickory, The
High Society, The
High, The
Hi-Spots, The
Hit Squad
Hoax, The
Hollies, The
Hoopla Baby
Horizons, The
Hornets, The
Hot Rods, The
Hotlegs

Hound God with a Tumour
Houston Wells and the Marksmen
Huckleberries, The
Hum of Good Machines, The
Hummer
Ian Crawford and the Boomerangs
Ian Curtis and the Dominators
Identity
Images, the
Imagineers
Imagineers, The
Impalas, The
Impossible Chocolates
In Crowd, The
Inca Babies
Incas, The
Incrust
Inner Sense Percussion
Inspiral Carpets
Interns, The
Interstellar Overdrive
Invaders, The
Invictors, The
Invincibles, The
Invisible Girls
IQ Zero
Irritant
Irwells, The
Isherwood
Italian Love Party
Ivan D Juniors, The
Ivan's Meades
J and the Melforths, The
J J and the Hi-Lites
J P and the Jurymen
Jackie Kennedy and the Presidents
Jacko Ogg and the Head People
James
James Bond and the Premiums
Jay Spearman and the Javelins

Jazz Defektors
Jealous
Jean Bidet and Bathroom Band
Jeannie and the Big Guys
Jerry and the Wild Four
Jerry Lee and the Staggerlees
Jerry Rogers and the Vampires
Jilted John
Jim and the Tonics
Jimmy Crawford and the Messengers
Jimmy Crawford and the Ravens
Jimmy Martin and the Martinis
Joe Roberts
John Cooper Clarke
Johnn Drake and the Admials
Johnny and the Avengers
Johnny and the Semi-Tones
Johnny and the Stormy Nights
Johnny Apollo and the Spartans
Johnny B Goode and the Hot Rods
Johnny Blake and the Admirals
Johnny Bright and the Rewires
Johnny Bright and the Sparks
Johnny Costello and the Lawmen
Johnny Dangerously
Johnny Daran and the Corvettes
Johnny Darano and the Strollers
Johnny Dark and the Stormy Knights
Johnny Dean and the Planets
Johnny Dean and the Shakers
Johnny Deen and the Crestas
Johnny Downes and the Dolphins
Johnny Drake and his Crewmates
Johnny J and B Sharp
Johnny Keeping and Lonely Ones
Johnny Law and the Lawmen
Johnny Lee and the Seekers
Johnny Mac and the Sporrans
Johnny Martin and the Paiges
Johnny Martin and the Tremors

Johnny Masters and Mastersounds
Johnny Mike and the Shades
Johnny Milton and the Condors
Johnny Moe's Rhythm and Blues Band
Johnny Paige and the Ventures
Johnny Peters and the Crestas
Johnny Peters and the Jets
Johnny Peters and the JPs
Johnny Silver and the Atlantics
Johnny Silver and the Cymerions
Johnny Silver and Thunderbirds
Johnny Sky and the Horizons
Johnny Tempest and Cadillacs
Johnny Vallons and the Dee-Jays
Johnson's Nephews
Jon Postman
Joy
Joy Division
Julie and Gordon
Just Sucking Cheese
Kalima
Kaliphz
Karl Denver Trio
Kathy and the Boleros
Kathy and the Conquerors
K-Billy
Keith Powell and the Valets
Kenny Damont and the Rebels
Kenny Stevens and The Blue Diamonds
Kevin Seisey and Claire Mooney
Kim Tracey and the Antones
King of the Slums
Kirk Daniels and the Deltas
Kirk Daniels Dominators
Kirk Sheldon
Kirk Sheldon and the Atlantics
Kiss AMC
Kraken
Kris Rhyan and the Questions
Lamb

Larry Avon and the Presidents
Laudanum Split
Laugh
Lee Allen and the Sceptres
Lee Castle and the Barons
Lee Curtis and the All stars
Lee Darrett and the Escorts
Lee Fender and the Topliners
Lee Paul and the Boys
Lee Shondell and the Premiers X
Lee Stewart and the Beat Squad
Lee Stewart and the Emperors
Lee Walker and the Travellers
Lee Zenith and the Cimmarones
Lemm Seisey
Lennie and the Teambeats
Linda Laine with the Saints
Lipids, The
Lisa Stansfield
Little Frankie and the Country Gents
Little Rikki and the Original Renegades
Little Walter and the Softies
Lobe, the
Lonesome and Penniless Cowboys
Loremel
Lorraine Gray and Chaperones
Lorraine Gray and the Olympics
Lorraine Gray and the Shakeouts
Lorraine Gray and the Toys
Lorraine Grey and the Questions
Loveland
Lovers, The
Lowthers, The
Ludus
M C Tunes
M People
Mad Daddy
Magazine
Magic Lanterns
Mainline

Mal Ryder and the Spirits
Man From Delmonte
Manchester Mekons
Manchester Playboys, The
Manchester Women's Band, The
Mandala Band
Manicured Noise
Marc Stone
Marion
Mark Peters and the Silhouettes
Mark Raymond and the Rayvons
Marty Barry and the Teenbeats
Master Jam and Owen
Matt Derry and the Stylos
MC Buzz B
McAllum
Meatmouth
Mediaters
Mel Dean and the Dean Aces
Mel Turner and the Mohicans
Mellotron
Membranes
Metal Monkey Machine
Miaow
Mighty Kyoga
Mike Brennan and the Testaments
Mike Cadillac and the Playboys
Mike Cameron and his Silhouettes
Mike Carroll and the Ramblers
Mike Curtis and The Set
Mike Everest and the Alpines
Mike Fenner and the San Antones
Mike McNight and the Phantoms
Mike Payne and the Misfits
Mike Sagar and the Crestas
Mike Sagar and the Quiet Three
Mike Sax and the Dominators
Mike Sax and the Vikings
Mike Sweeney and the Thunderbirds
Milltown Brothers

Milton James Band, The
Miss Danny and the Chrystells
Mistral
Mock Turtles
Molly Half Head
Molly's People
Moonshine
Moses
Mothmen
Motivation
Mr Smith and Sum People
Mudlarks, The
My Cat Dances
N M and the Bogstompers
Naafi Sandwich
Negatives, The
Neil Landon and the Burnettes
Nero and the Gladiators
New Fads
New Order
Next Step, The
Night Visitors
Noddy and the Toytown Rockers
Norman and his Cellmates
Norman and the Electrons
Norman Beaker
Northern Uproar
Not Sensibles
Oasis
Obimen
Olivia Twist
Omar
One Summer
Operation Guitar Boy
Our Salford Correspondent
Out
Pablo Panques
Paddy Melon
Pagan Chemistry Set
Panik

Paper Dolls
Paris Angels
Paris Valentinos
Parma Violets
Passage
Pat Wayne and Rockin' Jay Men
Pat Wayne and the Beachcombers
Paul Beattie and the Beats
Paul Dean and the Premiers
Paul Fenda and the Teenbeats
Paul Stevens and Emperors of Rhythm
Paul Young's Paradox
Pavane
Pavement Family, the
Performance
Pete and the Mohawks
Pete and the New Persuaders
Pete and the Rebels
Pete Berry and the Tornados
Pete Chester and the Consulates
Pete Maclaine and the Dakotas
Pete Maclaine and the Four Just Men
Pete Taylor and the Javelins
Pete Trent and the Travellers
Pete Wetton and the Dakotas
Pete's Faces
Peter Day and the Knights
Peter Novack and the Heartbeats
Phil J Corbett and the Coasters
Phil Lowe and the Swaggers
Phil Peters and the Swaggers
Phil Plant and the Plantes
Phil Ryon and the Crescents
Picture Chords
Plain and Fancy
Poontang and Hotshots
PP Messiah
Predator
Prime Mover
Prime Time Suckers

Prince Cool
Property Of
Pudding Spoons, The
Puppets, The
Puressence
Puritans, The
Purple Gang, The
Quando Quango
Quigley
Quivers, The
Ragin' Cajuns, The
Raging Storms, The
Railway Children, The
Rain
Rainbow Arch
Rainkings
Rainmakers, The
Raintree County
Ranchers, The
Rangers, The
Ratfink
Rats, The
Rattling Bones, The
Ravels, The
Ravons, The
Ray Anton and the Peppermint Men
Ray Kennan and the Quiet Three
Ray Malcolm and the Sunsets
Ray Marcus and the Deejays
Rebels, The
Red Hoffman and the Measles
Redcaps, The
Reg Coates Experience, The
Relatives, The
Remo Sands and Spinning Tops
Renegades with Wayne Gordon, The
Renegades, The
Resinous
Rev Black and the Rocking Vicars
Revenge

Revolution 9
Revolutions, The
Ricky and Dane Young
Ricky and the Jetzens
Ricky Bowdon and the Escorts
Ricky Den and the Fantoms
Ricky Ford and the Tennesseans
Ricky Lane and the Drovers
Ricky Norman and the Elektrons
Ricky Shaw and the Dolphins
Ricky Young and the Echoes
Ricky Young and the Fabulous Fourtones
Rig
Right Band, Wrong Planet
Riots, The
Risk, The
Roadrunners, The
Rob Storm and the Whispers
Rocket Jam Roll
Rockin Rapids, The
Rockin Slaves of Babylon, The
Rocking Jaymen, The
Roly and the Boys
Romany Rye
Ron Pickard Four, The
Rondecks, The
Rondellas, The
Rowetta
Roy and the Restless Four
Rubber Meks
Rude Club
Ruthless Rap Assassins
Ryles Brothers with Gay Saxon, The
Sables, The
Sabres, The
Sad Cafe
Salford Jetz
Sandstones, The
Sandstorms, The
Santa Fe Five, The

Sapphires, The
Satans, The
Scorchers
Scorpions, The
Script, The
Sean Campbell and the Mysteries
Sean Campbell and the Tremoloes
Seane and the Sonics
Second Sun
Secrets, The
Section 25
Seekers, The
Self Righteous Brothers, The
Semitones, The
Senators, The
Send No Flowers
Sensations, The
Seven Ways
SFW
Shabby Tiger
Shades Five, The
Shah
Shakes, The
Shallow
Shane and the Shane Gang
Shantells, The
Shape of the Rain, The
Shapiros, The
Shaun and Sum People
Shaun Hunter and the Falcons
Sheila Collyer and Smokey City 7
Shelbys, The
Shevrons, The
Shotguns, the
Shouts, The
Silks, The
Simply Red
Sinners with Linda Lane, The
Sins of the Family, The
Siren

Skol Bandeleros
Skyliners, The
Slaughter and the Dogs
Sleepwalkers, The
Slight Seconds
Slum Turkeys
Smirks
Smiths, The
Smokescreen
Snakes, The
Sneakers, The
Solo 70
Sombrero Fallout
Some of Them
Sonics, The
Sonnets, The
Sound Gallery
Sound Waves, The
Soundsations, The
Soundtracks, The
Souvenirs, The
Sovereigns, The
Space Monkeys
Spartans, The
Spectres, The
Spellbinders, The
Spherical Objects
Spidermen, The
Spinning Tops, the
Spitfires, The
Spyder Mike King Band
St Louis Union
Staccatos, The
Stackwaddy
Stalwarts, The
Stantones, The
Starlites, The
Starseed
Stateside Combo, The
Statesmen, The

Stationers, The
Steeltones with Ricky Adams, The
Steeltones, The
Sterlings, The
Steve and the Suspects
Steve Solomar
Stone Roses
Stonebreaker
Stonefree
Storm Beats, The
Stormriders, The
Stormy Nights, The
Strand Showband, The
Strange Brew
Strange Street
Strangers, The
Strangeways, The
Strides, The
Strollers, The
Stylos, The
Sub Sub
Sunchaser
Sunrise
Suns of Arqua
Sunsets, The
Sunspots, The
Susan Singer
Suspicions, The
Sussed
Swaggers, The
Swamp Children
Swamp Thing
Sweet Sensation
Swinbourne Swingers, The
Swing Out Sister
Swinging Lampshades
Swingtones, The
Swivel Hips
Symbols, The
Syndicate,The

T Dynamix
T'Challa Grid
Take That
Takeovers, The
Talismen, The
Tangents, The
Tansads
Taverners, The
Tearaways, The
Teasers, The
Teddy Bears, The
Teenbeats, The
Temper Temper
Tempests, The
Tempters, The
Terry and the Teenbeats
Terry Gordon and the Coasters
Terry King and the Saints
Terry Young and the Terry Young Six
Texans, The
Things, The
Three Dimensions, The
Three Dots and a Dash
Three Nuts and a Bolt
Thunderbeats, The
Tiffany and the Four Dimensions
Tiffany and the Thoughts
Tigers, The
Tiller Boys
TNT and the Dynamites
To Hell with Burgundy
Todd Miller and the Prowlers
Toggery 5, The
Tokens, The
Tom Hart and the Hartbeats
Tom's Rigg
Tommy Brennan and the Aces
Tommy Wells and the Delights
Toni Fayne and the Federals
Tony and the Baritones

Tony and the Scorpions
Tony and the Stormriders
Tony D and the Shakeouts
Tony Holland and the Packabeats
Tony Kaye and the Huckleberries
Tony Palandinos Rhythm Group, the
Too Much Texas
Tools You Can Trust
Torrents, The
Toss the Feathers
Tot
Trackers, The
Tractor
Tremors, The
Trevor Fayne and The Original Phantoms
Triads, The
Tribunes, The
Triffords, The
Trigger Happy
Trixons, The
Trolls, The
Troyes, The
Trycons, The
Tungstens, The
Tuxedos, The
Twang
United Mates of Hysteria
Untamed, The
Urban Cookie Collective
V2
Valiants, The
Valkyries, The
Vampires with Paula
Vampires, The
Van Der Graaf Generator
Vedettes, The
Vee VV
Ven Tracey and the Beat Squad
Venoms, The
Ventures, The

Vibrant Thighs
Vibrations, The
Vibratones, the
Vic and the Steelmen
Vic and the VIPs
Vic Brick and the Cements
Vic Elson's Teenbeats
Vic Patch and the Leathers
Vicky Lee
Victor Brox Blues Train, The
Victoria
Vigilantes, The
Vikings, The
Vin Atherton and the Jazzmen
Vince Bennett and the Galaxies
Vince Berresford
Vince Berresford and the Cheaters
Vince Earl and the Talismen
Vince Everett and the Black Orchids
Vince Harris and the Turmoils
Vince Martin and the Meteros
Vincents, The
Vindicators, The
Visitors, The
Vortex, The
Vulcans, The
Wailers, The
Walkabouts, The
Walkaways, The
Waltones, The
Wanderers, The
War Poets, The
Warriors, The
Water Monkeys, The
Wayne Fontana and the Jets
Wayne Fontana and the Mindbenders
Wayne Sheridan and the Centurians
Wayne Thomas and the Tonics
Wayne Wayne and the Trains
Weeds, The

Weeks of Sandwich
Weys, The
What? Noise
When in Rome
Whirligig
Whirlwinds, The
Wierdies, The
Wilde Bunch, The
Williams, Di
Wireless
Wirewood
World of Twist
Worst, The
Wyverns, The
X-L's, The
X-Odus
Yargo
Yennash
Yes Brazil
Yorker
Young and Renshawe
Young BroThers, The
Young Ones, The
Zenith Six, The
Zephyrs, The
Zero Cookies
Zodiacs, The

Bibliography

Abrams, Steve quoted in Jonathon Green, 1988, 'Days In The Life', London, Heinemann

Alfonso, Barry, 1992, 'The Beat Generation' booklet accompanying Rhino Records Compilation. Santa Monica, Ca

Amit-Talai, V && Wulff, H (Eds) 1995, Youth Cultures, London: Routledge

Bacon, Tony (Ed), 1981, 'Rock Hardware: the Instruments, Equipment and Technology of Rock, Poole, Dorset

Barker, M and Beezer, A (Eds), 1992, 'Reading Into Cultural Studies', London, Routledge

Becker, H S (Ed), 1963, 'The Other Side: Perspectives on Deviance', Berkeley, Free Press

Belsito, P, et al (Eds), 1981, 'Streetart: the Punk Poster in San Francisco', Berkeley: Last Gasp of California

Blacknell, S, 1985, 'The Story of Top of the Pops', Wellingborough, Northants, Patrick Stephens

Boyes, G, 1993, 'The Imagined Village', Manchester, Manchester University Press

Brake, M, 1973, 'Cultural Revolution or Alternative Delinquency' in Bailey and Young, 1973, 'Contemporary Social Problems in Britain', Saxon House

Cagle, Van M 1995, 'Reconstructing Pop/Subculture', Thousand Oaks: Sage

Carr, R, et al, 1986, 'The Hip: Hipsters, Jazz and the Beat Generation', London, Faber

Chambers, T, 1986, 'Popular Culture - The Metropolitan Experience', London: Routledge

Champion, S, 1991, 'And God Created Manchester', Manchester, Wordsmith

Chaney, D, 1993, 'Fictions of Collective Life', London, Routledge

Chief Constable's Annual Report, 1964, Manchester

Chief Constable's Annual Report, 1965, Manchester

Chtcheglov, August 1964, Paris, "Lettres de loin," I.S. No. 9

Cohen, S, 1973, 'Folk Devils and Moral Panics', London,

Paladin

Cohen, S, 1991, 'Rock Culture in Liverpool: Popular Music in the Making', Oxford, Clarendon Press

Cohn, N, 1970, 'Awopbopaloobopalopbamboom, London, Paladin

Communist Party of Great Britain, 1951, The American Threat to British Culture, London, Arena

Copper, B, 1971, 'A Song for Every Season', London, Heinemann Ltd

Davidson, S, 1976, 'The Penguin Book of Political Comics', Amsterdam, Van Gennep BV

Davies, H, 1968, 'The Beatles', London, Heinemann Ltd

Debord, G, 1977, 'Society of The Spectacle', Detroit, Black and Red

DeFoe, B George and Martha, 1982, 'The International Discography Of The New Wave', London, Omnibus Press

Denselow, R, 1989, When the Music's Over, London: Faber & Faber

Dickinson, Bob, 1996, 'Imprinting the Sticks', M Phil Manchester Metropolitan University

Economou, Konstantin, 1994. 'Making Music Work', Sweden, Linkoping University

Evans, Mike, 1974, The Hot Flash No 1

Everett, P, 1986, 'You'll Never Be 16 Again', London, BBC Publications

Everett, P, July 1975, The Hot Flash

Finnegan, R, 1989, 'The Hidden Musicians: Music-Making in an English Town', Cambridge, Cambridge University Press

Fiske, John, 1982, 'Introduction to Communication Studies', London, Methuen & Co

Frith, S and Goodwin, A, 1990, On Record, London: Routledge

Frith, S, 1982, 'Sound Effects: Youth, Leisure, and the Politics of Rock 'n' Roll', New York, Pantheon Books

Gallagher, T, Campbell, M and Gillies, M 1995, The Smiths, All Men Have Secrets, London: Virgin Books

Gambaccini, P, Rice, T & J, and Read, M (Comps), 1981, 'Guinness Book of British Hit Singles', London, Guinness Superlatives Ltd

Gillett, C, 1970, 'The Sound of the City', London, Sphere

Books

Goldman, A, 1988, 'The Lives of John Lennon', New York, Bantam Books

Graves, Robert, 1938, 'Count Belisarius', Harmondsworth, Middlesex, Penguin Books

Grossberg, L, 1992, 'We Gotta Get Out of This Place: Popular Conservatism and Postmodern Culture', London, Routledge

Guralnick, P, 1989, 'Searching for Robert Johnson: The Life and Legend of the King of the Delta Blues Singers', New York, Dutton/Obelisk

Hall, S & Jefferson, T, 1976, 'Resistance Through Rituals: Youth Subcultures In Post-War Britain', London, Harper Collins

Hannett, Martin, 1975, in The Hot Flash No 4

Hardy, P and Laing, D (Eds, 'The Encyclopedia of Rock', Vols I and II, London, Aquarius Books

Harker, D, 1980, 'One for the Money', London, Hutchison

Harker, D, 1985, 'Fakesong: The Manufacture of British 'Folk Song'', Milton Keynes, Open University Press

Harker, D, 1992, 'Bringing It All Back Home', Unpublished Typescript

Haslam, D, 1995, 'Reading Pop', Unpublished Manuscript

Hazelden, Glyn, 1974, The Hot Flash No 1

Hebdige, D, 1979, 'Subculture The Meaning Of Style', London, Methuen & Co

Heylin, Clinton, 1992, 'From The Velvets to the Voidoids', London, Penguin

Heylin, Clinton, 1994, 'The Great White Wonders', London, Viking

Hibbert, T, 1982, 'The Dictionary of Rock Terms', London, Omnibus

Home, Stewart, 1995, 'Cranked Up Really High', Exeter, Code X

Jackson, P, 1989, 'Maps of Meaning', London, Unwin Hyman Ltd

Jameson, F, 1991, 'Postmodernism', London and New York, Verso J

Johnson, G, 1981, 'The Story of Oi', Manchester, Babylon Books

Johnson, M, 1984, An Ideal For Living, London: Proteus

Books

Jones, D, 1990, 'Haircuts - Fifty Years of Styles and Cuts', London, Thames and Hudson

Keil, C, 1966, 'Urban Blues', Chicago, University of Chicago Press

Kelly, Edward R, 1979, 'From Craft To Art: The Case Of Sound Mixers And Popular Music', in Frith, Simon and Goodwin, Andrew (Eds), 1990, 'On Record', London, Routledge

Krantzman, Phyllis, 1983 'The Impact Of The Music Entertainment Industry On Austin Texas', Master's Thesis, University of Texas at Austin

Kristeva, J, 1974, 'The Speaking Subject and Political Language', Paper presented at University of Cambridge

Laing, Dave, 1985, 'One Chord Wonders - Power and Meaning in Punk Rock, Milton Keynes, Open University Press

Lawson, A, 1990, It Happened in Manchester, Manchester: Multimedia

Leigh, Spencer, July 1975, The Hot Flash

Levi-Strauss, C, 1966, 'The Savage Mind', London, Weidenfeld & Nicolson

Ludman, K, 1987, 'Making a Living as a Rock Musician', London, Kogan Page

Lyotard, J F, 1984, 'The Post-Modern Condition', Manchester, Manchester University Press Manchester Corporation Act, 1965

Marcus, G, 1989, 'Lipstick Traces: A Secret History of the 20th Century', Cambridge, Massachusetts, Harvard University Press

Matlock, G with Silverton, P, 1990, 'I Was A Teenage Sex Pistol', London, Omnibus Press

McGartland, Tony, 1995, 'Buzzcocks - The Complete History', London, Independent Music Press

McGibbon, R and McGibbon, R, 1993, 'Simply Mick', London: Weidenfeld & Nicolson

McGuigan, J, 1992, 'Cultural Populism', London, Routledge

McRobbie, Angela and Gerber, Jenny, 1975, 'Girls And Subcultures' paper, published in Hall, Stuart & Jefferson, Tony, 'Resistance Through Rituals', 1975, London, Harper Collins

Middles, M, 1985, 'The Smiths-The Complete Story', London, Omnibus Press

Middles, M, 1996, 'From Joy Division to New Order - The

Factory Story', London, Virgin

Mitchell, Tony, 1996, 'Popular Music and Local Identity', Leicester, Leicester University Press

Morley, Paul, 1978, Liner Notes - 'Live At The Electric Circus', Virgin Records

Morley, Paul, NME, December 2nd, 1978.

Murphy, David, 1991, 'The Stalker Affair and the Press', London, Unwin

Negus, K, 1992, 'Producing Pop', London: Routledge

Nuttall, Jeff, 1968, 'Bomb Culture', London, MacGibbon & Kee Ltd

Plant, S, 1992, 'The Most Radical Gesture', London: Routledge

Procter, M, 1954, 'Hell Is A City', London, Arrow Books Ltd

Rees, D and Crompton, L, 1996, 'The Q Book of Punk Legends', London, Guinness Publishing

Reid, J and Savage, J, 1987, 'Up They Rise: The Incomplete Works of Jamie Reid', London, Faber & Faber

Repsch, J, 1989, 'The Legendary Joe Meek', London, Woodford House

Rogan, J, 1991, 'Morrissey & Marr - The Severed Alliance', London, Omnibus Press

Russell, R, 1973, 'Bird Lives!', London, Quartet Books

Sampson Report, The, 1986, HMSO,

Savage, J, 1991, 'England's Dreaming - Sex Pistols and Punk Rock', London, Faber & Faber

Savage, 1992, 'The Haçienda Must Be Built', London, IMP Publishing

Shank, B, 1994, 'Dissonant Identities - The Rock 'n' Roll Scene in Austin, Texas', Hanover: Wesleyan University Press

Shapiro, Harry, 1992, 'Graham Bond: The Mighty Shadow', London, Guinness Publishing

Spinoza, Andy, City Life, August 1989

Sublime, 1992, Manchester Music and Design 1976-1992, Manchester, Cornerhouse Publishing

Tansill, P and Mairowitz, D Z, Eds, 1971, 'Bamn, Outline Manifestos and Ephemera 1965-70', London, Penguin Books

Thornton, Sarah, 'Moral Panics', in Ross, Andrew & Rose, Tricia (Eds),1994, 'Microphone Fiends', London, Routledge

Tobler, J & Grundy, S, 1982, 'The Record Producers', London,

BBC

Vaneigem, R, 1983, 'The Revolution of Everyday Life', Seattle, Rebel

Vermorel, F & J, 1989, 'Fandomonium', London, Omnibus Press

Walker, J A, 1987, 'Crossovers - Art Into Pop, Pop Into Art', London, Comedia

Warner, S, 1996, 'Rockspeak! The Language Of Rock And Pop', UK, Blandford

Wayne County & The Electric Chairs, EP 'Blatantly Offensive' on Safe Records, 1978

White, A, 1983, 'Convention and Constraint in the Operation of Musical Groups - Two Case Studies', (PhD thesis, Univ of Keele, unpublished)

White, A L (Ed), 1987, 'Lost in Music: Culture, Style and the Musical Event', London, Routledge & Kegan Paul

Willis, P. 1977, 'Learning to Labour', Farnborough: Saxon House

Young, J, 1992, 'Nico, The Last Bohemian', London, Bloomsbury

Interviews with the Author

Taped (T) or Conversation (C)

Boon, Richard,30 March 1996 T

Brown, Paul, 14 February 1996 *(Paul ran a folk club in Manchester 1964-66)* C

Brox, Victor, 10 December 1993 T

Carey, Scott, 05 February 1994 T

Devoto, Howard, 30 March 1996 T

Eagle, Roger *(DJ and broadcaster)* C

Fielder, Fred, 12 October 1995 *(DJ and broadcaster)* T

Harris, Andy, 05 February 1994 T

Hook, Peter, 03 July 1994 T

Hughes, Pete, 02 January 1994 T

Jon The Postman, 12 October 1995 T

Lee, James Gabriel *(Inspector, Manchester City Police, 1938-68)* C

Maclaine, Pete, 12 October 1995 *(Recording artist and musician)* T

Manning, Bernard, July 1995 *(Comedian)* C

Mitchell, Bruce (1), 30 October 1994 T

Mitchell, Bruce (2), 12 November 1993 T

Mooney, Eddie, 22 September 1994 T

Ryan, Tosh, 19 July 1992 T

Van Den Berg, Benny, 12 October 1995 *(Club owner and manager)* T

Whittam, Gary, 12 October 1995 *(Drummer, Herman's Hermits)* T

Wilson, Anthony H, 05 June 1996 T

Index

10cc, 8, 163, 246
808 State, 217, 233

A

A Certain Ratio, 176, 195
A Guy Called Gerald, 217
A Witness, 212, 253
A1 Music Centre, 188
Aaben Cinema, 210
Abbey Road, 162, 163
Abrams, Steve, 60, 64, 281
Acid House, 202, 216, 217, 218, 219
Adorno, TW, 239, 240, 247
Adventure, The, 227, 253
Affleck's Palace, 222
Africans, 26
Afro Express, 117, 134
Akers, Mel, 107
'Alan' (bootlegger), 58, 59
Albarn, Damon, 241
Albert Hall (The Royal), 11, 23, 54, 58, 59, 60, 81
Albert Square, 183
Alberto Y Lost Trios Paranoias, 91, 98, 103, 105, 108, 115, 116, 164, 167, 174, 231
Alfonso, Barry, 52, 64, 281
Alk, Howard, 58, 287
Alternative Music, 30, 91, 104, 281
Alternative Society, 104
American ('Threat to British Culture'), 10, 46
American (Bands), 212
American (Bluesmen), 31
American (Cultural Imperialism), 48
American (Forces, Burtonwood), 24
American (Forces, influence of), 71
American (Garage Bands), 126
American (Musicians), 25

B

D

Drifters, The, 35
Drones, The, 128, 142, 143
Drugs, 3, 14, 52, 68, 73, 77, 79, 80, 81, 165, 167, 201, 212, 216, 218
Dry Bar,173
Dub Nights, 199,
Dub Sex, 200, 211, 216
Dub, 210
Dublin, 44, 61, 94, 205
Duffle coat,10, 22, 24, 27, 219
Dunbar, John 50
Durutti Column, The, 171, 172, 174, 175, 227
Dwyer, Bernie, 231
Dylan, Bob, 10, 41, 48-49, 51, 53-63, 109, 123, 129-130, 188, 194, 230

E

Eagle, Roger, 14, 34, 82, 99, 102, 173-174, 184-187, 189, 242
Eastern Bloc, 222
Eat The Document, 48, 49, 56, 58
Eccles, 128
Echo and the Bunnymen, 36
Ecstasy, 14, 202, 215, 218
El Rio Coffee Bar, 31
Electric Circus, 139, 141-143, 153-156,198, 201,
Electro Dub, 202
Elektra Records, 54
Elizabethan Ball Room, Belle Vue, 153
Elleray, Caroline, 228
Ellis, Ruth, 50
ELO, 109
Elton John, 113
Elton, Ben, 92
English Folk Dance and Song Society (EFDS), 41
Enigma Records,178
Ennis, Seamus, 231
Ennis, Seamus, 231
Entertainments (Increased Penalty Bill, 1989/90), 84, 218
Erasmus, Alan, 170, 172, 174, 175, 176
Evans, Mike, 94, 96, 106, 109
Everett, Derek, 178
Everett, Peter, 33, 113
Eyers, Kevin, 108

G

Gallagher Brothers, 3, 230-231
Gallagher, Liam, 230
Gallagher, Noel, 3, 15, 229-236, 239
Gallagher, Rory, 37
Gallery, The, 202
Gambaccini, Paul, 19, 40
Gamblin' Man, 19
Gammadge, Ernie, 204
Gang of Four, The, 145
Garage, 168, 184
Garrett, Malcolm, 131, 136, 143
Garside, Ernie, 184
Generate, Dee, 138
Genetic Records, 176, 179, 180
Gerber, Jenny, 215-216
Gillespie, Dizzie, 183
Glasgow, 234
Glitter, Gary, 30, 32, 132, 202
Godley and Crème, 163
Golden Earring, 108
Goodman, Benny, 21
Gordon Is A Moron, 166
Gore Street, 188
Goth, 211, 221
Gould, The Reverend Baring, 42-43
GQ Magazine, 243
Granada Television, 30, 33, 37, 124, 131, 167, 168, 169, 197, 246
Grapevine Records, 177
Grass Eye, 97, 191
Grateful Dead, The, 110
Gray, Ellie, 216
Greasy Bear, 29, 99, 116, 189
Greasy Heart, 189
Great Rock 'n' Roll Swindle, The, 36
Green On Red, 212
Greenhalgh, Steven, 68, 77
Greenwood, Paula, 216
Greenwood, Walter, 44
Gretton, Rob, 166, 176, 177, 178, 179, 198
Grey Parrot, The, 210
Grilliopolus, Dimitri, 101
Grossman, Albert, 55-56

K

Kansas City, USA, 23
Kardomah Coffee House, 68
Kellet, Neville, 56
Kelly, Ben, 173
Keludine Amphetamine, 185
Kennedy Street Enterprises, 31, 246
Kennedy, Kevin, 37
Kennedy, Roger, 226
Kerouac, Jack, 51, 53
Kid Cadillac's Disco, 100
Kinder Scout, 44
King Tut's Wah Wah Club, 234
King, BB, 33
King, Spyder Mike, 98-99, 107, 188
Kinks, The, 229
Kiss, 110, 211
Kitchen Recording Studio, 211
Konspiracy Club, The, 203
Korner, Alexis, 186
Kozaritz, Imre, 34
Kraftwerk, 217
Kraken, 107
Kray Twins, 66-68
Kuti, Fela, 26

L

Ladybarn Folk Club, 1, 50, 51, 187
Laing, Dave, 118-119, 156-157, 214-216
Larkin, Philip, 34
Latham, Laurie, 174
Latham, Laurie, 174-175
Laurel Canyon, USA, 32
Lawson, Alan 18, 28, 65
Lazy Sod, 128
Leadbetter, Huddie (Leadbelly), 28, 41
League, Ivy 10, 25
League, Socialist Labour, 95, 96
Leavis, FR, 21, 40
Led Zeppelin, 160
Lee, CP, 175
Lee, JG, 113

R

Rock/Rock'n'Roll, 1, 6, 8, 10, 11, 14, 19, 23, 25, 32, 35, 38, 41, 54, 60, 62-63, 71, 90, 92-94, 97-99, 102-104, 107-109, 111-114, 119, 126, 131, 136, 144, 149-152, 167, 169, 172, 175, 190, 194, 198, 209-210, 215, 220-221, 230, 238, 240, 245
Rock-A-Billy, 19
Rogan, Johnny, 144
Roll With It, 237
Rolling Stone Magazine, 108
Rolling Stones, The, 42, 52, 63, 138, 185
Ross, Diana, 88
Rosselin, Leon, 51
Rough Trade, 14, 146, 151, 175, 192
Roulette, 19
Rowbotham, Dave, 170
Roy Wood's Helicopters, 202
Royal Court Theatre, 105
Royal Festival Hall, 28
Rubble, Barney (Joy Division), 92
Rushent, Martin, 180
Rusholme, 164, 184
Russell Club, The, (see also Caribbean Club, PSV Club), 172, 178, 210
Ruthless Rap Assassins, 211, 227
Ryan, Tosh, 17-18, 24-25, 31, 90, 94-96, 98, 103-105, 115, 117-118, 147, 153-154, 164-166, 173-176, 179, 183-186, 188,
Ryder, Shaun, 216, 231, 244, 245

S

Sackville Street, 76
Sad Café, 115, 167
Salaal (Owner of the Blue Lagoon), 184
Salford Citiy Council, 44
Salford Grammar School, 167
Salford Technical College, 154
Salford, 1, 44, 150
Salsa (Dance), 202
Sampson, Colin, Chief Constable, Yorkshire, 67
San Francisco,103, 188, 219, 222, 252
Satellite, 128
Savage, Jon, 131, 140, 151, 196-197
Savile, Jimmy, 89
Saville, Peter, 173, 175
Scally, 14, 215
Scallydelia 14, 209, 211, 213, 215, 217, 219, 221, 223, 244

Travis, Geoff, 151, 192
Trinidadian (culture), 26
Tropicana Club, The, 198
True West, 212
Tubular Bells, 109
Turner, Tommy, 18
Twilight Studios, 164
Twisted Wheel, The, 14, 33, 34, 68, 82, 183-187, 201, 242

U

U2, 3, 165
UK Subs, The, 193
UMIST, 90, 103, 115, 134
Unchained Melody, 19
Unknown Pleasures, 180-181

V

Valentinos. The, 37
Van Den Burg, Benny, 88-90, 121, 252
Van Ronk, Dave, 51
Van Verden, Karl, 89
Vaneigem, Raoul, 13
Velvet Underground, The, 9, 124, 126, 155, 160
Vicious, Sid, 36, 243
Virgin Records, 90, 107, 152, 176
Visions of Johanna, 61
Voice In The Dark, 161
Von Schmidt, Ric, 51

W

Wah Heat, 202, 234
Wally, 99
Walsh, Joe, 109
Waltones, The, 200
Warsaw, (see Joy Division, New Order and Stiff Kittens), 92, 142-143, 153, 155, 177, 178
Warszawa, 142
Watcha Gonna Do About It, 129
Waterloo Sunset, 101, 229
Waterman, Pete, 247
Waters, Muddy (see McKinley Morganfield), 27, 33, 41-42, 45, 186